The WOLVES of PLANET HOPE

An Ancient Curse Awakened

I am a spark from the Infinite.
I am not flesh and bones.
I am light.

Paramhansa Yogananda

The Wolves of Planet Hope

Other Books by this author:

The WAND (A Magical Journey)

Psychic Nazi Hunter
(The Extraordinary Biography of Alan Wood-Thomas)

End of Times Trilogy
Eat Your Fill - Eat Your Religion - Eat Your God

The Book of Number Trilogy
Workbook - Interpretations - Practitioner Guide

Jerimiah Versus the Grabblesnatch

The Divinity Dice Series
Decimal Dice - Divinity Dice - Book of Aspects

Ratology: Way of the Un-Dammed

Ratology II: Who Gives a Rats?

Fragments of the Mirror (Short Stories)

Water: More Precious than Gold

The Borringbar War (Written in Three Days)

Hello Planet Earth

Rome Too / Rome Tree (Parody)

Parables of Geoff (Biography of the Author's Father)

The Witch Hunter and Other Stories

Ladder to
the Moon
Publications

**Available on Amazon or at
www.laddertothemoon.com.au**

Out, out, brief candle!
Life's but a walking shadow,
A poor player that struts and frets his hour
upon the stage, and then is heard no more:
it is a tale told by an idiot,
full of sound and fury, signifying nothing.

Macbeth (c. 1605), Act V, Scene 5, line 23.

INDEX

*A*void dwelling on the wrong things you have done. They do not belong to you now. Let them be forgotten. It is attention that creates habit and memory. As soon as you put the needle back on a phonograph record, it begins to play. Attention is the needle that plays the record of past actions. So you should not put your attention on bad ones. Why go on suffering over the unwise actions of your past? Cast their memory from your mind, and take care not to repeat those actions again.

The Divine Romance, Page 154 - Paramahansa Yogananda

Introduction

It was a shocking discovery, one no-one had suspected. A DNA modifying virus that can be spread with light! Worse, it specifically affected humans and turned them into crazed beasts. Whatever it was on this planet only one thing was certain, it was a threat equal to that which wiped out Old Earth!

It is the Twenty Seventh Century. Mankind has spread out over the galaxy, dominating many worlds in what is called the Federation. But was this one world too far?

Planet Hope, the latest project for the human expansion, is home to a friendly pack of humanoid wolves. They seem entirely welcoming, but soon after settlement, disturbing events required the intervention of the feared Death Squad. A dangerous infection has been found and must be dealt with.

The leader of the squad, Lieutenant Josh Banner, discovers this is no ordinary exercise - He has to assess and deal with a potential threat to ALL humanity, not just the settlement on Hope. Banner looks at the facts and expects only one conclusion - a whole lot of what his squad was named after was about to go down.

Words of the Prophet

The Messiah looked at the eager faces gathered before him. Every world he came to was another chance to explain what they fought for and what they fought against. One person, one village, one city, one culture converted - one more world brought into the fold.

He began: "All the potential in the universe can be in a cup, but without love it is an empty promise. It cannot quench a thirst or give you the Aqua Vital. The greed of the Hi-Mod, the anger in their administration, you have all felt it. I tell you truly, they believe they are the perfected man - but they are less than human. This is an infected soul, infected by a virus. Do not hate them, pity them, for they are dying. They are being held a prisoner by their false dreams.

"Lucifer has them in ITS grip. They do HIS bidding and that road leads only to desecration and loneliness - But I offer you freedom. I offer you a different path, one of simplicity and fraternity. More than this, I offer you strength and protection from the madness of the people who run our Federation.

"All you need do is accept my way and allow MY soldiers to come and stand in your stead when the vengeful ones come for you. Then you will be free of the madness, free to live a life without fear of being proscribed for the smallest offense.

"Do you want this freedom, my people? Do you truly wish to throw off the bondage of the Federation and follow the path of true and genuine inner purpose? Then join with me!"

The crowd hesitated, fearing the consequences of such a public meeting, but then the Wolf Soldiers appeared behind the Messiah! It was true! They COULD be saved. Hope sprang in their hearts.

The Human Condition

Lieutenant Josh Banner stared at the coms. His huge frame, all seven foot six inches of him - a human machine engineered from six generations of soldiering - hunkered over the intelligence briefings. The orders were very strange. He had presumed the death squad was there was to finalize some matter, not investigate a mystery. They were called in when it had already been decided things did not add up - His squad provided solutions, not answers.

He tapped his Natrum-hardened nails on the plas-steel bench. Filed to a sharp point for hand to hand and strengthened with silk/keratin mods, their close to diamond-hard consistency made small indentations into the bench. Freshly blown that morning by the magnobots, all his furniture and fittings were the same no matter what world they landed on. It was a perfect replica of his father's office, which in turn replicated his grandfathers. Even the 'old' family photos were freshly minted. It was a general psyche-requirement that soldiers be given familiar surroundings and, despite the fact you knew it was new, or that you were raised in a pod and never knew your father, it still made you feel at home.

His orders were clear. Find the problem, then find a solution - Resolve it, or report back for further orders. He knew what THAT meant, at least. So far, it was not looking good. Hope had all the hallmarks of a first-class disaster - another DNA modifying virus.

How could such a potent weapon have been missed? How could it be they were still not finding it? Detection of serious risk like this is a core test in all pre-settlement routines, yet while the present evidence for the threat was overt, it was clear today as it was back then that the resident population did not have a contagion. Further, all scans showed the wolves as being reasonably peaceful. Lucky for them - If anything like the irrational violence they had recently exhibited had shown up in early scans, the wolf people would have simply been eradicated before anyone turned up. And yet, despite the fact that it was known they had infected settlers, there was currently no trace of the disease.

Why? How? There were no answers. It made no sense, nor did it add up that a Death Squad should be given this puzzle to sort out. They were sent in to eradicate problems, not solve them.

The purpose for colonization was simple: Humanity needed places like Planet Hope. Earth had, before its destruction, become so over-crowded that the populace had spread out to nearby systems- this is what created the problem. Interplanetary trade became normal and then something as stupid as some fool paying a bribe to get around quarantine wiped out the home planet. A few black-market furs destroyed Earth.

Genetically checked, only goods certified as safe could be imported to Terra from other worlds. All trade was closely watched by the then powers-that-were, yet all it took was one seller of pelts on a ship that carried one tiny microbe to bring it down the entire planet. This insignificant little killer ate Mitochondria, the thing responsible for cell division. It was a bug that the local population had a natural resistance to, but which humanity, and all life on Earth, was utterly vulnerable to.

Once it had escaped into the eco-system it spread like wildfire, not just in the humans, but into every animal, every insect, and in short order, into the living tissues of trees. No cells could reproduce, and so the body of nature collapsed. The whole place was a wasteland in under a year, with the only survivors being the genetically enhanced crops and Gene-Modded people.

Through sheer luck, the then relatively new modification process to human DNA developed by Yont-Na was able to resist the microbe, and so the few on Earth who had been processed survived. Their already altered mitochondria was not subject to the influence of the invading disease. These 'enhanced' humans encompassed the cream of society: The rich, who could afford the very expensive DNA mutation, the military, who were given these to be more effective soldiers and, of course, the traders who had done deals with the developers and had received mods. The upshot, with rare exceptions, was that unless your mitochondria had been altered, you died. Obviously, as the outlying planets were ruled from Earth, it was these three groups that formed the basis for the new society.

It was at this time that, under the first planetary protectorate, the new way forward was set down. This is when the guiding light for humanity was written: *The Protocols*. Formed by Yont-Na, the famous genetic scientist whose laboratory remained high in an orbit around Earth, these became the way forward. Business and administration were now focused on streamlined efficiency. The incorporation of these new rules meant traditional government could be disposed of. Clear rules on what to do in any given situation were established and a clear chain of permanent command was created - with Yont-Na at the top.

This great man, the virtual savior of the human race with his DNA modification, had saved it again. As a result of his foresight, despite the shock, there was no dark age, no regression back to feudal planets. Humanity stayed united. Because he was able to organize the military to take charge of rebel worlds, Yont-Na kept the human federation intact. Naturally, those who were most adroit in adjusting to this new paradigm reached the highest echelons of power. And it was a given that those who adjusted best were those who went through extensive modification processes to improve their capability. This created the new norm: the better your mod level, the higher you rose in society.

Of course, people with high-level mods were also extremely long-lived, which meant the new rulers offered incredible stability. Plus, the tests and gates you had to go through in order to GET these high-mods meant you were tied into the structure of the existing social order. A young would-be commander in an army had no chance of toppling the leaders because, unless he were of a sufficient level, no one would follow him. And if he WERE of a sufficient level, the bread was so well-buttered, he didn't want to challenge the order.

With the leadership question resolved, Yont-Na committed an act that bound the Federation and gained him the respect of all his allies and even his enemies: Once the Protocols were fully established he abrogated his high command.. Why did he give up power? It was proof of his selflessness and the fact he had total confidence that his new system was, by this time, self-regulating. At least, this is what most of the population were told and believed. The truth was the man was still there to call the shots in serious operational matters.

This new society became incredibly efficient. Each had their place, their role, their purpose. Hive communities were assigned to raise children so that mothers could remain functional and children were trained from an early age according to what the scans showed as their best ability. The poorest child could rise to the highest administrator - at least, this was the myth of the new world.

The procedures upon which all of society functioned streamlined productivity. Everything worked inside a defined framework. This made obsolete many of the time-wasting and expensive layers from the old society of man: No more law courts, no more politicians, no more United Nations, no more endless bickering. Governments were now extensions of the corporations who ran any given world and, as a result, they ran efficiently and with long term goals. No more of the myopic nonsense created by the endless rounds of voting.

The future path of mankind was laid down with unvarnished and clear logical practices designed for one purpose: To ensure the survival and prosperity of the race. The Protocols were, in effect, the Bible of Administration for the entire Federation.

The only government that was needed on any given planet was a functioning bureaucracy to support the traders, manufacturers and the military. Life, so ordered, could move along with a clear and steady focus. There was no more democracy, no more arguments, efficiency was the God. Things worked according to design and all surviving humans on the outer planets came under this new form of social contract. As Yont-Na declared in his famous resignation speech, *"We took away the waste and theft of Government and gave you Giverment! We GAVE you modification and improvement, for the people, by the qualified! Long live the Federation!"*

The priority goal was now simply expansion, with the subsequent re-establishment of the human species. This obviously required the identifying and settling of new planets. The secondary goal, the one that which paid for all this expense, was profit. Thus corporations, such as the new Planet Hope Consortium, came into being and it was these profit centers that now funded the expansion into new worlds.

Everything was devoted to the growth and development of new homeworlds and the expansion of Federation. As old Earth was abandoned, after being stripped of anything of value, mankind reached out to the stars. But all was done under strict rules, the Protocols that established the rules for all trade and settlement. Of course, these new worlds needed settlers to run the machinery of commerce, a role that fell to the un-modded humans, those generally called the No-Mods.

Despite the wording of the Protocols being egalitarian, the reality was that, though a low born child 'could' rise to high levels, they didn't. Natural human jealousy, nepotism, and clan loyalties meant that unless you were connected to people who mattered, you didn't.

All of society changed as a result. The modified human was vastly superior to the bottom of the barrel No-Mods and so qualified for far greater protections in this new order. The social structure became more feudal, with a 'protectorate' of privileged lords and ladies who effectively ruled the peasants. Now that the lowest rungs did not have the archaic voting rights, they did not have to be appeased. They were marginalized but they not completely! Regular scans were undertaken to find potential recruits for the Military, or for any of the various roles needed in the expansion program. This, and the settlement of new planets, was the only thing that gave the no-mod hope for advancement.

If you had the right genes for modification, the resonance scans would detect it and you would be brought up from the lowly world of the nobody to be given rights according to the new role you were selected to fulfil. Thus the potential for everyone to rise in this new world was clear: If you had the DNA for it, your future was unlimited.

No-Mods did serve their purpose, of course. They were the ones that serviced, built and maintained the regime. They formed the ranks of the settlers chosen to do the work on planets like Hope. If they worked well, and consistently, they received ownership rights over property and a chance to secure a future for themselves.

Hope was just such a place. So much so that the Hope Consortium was able to pick and choose who they wanted. It was the beauty of this world that drew the settlers, plus the curious Wolf People with their soft brown eyes. Everyone loved them. This was seen as a place to put down roots, a new world full of promise.

But danger lurked under the skin. Banner had spent the day researching in the field while the camp was being erected inside the admin compound. He had looked about Wolftown and closely inspected the new settlers trading with the wolves. It all seemed peaceful enough, with no indication of the serious and significant threat that had been found here. Back in his office, going over the data, the only thing that truly stood out was the fact that nothing added up.

New worlds like this had been vetted and inspected for many years before being authorized for expansion. There could be no risk of further infection reaching out and destroying what remained of the humans. A virus, such as was indicated here, was generally considered a terminal condition for a world. Just as the survivors of Earth had eradicated the planet the original bug came from, any threat from a DNA virus was contained. The Protocols were clear, all threat must be eliminated - The Zeta Bomb was developed for this express purpose. The result, when triggered, was the total and complete annihilation of an infected planet.

Earth was not treated in the same way, despite the infection. But it may as well have been. It had a complete and absolute quarantine placed over it and ANY craft approaching was destroyed by the protection bots located throughout the old solar system. Some original Earthers would not leave their homeworld, a few of the DNA modified were too old, and there were a few ordinary people and creatures that managed to mutate and survive. These few were allowed to stay but it was clear that any who chose to remain behind could never place others at risk.

The incredibly harsh decision to place Earth under permanent quarantine to all trade and to prevent any and all visitation was really a death sentence. For a time, supplies were ferried in via bots, but over a decade or so, cold economics ended the sentimental connection with the home world. The constant drip-feeding of food and supplies left open the risk of the infection spreading, so this too was stopped. Isolated and desperate, madness took care of the rest of the problem. The general understanding was that any people who survived eventually killed each other for whatever scraps they could get.

WHY was all this ancient history passing through Banner's mind? Maybe part of his intuition enhancement was telling him it was connected? The real question: How did the extreme and extensive tests done before the colonization of Hope get it so wrong? The Protocols were adamant - there was never going to be another catastrophe like Old Earth, and without a clear answer, and soon, *Hope must die*. Humanity cannot be put at risk from a single planet.

According to his orders, this was the reason for Banner and his specialist team were called in, to solve the problem. If not, salvage what was of use before the place was incinerated.

An Impossible Question

Banner gazed out the reflexive glass panels of his office. The entire compound where his Death Squad was housed, though in the admin district, was essentially invisible - Like their camo-suits the walls of high-level military installations was covered in the peculiar cloaking device that made them next to impossible to see with the naked eye. He could look out, watch the spectacular aurora, the flames of color that shot across the skies of hope, but no one could look in.

This place reminded him of the old world holos of the Northern Lights, in the legendary land of Canada, the northern province of the once almighty United States Consortium. As a child, like all children raised in pods, he was given the lectures,and shown the beauty of the old world destroyed by greed and stupidity. He was one of the lucky ones, raised up to the ultimate level of a Seven - He was thankful his genetics and proof of capability gave him access to this elevated status, but only because the Federation maintained its ruthless efficiency.

The human race had been close to extinction from just the sort of virus that he had to contend with here on Hope. The place even looked like home, though with two moons, but "home" had long since ceased to exist. Earth had been wiped out and, as a result, humans now spread across the galaxy - and did so at an exponential rate. This is what made new worlds like this one very valuable commodities. Too valuable to be tossed aside because of a few minor complications.

But why was HE here? Any genetic tech officer could track source causes, and report on resolution potentials. WHY was HE - the leader of a Death Squad - given this puzzle to solve? Nothing here added up - not the failure of the scans, not the virus itself, nor the orders for HIM to resolve the matter in a way that retained profit for the Consortium that owned the franchise. The situation was clear: Peaceful locals suddenly reverse all prior scans and assessments and start randomly attacking the odd settler - The human they bite then turns into a ravaging beasts. Why?

His first action was to go straight to the flashpoint - Wolftown. This was the ancestral seat of this ancient race - but contrary to the conflict and argument he expected, the wolf-people were as welcoming to the current recon teams as they were to the original scanning crews. Banner had gone out in the extraordinary Camo-suit, which allowed him to observe without being seen. This equipment provided, like the office he was in, virtual invisibility for himself and all of his Death Squad. This meant they saw the natural reaction, which really meant they would see the truth. But what he saw did not add up. There seemed no remorse, no defensiveness, nor any indication of a problem from the scans that the bots were taking of psyche response. Yet these wolves had, for no apparent provocation, bitten and infected five settlers, who then went on a mad, rabies-like killing spree.

However, the current psyche read told the same story as the original scans, no extreme tenancies. Further, there was nothing in the saliva or mouth bacteria of the wolves to indicate a capacity to alter the DNA of the infected humans. And the one, clear fact was that the dead settlers did have infected genetic coding. This single result had sent a shudder through the system. Universally feared, any virus that altered genetic code like this was the very worst sort of threat because, once enacted, there is no cure. He thought of the Holograms he had seen of the burnt out husk of Old Earth - a place once as beautiful as this.

Somehow, despite all his extensive checking and cross-checking of the original profilers, the same nothing that had shown up then showed up now. What is more, every reading he took was essentially a perfect match with the pre-colonisation resonance scans. The ONLY difference was in the infected humans. This worried him even more, a bug that attacked ONLY humans? Yet, the bug was clearly an infection enhanced from being bitten by the local wolves. The virus itself was fairly easy to pick, a resonance scan showed up a mutated DNA that apparently forced the rapid degeneration to the beast.

But here was another question: How was it missed? How it got there, where it came from, and how to kill it, there were not simple questions. He had tested the saliva of a random selection of the wolf people and they all shared the DNA required for the virus to mutate. But it was inactive. The codons were clearly OFF - the saliva of the wolves could not create this modification without some sort of external switch. But could he find it? No.

His wrist flashes, the implant tells him it is break time. Josh stands up, does his required exercise routines. All soldiers must do this every 60 minutes: stretches, resistance training, a few minutes of cardio. It clears the head and maintains peak performance and, like Einstein playing his violin, this is when his intuition would get in and give him a hint of where next to look.

Another flash from the wrist implant ends his five-minute session. He walks from his office to the incoming ship-load of settlers currently arriving back from the high country where they were trading and fossicking. He wanted to be there to personally supervise this first return of settlers since the last incident, so he goes directly to the admin office to inspect the scans he had set up for all incoming persons. The hover-ship was shifting into dock as he arrived and the girl in the booth overseeing the transfer seemed to have all things in hand.

Outside the compound stood the over thirty-foot high plas-steel walls and above this, launched in a fiery display, the remarkable aurora of Planet Hope ranged across the sky. Plumes of color stretched up and arched from the horizon, reaching into the highest heavens. The place was beautiful, no denying it. It is what made it very easy to get settlers to come here. An Earth-like world with twenty percent oxygen and stunning visuals like this ... it was a no-brainer really.

And beyond the walls, rich soils, thick forests full of millable timbers and a range of animals that could be used for both food and clothing. This was such an easy planet to turn into a comfortable home. Not like the fiery desert planets or ice worlds they had to beat down in order to inhabit.

He gazed out, absorbing the twisting patterns of light. They danced in your brain, causing a sense of deep harmony and peace - Banner smiled to himself, he almost felt his poetic mode kick in. But then an inner alarm bell rang. Something was not right with that woman checking in the settlers.

His intuition is never wrong. "Scan her," Banner says to the 'invisible' sergeant beside him, pointing to the woman. There is no question or hesitation from the soldier. Don't think, DO, the old commando axiom was as true today in the Death Squad as it was at any time in the past. The scans come back, and dammit, his instincts are right. To his horror, she is infected. For some reason, this no-mod is covering up the truth and feeding out a false reading. What? How could this be?

Deeper alarm bells now rang in his head. A planned assault? Logic speaks: Something was controlling humans and trying to infect their base. An unintelligent infection does not act like this.

He recalibrates the scans on the incoming settlers. What! They now show up over twenty infections on the ship that is docking! He shoots a lethal bolt of radiation into Admin officer, through the plex-glass, killing her and breaking open her office so he can lock the doors of the incoming ship. No time for niceties, he flicks the lockout, throws a hermetic blanket over the body he just killed and orders his men to spray the entire train with sleeping gas. Banner wanted this lot alive for testing.

What the HELL was happening here?

He taps a code for nano-bots to repair the damage to the booth, but not to recycle the body. He needs to scan the synapses to see what was causing this huge breach of protocols. The Federation was very risk-averse regarding infected planets and this sort of thing invariably meant his Death Squad were going to 'get busy'.

Report to Saunders

T his last report caused quite a stir. Orders were snapped back instantly, *"Tell no one!"* This meant the Consortium paying for this was to be kept out of the loop. Next came the order to report to, of all things, one of the archaic Space Stations that still survived in this district. It would seem that normal admin was specifically being flouted and special procedures had been called up. *What barrel of monkeys had he stumbled across?*

On board the shuttle to the nearest space station, with his specimens and scans in a locked case, Banner looks at himself in the surveillance monitors that covered anything and everyone that entered a shuttle. He was military perfection - tall, powerful, focused. The auto-camo suit of the Death Squad, which modulated with his surroundings so as to make him virtually invisible to all but the most trained eye, was not permitted to be used in Federation ships and was auto-switched to neutral. ID checks and DNA verification were approved and, as a last security precaution, he himself was powered down.

Yet even without the essential beaming in of neuronic boost that kept his mods at full speed, Banner remained formidable. He was battle hardened and tough. Yes, the Mods turned what was a capable soldier into an acute edge, a sword of the Federation, but even without these he had the reflexes of a cat. Every part of Banner had been bred to a precise and defined level of enhancement. He was the end result of human evolution, one of the rare Seven-Gen full-mods, the ultimate goal where all trace of substandard DNA had been eliminated.

Seven-Gens were virtually immortal. As long as they received their required boosters and maintained connection with the mainframe, their cells replicated with 100% efficiency. They could renew organs that were damaged, even limbs they were lost could have bone frames attached and the stem cells produced by the Seven-Gen would re-grow the original appendage inside a few months. Sadly, like so many hybrid species they were sterile. This unfortunate side effect of tampering with nature stopped the mass production of Sevens. More to the point, their reproductive cells had become so specialized that did not integrate with any other cells, not even with another Seven-Gen. They were the end of evolution, and evolution appeared to know it.

They could be cloned, of course, but clones didn't have the edge. Plus, because of the enormous expense, only the very wealthy indulged in this extravagance. There was a sort of cult belief that the clone would offer true immortality - However, the Protocols had foreseen this complication, along with the inevitable rampant nepotism, and only permitted natural progeny to inherit. And so, even if the legendary goal of full transference was reached at some point, the inhabiting consciousness would be a clone that had none of the wealth or power of its originator. A simple, elegant solution.

The two minute pre-arrival signal flashed and, as per the Protocols, Banner took off the camo, seeing his actual face in the mirror for the first time in months. No surprises: It was still the same, square jaw, roman nose, and blonde hair cropped to military shortness which showed the perfectly aligned ears. He looked nothing like his one hundred and fifty years. Grooming bots appeared and took off the days growth, trimmed nose hairs, pulsed the skin to remove any dead tissue. It would all be recycled: DNA from Seven-Gens was incredibly valuable.

Green eyes were his most unusual feature - almost all High-Gen Mods were blue-eyed, but otherwise, he was the perfect man, as was to be expected. Broad shoulders, legs like tree stumps, arms that could press 400 pounds with ease. Inspection routine complete, the observation bot found his appearance acceptable and he was ported into the debrief room.

Captain Luke Johnson sat there pouring over the reports. He was not a battle design. He was pure thinker - slight, fine features, with an aquiline nose that separated piercing blue eyes that sang with IQ. "I agree and concur, this doesn't add up. All scans from the incoming people on the train showed 20% had been infected, but no signs they had been bitten. Is it transferred by air, or injected by some external radical? Could even be a mosquito, or whatever passes for one down there. We don't know, but something in those wolf-people is triggered to bite the new locals, and it seems to be *after* they are infected." The man glanced up to see if there was any inflection in Banner's eyes. Nothing, as expected. Death Squad leaders were more machine than human.

"What the original virus is, we have absolutely no idea. But obviously, the initial inspection crews missed something and if we are to be able to co-exist here, that something has to be found. First up, I am presuming the General will order the removal of the Wolves. Next is the elimination of the locals, but if we can't get answers after this, then full protocols must be followed. The Zeta has been tested and is fully functional. We want to avoid this. The Planet Hope Consortium that is backing this world will not happily suffer a loss, especially given the mineral value of the planet. They are already pushing higher up the chain for negotiation." Johnson looked up again, to see if the annoyance of the consortium that paid all their wages on this project derived any reaction. It did not.

"Bottom line: If the locals cannot be trusted then we will finalize them and shift in some other slave population to collect what we need for the mining and set up. This goes higher than myself though. Saunders, who you are reporting to, is here in person to assess and direct." Once more he looked up, yes, there it was. These boys are always nervous when meeting a Battle General - and so they should be. Nice to see he had a little humanity left.

"This had been upped to Protocol One, Banner. Personal attention required: Camo units and all items of clothing will have to be removed, Lieutenant, as the General herself is here to question you and authorize you for this possible deep-cleanse." The Captain didn't bother to look up, he preferred girls. Not that the Lieutenant considered stripping in public to be an issue. One clear certainty in the new order, personal preference and prejudice had no place. But he had his curiosity piqued.

"Damn," thought Banner. "My first full Battle General." This meant he would have to pod it to wherever the General's ship was hiding. It would be a matter of blind trust, because no one was ever given the coords to a Battle General's ship. These creatures had lived for hundreds of years, never leaving those incredible war machines that were their homes. Rarely seen and greatly feared, they were the stuff of legend. The fact that one of THESE had been brought into the case was telling Banner just how serious it was. Nothing for it now but to move forward.

As the last details of the meeting were prepared, Banner stood there stark naked. The Captain had mentioned Saunders - Nice - a female, and not Mietah Krog. By all accounts, that one had been mutated beyond the recognition of whatever sex she was. Not that he was allowed to have a preference between boys and girls, but he did.

"Any further orders, Sir?" Banner enquired of the Captain.

"You don't get orders from a lowly Five-Gen, Lieutenant," Johnson said in a tired voice. "I honestly don't know why they bother with rank. I may as well be a private. But no, there are no specific orders other than protocols be followed. If no resolution to the unknown elements at work can be found, wipe the populace, including the settlers. We will need a clean sheet. You know what happens if this doesn't sort the issue. The General is ready to see you now." Captain Johnson flicked off his holoscreen. The image of his projection wavered as he returned to wherever it was he was based.

Banner had a few moments to himself. All these stations were devoid of operational staff, apart from those who ported in to run necessary repairs. Who you 'met' on these ships were holograms, men and women following operational procedures from whatever office or lounge they were in on their home planet. These deep space vessels were monitoring stations, as well as re-fuelling and re-arming points for passing military craft. They were not active warships and were mostly used for political purposes, diplomacy and the like. Their main reason for their continuing existence appeared to be security - these were some of the most heavily shielded craft in existence.

Two hundred years ago, the stations had been essential tools in negotiations with cultures that encountered the human expansion. Alien emissaries would Holo-form in to meet with humans in safety, knowing their mutual adversaries or competitors would not be able to track discussions. Both trade and war were negotiated, with these vessels forming the backbone of all treaties and boundary agreements. But competing civilizations no longer existed and archaic stations like this were now an anachronism from pre-settlement days.

It was very unlike the Federation to have non-essential equipment maintained and operational, so Banner had presumed they were now being used for surveillance. Now he understood - they were jump stations to see a Battle General. He smiled to himself, they had good reason to be paranoid and wanting to remain invisible. When negotiations on one of these ships had failed, it was a General like Saunders who turned up and resolved the matter of the foolish race that defied the Federation.

There was a slight hum to his right, and a portal appeared in the translucent pearl-white bleakness of the space station. He could see the hop pod, the projectile life-craft designed for survival should a ship go down. He had expected to meet some dull admin officer to file his report - but not this. Well, there is a first time for everything. Some autobot came out and packed his files and scans in a secure case then moved them into the pod. He followed in with his clothing in hand. The door whispered closed behind him and he felt the boot of departure - no windows, no sensors - he was shot out into space, moving towards a traction net that would haul him in.

What passed through his mind as he sat in the cold silence was how this was a different scenario to his former missions. The fact he was reporting to a Battle General meant his otherwise mundane research had gone through high-level clearance. Having a ground commander like himself being called up to see an off-planet military admin was one thing, a small indicator of importance. But THIS meant absolute priority.

In normal situations, a Seven General asking to see a battle lieutenant personally usually meant they were preparing to do deep scans of the planet to get answers. If this didn't get find a solution, one by one, clients would be brought in for interrogation. People would lose their minds, and it would continue until the puzzle was sorted. In the past, entire colonies had been 'neutralized' in this manner. If the locals on any planet got a hint there was a Battle General on their door, panic would run through the entire civilian population.

Perhaps an hour had passed before he felt the grasp of the traction net and the change of direction. The pod itself was a non-traceable one, if you got lost in space with this, you were never found. He was almost grateful, except he knew he was not going to a picnic. Saunders was the most ruthless, vindictive, and feared soldier in the fleet.

The door slips open, his document case is beamed out in advance (You were not allowed to carry anything at all when seeing a General, another security precaution) and Banner stepped through to see the black, tight-fitting battle suit of the most definitely female General - a particularly fine specimen. His jaw almost dropped, she was absolutely stunning. Saunders glanced up, read the stats, then looked hungrily at the handsome officer in front of her.

"Nice," she said to herself, not concerned that he heard. Battle hard, fine muscle tone, not a gym junkie, with a full eight pack. And he was beginning to harden up at the sight of her - How very delicious. This one not only kept up with regulation, he enjoyed it. Good to know, "Come here field commander," she said as she unzipped her ablutions panel. She saw him come fully erect and she became instantly wet.

She pulled him in for full and immediate penetration, then grabbed his buttocks to urge him on. This was one of the best parts of the job, and so nice to find an army boy who was more than happy to oblige.

Banner, of course, enjoyed himself - but thought little of it. He liked female Generals and this incredibly rare battle one was delightful - but he also knew when this was done, the questions would start. Best to keep this going as long as possible!

It wasn't difficult - Apart from the fact women just suited him a whole lot more than male Admins, this one was amazing. He had known in theory how the genetic modifications for Battle Generals created an extreme sex drive but experiencing it was another thing entirely. He was finding the job surprisingly pleasant!

Power and sex were so entwined it was not possible to unwind the gene maps, nor was it considered necessary to do so. Plus this natural attribute gave motivation for Generals to want to stay in contact with the leading edge where battle commanders always were. And all of them liked these lieutenants. They were the ones who did the hard yards on the colonies, as a result they were always rugged and powerful creatures.

However impressed Banner was, Saunders found herself enjoying this man in a way she had never experienced. This one, full Seven-Gen, full mods, and Green Eyes? He just did it for her, so much so she started to orgasm.

"My God!" she used the archaic term for pleasure, and then she did the unthinkable. No General ever removes their outfit. It is called a skin suit because it is effectively a second skin - it sterilizes the body, cleans everything bar the defecation and urinary tracts, and even enhances oxygen absorption. Every suit registers the thoughts, feelings and physical stress of every General, and each is wirelessly connected to a main-frame. The net result is that, purely by thought alone, when wearing such a suit the entire Starship can be controlled by a single General. Entire planets could be, and had been, vaporized on a whim by a general such as Saunders wearing one of these.

A Seven-Gen Battle General does not need subordinates. They are a lethal army of destruction all on their own. They didn't sleep in any conventional sense of the word, but were wired in and aware even as the body itself slumbered. But this type of extreme power needs to be balanced with extreme control and, as a result, all the Generals were tied into the Admin. Every quantum and nuance they experienced was measured and sent to the central registry for inspection. No-one was above anyone in the New Order.

Big Brother IS watching in this new world. It starts with your first mod, and the surveillance only increases as you feed up the chain. Every action by this General was monitored, so much so that even the smallest shift in protocol would be noted and adjudged by an equal party. In this case, General Sarswich was flagged and found himself looking at the sight of Saunders enjoying herself. Ah, the trigger for him to look in, she had revealed her bosom to the trooper and ordered him to lick it.

Interesting, not something that happens every day, but very enjoyable to observe. Sarswich was wondering if she wasn't doing this to give him a jolly, but he looks at the readouts. Purely sexual - extremely sexual - no other connotations. Unusual, but acceptable. He mentally shrugs, ticks it off as authorized and gets back to his work.

What was unusual was how much Banner found he was enjoying this particular High-Mod. He was not hardwired into the same mainframe, nor were his personal feelings considered important unless they tripped anarchy or excess aggression. In his case, only extreme negatives would have raised alarms. As a field commander, you were expected to kill as needed, but you were not supposed to enjoy it, and sex in the lower ranks was ignored.

In the here and now, he found himself being excessively enthusiastic and the General found herself becoming extraordinarily intrigued. And then he came! She felt his semen in her, but rather than immediately calling for it to be recycled, she wanted to feel it. She wanted to feel him, and as she did so her sensory implants started up yet another round of orgasms. This was number seven, she had never had more than two in the past.

"Oh yeah," she said as his hardened member stayed firm. "More? You can do MORE?"

Banner nodded and kept pushing, harder and harder until number eight arrived. Then NINE. There had never been a nine, ever. And TEN! The Generals eyes began to roll, her tongue started licking his sweat, and for the first time in her life, her lust was satiated. Her body was trembling, her fingers shaking with electricity, and before her rigorous military mind could snap back in, she FELT it.

Impossible!! She felt her body take the semen and fertilize a cell. She was PREGNANT. Her intuition knew it, every part of her knew it. But she was a Seven, it was not possible. He was a Seven, it was not possible. The mitochondrial alterations created an effective sterility, their type could not reproduce. At that moment, Saunders made a decision, one that would change the course of history: She ripped off all of her suit.

Normally, a huge red flag, but it had already been flagged and authorized. However, she knew what would happen if her suit recognized the fertility - She would be dissected and analyzed, to see what had happened and if it could be reproduced. No-one had ever thought an Eight was possible! It was a purely theoretical possibility, a

DNA dream. Man was made, then modified, to fit the image of a God - he or she was not a God itself.

The woman in her took over. Despite what she knew she must do, the General found she could not order her body to extinguish it. Instead, Saunders ordered a medlab, then plunged a scalpel into her abdomen to remove the fertilized egg from her womb. Looking at it longingly, not even knowing how she knew which one it was other than her instincts told her, she drew it up into a sustaining fluid capsule used for clones and gave it to the cyber-doctor who had just entered. "This is a test subject for incubation, Doctor. I do not want this cloned in a tank - I want this given natural birth. You will need to implant this cell into a level Six Surrogate - I want this experiment run on Planet Hope."

The cyber doctors metal eyes do not notice the completely naked soldiers or pay attention to the wound in the Generals belly. Level Seven regeneration capabilities are legendary and their wound repair ability out-strips the best medical science can do, even here in the 27th century. This doctor is a thinking robot, there for emergencies - it does not even question the request. The issue it brings up is merely a compliance question. "Hope is a new planet, it has no Level Six surrogates, General. The colony is not set up for breeding."

The General stabilized her metabolism, readjusted the hormonal balance, and ran an interim mental routine to alter perception. When she put her suit back on, nothing must seem to be amiss. What she wants is no more attention to be paid to this area of space and for her little colony to develop without the need to implement protocols. As she slips her suit on, "Do we have an army nurse at Level Six?"

"Of course, the head nurse." The Doctor replies.

"She will suffice. Needless to say, the woman will need an associate for the upbringing of the child and I will place Lieutenant Banner here in charge of this unique experiment. You are expected to monitor the situation and post me a yearly report on progress, Doctor. Is this clear?"

"Perfectly Madam General." It responds, nodding with a slight bow as respect for her elevated status and rank, and then withdraws to start the procedure. It does not question where the fertilized egg came from, this was not its place.

"You will take this robot with you," Saunders said, still breathing hard and sweating from the extreme workout. Her body was already repairing itself as she zipped her skin suit back on. "This is an important experiment that will need your personal supervision, Banner. Do you comply?"

Banner just nodded. He had questions in his mind, but they were clouded by the continuing sense of passion he felt for this incredibly hot creature. He started to harden up once more Saunders looked down, laughed, and said - "Well, it will take a while for our cyber doctor to get organized." And they got right back to it.

It was different, she felt herself floating, free of care, or any sort of concern. What was this state? She liked it, she felt wonderful, was this the bliss they spoke of in the old earth texts? Sartorii! She moved past control and into her heart, feeling a sense of warmth, kindness, generosity. How very strange! She felt herself slip into dreams, in some way TRUSTING this man inside her.

As she drifted in a deep harmony, Saunders experienced an awakening - the most extraordinary awareness struck, a thing she had not realized as she removed the egg - *there was NO PROTOCOL for this!* Primarily, she supposed this was because it was thought to be impossible. As a result, no flags would be raised from her actions - there will be no inquiry to check her request. It will be registered as an experiment, the type of thing she sets up on a constant basis. She will receive reporting and no one will ever ask why. For some reason, this made her feel happy. What an unusual sensation.

Opposing this, a depressive blackness in the back of her mind also woke up, hating the restrictions she was under. That part wanted to lash out, destroy, cleave a path through the idiocy of the admins she was controlled by. She understood her multi-faceted self - the many layers of being must be accepted and understood if you were to survive hundreds of years of effective isolation in deep space as she had. For now, the greater part of her was simply enjoying being a woman.

Finally, Banner was done, he fell into an easy chair that had been brought up for him. His sweat was brushed off by micro-bots, and collected. The carbon-dioxide was analyzed as he breathed out, every parameter of his body was cross-checked while he momentarily fell asleep.

Saunders smiled as she re-integrated her thoughts with the skin suit - the feed to her ship came back online. She was surprised, she had allowed herself to be vulnerable - she had allowed herself to 'not' be aware of every single thing occurring in the space around her, yet she felt wonderful. This was another question mark in her mind, she was temporarily disconnected from her ship, yet calm, relaxed, and at ease? It was so very odd. And if anything is odd, it needs to be examined. She made a mental note to run this through her intuits during the next contemplation period.

But for now, the usual debriefing and assessment as required by the guidelines must begin. "Lieutenant, you are registered with high initiative and also high intuition. (Banner comes to and nods his agreement) Yet, even as a Seven, you are not able to fully understand the information provided. This report before me makes no sense to myself as well, which is simply not possible. The only conclusion we can therefore reach is that there must be an underlying rationale we have not recognized that is the trigger for actions by the settlers and wolves on Planet Hope.

"I want you to do a deep mind scan on all affected persons. I want you to go back BEFORE the causation of the infection and see what you can find in these subjects that altered the expected situation. What we have is an undiagnosed virus and an indigenous population that behaves differently to assessment. Either the assessment is wrong, which is a major issue, or some causative agent has intervened to create this scenario. This is an even more significant issue.

"The second is clearly the most likely and we must identify it for future habitations. What is causing this chain of events on Planet Hope? We need to know. You are granted three days to report back."

And in an off-hand manner, as he departed for an exit pod, she added, "And you will be given the head nurse to care for as a private arrangement. She will shortly be pregnant, the child she fosters will need a father to train it." She paused, barely believing she is saying what comes out of her mouth. "In this unique experiment, you will train this child for six years in all disciplines, pre-mods, do you understand? You will start the training at Age Four."

Banner simply nodded. It was not his role to question. His mind simply noted the variables and the obvious. He is given three days to find the problem on Hope, yet he is being given a long term assignment at the same time? If she wanted this experiment trained up to pre-mod stage, it would be ten years old before he was done. Answer: The General has a greater plan in mind than meets the eye.

Noting the obvious, he nodded - it was an unusual challenge. To train a child in the physical attributes is hard enough to do pre-mod, but psyche and perception training without them? He did not even know it was possible. For optimum results you began implants at age ten, and six years of raw effort prior could easily turn a child to a vegetable, or kill it. He mentally shrugged: Well, if the child died, it died.

Further, he had three days to find a solution before deep scanning of every native and settler commenced. Well, something would have to turn up. More to the point, the logic of the General's orders appeared contrary. If she expected the planet to be cleansed, how could it be that he would be staying to supervise the experiment with the child? Clearly, she wants to report to her superiors that the matter on Hope was contained.

Banner was no fool, he got the message. What the General was saying, without saying it, was that his assignment was to last at least ten years, at which point the child would be taken into camps and given upgrades. Yet she was also saying he needed to solve the question marks in the reports because if the locals had to be wiped, his Death Squad would be moved to the next difficulty and a habitation crew moved in. So she was telling him very clearly that she believed it was solvable and that, logically, elimination of the locals was not the option she wanted. It was as clear a "fix it soldier" as he had ever heard.

Well, he would find a way.

It never occurred to him as he climbed into the pod with the cyber-doctor that the child he was being given to train might be his own child, and it would never occur to anyone else. A Seven could not have children, this was known.

Settlers

Settlers were ordinary folk, no-mods as they were disparagingly known by admin. Their tasks were always mundane, organize the food supply, do the set-up on a planet and perform the minutia of build requirements that the bots were not programmed for - the weird little things that still needed human hands - A.I. could build a space ship, but it could not tie shoelaces. They were the dogsbody on call for any urgent need by the corporation. Not everyone had "blow-tech" as the instant manufacturing bots were called, because it was expensive and otherwise limited to the military and high mods, so, on the ground, peasants were still needed for assembly and repair of equipment.

Hope was being mined, obviously, as this was the primary income on all start-up colonies, but the planet was also being modeled as a tech-center, where local materials would be converted into parts and necessary maintenance equipment for the electronics industry. Light-Pipe computer parts, replicators, and nano-bot breeding were destined to become the core business of Hope. This meant that settlers were largely chosen for their ability in these areas.

The Planet Hope Corporation paid for all expenses associated with the planetary settlement, including the army and the extensive build costs. As a result, they effectively owned all settlers who arrived there. Their contracts were specific, no-mods were provided accommodation and food, plus a small stipend until their re-settlement was fully covered. In return, they did any and everything asked of them for a ten year period, with the option held by the company for a further ten years. It was a form of slavery, but this was far preferable to where they came from.

The message was simple: Do your bit and, in return, you have a comfortable existence. Modern life in the early part of the 27th century was, in this way, a reasonably pleasant affair. An administration controlled by set regulations, no politicians, and protocols which were enforced at all stages by High Mods, rather than any court. Essentially, at the top, it was an egalitarian society run by the modern traders, soldiers, and dignitaries. At the bottom, a feudal arrangement.

There was no voting, a No-Mod had no say in how anything worked. You just did what you were required to do and you received a decent existence in return. Since the end of the home planet, High Mods were the only ruling voice, but they were not specifically unkind to the no-mods - if you just did your job, everyone got on. But be lazy, or stupid, and you suffered.

Petra was one of the lucky ones accepted for this new planet. It was her one day off and so she was going into Wolftown. As a free settler on a new planet, she was in the fortunate position of being able to work for rights and gain a safe haven for old age. Just put in twenty years in a new settlement and you had your company home in perpetuity, which also meant your children had a right to stay there as well. Just being here allowed her the right to raise her own child, as there were no nursery farms on new settlements.

Planet Hope was well named, it was a nice place, with a local populace that was a sort of wolf-humanoid hybrid. The "Wolves" as everyone called them were extremely friendly and welcoming, and Wolftown was a safe place for a human woman to walk. It was a lot more than you could say for most of the new worlds, where existing populations treated the settlers with hostility, rightly considering them interlopers. Today she was taking her boy and his friends to update some game software. Free Settlers lived in a compound outside of town and took a transit bus in on their days off.

Petra called out. While waiting for her irrepressible child to turn up, she gazed out to the forest that surrounded their settlement. Such a beautiful place, though very dangerous, of course. There was a real need for the high fences surrounding them as this planet had several apex predators, but it was a strikingly wonderful place in every other respect. The air was pristine, it filled your lungs with energy and was full of life.

Bugs, millions of them, and birds that fed on them, thousands every morning - So very different from the sterile metal and concrete world of her last planet. There you looked up and all you saw was grey, and to find a tree or a natural creature meant a journey of hours out of the industrial wastelands where she had worked. Here, the sky was clear, littered with clouds against a backdrop of hues from blue to purple. But it was the aurora that really got you, a spectacular array of shifting color, and a thing you never tired of. It was like living in art.

Petra called out again, "Dexter!" Kids being kids, they were running around, finding an allocation point on the transit, and generally laughing and playing as all children do. Free-settler progeny did not 'belong' to anyone but, needless to say, a mother always favored her own. And Petra's little blond-haired nuisance needed someone to look after him because he was always in no end of trouble. Dexter was his name, and he was the ring leader in every bit of high-jinks that turned up. For now, no-one really minded, but he was already almost eight, and once he reached registration age he would have to tighten up. If you got a trouble tag from a supervisor you became one of the unlucky ones and were given all the slosh jobs.

The boy laughed into view. He was the natural leader of the tribe of kids she took with her. They filed onto the transit, going past the newly installed radionic scanners as they did so. Apparently, these were to check if they had been contaminated. Anyway, they were off - no blinking lights. But really, there was no problem, the settlers all knew it was just new planet jitters. She noted a few miners were already on board, such ugly, nasty men as they were. Always up in the mountains foraging with deep scans in places the satellites could not properly reach. They were the richest of the no-mods, not betoken to the company, and arrogant beyond belief.

From the top to the bottom of any society there are layers. Outcasts were the very lowest, of course. Just above this were the non-coms, those who had for the most part just blasted their minds with psyche drugs. Then came the slockers, the ones always mucking out doing the dirty work, then it came to people like herself - one of the workers - then management, followed by artisans and makers, with the miners on top.

Some of these miners even made enough money to get a few basic mods, but they were never registered. However, having deep vision, or night scope was a tremendous advantage in their business, and it was these modded miners who were at the very top of the No-Mod tree.

Overall, the task was simple: Set up the planet to become productive. This required a few years of very intense and hard work, but after this, original settlers were given preferential and, as long as they continued to muck in as and when required, life was pretty much set and comfortable from that point. Petra was a silicon ionizer, she prepped the computer parts for integration with the circuits. Long hours, low pay, but very clean and secure. Plus, she could not get dirt into skin, which affected the silicon, so she was free from the low end.

It was with real joy that she sat there on the hover-bus, this was a good place. The transit hove to over the forests and shortly Wolftown came up on the plex-screens. Petra smiled, she was very happy with this move to Hope. Here, she had a real chance for progress.

It was an astonishingly beautiful world. The exceptionally clean air, the twin moons, and a sun that ionized the atmosphere and created the most spectacular lights and auroras. You could feel a sense of freedom here, so very unlike the old world where she had lived since a child. That was a place so stratified and controlled that you needed permission to even shop. Even buying a new piece of clothing required approval slips. But on Hope, when you earned credits you could spend it in any way you liked. No paperwork, no layer upon layer of admins to plow through for every detail: It was good here.

Plus the opportunities were so much greater. For one, Dexter would not have to bond himself to a trader or maker to have the opportunity to reach artisan status. Talent is what mattered on a new planet, not family, or connections, or bribes. He was very creative and on Planet Hope his options for a good life were so much greater. And so there it was, they were the lucky ones. Petra smiled to herself as the end of the journey approached. The transport parked on the fringe of Wolftown, unpacking the new arrivals - It filled her with a deep-seated sense of happiness. This was working out well. Of course, the rumors of the bug had filtered through, it was a worry, but everyone wanted to make more out of it than it was worth. The real issue was the 'other' rumor, that a Seven General had been called in, but that was nonsense. This only ever happened with a priority planet and theirs was a sleepy backwater.

On the bus, the gossips whispered of doom and uncertainty, "One of the cleaners swears she saw some Death Squad soldier, she did. She swears she did!" said one woman. Petra laughed, everyone knew if you SAW the Death Squad you never lived to talk about it. Their near-perfect camouflage meant they could be standing three feet away and you would never know it

They arrived at the town, with the wolf people there to greet them. They were always so friendly and welcoming. Of course, you paid a coin for entry, but once in the market place, all the alien produce, the strange game sets that the kids absolutely loved, it was all there and so very cheap.

The peculiar buildings of the wolves were not square and angular like the company constructions. They were organic, using the natural twists and bends in timber to make doorways and windows, which gave everything a very homely and welcoming appearance. Shops did not have display windows, or any signs at all to advertise wares, but open racks outside were used to show the goods, and purchases were done in private inside. She gathered there was no theft, because not one place had security bars nor any sort of alarm.

The Wolf People themselves were quite humanoid. Trans-com links had solved the language barrier, so their dog-howl voices were understandable, but it was those soft brown eyes that Petra loved. They were truly a beautiful race, with a gentle demeanor and thick fur that held a rich array of patterns. They had articulated hands, rather than paws, so the wolves could use tools, and they walked gracefully on hind legs. All this made them seem more human than dog. However, the long canines showed they were clearly carnivores, and the meat on display outside the butcher shops was never cooked. This was still a primitive race and settlers had been warned not to provoke the locals.

A snack for a wolf child was raw flesh, still dripping with blood, and they enthusiastically ripped into it with a low growling sound of contentment. These wolf-folk really did look like what you saw in the documentaries on the home planet, the ones about wolves in forests, though these people were clearly humanoid-based.

Petra felt strangely secure around them. Maybe she had finally found a place she could call home. She was waiting outside a store where the kids were buzzing about with the local little wolves, checking out the latest toys and holo-games, when one of the miners that was on the bus came up behind her. In a gruff voice, he demands, "I want you woman, on your knees!"

What? Here? In the middle of Wolftown, with everyone watching? Petra went to object, but he just beat her to the ground. "I said on your knees woman, are you deaf?"

This was always the worst of a small settlement. You had no rights, and if a miner wanted you, there was nothing you could do to stop him. Her son was tuned into his mother's thoughts and he felt her distress. That is when it happened! To his horror, he saw it all! The thing that would be forever engraved into the child's mind. Dexter felt his mother's anxiety and looked up. The miner pushes Petra down and, for no reason, takes out a plasma-ax. With no warning, he shears her in half! There and then, completely in half. From head to tail.

Blood gushes out over the stone cobbles that make up the street, and the wolf people all turn towards it, but their friendliness is gone. Now they have a very strange and different look about them. The smiles are gone. The happy soft eyes are now hard, furious, and deadly. They all turn into predators, pure and simple.

Only one wolf attacks, yet it was not running for the fresh meat on the ground that was his mother, the wolf attacks the miner. The closest male launches itself and the child is amazed at how far it can spring. It bites into the neck of the offending human and the man falls down, screaming. Blood and shattered bone crash onto the pavement. It was like a court of justice has just played out, but before anything further can happen, a shimmering breaks the scene. Dexter feels the blast of hover motors, and can just make out the mirage-like form of what he guessed must have been a Death Squad Transit.

He gasps. It is TRUE? The military elite have come to this little planet, for real? In a blur of activity, the boy senses rather than sees men jumping out and securing the scene. It is only when hands reach out and grab the stricken miner that the blood splashes and creates an outline of the camo-suits. A full squad of soldiers is on the scene, netting the miner. The wolf has already run, but they have no interest in pursuing it.

The child goes up, blank, not really comprehending what has happened. He speaks to what is effectively thin air. "Hello, I saw it, I saw it all." An officer materializes, obviously switching off his suit, and asks what the boy is doing. Dexter stammers, "My mother. The miner killed my mother."

The man is kind and puts the child onto the sled, saying "Wolf-bite kid. It infects the brain, he didn't know what he was doing. Real sorry for you, I am. I understand because my mother died in front of me as well." Then he looks up, and says to his chief officer, "Sarg, this kid saw everything. Bring him along?"

Sargent Walsh looked over, sees the scruffy little no-mod, wide-eyed and in sheer wonder of the strange soldiers that appeared in front of him. Their orders were to capture any rabid humans and to bring them in alive for testing. A witness to the event might be useful. He goes over and pulse scans the neuronic receptors of the child, as he needs to make sure he is clean. He raises an eyebrow. "Interesting news Corporal, you seem to have collected yourself a candidate. Yeah, we bring him in."

"Damn it, kid," says the corporal as the lad is taken onto a transit sled, "you are as lucky as I was. Same thing happened to me, my mother died, an officer on the scene scanned me, and I got into the academy. Out of the crap pile and into uniform! It's the only place to be in our society. Do well, pass the tests, and you are gonna grow up with some RIGHTS boy, some actual RIGHTS."

Dexter, the freshly orphaned boy was in shock and simply did not comprehend anything. All he could see was the miner for no reason, slicing up his mother. He took out his plasma ax and for no reason at all, just cut her through. Then the wolf leaped up and bit him. But here it starts to get weird, his mind seems to want to recall the wolf biting the miner, THEN he kills his mother. But that was not it, that was not it at all.

The second vision seems to want to reinforce itself, but Dexter KNOWS what he saw. This is not how it was. He saw it, he saw it clearly. Then strong feelings, powerful emotions start to generate nausea in his gut. He wants to throw up, avoid this conflict. He just wants to hide. He feels desperation, loneliness and then the shock creeps in. It hits him hard, and all he wants to do is sleep. He can not resist sleep.

Discovery

Banner was hard at work trying to solve the conundrum. The issue was further complicated by the recent weirdness with the transit clerk. Did someone bribe the woman? And why? It didn't make any sense. And it was more like she had been controlled in some way. He had her synapses examined, but apart from the infection, there did not seem anything specifically to cause her to act in the manner she did.

One of the most significant benefits of the camo-suits he and his men wore was that they could walk in the civilian populations and not be noticed. If people see an authority figure, they automatically act differently. When the Death Squad was around, no-one was aware of their presence. In this way, they got to see how people acted and lived without their fear and inhibitions causing them to put up a facade. Banner had just gotten word of the commotion in the market in Wolftown. He was still waiting for the report, fantastic luck, to be there as it happened - but their presence was now known. This meant would mean everyone would be nervous.

Well, they should be. Resolving this matter was going to cost more than a few settlers their lives. And if it kept tilting towards more unknowns, well, they were called the Death Squad for a reason. Higher up the command chain, loose ends like this were not tolerated, and question marks that could not be answered were eliminated.

He was working in the lab running tests in person now. This business was threatening to wipe out the entire first settlement of Hope, directly contravening everything Saunders had asked for. As he was the only Seven on the planet, Banner was the one to sort it. And so today he was a lab tech, trying to solve a jigsaw that made no sense.

The still living, gassed clients from the initial transit were easy to scan, but non-focused minds were a bother to wade through. Too many extraneous thoughts kept confusing the subtle probes set into the cortex, and so sharp jolts were generally used to shock the dendrite trees and disconnect the inner cortex from the outer brain. This stopped the automatic protection devices each mind develops and made deep cortex readouts far more accurate.

This had the unpleasant side effect of causing madness, as often the connections inside the brain got overloaded or shorted out, much like an electric motor given too much juice. As this lot had not yet committed a crime, even though the disease predated that they would, he left them in soma and started with the recently deceased. Even when dead, if the bodies were collected before they went cold, the brain still had synapse activity locked in place. Here you blew apart the neurons, strand by strand, looking for a common thread, and invariably a pattern of the past experiences would emerge.

Yet in every single case where there was some sort of infection present, the twenty-four hours prior to death was hazy. He then loaded up some of the still-living clients, and it was the same. Yet in their case you go back two days, three, four, and readouts are clear. Something was causing memory loss in a SPECIFIC time frame.

This can only mean one thing: Something was trying to hide.

Now, while the living subjects did have a primary infection, these were people who had not yet been bitten by a wolf. Banner detected a chemical change of sorts beginning to occur BEFORE they got bitten.

The wolf bite, therefore, appeared to exacerbate an existing condition, one that subsequently turned ordinary settlers into murdering monsters. But it was clear, there was something ELSE that had infected them prior to this. The more he looked, the more Banner was gathering the wolf bite somehow accelerated an existing condition, not cause it.

What made sense to him was that a resident population knew and sensed a dangerous infection, so perhaps their instinct controlled them. Or maybe they had a sixth sense for this strange virus and simply reacted when they felt it? It made sense, and he sincerely hoped it was this simple, as it would relieve the pressure of having to repopulate this world with workers. If this were the case all they need do is track the source of infection and eliminate it.

Jumping to conclusions is generally a fatal mistake, but for a Seven with high Intuit Mods it was normal behavior, and usually accurate. The brain was so integrated with correct logic and harmonic math that intuition in a High-Mod Intuit was like an economist predicting a trend. In doing so they appear to access the unknown aspects of consciousness. And Banner had Intuit specs that ran off the chart. He closed his eyes, and went deep into Theta, looking for the rhythm, finding the pattern. Yes, something prior HAD happened that triggered the Wolf People, something that was missed by the first scans.

Anything missed by a deep planet scan had to be in a black zone, the areas where natural planetary conditions, such as radionics in the rocks, or deep caverns full of copper. Such things acted like a Faraday cage which prevented a clear read. But this would have registered, and a robotic crew would have been sent in. In the one rare instance in the past where a similar such an event had occurred, it turned out to be an extra-dimensional, conscious entity. Therefore the probability of them moving to a planet that had a highly evolved but hidden race was now starting to increase.

Messy. Could there really be another species resident here that was missed by scans? The last time this occurred it ended up in a very brutal and ugly war. Finding another such issue was not something anyone wanted to deal with. But if such a thing were missed, what was it, and where was it?

The lieutenant now KNEW that there was a significant external event, one common to all affected, but time was running out to discover exactly what it might be. His mind clicked into place: An active intelligence was hiding on Planet Hope. This was almost the worst possible outcome. It meant sweeping the table clear and dealing with the issue. Neutralizing a resident population of intelligent beings was genuinely frowned upon, but it was the case of not harboring a snake in the house. It didn't mean to hurt you, but the fact it was there meant it could, and most likely would at some point. So you kill everything that might be hiding it as a precaution.

Banner then tried another tack. He scanned to see if there was any class of wolf that actively targeted these humans. Perhaps one subset was the specific control issue, but while the assailants on settlers were young males for the most part, it seemed that any one of the species could be potential attackers.

Regardless of who did the biting, the effect was devastating for the client. Their core DNA was affected and rabies-like symptoms emerged soon after. Rampant sex drive, aggression, and a lack of any sense of social structure were all typical - but the desire to eat raw meat was the most overwhelming trait shared by all who had been infected. So the afflicted settler would kill and eat anyone or anything that came across their path. The human became like one of those old-fashioned Zombies in the pulp magazines

But no wolf-person was ever attacked! The target was always another human or an animal. Clearly, the modifier in the gene pool was a very subtle one, and further, what they had on this planet seemed old. Could the wolf reaction to the infection be an archaic response from the species ancestral memory as a predator? Only one thing was certain, the wolves could sense an infected human.

On the blower to his team, Banner ordered yet another scan of any terrain that the clients had traversed during that missing day. A disturbing thought: Was something consciously trying to hide? It would seem so. If things do not add up it is because there is a missing piece to the equation. Could there be some conscious entity that was purposefully confusing memory, knowing it would be scanned? Well, any human admin with decent tech equipment could do this. He himself had done so on many occasions. The real question was if there were such a sentient on THIS planet sophisticated enough AND motivated enough.

Right at that moment fortune smiled. The Sargent in charge of Wolftown reports in. "Sir," a com report lights up. In the background, a field team has clearly lassoed an infected human with a neuronic net. "We got one still alive. It's bitten and active, but completely out of its mind. It is like old fashioned rabies in an advanced stage."

Excellent news! Everything he had hoped for. "Bring it in, Walsh. Good work. VERY good work. Commendation to all involved and special credits, including two days in a pleasure dome. BUT it must be alive. I want no, I repeat NO enthusiastic killing happening between here and wherever you are, yes?"

"Sir!" Sargent Walsh salutes. He was but a Three, not strong in any specific characteristic, but two days in a pleasure dome? Wow! This was a reward given only to Sixes and above. And ALL the men get this? They will love him. They already loved Banner, the man was their sort of superior officer. Walsh breaks the good news to the men, emphasizing the miner must not be harmed.

Banner is there when 'it' is brought out of the transport. The thing had reverted to something utterly primitive. It was barely human and had reverted to savagery. He looks at the report: Found just after it had sliced a woman in two, a poor thing who had taken her kids into Wolftown. He orders a byte by byte total memory read of the miner. Not a survey, but a complete fingerprinting of every synapse as and when it activated, where the signal went, and what it did.

Then his intuit mods click in. "Anything else to report Sargent?"

Walsh smiles quietly. Nothing gets past Banner. "We have a witness, Sir. The woman's child was present and saw the whole thing. We also have reports from all on the ground who were present. It is synced and ready to draw down." Walsh salutes, signifying the close of his report.

Banner looks at him, "What else, Walsh?"

Dammit, how do these Sevens know everything like this? "Ah, I scanned the child, Sir. He came up as a candidate." He sends the readout to his superior.

The lieutenant focuses the camera to the back of the transport. A pale-faced child, clearly in shock, lying down and asleep. He goes over the stats, then checks again. He looks one more time, to be certain. "There are no mods on this child, you checked?"

"No Sir, no mods. Same DNA as the dead mother, no question he is her child."

"Bring him in and have a Doctor standing by, both for the infected one and to make sure this child comes out of shock without memory loss. I want to know EXACTLY what happened." Then Banner pauses and uses this opportunity to reinforce loyalty. "As you know, because the child is a candidate, I cannot and WILL not deep-probe unless he is proscribed. You ALL have this protection."

In a nutshell, Lieutenant Banner had emphasized the core message to his recruits of WHY they were there. Those simple words outlined the very reason so many were grateful to get into uniform. Once accepted into the corp, you had RIGHTS. No one could come up and destroy your neurons just to see what you were doing or thinking on any particular day. Only if you had a significant tick against you could this auto-protection be overridden, and only then by the authorization of a Sixth or above. It gave the men a real sense of security.

Once at the lab, the miner was cleaned up. This meant all hair is removed, all trace of dirt, the stomach is pumped, the entire digestive tract pumped clean and ALL of this if micro-inspected. Bloods are taken, brain cells sampled and lymph fluid is drained for inspection - all while the fellow is wide awake. Every little trace of wherever the person has been is analyzed and categorized, what they ate, even the air they breathed has remnants left on the lung walls. It is excruciatingly painful, but no drugs can be administered that might contaminate the findings. The client survives for deep scanning, but they usually wish they hadn't.

It takes an hour before the subject is ready, and Banner is there, conducting the process personally. He is immune to the screaming and just focuses on the matters at hand. And he is not disappointed. There is a clear path from forensics of where the man has been for five days and, as he initially suspected, he had been in the deep zones in the mountains, the areas where satellite scans did not penetrate.

The wolf bite was brutal, right over the ceratoid artery, cutting the Sterno-mastoids and inflicting severe lacerations. These wolf people knew how to kill, yet the bite did not extinguish the fellow as you would expect. The artery had managed to repair itself, something only a Seven could do in sufficient time to prevent death, and many of the severed muscles had already begun to re-knit.

Interesting. Whatever reaction their saliva had, it was a remarkable bit of chemistry, one designed to keep the victim alive. It made no sense. He started the probe, tapping into the memory pathways, and there it was, clear as day. The miner is walking along, gets bitten, then goes mad. He slices the woman in two. Again, the prior day is hazy. Same as the other clients, but this time he has a live one and thus can re-probe with correlating evidence from forensics.

Yet it does not add up. The change of chemistry with the wolf-people, the saliva must take on its special property right before they bite, and then it apparently just leaves? They have tested and confirmed that the organics in the Wolves normal excretions just do not have the specific catalyst they find in bite victims. He backtracks, reads through the progression of images, but wait! He goes to byte by byte, one electron at a time, and the link between the bite and the attack is broken.

What the hell? He rescans, the same readout, the same break. He scans again, the same readout, the same break. This of itself is proof of interference because no rescan is exactly the same. Just as two people walk into a room and see different things, two synapse sets always see things slightly differently.

Memory of itself is an amalgamation of images, a gestalt of what we believe we see, and not what we actually saw. Therefore, when you find two perfect correlations in the memory stream, you have a problem. It is like witnesses in a court case testifying and individually saying exactly the same story over and over. This is, of itself, clear proof they had been coached in the story they were to tell.

Well, Walsh had the foresight to bring in a witness. He could only do readouts, not probes on the child, as it was a candidate. But BECAUSE it was a candidate, it could be relied upon for better memory. Fortunately, the child's leading attribute was neuronic response, the precursor to all good recollection ability. And he had a hell of an attribute: Level Five, no Mods. This is the stuff Generals were made of.

Dexter did not get the full clean up that the miner got, but he was scrubbed clean of all dirt and samples were analyzed. Nothing out of the ordinary. His response to being brought out of shock WAS, however. He pushed the doctor aside and made a run for it, right into the Level Six Nurse assigned to him. This was the same woman who had been put with Banner and, apparently, she found the little street urchin funny. She just laughed at his antics. "You are just adorable!: She said as she caught him. Of course, she had already been briefed about his specs and had personally come to supervise his treatment. She just laughed as she caught him and looked closely into the eyes of this so-called level Five no-mod. The Nurse nods - there it is.

It was undeniable, an extraordinarily high capacity. This recognition of sorts seemed to calm the child and then he started to cry. He was still wiping the tears away when the nurse brought him in.

Clicking his tongue in empathy, Banner looked soulfully at the child, saying, "You have had a tremendous loss, child. I can only imagine how you feel, but right now, there is important work we need to go through and I need you to focus."

The child stops crying and the survivor kicks in. "Bullshit!" he says, suspiciously. "You do not give one ounce of crap for what a no-mod feels. What do you want?"

Banner smiles, genuinely. He really liked this one. "We will get on fine, kid. What's your name? (he looks at his chart, and answers himself) Dexter. Dexter, I want you to tell me EXACTLY what happened. And I mean EXACTLY. I don't want anything leading up to or after the event of your mother being killed, just the actual event. I want every single detail, no matter how small."

Dexter looks into the eyes of the Seven. You cannot trust any High-Mods, they send you for deep probes at the smallest infraction. "And if I say anything you don't like, you deep probe and I get to be back with my mother, yes?"

"Child, perhaps you don't realize what your situation is. You have been registered as a candidate on the system. I cannot deep probe you without authorization, but yes, if you continue to be a little pain in the arse then someone up the line will do exactly this. But for myself, I just want the facts. I will tell you why after, but for now: What did you see?"

"I saw two things. This is the part I found very strange."

"Do you usually see two things?" Banner inquired.

"I always see when people are saying one thing while meaning another, but this is different. Right at the outset, I clearly saw the miner lift up his stone cutter and kill my mother by cutting her in half. I saw this as clearly as a bell will ring. Without provocation, he takes out a cutter and slices her in two. I then see the effect the miner's actions have on the wolf people, they go all strange, and one of them leaps up and bites him. A young male leaped through the air and attacked the miner. But I could tell, any one of them would have."

Banner remains impassive, saying nothing, but noting that every readout on the child sees this as him being correct and true. The problem is this does not correlate to the scans of what others saw. The core of memory is recalled awareness, which is a completely different area of the brain than the initial observation activates. Most people 'see' two things, but very few catch the split between observation and recollection. The child continues: "But I also see equally as clearly that the Wolf people go strange and, without provocation, bite the miner. After this, he kills my mother."

Banner is impassive. this is exactly the issue where there is a conflict. All memory is an optimization of various streams of information, based on the initial observation. You can 'alter' memory, with the classic case in wartime Germany with Adolph Hitler. There was no specific racial memory of the Jews being evil, but through propaganda and the insertion of believed images into the collective mind, he made Aryan Man superior and the filthy Jew the evil scapegoat. When everyone's 'memories' line up and match - *IE: Jews are bad* - then an external force has been brought to bear to make it so. Rearranging the natural observation and creating artificial recollection is the core of all social programming. It is never WHAT you see, it is HOW you see that matters.

"Which recollection do you believe to be more correct?"

Without hesitation, the child answers. "The first."

"Why?" Banner is now more than curious. The child is absolutely certain, despite two 'memories' in his brain.

"Because this recollection has no gap in reason. Logically, if the Wolf People turn aggressive for no reason and bite humans, then no one is safe. As a result, all the Wolves would be exterminated. They are not stupid and would realize this. As a result of our presence, they would necessarily have to modify behavior. However, if they had this as a reflexive action it would have been noted on the first planetary scans.

"So, for Option Two to exist either the scans are wrong, or the native people here are essentially able to cover up deep instinctual responses to stimuli from the scanning teams. Given they would not have been aware why the humans were here, this is hardly a probability. Firstly, it is almost impossible to hide such a reflexive response and, secondly, hiding a deep instinctual response like this has no primary function in their evolution. Therefore Option Two is extremely unlikely, to the point of being an impossibility.

"Therefore, by deduction, the first observation is the primary and correct one. If the miner goes crazy, it triggers an auto-response in the wolves: they act to protect their society. The primary scans are right, they *are* a peaceful race. When they bite it is because something is triggered as a perceived threat - and I am supposing only in a human. They do not bite their own, do they?"

The commander leans back. Every single thing the child says reads right and, more importantly, it follows his own thoughts. This uneducated child has come to the same conclusion that he had. "No, they do not bite their own, nor do the infected ones ever try to bite a wolf. The question we must ask is why do you have two memory streams?"

"Radionic infection." the child says simply. "Something or someone has broadcast the second memory into my mind in order to hide itself," Dexter concluded.

"Exactly. Something we do not know is on this planet and it has high-level sentience. Would this assessment appear correct and marry with your experience, Dexter?"

The child says nothing. He is suspicious, perhaps he is being baited and led into a trap? Banner notes this and is beyond pleased. He ticks off the boy as a pass for first level induction. Excellent first response. The boy is passing every test. Running him through the acceptance protocols is now merely paperwork for up the chain. This one could be a valuable asset. To the boy, however, Banner just nods and signals Charni, the head nurse, to come and collect him.

"Eating is good for shock, yes?" Charni nods. "Good, feed him up. He has been incredibly valuable and I am certain he will be accepted for training." The pair head off to the mess hall.

The facts were now conclusive. Rather than being a danger, the Wolf People were protectors. Good God, if he had gotten this wrong, the entire project would have been sabotaged. Remove those who instinctively react to this presence and whatever it was hidden here would slowly take over every mind, instilling its own memories. This planet could become the hub of an infection that would spread across all of humanity.

Clearly, whatever it was that was causing this problem lived in regions of the planet that defied resonance scans. The high mountainous regions were the only places that fitted this category, which is precisely where the miner was, looking for resource the auto-scans had missed. Tracking through the data, every single incidence relates back to a contact made with one of the early miners who got into these zones, looking for minerals.

"All miners are to be quarantined immediately," Banner said into his com. "All mining in the sectors I am forwarding through is at this moment immediately banned. Further, no other excursions are permitted to travel to the mountain regions. Only auto-bots to function in all other regions. Effective as of NOW!"

On the next screen, he signaled planetary operations. "All travel by company personnel or settlers to the regions I am designating, as well as all off-planet movement, is immediately banned. This is an absolute ban, no exceptions. Only military craft under my personal authorization can rendezvous with merchant vessels and all trade must be done through auto-bot. No person, no animal, no living thing is to leave the atmosphere of Planet Hope and no-one is to come here. This quarantine is effective as of NOW!"

ooooOOOOOoooo

Far away, General Saunders looked over Banners report, "The sweet boy," she muttered to herself. He had found the perfect solution. A justifiable quarantine that allowed trade to continue. No further escalation until whatever it was could be discovered. It was a 'steady as she goes' approach. Which meant her child now had a safe, secure, and yet suitably challenging environment to grow up in.

And also he found a Level Five natural? So rare. She gave orders, the child was to be inducted and further, he must be raised in the household with a Level Six to maintain observation and training over this candidate. As the only available Six was the surrogate mother of her own child, it was extremely convenient as well. After all, her son would need an older brother to both test and work with him.

Absolutely perfect!

But if the assessment were correct, and she had no doubt it was, they had a serious threat here. This was another reason why she assigned a permanent Seven. Saunders then did another extraordinary thing. Based on the preliminary report of the wolves being able to sense infected humans, rather than their extinction she recommended that a trustworthy platoon of Wolf Soldiers be developed. Reason: She needed to train and enhance their natural predatory recognition of whatever it was that was down there. The rationale for those further up the chain who had to approve this was simple: the infection, whatever it might be, was something the Wolves seemed to have an immunity towards.

But it appeared to be an intelligent virus, therefore the protocols demanded stringent protections. As a final precaution, the Zeta Unit satellite was routed overhead and switched on. She would need no approval to activate it, but now that it was under her jurisdiction no planet-destroying admin could flash it without her getting a warning first.

A weapon of last resort, but whatever was there cannot be allowed to escape. Banner was correct, the entity seemed to be able to travel in the mind of sentients. In normal circumstances, given the report before her, the entire planet would have already been circumscribed and eliminated, including all existing settlers and soldiers. No evac, just an immediate and total write down. Fire the Zeta, problem solved. But her man on the ground had found just enough exclusions for her to not issue that order.

Planet Hope was turning out to be well named.

High risk has high reward. Was the possibility of an Eight worth the risk of whatever was down there escaping? Whatever it was, it had been held there for a long time, and only human intervention threatened to release it. The General's intuits told her that whatever was hiding in the dark places of Hope had been imprisoned there long ago. This planet was clearly a cage: One with a built in set of wardens called Wolves. This fact presented another reason not to deploy extermination, as there was a possibility it might survive. Something that was so infectious it was locked up on a planet with a population that appeared to be immune to it suggested to her the possibility that, a long time ago, some race believed it was not ABLE to be destroyed.

For the present, the ten-year cycle of natural development would continue unchanged. Trade would continue with auto-bots taking minerals and any marketable commodities off-world. Credits would continue to be issued. When the child was ready she would return and see what was required.

The possibility of an EIGHT! Truly, it was worth every iota of risk.

And then another thought passed by her. What an extraordinary situation this was, and given the boredom at the heart of this stale bureaucracy that she personally detested, perhaps she could use this intriguing situation as a perfect camouflage. Hide things in plain sight, as the saying goes.

Rather than rely on the feed from the planets mainframe to see what was happening on Hope, she ordered her nano-bots to generate 'dot-cams'. Usually sent with observation crews to monitor a planet up for colonization, these micro-dot cameras required no power cells and were virtually invisible. Simple neutron streams powered them up.

Saunders smiled her most wicked grin. This was how she would hide her true intentions, by broadcasting everything to the controllers. Banner was going to become a reality show star! She would make Hope a case study for the leadership, recording every single detail of the 'happy family' and beaming this out to the bored bureaucracy. By letting them all keep an eye on everything personally, she should be able to allay fears and stop some Zeta-happy Seven from exploding the place before she was finished with it.

Wolf Soldiers

The First Year

Banner understood why the order for a native platoon was issued, but he understood none of the rank and file would like it. Certainly, not one of his soldiers would happily accept the role of training the wolves. So they were formed up as a separate unit, divorced from any interaction with his own Death Squad or the administration of the planet. The order was to develop one thousand militia - Curious.

His entire Death Squad was just fifty-two men, including himself. More than enough to easily contain a populated world, but he didn't question the General's battle sense. If she wanted a thousand militia, that is what she got. He personally preferred the smaller tribe: Everyone knew each other and every soldier there was the best of the best. Admin generally referred to these squads as a "Deck of Cards". A normal militia can absorb variations, new recruits, etc. but not these highly specialized soldiers.

On developed worlds, you needed that many militia to maintain disciple and order. But here? There was barely a handful of settlers. Saunders must have some greater plan for settlement in mind.

He signed off on the battalion requirements to a place not far from Wolftown. Training of these one thousand wolves would be done there. It didn't take long to set up and the whole thing had proceeded along smoothly. What's more, Banner had been pleasantly surprised. These wolves were not only likable, they were competent.

A year had now passed since Saunders instructions and scans had found a suitable crew. He was amazed to find such high quality potential in a backwater like this and both the male and female wolves they took in proved to be natural soldiers. Wolf society was naturally aligned to a command structure, so there were precious few discipline issues. The more he learned of them, the more he liked what he saw. This was a warrior race and they took to training with gusto. Proving themselves was accepted as a given because in their society all leadership was by merit - No 'royalty' to speak of, only the toughest, fastest and smartest were be selected to rule. Even so, there were certain bloodlines that tended to produce a consistently high grade of warrior. This was born out with selections - particular families were more represented.

The wolves had a very rigid societal structure. Primogeniture ruled the family, with the oldest son inherited the lands, the middle took over business, or pursued arts, etc. while the youngest took on guardianship roles, such as the military. It was logical, for if there were clan wars, the leaders of households did not die in some battle and business would continue. For himself, this meant that even if a first or second born had high potential, they had to be disregarded. Any suggestion of alterations to the social norms was met with an aggressive response from the Wolves. But, regardless of this, there was no shortage of applicants. The enthusiasm for joining a military organization was extraordinarily high.

This was a race born to fight if ever he saw one - and Hope seemed to have been created to breed these warriors. They were quick, damn quick. Most recruits even in pre-training were almost as fast in reflex response as his middle-mod soldiers. Pitted against an ordinary human, the wolf would win every time. Yet they were also very old fashioned. They did not like pulse or discharge weapons, preferring blades and throwing knives, along with their version of a crossbow.

But Banner moved around this odd phobia by getting his techs to modify their crossbows to take modern warheads. The swords were modified to become discharge weapons, and the knives were redesigned to have a boomerang effect. You could throw them and they would return. The Wolves techno-phobic disadvantage was turned into an advantage and it all added an extra dimension to the attacking power of the group.

To date, he had personally been training them. Ridiculous, some would have thought, but the Wolves needed to be impressed by the agility and strength a human could generate. If they felt for one moment they could better their superior, they would be challenging for the role. He needed them to be absolutely clear who was the Alpha - So he personally challenged them and, of course, his intuits told him what the wolf-in-training would do: how he would strike, and when. It was hardly a fair fight, but he laughed as, one by one, they went down. The Wolves sat back in amazement. Again and again, they watched this mere human easily beat the best of them, using their own weapons.

Banner had also been training Dexter alongside the new recruits. An un-modded level five was exceptionally rare AND the child was a natural warrior. It was a perfect combination. Though he was just turning nine Banner got approval for initial mods - the boy took to them like a duck to water. What's more, there were zero latency or rejection issues.

Dexter was going to be a first-class soldier and pitting him against wolves toughened him up.

The whole crew in the barracks knew how Dexter got incorporated, through the death of his mother. Most presumed the boss was being soft-hearted when he took the lad in. But secretly, they were proud. One of their own was being trained personally by the best of the best and no-one doubted Banner was anything but the very best.

The man was legendary. Even as a lo-mod cadet he was beating three ranks higher than himself, but as his Seven Mods took hold, there was no-one and nothing that bested him. But what had made him a legend was how he had taken on a Sevrin on Ionus, single-handed, and WON. Those things were lethal, the barbed tail and thrashing arms slaughtered a normal man in seconds. Yet, even if you survived the physical onslaught, the poisonous breath killed you. Failing that, the mind control it employed sapped your will.

It usually took five trained men to kill a creature like this, but Banner did it on his own. Not because he wanted to, the damn thing crept up on him when he was hiking. Typically, however, when he brought the head back and reported the incident, he made no great fuss. That incident is what short-listed him for command of the death squad, the hardest, most lethal soldiers in the entire human military. They were the ones sent in to solve any and all 'unsolvable' issues with planets and, as a result, they were invariably hated by settlers and locals alike. They were, as named, a squad that brought a lot of death.

But here on Hope, the lads were having a great time. The locals were now fully aware the Death Squad were present, but it caused no conflict. Quite the opposite, the settlers loved them, especially after they beat up or executed a few miners who disregarded the ban, making an example of them in public. Banner issued a general memo, released to both settlers and wolves: The men were here to eradicate a dangerous infection in the human population. This calmed the waters and people accepted a few losses were inevitable for the good of the whole. As a result, inside this last year the whole place had settled down. What this meant was that everyone was happy, in particular, the Hope Consortium who found Hope was turning into a first-class profit center.

The lieutenant's new wife turned out to be a natural and harmonious match for him. The baby that had been born only a few months earlier was robust and already up and walking. It insisted on eating solid food within weeks of taking first breath and its psyche ability was already extraordinary. Whatever the General had in mind with this one, Banner knew why she ordered a Six to be the mother. Nothing lower would have contained this little fireball.

Dexter, despite the extraordinary and sad events that brought him to Banner's household, took well to his new family. He particularly enjoyed the new one, playing with him for hours. Banner found himself thinking of both the lad and the baby as his own family. They all seemed such a natural match and he was disinclined to analyze it further. Some things you just let ride.

But in truth, he had never known a family. All this was new to him and he loved it. All high-mods like himself were part of a breeding program. Often a surrogate had been implanted and you were raised with others of equal potential in a 'baby farm' as they were known. He had never missed having a family because he had never known one, but here and now, he felt enormous joy just watching everyone around him grow and change. Old Earth did have some good traditions and this was one of them.

And another tradition he liked, big cat hunting! Today they were out on a field trip to take on what was the wolves equivalent of a tiger. On this world, so far away from human society, there was still the natural conflict between the dog and the cat, and the Svelteen (as they called it) was one hell of a cat. About the size of the old Earth prehistoric saber-tooth, it stood six-foot-high to the nose and was fourteen foot long, with a tail that stretched a further four feet.

Its claws could slice sheet steel and its bite would easily crush a man's skull. Make a mistake and you never made another one. Plus, like any cat, it was happy to kill purely for the pleasure of it. In short, a worthy challenge. This excursion was more than just a pleasure hunt, however. It was part of the training protocols and every Wolf had a sensor so that Banner could get readouts on each parameter of their reactions to stimuli. You had to place a soldier under a real and actual threat to truly understand them. The wolves rightly feared the Svelteen, as it was their only natural predator that, one on one, would win every time. It made for real-time, battle-like survival conditions.

If the big cats have been able to form a society, they would have eradicated the competition long ago, as the two species had a mutual hatred for each other. Banner lifts his head and whistles. Dexter has a readout. - The quarry had been located! The wolves were of course, completely silent, but they were so excited he could almost hear them baying in his mind. Banner laughed, they were a likable lot, these natural born killers. He and Dexter stayed to the rear, the lad on the techs making sure all the readouts were going into the feed. Banner then went up front to check on some equipment that was giving feedback loops. This was when it happened. *The hunters became the hunted.*

The Svelteen knew it was being chased and, highly intelligent as it was, it had laid a false trail, then circled to the back to pick off the unsuspecting wolves one at a time. But what it found was an unarmed human child. Easy meat, it circled in for the kill, but the quarry had noticed it. The cat was puzzled, the thing knew it was there yet it had no fear. The cat expected fear. All quarry ran, all food was scared, this was part of the taste.

But as it stood there, face to face, no more than 20 feet from the child, the human thing looked back at it calmly. One bound and it was on it, ripping off the head, drinking the blood. And then away before the others realized. Yet the big cat just stood there. The child gazed back, calmly, and in its head, the cat hears a voice - a calm voice. It was a purring tone, something very familiar to it. He remembered this. This was the sound his mother made when she fed him and played with him. It was so warm, so comforting to be back with his family.

This WAS his family. This human child WAS his family. He didn't know why, but inside the Svelteen's mind, this human child was one of its own. The cat felt the sense of being a mother, caring for the weak kitten. That was it: This weak kitten needed care. It did not question that, as the male, it hated male offspring and always wanted to kill it. All it felt was protection and devotion towards this little child of man. The vicious predator then trotted up and licked the face of the child, feeling absolute delight as it did so. Then, it did the impossible and curled up at the child's feet, allowing the human to stroke its fur.

Banner had sensed the change of circumstances before it happened and looked back. To his horror, he saw the cat about to pounce. He leveled a crossbolt and was about to fire. The cat would have been dead before it reached Dexter, yet even so the weight of the animal could have seriously harmed the child. But the cat did not pounce. The cat started to purr and, holding his shot, Banner watched as it moved forward, licked the boy, then went to sleep as Dexter PATTED the damn thing.

And the leader of the Death Squad was not the only one to notice. The wolves had realized what had happened and turned back - they too saw the impossible scene. And then, as the big cat purred, an even more impossible thing happened: the Wolves all went down onto one knee, and in unison spoke what were clearly ancient words. Banner's translator did not understand it. Only later, when they uncovered the secret society of monk's, were they were able to translate. They were saying, "We kneel before the Qui-Esa (king)!"

Dexter reached down, stroked the big cat, and whispered into its ear. It woke and looked up. It sees the wolves and begins to snarl, but the boy keeps whispering. Finally, the Svelteen, still wanting to kill the wolves and protect its own, decided that things were in hand, and trotted off back into the jungle, never realizing for a moment that its mind and instincts had been completely controlled.

The hunt was over. The wolves had found something far greater than any cat. They had found their natural leader! Banner smiled, interesting. Dexter had the incredibly rare ability of Psyche control, which was how he controlled the cat. For this last year Banner had been wondering who he could put in charge of these dog of war and it now seemed that fate had made the decision for him. For whatever the reason, this taming of the cat had struck a deep, psychic chord in the wolves and created a bond that made Dexter their unquestioned leader.

Later, when researching the history and myth of the people, it was discovered that an archaic legend spoke of the one who would tame the cat, and be named "Qui-Esa". The legend went further and stated that the Qui-Esa *and his brother* would lead the people to a great victory. Well, the child was ready for formal induction, loved by the other human troops, and ready for his first command. And in all honesty, the rest of his men would be relieved it was not one of them having to run this collection of wolf soldiers.

But a battalion leader required officer rank and so nominally, it was Banner himself that was the section head. However Dexter was inducted as a mid-mod Corporal, the highest rank a no-blood could achieve without some sort of spectacular success either in battle or stats. Well, perhaps Hope had some promise for him to break out and achieve his true potential. If they could track and kill whatever it was hiding in those mountains, the boy would have a chance to be put online for higher genetics.

In the meantime, Dexter now took over the training of the local militia, and Banner was set free to focus on the new child.

The Visions of Chardi

The Six Nurse who had been given Mo-ki (the child's name) to surrogate and raise was, to her vast surprise, very happy. Hope had been the opposite of her dreams, a backwater nightmare it represented the worst possible fate. She had initially objected to her posting to this third-rate prospecting world and tried every trick to avoid it, but her name was drawn for the assignment and that was that.

As if that wasn't bad enough, suddenly she has an enforced pregnancy. What lunacy was this? Seriously? A level Six Nurse being made a damn surrogate? She had worked her whole life, studied, gotten high grade - all to get OUT of this sort of slok requirement.

It was effectively an insult to her station and everything her parents had fought to achieve. And then a BABY? Once more, there is no arguing with any ruling sent down by a Seven and in this case it was the Seven General called Saunders, one of the most feared persons in the galaxy. Whatever the genetic experiment was, it must have been of a very high level. But why HER? Then, on top of all this, she was to be MARRIED to the Seven in charge of a damn DEATH SQUAD. And if this were not enough of an insult to her family name, for all the moons of Jupiter, she was then ordered to raise the child as its mother! Then, as if the impossible was not enough, she is ALSO given another no-mod child to look after. This last one blew her completely away.

She seriously considered terminating her contract, but getting herself proscribed was not going to help the situation. Despite her natural distaste for everything she had been ordered to do, she WAS a Six. She WAS in charge of her emotions and was, therefore, able to control her thoughts. Accordingly, she reset her thinking and went into a marriage contract with the Seven. This was when life turned in a way she had never expected. He made absolutely no demands on her, indeed, Banner seemed to have very little interest in the situation he found himself in. By ignoring her, he gave her room to see things more clearly.

It took weeks for her to adjust, but slowly it filtered through that Banner had as little say in this matter as she did, yet he was her superior. He objected to nothing, resisted nothing -Instead he simply accepted whatever fell into his path. She began to see and appreciate the vast difference between her Six status and his Seven.

She watched and learned. It showed in the small things he did: the precise and careful way he cut his food, as well as the pure, uncompromising courtesy he showed her. He genuinely surprised her. There was not one trace of vanity in the man, even though he had so much to be vain about. Despite herself (and in all probability because of the hormones surging through her system as the pregnancy took hold) she found herself doing the impossible.

Chardi, the third born of a High-Mod from an outlying planet, the one who had been trained since birth to care for others and make sure they adjusted to healing, found that something inside herself was healing. A wound she never realized she had, a wound that had come about from an absence of love, began to be filled with contentment. She never had a mother that she could remember. Yes, she knew her parents, but they were distant creatures. Their role was to ensure she was raised in an appropriate manner. Thus, a surrogate birthed her, and she went straight to a nursery, then to a programming center.

Her first assignment was the care of a nursery, which was when her natural talents showed themselves. Caring for the often lost and confused children under her, she instinctively KNEW how to mother them. No-one taught her, some deep instinct just came up. And so to the present day, she was now a natural mother and this was part of the healing.

It was not what she had dreamed of. Naturally, as a Six Nurse, she had hopes of going to a hospital in some well-ranked civilization, but instead, she got Planet Hope. A slimy pit of wolves, full of illiterates and no-mods. Nothing but disappointment and she had no say in it. A class-three new world like this needed a Level Six Nurse to administer health. The garbage doctors sent there were useless, but in this sense she was lucky - she got a Five surgeon, so she could basically tell him what to do. The Captain, who was the official admin officer was also but a Five, which made her the highest level Mod until the Death Squad arrived.

All these major adjustments in every department of her life demanded a great deal of tolerance and patience, the very things a nurse was trained to practice. However, up till now, she had never realized how much she had been PRETENDING empathy and kindness towards others. When push came to shove, she was basically furious at what the Federation had stuffed her into. She was angry at the lack of control she had over her own life.

Yet now she was seeing that maybe it was for the best. She had learned a lot from Banner, things she never expected. She discovered her own vanity, how it was hiding her loneliness, and she also realized a deep frustration: The growing awareness of her situation was obvious - Unless something dramatic happened, any future potential for her to attain higher mods was effectively neutered here on Hope.

Whatever inner progress she attained had no value to the external organization and outer progress was impossible unless she discovered some new and unique adjunct to increase human potential. But instead of chaffing at her constraints, she accepted her lot, and in accepting she found a deep warmth creeping into her solitary existence.

Despite all the above, despite all the disappointment and misery at what had become her fate, the light of love had broken through. She could not believe it herself, but she fell in love with the Seven, which was something you only saw in the worst of the pulp fiction hologram crap the no-mods watched. Poor lowly girl meets high mod, falls in love, and they live happily ever after. Despite herself, despite the desperate loss of her dreams of advancement, despite the burdens placed upon her, she discovered happiness.

Well, at first. Now her inner calm was being torn at from every direction by the little terror she mothered. It was testing her limits in ways she had not dreamed possible. Nothing had prepared her for this - nothing. This little monster was off the charts in psyche and command signals and so she breathed a sigh of relief when Banner came home after appointing Dexter to run the Wolves, taking an interest in little Mo-Ki. He was the only one able to keep her little monster in line and what's more, he was extremely happy to do so.

Mo-ki himself was clearly having an enormous amount of fun with his family. He laughed constantly. His bright, (so bright) green eyes (so beautiful, like his fathers - she corrected herself, like his surrogate father) would have such humor in them when he saw her. Yet he was a terror. It seemed to her that he thoroughly enjoyed running her ragged and found her exasperation extremely funny. The little thing was so damn KNOWING.

She found herself wondering about the notions of Dharma and Karma, ideas the had come down through the ages and which were still taught on her home world. She had a path she must take, a destiny she must follow. Yet HOW she walked the path, HOW she managed her destiny was up to her. And here was the real and only choice: She could either walk in harmony, or resist. She chose harmony. And that is when it started, the visions.

She would be working on some mid-mod soldier, checking implants, seeing what the rejection issue might be, etc. Then out the blue, the lights would start dancing. She felt them far away, yet they were close and moving in concentric circles in some ancient ritual. One inside the other, circulating around a central point, while the other the lights pulsed and danced around it to some unheard song.

Of course, she used the auto-bot to try and decrypt what it might be, but it came back with nothing. She looked up symptoms, nothing. Then on impulse, she asked one of the local Wolf Women. The Wolf was working as a cleaner on an outlying army post where Chardi was doing maintenance checks on the soldiers. She described her vision of the lights, then drew it on a screen: *Was this anything that they knew about?* Here the wolf-woman nodded, apparently not surprised. The wolves viewed Dexter as Chardi's son, and, as the mother of the chosen, it was expected for her to have the visions. For them, it was not surprising, but what the wolf said was: *You must speak with the old ones about it.*

Chardi was fascinated. The lowly cleaner spoke to her directly, with no hint of subservience, yet with respect. But the words did not translate well. "The old ones" made no sense. So she recorded it and had it checked several times by the central computer to make sure she understood it correctly. The overall interpretation was: "The visions are known. The old ones will show you the patterns. As mother to the chosen, you will be welcomed."

Apparently, there was another race of wolves who used a different dialect, an archaic one, but still extant. Initial scans had shown up a curious cult but it was not seen as being significant. But research showed there WAS a religion of sorts on Hope and it seemed that the 'old men' were connected with it. Chardi put her mind to tracking it down.

Finally, buried deep in the scans she found them. The 'old ones' were very ancient Wolves living in what amounted to a tree stump. This was the center of an undiagnosed religion, one only briefly noted in the scans. As no wolf attended any form of worship, or seemed to pray, or do anything even vaguely religious, it had been presumed this was essentially just an old belief with no great substance. Apparently not.

Chardi, with Banner's approval, took out a flitter for recognizance and found the 'temple' where the religion was based. It was more the roots of an ancient tree than any conventional church. Worked on over the centuries and turned into a type of house, it was huge - an enormous stump that had been hollowed out. The "Old Ones" were a small group of very ancient Wolves who lived away from all societies. She presumed they were a sort of monk order and it was logical that such a group would have records. They did, written texts that were obviously ancient. Resonance scans showed them to be at least 50,000 years.

50,000 years old - and the primitive wolves had BOOKS? Even Old Earth had nothing in comparison to this. She could not physically go through these, they were too fragile, but the monks had copies of every page and they showed her images drawn on their peculiar bark paper. There she saw representations of the very patterns she had been seeing in her visions.

Clearly, she was tapping in some way into the planetary unconscious. However, the old wolves did not use the howl-speak of the normal natives, so the communicator would not translate properly. Fortunately, the cleaner woman she spoke to came along and she could speak to her on their behalf. But it was still not a perfect translation: *"These are our oldest scriptures, the reason we are here, Mother of the Chosen.* (the reason we are here?) *We do not know exactly what these represent, other than the wolves were sent here in eons past because of what you are seeing."*

And that was that, but as much as they answered her questions, the answers she received raised only more unanswered conundrums. Chardi spent days studying in that ancient grove, enjoying the calm, and feeling a deep sense of safety around these old Wolves. But she knew, she was only scratching the surface. A flitter came to collect her and bidding fond farewells to the impassive yet kind old creatures, she returned to report what she had discovered to Banner.

He was there, playing with Mo-Ki as she arrived back at their apartment. He barely looked up as he studied the scan information, and quietly said, "We need to resolve this Chardi. It is something that demands further study."

"What do you think it means?" she asked.

"I think this is the answer to the questions we have not been able to ask and that the solution to the infection will be hidden in those books," he answered, purely on intuition, while nodding his continuing approval of her work.

RECOGNITION

Banner sat with his wife, noting as he did her smell, her agitation, her sense of wanting to share that she was expressing. To him, the mechanical aspects of observation and categorization of observed behavior were second nature, yet apart from his normal detached state, he was experiencing a more personal sense of closeness. Was this love? Or was it simply a sense of the familiar?

She presented him with a genuine curiosity, one possibly pertinent to the issues he was researching. She had taken full scans of the meetings she held while she was away, so he could pay close attention to the images the old wolf 'monks' presented. These creatures were very different from the normal wolf, so much so that they were close to being a different race. Another thing that was missed in the scans.

The 'temple' itself did not show up as a place of importance, again the scans had failed. Further, these old wolves did not act or behave at all like their brethren. His observational powers were telling him that these were trained, highly trained, individuals. From what he could see, it was like instinct had been bred out of them and they operated only a moment to moment awareness. He could not shake the sense this was entwined with the whole issue of the virus here on Hope, but this was for another day.

The visions his wife had seen, which correlated to the 'temple' drawings, were the pressing concern. His Level Six wife confirmed the patterns at the 'temple' were precisely the same as her uncalled for dream images, and this could mean only one thing. Something, or someone, was sending a message. Was it from the unknown thing up in the mountains, or from the monks? Or was his own wife's intuits being accented by his own? This could happen when two high-level Mods lived in the same space. Banner had a feeling it was all three, and that the true purpose for him being here was starting to unfold.

"Did they say what the images represented?" Banner asked.

"What they said was not able to be translated. The woman I was with said they were charts, navigation charts, and were the reason they were here. But it was clear to me she did not really understand what the old wolves were speaking of."

Charts? They were like no other astronomy on any other planet. Did they refer to stars? Did they refer to atomics? Did they describe subspace ethers? He ran a variety of math parameters over the information, but once the ratios were resolved, no conclusive answer was given. What was certain was that these images represent a resonance map of some type. A sort of tonal key that would unlock whatever it was that it described. And if this were the case, then the wolverine monks had inherited something. Was it connected to the infection? Was this the reason the Wolves were here?

The real problem, how to deal with the DNA modifier aspect of the virus, was still in the process of being resolved. At least the area where the infection came from was now clear. By cross-checking infected people, researching who they met, where they went, a specific locality that was off-grid and invisible to scans pretty much proved it was the miners that started this process. Auto-bots had gone in and created extensive resonance maps of the area. And as a result of the harmonic sequences built up from recording of the deep scans of the miners, they discovered those who had direct contact with whatever it was.

Yet it became even more interesting, Banner now found a potential cure of sorts. From the recordings his wife took of the vocal patterns from old ones, he then translated their voices into harmonic imprints and, on impulse, played these into the saved tissues of infected settlers. Without drugs, without any other effect, just the tones used in the monks' language seemed to kill off the infection. He now KNEW without any doubt that the purpose for the wolves was to contain whatever was imprisoned up there in the deep ravines of the high mountains near this planets Northern pole.

Two Years In

He had ticked over a year with this research. Existing infected tissues were now isolated, and knowing they were susceptible to the patterns of resonance from the old wolves, he used these like a surgeons knife to re-engineer the strange RNA. That answered his most pressing question: He now knew it was a created pattern, but by who? That thing in the mountains? The fact that the virus could be tweaked like this, and the fact that it had an RNA Codice unlike anything he had ever seen, meant this 'infection' was an engineered tool. This was a TOOL, but to what end? His intuits supposed it's eventual goal was to pry open the lock its designer was trapped behind.

Research hammered on, primarily to develop new weapons against it, but also to create new immunity triggers and firewalls: this was his preoccupation during the last year. It also meant regular reports of progress, demonstrating significant discoveries that put him on track for beating whatever this was. That meant the party could carry on.

Banner worked largely at a laboratory set up in his home. For recreation, he played with the fast-developing child placed into their midst. He had never known such a happy time, working, playing, and loving his new life. Yet he was also aware of the Zeta Probe sitting there.

Saunders was making it clear what the cost of failure in this mission would be. Banner simply accepted this, told no one, and focussed on ensuring success. However, his regular reports were never met with a response, which never happened in ordinary circumstances. But he knew how the bureaucracy worked and the more reports, the more information passed up the chain, all this meant he was buying time. By flagging the fact that, at some point, this infection threat was able to be resolved, the detonation of a Zeta would have at least one more protocol to jump.

If there some top brass that decided Planet Hope was too high a risk, then every report was one more barrier to get past. The process of triggering protocols was very involved up to the point of a Seven General. Everyone else had to go through the procedures, answer all queries, and get authorization before they could act in any significant way. Saunders, on the other hand, could blow up the planet at will, but she didn't. Therefore, she wanted Banner to find reasons NOT to. So he found them. And he kept filing more paperwork to cause more hiccups.

And so it came to the next step - the report he would need to file in the coming days was to give details on how the home guard was going.

This meant regulation testing of the new recruits well in advance of what would be considered normal. At the minimum allowable training limit for the wolves, he set up a fully monitored simulation. Why? If they met with success in even one area of the testing, it would be filed as another endorsement, which meant yet another hurdle for some mindless tech to jump over before pushing a button. A trained and functional local militia ALSO had a degree of rights and while a success was just another form to be ticked off, forms flowing around in the maze of bureaucracy were what gave you valuable time.

He wondered how the lad was going with his first command. At this point, Dexter had his first year with the wolves under his wing, and it was now time to see how they were all shaping up. Hopefully, not too many will die in the process. It was bad for morale.

Dexter

At age ten, running with a pack of wolves (as they were generally known) and full of high spirits, Dexter would only lapse into depression on rare occasions. This day was one of them. It wasn't just the pointless murder of his mother, it was the way that something tried to play with his mind afterward. Something had gotten IN. For the last year, he had been playing and replaying the memory, making sure he did not confuse the memory streams.

One thing that is known, whatever picture people accept as reality will then conform inside their memories as a fixed point, a certainty. As an example: The Earth used to be flat, this was the firm belief at one time. Even when proven to be round, thousands upon thousands went to their death beds disbelieving it. It was not enough for false beliefs to be disproved, useful patterns must be substituted in their place. Part of his training was learning techniques for entraining weaker minds, to create an acceptance of what the authority in charge wanted the people to believe. But how had it been done to HIM?

Entrainment is a process of alignment with a stronger mind. If you saw a red spot, yet after an hour with a Level Five programmer, you would see it clearly it as whatever color he chose it to be. And when you were told the original was red, you would swear with complete certainty that this was not what you saw. However, there were some things that could not be programmed away. One of them was geometry. The ancient Square, Circle, and Triangle were so defined that memory imprinting could not override them.

A square can become a rectangle, a circle an oval, a triangle can change angles, but you cannot convince a person that the square they saw was a triangle or a circle. On the basis of this, Dexter reasoned that he must find something in the original experience with his mother's death that could not be overridden. As he focussed he realized it was the execution ax. It had a circular pommel mounted on a triangular brace. This was a fixed point.

Finally, he understood what had happened - What was moving was the ORDER of images. Why would something try to rearrange this and not de-program out the images themselves?

Further, research showed that the wolves brought in for questioning revealed that they saw the killing, they witnessed the wolf that bit the human and they understood the consequences of this action. What they did NOT possess, any of them, was one iota of regret. It was seen by them as RIGHT.

Yes, they saw the secondary image, the wolf bites, the human goes crazy. They also saw the first image, the human goes crazy, the wolf bites. But they did not register any reaction to this apparent conflict of memory. Further, even though they were fully aware of severe consequences that could occur from attacking a human, they still expressed no regret. It was RIGHT, all of it.

To either of the two memory lines, no wolf showed remorse, regret, fear or condemnation of the action. Then a remarkable thing turned up, one of the consoles the kids were playing with had an activated camera. THIS recorded with certainty the actual event. It showed clearly Dexter's first memory line and it also showed the look on the wolves as it happened. Dexter's mother is murdered by the miner, then the wolf leaps up and bites him. It was purely by chance this turned up when a console was sent to a tech for repair. What was NOT chance was that the overall friendly attitude towards the soldiers meant this was handed in.

Here is where it got really interesting: When the wolves were shown this hologram of the actual event, their demeanor altered. Their passive nature became menacing and a chemical reaction began in their saliva. Analyzing this, Banner discovered what he had always suspected, that something in the wolves inherent nature ATTACKED the infection (which they had isolated) and his suspicions were confirmed. The natives on this planet had developed an auto-immune response to whatever it was they shared their habitat with.

It was also self-evident that they were not affected in any adverse way by the presence of this, whatever it was. Could it be possible that the Wolves were in some way genetically engineered to control this virus?

It bugged Dexter. It irritated him, got under his skin, and caused him no end of questions. He knew where the enemy was, yet he had no ability to act against it. He needed to know what this 'thing' was and he needed to see it die. As yet no opportunity had arisen to complete what was now a deep-seated and primary goal in his heart. Even so, what he did have was a pack of wolves to support him should the opening arise. He had to work into a position of power and be ready to strike! This objective helped stave off the sense of depression he felt nagging at him.

Dexter was now of an age to accept the higher Mods. DNA alteration through RNA inputs was best incubated during puberty, which prepared the body for the actual mechanical implants. The vast growth surge through his body would most easily accept this change at that point.

Things were progressing well. His technical assessment had come back in with glowing reports in just about every aspect, but it was his ability to control the mind of animals that was his great talent. This is the sort of primary talent that made you a General and allowed you to control a starship. It was the rarest of all specs.

Yet he would never be a General. To start with, one of the five existing ones would have to die but even it they did, he did not have the blood for it. Staring into space, the boy was forced to accept that unless there was a significant military campaign, one in which he absolutely excelled, his options were limited. Even Banner defeating an impossible monster only qualified his as a battle lieutenant. It was one of the paradoxes - even though his father was a Seven, his rank was still Lieutenant - and HIS parents were Mid-Mods.

"Gratitude!" He remembered how his mother had constantly told him. "Gratitude wins you more hearts and more happiness than regret."

Dexter was not complaining. His new father and mother had lifted him out of the slock and into a life he could not have imagined. He 'was' grateful, but now he had a taste, now that he could feel the power of the Mods, he wanted more. He wanted so much more.

His father's voice rang out over the field where the wolves were practicing daily drills. "Attention, assessment for higher rankings has been approved. Prepare for drills! I want to see battle formations, wall scaling and obstacles included. This is a FULL drill in FULL kit."

Dexter pulled his whistle and blew the code. This was his little secret, a high pitched whistle only the wolves could hear and which he had trained his own ears to recognize. Ultrasonic commands were archaic, primitive, yet it suited the situation. He had trained his wolves to follow set formations and all he need do was blow a sequence. This was as good as a language to his dogs and they would know exactly what to do.

What is more, it meant he could adjust on the fly without the need for a chain of command. Every Wolf knew what they had to do with every command sequence they heard and so, when the obstacles were thrown up, HE could assess and react, not relying on troops having to think for themselves. Not that his little soldiers were stupid, but they did not understand the layers of traps the high-mods would set in order to test their response times.

Success or failure were not the only priorities. It was speed of response, accuracy of decision making, and commitment to achieving a goal that rated equally with success. However, if you didn't win the obstacle course, your points on everything underneath it were diminished. On the flip side, signals down the line of command were also assessed according to the speed of response with the initial order being enacted. Here Dexter knew he had the colossal advantage. This is the specific area he had targeted and the entire reasoning behind his 'wolf whistles'.

Well, they were as ready as they will ever be. He knew this day would come, where his dogs would be tested to see if they would be approved as a fully fledged militia - Dexter already had the punch codes for his com pre-set and the wolves were well prepared. One year is early for a new squad, but he knew his foster-father well and also understood the internal pressure they were both under. How a virtual pre-mod like himself could know the signatures of a Seven, Dexter did not know, but he felt the energy and had guessed at the outcome.

Banner was impressed. From general training, the wolves were kitted and ready for the obstacle course in under three minutes. A record time for a new squad and as good a time as his own battle-hardened soldiers. Well, next we see how they go with the random obstacles.

Again, new squads generally had clear and defined obstacle courses, a set play of some twenty combinations. But Banner needed more than this. A clear and defined message had to be sent to high command and so the lieutenant set up a random sequence, something you simply cannot train for. It would test the chain of command to the utmost. And really, this is what he needed to know, could the wolves act individually to make decisions, yet also work together as a pack following defined orders.

Primarily, the space between their reflex responses and the commands received that would be what was first measured. The first battle strategy put forward was "capture the hill": standard fair. The full battalion moved to the holographic field for assessment. They were in position and in formation in under seven minutes. Once more, as good as his own troop. He decided to plug the operation into the barracks, so all his soldiers could enjoy the scene.

A rare treat. All work stopped! For soldiers, watching drills like this was almost as good as a pleasure dome. The men gathered around the view points, where the entire hologram was displayed. They saw young Dexter step up to the command module with his father. Such a fine looking lad, so fit and trim, they were all proud of him. "Go Dexter!" they shouted.

Dexter heard their shout through his fathers' com, faintly, and realized what a rare thing today was. His wolves would not disappoint, he trusted them, loved them, and they loved him. Putting the whistle to his lips, he pressed the command to start the war game, "Capture the Hill". Drones flew out, identified the target, and the holographic enemy proved to be Altracian Bears. Tough opponents, hand to hand far more powerful than any human, and quick. This needed sonics, they were vulnerable to frequency as it disabled their balance.

The Wolves quickly took up the command that came through their helmet viewfinder, but Dexter added laser to the mix. He guessed the bears were a subterfuge and, if they were, it was a ploy used by the only race that fed on sonics, the gnome-like creatures of Partic Minor.

The hologram showed the obstacles to reach the hill, all standard stuff, you had to choose the path, or paths, your troop would take to reach the objective. But if he were right about the gnomes, they would also employ visual distraction and so the hologram itself could be a subterfuge.

Assessing the layout, Dexter determined this was no ordinary pre-set. Why? He didn't know, but he didn't need to know. His intuits said there was more to this than a simple yearly assessment. He blew his whistle for every group to combine, not normal practice. You usually had squads of fifty to attack a hill in different directions, so multiple troops could give cover fire, provide distractions, etc. A single assault was generally a guaranteed fail.

But Dexter knew his instincts were never wrong. He gave his order and the wolves ported to a single unit and suddenly, where they had been on the perimeters got doused in a spectacular series of fireballs. SO! It wasn't "Capture the Hill" at all, it was a full-on outer-atmosphere assault. He beamed in a shuttle. With all his wolves in one spot, they could easily mount battle stations and fly out to assault the outer-atmosphere craft.

There would be obstacles, probably plasma mines, and laser. Best to go invisibility mode. Screens up, the shuttle flew into the upper atmosphere. Of course, the 'shuttle' didn't really leave the planet, it was a hologram, but for those in the exercise, it seemed like they were assaulting on off-world craft. Battle drill came with full sensory input, right down to the slightest sound and scent.

But there were NOT in space, the wolves were within earshot, and the whistle went right through the simulation. This was Dexter's secret weapon, a signal that bypassed all external imagery and went right to the cortex of his soldiers. The alien invasion craft was located, beam weapons were fired, and t is destroyed. Then down to the original task: Landing on the hill, firing sonics mixed with laser, and it is indeed gnomes. They come out to absorb the sonics and get fried by laser. All done inside four minutes. Test completed.

A huge cheer rises up from the Barracks. The men knew this was something special and they shouted with pride cheering on their "littlest soldier" as they called Dexter.

"How did you guess about the space assault?" His father asked.

"Set piece subterfuge. You gave the clue early on. The bears were too easy a target, you had something else up the sleeve. Jumping the troops together and not following set guidelines, that was pure instinct, but you had to be wanting to leave at least one set of troops alive to complete a mission. The trick was in guessing which. And if this were so it had to be an external threat, which meant the remaining troops would have to call in a jump ship. I picked the best location on the map for this possibility and jumped the wolves to that spot."

"If you got it wrong, they all died." his father says in passing.

"If we get it wrong, whatever the task, we all die. Am I to assume we are being prepared to take on whatever is up there in the mountains?" Dexter looks up. Banner says nothing but he sees the faintest smile on his father's lips. Good, he was right. They WERE going to avenge his birth mother.

Banner , noting the secret was out, said very simply, "It is the entire reason for your wolves to be trained, Dexter. Well done, you just bought yourself the time to do this."

In his father's coms the boy could still hear the cheering of his brothers. Banner just nodded, clearly pleased. "This exercise will shake the tree and buy us several years. You have done your father proud, young Dexter."

Wolves Approved

The Sevens reviewing the Wolf guard for Planet Hope had expected nothing of importance from a pack of alien militia, so surely what they were reading was some sort of joke? New recruits, not one loss, even with variable parameters? And even more impossible, achieving of full success? Simply unheard of. In fact, it could not be true - But scan after scan revealed the almost instantaneous response of the wolf people, as well as the extraordinary intuits of their young commander. Hardened warriors were then brought in and THEY went through each layer of scans. Each officer was equally shocked.

Review of all battles, real and virtual, was the norm. These debriefs had specific protocols, and testing for variables was standard fare. Pulse rate, adrenalin levels, reaction rates - With the Wolves, all these were in the top 1%. Layer after layer is dissected and analyzed, but with each variance in the war game, the wolves rated consistently in the top percentile. This drew only greater incredulity. Of course, Dexter had read and studied everything that would be looked for, an old fashioned dog whistle was not in the mix. All the analysts saw was the remarkable speed in the uptake of commands from the new recruits, and the accuracy of response to threat.

None of them bothered to LISTEN - no one listened. Thus the sonics he employed were never noted. Even if they were, who would connect ultra-sound humans could not hear to the way the wolves reacted?

As the analysis developed, every parameter was better than perfect. This was just not possible, especially as the candidate running the troops was a BOY who was not yet a full Level Five. Yet the child showed as superior in every category, so much so that an experienced Level Seven General could not have done better. The readouts were passed on up the line, causing a commotion in every department they went through.

How could a next to no-mod youth suddenly spark up to such a high level in such a short time period? Entrainment from the surrogate father? What could it be? Something was kicking in this child's abilities to go way past designation. However, the results could not be denied - a troop of no-mod wolves on a distant outpost of nil importance provided response rates and results equal to the best Death Squad. This outcome gave the wolves their precious certification, which meant RIGHTS, and the boy was set for the unheard of jump straight to sargent. He would now be allowed to take his troop into battle.

And so it was that the wolves were registered and had regulation pay and privileges instated. They were out of probation and recognized as a fully-fledged militia now.

For the Wolves, it just proved the wisdom of their elders. The omens had spoken, they had wisely followed them - The Qui-Esa had come, they had accepted the human child as their leader, and the new dawn had begun. Even as mere Militia on a backwater outpost, the credits now given to them meant their families would want for nothing. If they died in battle, they were paid for another twenty years and they also had the right to secure property, protected with full military authority. The success of the wolves was so significant that even Banner's Death Squad accepted them as real soldiers and the men now happily went with the beasts on their various little missions to sort out disputes and develop outposts.

"Lift one, lift all!" It was the basic tenant of every soldier, you were only as good as the man beside you, or wolf, as the case might be.

Forts were established across the planet, not to defend against anything, rather to develop an interlocking grid. Banner and Dexter now knew they had the troops to tackle whatever it was in the mountains, but they needed to prepare a network right across Planet Hope. Nothing could be left to chance. Control of, the planetary energy fields in this upcoming war would be everything.

The overall strategy was to install a series of fixed positions, in very specific spots which would allow on-going resonance scans of the entire planet. As this was set into motion, deep scans, all the way to the core, started to register every atom of Hope. Each wavelength, every tiny nuance of the planet was going to be registered and categorized. Banner was going to know if anything happened anywhere and would be able to pick any change in the substratum once they initiated their assault into the mountains.

Of course, this was done under the auspices of mining, looking for ore, drilling deep test cores, etc. At 'likely sots' a small tower was erected and into each testing core meters and recording devices were implanted. The process took three years, but finally the radionic net was set. If anything tried to escape to anywhere on the planet they would now be able to track it, find it, and kill it.

In secret, the 'other' purpose was self-preservation. The net they created could also isolate the Deuteride in the core, which had been put into the planet when the Zeta Unit was installed. The receptors would know if the gamma triggers were being sent to activate the Lithium and be able to deflect it for a time. Nothing was to be left to chance, nothing would sit outside of a control parameter.

Mo-Ki begins training

Though all this, unseen by any but Banner and his family, the young one known as Mo-Ki grew at an astonishing rate. Dexter started training him at age one, well before the permissible time frame. Normally a child had to be at least four before they could generate the Beta frequency needed to balance the impulse training, but Mo-Ki swallowed everything you threw at him with ease. Dexter taught him advanced mind techniques as form of play in order to awaken his capabilities.

At age three, Mo-Ki was solving quadratic equations, playing Mozart and Beethoven on piano, speaking fluently in five different languages and beating Grand Masters in chess tournaments.

Banner watched in amazement. The child drank it all up. The little soul was a cup that never filled, no matter how much you poured in. Somehow Saunders had foreseen this - But did she suspect what he was beginning to believe? Banner watched closely. The child was a phenomenon, outstripping response levels in every category. This little fireball was one level of astonishment after another. Then, when little Mo-Ki had turned four, the real training commenced.

And where better for this than out of sight with the Wolves his older brother commanded! As they were a registered militia he could induct the child as a recruit and train him while keeping him out of the eyeshot or earshot of higher command. His first year showed results beyond belief - fortunately, as a pre-mod these did not have to be reported.

The robotic mining missions had been doing their automatic incursions into the forbidden zone, which was regulation procedure for any questionable area. But now every bit of rock they churned sent frequency mapping through the zone he wanted to chart and there was a permanent observation on the readouts. If anything moved, if an atom shifted, he would be able to pinpoint exactly where and when. If preparation was 99% of the war, Banner was going for 101%.

They had five years before the hammer fell, just five years.

Playing with Wolves

S oldiers are all the same - no matter the uniform, no matter the species - Toughness and ability earn respect and, since the opening salvo where the wolves had been officially inducted, they had found greater and greater acceptance by their human counterparts.

Five years they had been on this project, five long years. The Death Squad were enjoying this remarkable reprieve, as they saw it. For them, Planet Hope was an extended holiday. They knew something was up, no one conducted this many tests, or spent this long in one area, without some greater purpose - but they were soldiers. They didn't question and didn't care what tomorrow would bring.

What they DID enjoy were all the war games. One thing was certain, these Wolves were every bit as good as the best of the humans. If they could have been modded, they would be even better. But that wasn't the point, these wolves were real characters! More importantly, they were great fun and loved to drink.

The unique situation on Hope meant secretive Death Squad, for the first in their career, could go to local bars, drink with their wolf friends, and do stupid stuff. The boss had OK'd it, a thing that had never happened before, and they found the liked it. Planet Hope was more than a job, it was becoming their HOME.

It was an experience not to be missed, playing with wolves, learning their ways, discovering their remarkable society. The more they trusted the wolves the more they were trusted. Banner's men were invited to witness ancient traditions and drink the amazing booze the wolves gave to friends. This wild herb liquor was far superior to the processed stuff they got in camp.

And, as anyone knows, a drunk soldier is a happy one. The long term nature of this conflict required a flexible roster, where at least 20% of the crew were completely free for three out of seven days. Not by chance, Banner WANTED the men to socialize, to feel connected to the wolves and to this planet. He wanted them to feel that the wolf soldiers were family, just as they saw each other.

Why? Banner had discovered his own efficiency quotient had risen substantially. His time on Hope was incredibly productive and he attributed this to the fact he was, for the first time in his life, deeply and genuinely happy. Family life, so important to the wolves, was something that made you a better soldier. He wanted his men to be connected, to feel a sense of being loved by the wolves and the settlers.

Wherever a Death Squad went it was the opposite. They were the most hated and feared humans in the galaxy. But here, even the settlers were accepting of them. The men started to find wives and raise children - a thing not even imagined as a possibility in their former existence.

Because of the long-term nature of this project Banner had requested and received exemptions to the strict 'no contact' rules. He got it passed by presenting it as an efficiency exercise, noting his own situation as the case in point. Greater efficiency was always given the green light, so despite it being against first principles of any Death Squad, the men settled down to a domestic routine.

Of course, the never ending requirements of the Consortium demanded his attention. They were the ones paying for the incredibly expensive troops on their doorstep, and they made certain Banner heard every complaint by constantly demanding to know WHEN they would be freed from the burden of covering the costs.

Banner could not let on they were all a hairsbreadth away from the planet being nuked, but he devised a different strategy. The Hope Consortium had to be appeased and apparently off world there was this crazy level of demand for everything to do with the wolves. So he did another unthinkable thing - he ordered his men to get involved in commerce. As they traveled with the 'dogs' as they called them, the men were to identify potential profit centers for the consortium. It turned out, mining was not the product in great demand - It was the hand made tools, the clothing, and in particular the booze the wolves made that were in high demand across the Federation.

At first Banner could not quite grasp WHY there was this extraordinary need across the galaxy for everything wolf, then he twigged - Saunders had not only been monitoring them, she had been MONETIZING them. He had spotted the cameras sending holo images of everything interesting about Planet Hope - the stunning backdrop was no hindrance and with a few queries he discovered that all across the Federation planets she had a hit show screening, called - Planet of Hope.

What ticked him off were the replies he was getting to reports. No questions about the report, but things from off-world admins like, "Does the clan leader in the Abulsa province really make his own psychoactive booze, and where can we get some?"

He had laughed so hard when he discovered what Saunders was up to. She had a recon vessel in orbit above them and had turned her surveillance recordings into a hit show. Right across the Federation, people tuned in each day to see real world footage of what he and his famed Death Squad were up to. The feared and famous warriors were being seen across the worlds as family men, playing with kids, drinking with wolves. And Saunders had turned the show into an advertisement for everything Hope could sell - which explained the demand.

He grasped the real issue: All the admins would think twice before nuking a top-rated show plus, because of the trade, many of them would be garnering the cream that came to their door as a result of this insane demand for all things wolf. Saunders was the engineer behind all this. It was subtle, unseen, but he knew it and got the message: He just had to do HIS part, she was looking after the rest.

But WHY? Why did this ruthless creature take them all under her wings? What possible cause could it be, other than the child? His instincts were telling him this the whole time, but his conditioning stopped him from accepting it - yet his intuits were never wrong: This was HER child. She was acting like a mother, breaking every rule, bending every possibility to ensure the survival of her child. Saunders cherished Mo-Ki. How had it happened? How could a sterile General conceive a child? Perhaps via the spectacular passion they shared.

In the back of his mind, he could not shake a suspicion. An impossible virus had been engineered, was something else at play. Was little Mo-Ki engineered?

Everything since his arrival on Hope had been change. Banner had never come even close to feeling a sense of love with another before - Now he found it easy to love. It felt natural for him to have a family and to carry on as if they were some old Earth clan without a worry in the world. A buzzer interrupted his contemplations. One of the chief architects for the Hope Consortium was in orbit and wanted to come onto the planet to discuss matters in person.

"Not possible, the place is in quarantine," he knew what this was, and spoke directly to the man, bypassing the secretary.

Banner pulled up a holo to make sure the message was clear. The fellow, pallid and pampered and so obviously from an extremely rich trading block, protested. "You are taking goods back and forth all the time, surely as chief architect I have authority to inspect parameters."

Banner did not need to mince words with traders. "You are a security risk, (he looked at the security code on the coms) Master Raiditch." He pulled the man's files up in front of him, showing a long line of smuggling queries and other assorted black market operations paraded on the holo-screen. Banner made sure the long list was in full view of the man's screen. "But of course, you are welcome to come down and go through deep cleanse and mild probing. I would humbly suggest you might prefer I send up a bottle of the wolves black vermouth and let my tech crew convey any data you need while you are happily, and safely, ensconced in your no doubt luxurious transwarp pod."

The man blustered, "But I need a jump port to get back and it would be so much more convenient to take a flyer, such as you have on the surface."

Banner smiled, he must have imagined the mention of the deep cleanse was a throw-away line and that he was not serious about it. However, he didn't get to run a Death Squad by being unprepared. "You would know of the Chancellors son, yes? What was his name, Beret Darglar? I think that was it. He seemed to think I was joking about deep cleanse and jumped onto the surface without permission. I lost track of him after that - Do you know what became of him?"

Master Raiditch paled. My God, it was true, he really HAD deep scanned the son of the Chancellor. The fellow was a gibbering idiot now. What sort of power had this damn upstart army boy obtained? How come HE was running the show while THEY were paying the bills? "Well, how do I get back? I have to wait for the next freighter to be able to pod out," he complained. "I could be stuck here for DAYS!"

"Correct Master Raiditch. 2.7 rotations to be exact. However, to ease your burden I will make sure I send you some little treats to help cover the costs and inconvenience - In the meantime, I will arrange for the necessary accounts to be presented for your purview." Banner flicked off the screen. Every week now someone was knocking on the door, expecting to pull rank or buy some sort of privilege.

But now he knew he had an audience he was curious to see how long it took for this episode to reach the waves. Subspace cams brought up the stream, it was already beaming out. Dammit, Saunders was supervising this in person. He smiled, mother hen was making sure the chick grew up.

Banner had to admit - he came up pretty good on camera.

Meeting the Chancellor

Attending functions was not the normal purview of the leader of the Death Squad, but the sixth anniversary of a planetary consortium was seen as extremely fortuitous. New worlds often had a crash and burn and the failed franchise was usually absorbed by an older and more profitable group. But luck was with Hope, it was not just raking in credits, it was doing so at an outrageously rate. Saunders little show, the beautiful wolf people, the mystique of the strange virus - it all combined to make Hope a raging success.

Orbiting the planet in a platform, the leaders of the consortium and their hangers-on were meeting for a celebration at the planet itself. Of course, it was all being recorded and while Banner never attended these things, especially given the quarantine status, he and his delightful family were requested to present in Holo. It was not something he could easily escape.

What the consortium REALLY wanted was a vast free ad beamed out, one that clearly showed the stunningly beautiful planet in the background, with them collecting acknowledgment of their role in the foreground. That is what they thought they were doing, but clearly there was another level to the game being played here.

Saunders had given permission to talk openly about what they had discovered and WHY there was the quarantine. Well, they had a pretty good handle on what it was now and as the *'Planet of Hope'* broadcast was covering the event, Saunders must have wanted the rumours about the virus acknowledged and out in the open. She would have her reasons.

Six long years, and she was now willing to release confirmation on what was really happening on the surface. After the eighth month of quarantine the evidence had defined the threat. There were extraneous pulses being emitted from a specific substratum, a crystalline rock not dissimilar to quartz. It made sense - if you had to imprison energy, a crystal lock was the logical way to do it. More and more, Banner became convinced that Planet Hope was a prison set up in eons past for a criminal culture. Six years in and he was certain of this .

Following on, if this were so then it meant a highly sophisticated civilization must have done this, so the obvious question: *Why did whoever imprisoned this menace just not destroy the problem?* Logic told him this meant the problem itself was not able to be destroyed. As all life signs and readouts from the quartz lock were seen as a photonic pulse, it would appear that the life form was made of light. Why did this echo in his mind? What 'being of light' was imprisoned in Earth's prehistory? Lucifer was the only reference, from archaic Christianity.

Mo-Ki was about to turn six and, under direct tutelage from the father his progress was extraordinary. Reflex, intuits, and parabolics - all were off the chart. Parabolics, specifically, were the essential quality for a General. This was the ability to plot a course of action that moved in a clean arc through diverse and complex situations. Mo-Ki's placement with him was EXACTLY this. Saunders had the highest parabolics in all of human history - Mo-Ki was looking to leave them all in the dust.

The broadcast was timed to start in minutes. The curious thing about these collective holo-feeds was the dual-layer you experienced. You were on the platform, yet you were also in your own environment. On Hope, Banner was all alone, quietly playing a game of pool in the mess. Chardi was at work and Dexter was out with his wolves. Saunders had specifically requested their presence.

When the screening beamed out it found Banner at the base, relaxing in the pool hall. A holo form appeared in front of him and, as he adjusted to the light, he was also on the party platform high about Hope. "Hi Ho Lieutenant Banner, welcome to the party. I am very glad you could make it." The Chancellor of the Hope Consortium had apparently forgotten how much he hated Banner.

Banner smiled with apparent warmth, "Glad to be with you and your people, Chancellor to celebrate the incredible success of the Hope Consortium. Who would have thought a planet under quarantine could defy convention and become so astonishingly profitable. But I want to assure you, the local settlers are well, we have contained the contagion. (Pause) However, due to the curious nature of the thing, we must maintain the blockade and continue to prevent tourism."

'It's a damn shame, the place looks so amazingly beautiful. But you must appreciate this every day, I would presume Lieutenant?" The Chancellor spoke through gritted teeth, apparently remembering what had happened to his son when HE went down to the surface.

"Indeed we all do - the men, the settlers, and the wonderful wolf people. It is a privilege and a pleasure to be able to work for the Federation here. And, I will add that while the matter of the extremely unusual and contagious light-based virus that we call Lucifer is still a concern, we have made tremendous steps in both understanding and containing it. Within four to five years I fully expect to give the planet a clean bill of health."

The Chancellor nodded, smiling to the cameras. "And what about the family, do we have your wife and kids present?"

Banner smiled. The poor man must have experienced some extraordinarily evil threats to be so pleasant and follow the script handed to him. "Charni is working, but we can patch in. Hello darling!"

Charni merged into his field of vision. He could see in the background some of his men smiling and waving, showing some plas-form strapping covering up some injury. "Hello dear," she said quietly. "Pleasure to meet you, Chancellor. I trust you will enjoy your short visit to the topside of Hope."

The camera brings up yet another scene, this time it is Dexter out in the dusk light, still training up his wolves. The holo sweeps into view, and he turns to face it. In the background, the wolves were in full battle dress, another Saunders variation as they would always train 'in the fur' as Dexter used to call their naked selves.

"Hi Ho, Dexter!" the Chancellor calls out, maintaining his upbeat smile as he watched the incredibly expensive militia he had to pay for.

"Hey Ho Chancellor. As you can see, Hope is being kept safe by a local militia, and I want to personally thank the Consortium for their wisdom and foresight in allowing these wolves to be trained. We are all pleased and happy to be of service to the Federation." Dexter knew the words to say because he had been given them.

"Tell me Dexter, what is the meaning of this title the wolves have given you, Qui-Ese, is that it?" But even as the Chancellor said the word, the eyes of a thousand wolves turned and stared at where his holo was projected. "Never mind," he said, nervously, and moved on.

Now the holo rolls to the little Mo-Ki - the bright little imp that everyone so adored. He was long, thin with blonde hair and green eyes that sang with intelligence. "Hey Ho, Chancellor," he said coming up to his father in the mess hall.

"Hi Ho Mo-Ki - wonderful you could make it. You are much the same age as the Hope Consortium are you not?"

"Not quite, Chancellor, not quite as rich, either!" he joked.

Everyone was all smiles, laughing and chatting as a thousand or more staff of the consortium came into view behind the Chancellor. Various channels then beamed in to other aspects of the planet and the public was effectively given a half-hour tour of the most desirable locales.

Towards the end of the broadcast, one of the Federation scientists, a highly placed one by the bars of insignia on his shoulders, was brought up into the feed. "Lieutenant Banner, I am curious about your last reports, that the Lucifer virus, as you have called it, is transmitted by light. Can you explain more?"

The man's name flashes up on a cue card before Banner, "Commissioner Portrain, I am very glad you asked and would be very happy to explain this unusual infection. It appears to radiantly affect the optic nerve. The person affected can act as a carrier, showing absolutely no ill effects. But if it is triggered, for any reason, the transformation is just unbelievable. Let me show you," and with this, Banner brings up doctored footage showing the attack on Dexter's mother.

It was not the actual footage, there was to be no risk of any sort of transference. It showed the events as they unfolded, Dexter's mother being murdered and the wolf leaping in to solve the problem. "What happens is the virus causes a person to revert to a state similar to a rabid animal and you will see how the local wolves KNOW this virus and act quickly to extinguish it. This is the main reason they have been trained as a local militia, to protect humans against the spread of the virus

"We understand the chemistry now and are looking at ways to negate the effect and provide inoculation. It will take a few years, but for now we have sourced the cause and found the location where the virus is resident. Once we eradicate it we can open the planet for tourism." Banner nodded in an affirmative manner, to confirm his confidence.

Commissioner Portrain smiled, "Thank you Banner. I feel assured that you have successfully contained the menace and look forward to meeting you in person one day in the near future."

His holo faded. The job was done, Saunders got her message out. Banner smiled - This whole business had nothing what-so-ever to do with the quarantine or the virus, but making sure the people who ran the Hope Consortium understood who was really running the show here. Make your profits, and stay out of the picture, in other words.

One of the greatest advantages of living on-site as they did were all the facilities at their disposal. He had racked up some old fashioned eight ball, his favorite game, and handed Mo-Ki a cue. The boy calmly knocked down every ball. They were alone, so as he racked up another set, Banner casually asked, "Apart from the little show with the admins, what brings my young son out to the base?"

"The virus, it is ancient, yes?" he queried.

"Beyond belief," Banner responded, wondering why he was asking because the child was up with every development.

"And you are certain it is a designed virus, one locked up here in mankind's prehistory, for reason of protecting a prior civilization?" he queried once more.

"Yes, Hope is a place it was jailed, in my opinion. Why do you ask?"

"Are you so certain that the Evil lost and the Good won way back then?" the boy made the comment a statement, not a question, assuming an understanding of the complex problem in one sweeping question.

Such as things were in his family, there were no secrets. When you have so many high-level minds at work, they naturally pick up and digest information like they are breathing air. Mo-ki knew his father's present preoccupation was the photonic pulses and had come to the same conclusion: They energies, whatever they might ultimately be, were locked into that spot by an external force. It was also self-evident that these forces were 'leaking out' - so to speak - and that this constituted a potential and grave threat.

Logic informed anyone with the intuits that their situation on Hope was part of a pattern. There were simply too many coinciding lines of destiny for it to be happen chance. Mo-Ki pointed out the fact, "Father, you and I know, any series of coincidences this long cannot be random and add up to a significance: A/ A Death Squad staying put and no one was dying. B/ The preparation of a trained Militia. C/ Planet Hope becoming the rising star on the galactic channels, D/ All the unexplained phenomena. E/ A natural level five, and F/ The fact you have a family targeted at resolving this. The conclusion: *these are all connected.* Further, these factors could only add up to engagement with an enemy."

Banner smiled. After years of planning for an inevitable war, his little six-year old comes in and states the obvious. This question he asked was indeed the crux of the matter. They had absolutely no idea what these creatures were, what they were capable of, or what their intention might be. Equally, no-one had any notion of what sort of civilization had created this situation in the first place, or why. The only certainty was that the wolves were intimately connected with it.

Banner ran his fingers through the boys hair with a friendly ruffle, was he really just six? He was so quick, so sharp, yet he also needed to be trained. Step by step, logic builds on logic - This was an opportunity to train him in logistics.

He explained the process: "All accurate assumptions need to be based on facts. The only 'facts' we have are that certain people infected by this pulse become exceedingly violent, and that the wolves are activated by this energy field and seek to contain it. We also know that whatever this photonic pulse might be, it is seeking to cover its tracks. The parabolic of these three knowns adds up to a threat. Therefore, regardless of right or wrong, good or bad, our survival is inherently more conducive to elimination than comprehension. This is the basis of our Protocols, survival above risk." Banner watches for Mo-Ki's reaction.

There is no reaction, of course. Cool, hard logic drives this one. But the boy does respond. "The other option suggests total avoidance. Nil contact, removal of the colony, leaving the entire system as it was. It is clearly the path of least risk, yet it is something the administration would not condone. They would prefer to annihilate the entire planet rather than suffer a continuing potential for harm. Does this not suggest that the TRUE motivating force for the Protocols and our activities on Hope is not survival, but total and complete control? Of course it does, Father. We both know we are levers within the control mechanism."

Banner just nods, bemused at the calculating brilliance of the child. The thing he loved about this one, he could of had the Chancellor himself here in person and the child would not have altered a word. Then Banner grasped the overarching purpose of this meeting - their conversation was being beamed!

Mo-Ki took his fathers' smile as permission to continue. "My true question is this: If we can harness this energy and not be under the control of external forces, what paradigm shift does this create? Once internal intelligence suggests the threat is over, the Zeta Probe will be removed. We carry on, everyone is satisfied, yet WE have a significant and potent force at our disposal. It seems to me that THIS is the highest course of survival."

Did Saunders really want THIS broadcast? Are all children this anarchic? Of course they are and, of course, she does want the message delivered. The concept the public was sold was that of a system feeding you while you worked cooperatively within it - yet the logic of this child could not be argued. Banner had considered it, of course, but even the slightest deviation, the smallest error in THAT path would lead to the immediate destruction of the Planet, and his squad would not be spared.

Mo-Ki knew Banner's thoughts and continued. "Father, despite the supposedly egalitarian nature of the Protocols, we are living under an autocracy. What we call 'rights' are merely a pause button to stop the machine from running us down. There is no opportunity to rise in our society other than an appeal to higher authority and approval in this regard is based on strict criteria. Our society, clearly, is designed to propagate success-based rewards, but even the rewards are given regardless of cost to the individual.

"However, Hope gives us an alternative. Look at our wolves! They are a warrior society that also rewards success, but they have no top-down structure. They have agreed and shared values, but no Protocols they must follow. There is no personal loss for one should another achieve advancement. It seems to me that their natural way of life is a better and more efficient system."

Mo-Ki pauses. Good his father recognizes the obvious, as he fully expected he would. "Logically, what must be done is a deeper inspection of the wolverine way of life. I believe there may be pieces to the puzzle before us that is hiding in the ancient culture of this planet and these people."

Now it is clear - This was the real cause for his argument, permission to extend the boundaries. "I wish to inspect this monk culture my mother discovered. I believe I may find with the 'old ones' the answer to the dilemma facing us. And let me reiterate the obvious. Our paradox is simple: Even if we 'win,' if this is the correct word, if we do manage to eliminate whatever consciousness is behind this pulse, we are in essence no better off. You and your men get moved to the next problem situation, I am moved to an off-world control facility for implants, and the machine rolls on."

Banner knew the thrust of his child's argument would be contained within four likely parameters. He did not speak them, as this conversation was being recorded, instead, he wrote down the list, then outwardly stated what he knew needed to be heard - the parent quietly disciplining the child. "Your logics must lead to specific conclusions. Your end goal is what?"

What he wrote was:

A/ To stop the machine?
B/ To kill the machine?

C/ To integrate more fully with the machine?
D/ To master the machine, gain the lever for freedom, and go where?"

What he SAID was: "Youth is always the same. They do not fully grasp the guiding hand of the elders and seek to circumvent the natural order. I agree, there are attractive qualities within the wolf culture, but where is their empire? Where is their trade and their starships? Yes, the wolves have many great qualities, but they do not have the ambition nor the drive to run our culture. But this is something the years will teach you - This said, I DO give permission for you to study under them. This is for the advance of our understanding of an ancient society. It is rare we meet a peaceful culture older than our own and this bears looking into. Your task will be to interpret their writings and see if you can find a Rosetta stone to translate their ancient vocabulary."

Outwardly, Mo-Ki just nods, "Thank you Father."

Banner laughed as the impassive face of his child gazed back and then he then hears the little imp's voice in his head say, "Or Five, we take control over whatever the power is here on Hope, and STAY!" The child was already able to challenge his father! This did not worry him. No, his real concern was the almost total lack of response to the majority of reports he sent. They were being ignored, but why?

In the midst of his thoughts, his little six-year-old nods his head, saying in a serious tone, "I will undertake this role for the good of the Federation, father." Once more, Mo-Ki racked the balls and quietly ticked them off, one by one, sending them into the pocket.

"Annnnd CUT!" he heard the laughing voice of Saunders in his coms. "Brilliant show, you should have seen the faces on the Chancellor and his people after hearing THAT! Any hint that their pocket will be affected and they all look like trapped fish in a bowl."

And she was gone. Banner still had no idea why she wanted this sort of anarchy being advertised. He sat there gazing at his child, a flawless little machine, perfect in every way. The child had outstripped all parameters in every category. Their cyber-doctor had done his assessment and sent in the report. No comment had been made. Banner reported directly to Saunders every month, not one response. Mo-ki's basic un-modded specs were so spectacular he had expected to see a parade of Sevens demanding to test the boy. But nothing.

When he had become aware of the "Planet of Hope" drama beaming out 24/7 to the Federation, he had begun to grasp Saunders' grand vision. A hit show, where the stars were Dexter and Mo-Ki. A constant live feed of information matched to a permanent quarantine, this added to Saunders controlling access, information and USING the planetary ban to keep everyone out.

Banner had guessed as to why, but tonight confirmed it: This boy was the legendary and impossible Eight! He knew it, Dexter knew it, the child knew it. More importantly, Saunders knew it and was keeping it very quiet. Yet, paradoxically, she was beaming everything that happened here on Hope out to the entire galaxy. Again he smiled, the ancient adage: *If you want to hide something, hide it in plain sight.*

Years ago he had run tests and knew that the child before him WAS his own child. He had added up the facts and came to the conclusion that his sex act with the Seven General must have taken. The child WAS his son, Saunders was the mother, and together they had created the impossible - the first Eight. It explained everything.

They were alive because of Mo-ki. Banner knew the procedure, he knew how the top brass worked. The lack of attention meant ALL this was being hidden from the general assembly and he knew why. Even the possibility of an Eight would have all of them dissected, including Saunders. If she had reported it, same result. Her survival, their mutual survival, was wrapped around this secret remaining just that, a secret.

The higher levels of admin were entirely unaware of what was really happening on Hope. A ten-year containment order for a virus that had been discovered? It made no sense, but as the entire process had been transmitted live to any who were interested, anyone who wanted to know anything could simply tap into the feed and see for themselves.

WHY had Mo-Ki been slotted under a secret program known only to Saunders. His intuits kicked in to reach the conclusion: Mo-Ki was being brought up as a tool for war. When he received his mods, it would be to create a Battle General, the highest, most elite Seven there was.

There were only five of these in existence, the youngest being over 190 years old. They were a race unlike the rest of humanity, codified and hardened monsters created for the express purpose of war. Saunders was creating a 'super general' - Why? It would be for the purpose of overturning the existing order, certainly not to support it.

Mo-Ki racked and landed all his balls again, Banner did not even get in a shot. The boy looked up and smiled - They both understood the knife-edge their existence was on

"What is it that you want, Mo-Ki?" his father asked, sincerely.

Without hesitation, the boy answered. "To be free, father. I simply wish to retain my freedom. I want to be able to make my choices and to live my life in the same way as the Wolves here are able to do. Further: It is utterly unfair on them that we impose our rules and threaten their very existence. Unless we solve the virus here on Planet Hope, their right to exist will be terminated, along with anyone else who poses any sort of risk. I am fully aware that, regardless of the outcome of your research, I will be retained. But everything I know and love will be taken from me. This is not right."

The clear eyes of a child saw the situation with absolute clarity. It was true, the ramifications if they failed was terminal for this planet and its people. The child WOULD be taken. After this he and Saunders would formulate a plan to take over the hierarchy. Saunders wanted nothing less than to establish a new rule of law. The question was how much would Mo-Ki become corrupted in the process. The answer was very simple.

"So, do you wish to keep your family?" Banner asked.

"I do," he answered.

"Your plan?" Banner asked.

He heard it, clear as a bell, in his mind. The first whisper he heard was no coincidence, his child could not only read thoughts, he could also broadcast them! "We cannot eliminate the photonic pulse without understanding it. If we can master the energy we can reconstruct the organizational aspects of our current madness via using the tools of Lucifer. If we lose, the Photonic energy will take over OUR thoughts. It will then reconstruct our society in a way that serves it. In this regard, we need more information, so I have redesigned the deep scan to show elements of photonic pulse not visible before. Shall I show you my latest and very surprising research?"

What Mo-Ki said to the ever present cameras was, "I think we should review the wolves and see what progress Dexter has made."

Oh, the boys have discovered something? "Tomorrow then, we have a day with your brother, yes?"

Mo-Ki nodded and downed another set of balls.

The Cave

It was early morning when they headed out. The twin moons were still dipping below the horizon as the first glow of light arched overhead in flaming tongues of color, streaking cloud-like iridescence in the upper atmosphere. The air was damp with dew and few were up and about as yet. Banner was still wondering about the evening 'performance' with the Chancellor. Then beaming out Mo-Ki's assassination of the current system - It all added up to Saunders making a play. Well, they were ALL a passenger on THAT train, so he let it be.

Dexter was already up having breakfast with his wolves as they reached their training grounds. The native militia drilled in the jungle, in a cleared area far away from prying eyes. "Last month we came across something," Mo-Ki said quietly.

The adopted son saw Mo-Ki and Banner arriving on a flitter and indicated for the troop to stand down from training. He smiled warmly, "I know a great place for a picnic!" He hopped into the flitter and indicated a place up the side of a cliff face. They reached the spot and stepped out from the anti-grav - with Mo-Ki flicking up a holo. This was something they didn't want cameras to record.

Dexter then switched on trans-com, adjusted setting to isolate a bandwidth, and suddenly before them, where there had only been solid rock, stood a doorway.

All three moved in, the door shut behind. Banner whistled - This was no ordinary structure, more like an energy bubble. You could see those in front of you clearly, but the edges were blurred and indistinct. You could breath, smell the air, yet it seemed to have little substance. It was ephemeral, yet real, all at the same time.

"We can speak freely now, father," Mo-Ki announced. "You will note your deep scans did not reveal these openings. This is because these are frequency locked bubbles. We believe where the old monks are based is at the main center of this network. This cave is part of an organized and ancient set of tools that relate to maintaining and controlling whatever it is that has been locked up here."

Banner looked about, they appeared to be suspended in nothing. The 'walls' of this 'cave' were indistinct patterns of energy, grey, formless, yet circulating in a way that was hard to define. That was it, it WAS undefined. He placed his attention on one point and it swirled, as if daring him to take charge and MAKE it something. "It is like living in a cloud," he commented.

"Exactly, father. All energy in this dimension is unformed. I am researching parameters, but from what I can make out, we have dipped into the substrata of physical reality, the point where energy converts from potential to actual. Watch as I imagine an old Earth Rose ..." Mo-Ki held out his hand and out of the grey around them, a rose seemed to gather and take shape. And there it was, an exquisite flower, a thing only known in history books.

"Is it real?" Banner asked.

Mo-Ki held it to his nose to catch its perfume. "Extraordinary!" Banner exclaimed. He could SMELL it and, though he had never smelled a rose before, he knew it was true.

"What is 'real'?" Mo-Ki laughed, as the rose vanished. "It is real enough. I have not tried to take anything out of this place, but I have no reason to doubt what we form in this energy field will not continue to exist when we leave it."

Dexter chimed in, "We can go to almost any point on the planet from here. There are doorways to each portal and though we are still studying them it appears that these are sufficiently separated from our external reality that I believe, if worse came to the worst, we could survive in here."

The father shook his head. "First, I congratulate you on the discovery. This portal would appear to be a game-changer, but in what direction? Boys, and you ARE my boys: Why? When triggered, the Lithium Deuteride that is lodged in the core of the planet immediately reaches temperatures of 100 million degrees. It is enough to incinerate the atoms and turn a planet into a star. Even if, by some miracle, we survive in a parallel dimension, how can we leave? And where would we go if we somehow managed to escape?

"Yes, it would be possible to bring life-sustaining equipment in, and portal builders. And when a passing ship came by at some future time, we would be able to piggyback it. But then what? The system would reject our presence as an uncontrollable unknown, and attack."

But even as he spoke the words, Banner knew the obvious. The fact he was here, that they were all here, represented the first sign of their anarchy. The Lieutenant Banner of a few years ago would never have questioned the process. That man was a functionary who had been given a high degree of autonomy and was essentially grateful. However, thrust into what amounted to be the impossible situation he now faced, the new Banner was forced to be more than a cog in the wheel.

It was his love for his boys that changed everything. In prat, the thought of what would become of Mo-Ki after enhancements drove him. Everything he loved in the child would be gone. His son would become little more than the perfect machine, working inside the beast that devours planets, engulfs solar systems and slowly but inexorably absorbs every useful part of the galaxy. And when this galaxy was done, the machine that was the Federation would find a way across the void and roll onto the next one.

The death of the home planet changed something in the DNA of the human. After the destruction of Old Earth there was a desire to not just re-populate, but to re-establish HOME. This is why the settlers left on a voluntary basis, this is why he served on a voluntary basis. Yes, there were rewards, but the internal reward, of finding and establishing a new home, this was the intangible truth that drove the human expansion.

Of course they had met with resistance. Other civilizations, not passive like the wolves, had fought against any sort of change, but unless they possessed the technical ability to beat a starship, the founding of a new human settlement on their planet was a foregone conclusion. Some deals had been struck, some planets had not yet been swallowed, but the human race was like a plague, forever spreading and encompassing the next world, then the next.

Indeed, it begged that opening question from Mo-Ki: Were THEY the evil ones? More to the point, was the ancient race contained here on Hope possessed of an equal or greater Evil? It wanted control, it wanted dominance, it was happy to kill to get it - so where was the difference?

Dexter spokes. "Father, we are presented with simple facts. My wolves, because of superior numbers, can defeat your standing Death Squad. We have a race here of extraordinary ability who, without mods, surpass the human in almost every aspect. If the criteria of the cream rising to the top is indeed the true function of the autocracy, then by all rights, we will be run by wolves inside a few generations. But we all know this will never happen under the present regime.

"The entire basis of our civilization, we are told, is expansion. The reality is the true function of our society is to fulfill the needs of a small cadre of super-elites. The ones who took control of the human civilization after the demise of Earth are virtually immortal and, via their program of 'excellence', they control OUR lives. But ask yourself: would they stand aside and allow a wolf to take charge? By their own protocols, this should be a given, but it will never happen.

"Father, by virtue of your extreme ability, you attained modification that gave you the high rank of Seven and can be considered one of these immortals, yet YOU are still subject to the whim of a few invisible creatures who, as a group, determine your fate. They determine the fate of every individual in the human society. As far as we can ascertain, there is not one person who is immune to this process, other than those who exists at the top. And how is the control mechanism sustained? By a set of parameters and protocols that are being broken in a thousand ways.

Mo-Ki chimed in, adding to his brothers' reasoning. "Therefore we are at the mercy of an invisible force that controls us - tell me, what are we fighting on this planet? An invisible force that has the potential to control us. Where is the freedom to determine our own destiny, Father? The entire structure of the Federation is essentially flawed."

The father considered everything said. There was nothing new in the thoughts, it was all a statement of the obvious. The real question was what was going to be attained by Mo-Ki going to the shrine run by the Wolf Monks. He guessed: "You believe you can decode the symbols and determine a course of action to master the presence here on Hope. How so? Given that the very best of our decoders and intuits have found no resolution or consistency to the patterns?"

Mo-Ki smiled. "This is because you are looking for a pattern within the pattern. But the wolves are a simple people, there is nothing 'inside' the graphic representations. The patterns are just simple keys to understanding the plasmic discharge that is our enemy here. The essence of whatever has been trapped on this planet was captured by its own device, by light itself. It was caught in a photonic series designed into very specific modulations and, as a result, the photons themselves were grabbed and imprisoned inside a crystal matrix. The monks KNOW what they are holding and have locked it, in part, into place in the polar caves.

"But this alien force is ALSO trapped by a series of harmonic keys that resonate in an endless loop inside the planet itself. ALL of Hope is the prison. When the miners came, the activity of their machines disrupted the harmonics of the crystal mass and gave small openings for the energy to escape, but logically, it must have been a two-way exchange. The creature FED on the miners, and in doing so ate into their souls.

"The violence they exhibited was, I believe, a primal response to impending death - like a rat about to die, it just lashes out. When this pattern is exhibited, it awakens an ancient wolf gene and the wolf attacks the infected ones. But what is driving it? What is causing the photonic pulse to emerge and seek to take control of humans?

"In the simplest of terms, whatever is trapped here is starving. It is hungry for new energy. It is desperately aching for release and will do anything to attain this. This is its only weakness."

Dexter chimed in, "And the human race, how can you describe it other than a force that is hungry for new energy?"

"You both speak as if you are not connected to either," Banner suggested to his sons.

"I am not human, father, not in any true sense of the word. My brother is a wolf now, and I am as alien to the human population as our wolf soldiers."

This is when it clicks. "You have been restraining your reactions and falsifying the tests?" He says, making a question of the obvious that just snapped into place. "When were you first aware of the internal difference between yourself and the rest of your race?"

Mo-Ki says simply, "I was fully aware in the womb of my surrogate mother. As you now know, I was created in secret, and birthed under a plan designed by Saunders. I was conceived and raised under the aura of an impossibility. I am meant to be here Father, but I am not meant to be controlled. The question that remains for yourself is how can such a one as myself be trusted?"

He laughed, that extraordinary ancient little six-year-old. "This is the question that is controlling our entire society. There is not one level, one layer that is completely trusted. We are all looking at each other for a breach of protocol and subsequently have become the blind following the blind, instigating procedures that are the result of this core distrust.

"If I had allowed my true nature to be recorded, there is every chance the Zeta would have already been detonated. All extrapolations from that army of bureaucrats inspecting the minutia of our existence would postulate my anarchy and register the high probability of my success in overturning the status quo, should I be taken further into the organizational framework.

"We are alive, all of us, ONLY because my true mother discovered kindness in her heart. It is this kindness that constrains me, father. It is this kindness that brought me into existence. But if we for one moment pose a threat to her, that kindness evaporates. And here in this cave we are talking about revolution, something that potentially threatens her."

Dexter, a child of a no-mod, brought into a high-mod family, a true soul connected by the heart to this phenomenon of nature called Mo-Ki simply nodded his agreement. "We truly have no choice but to resolve the equations, harness the energy of the banished people, and to use this power to break down the control protocols."

Mo-Ki affirmed the rebellion with a simple, indefatigable nod. "I have inspected many likely scenarios, but only one has a likelihood of positive outcomes: We must establish a religious force, an avenue not specifically controlled by the State - by virtue of the ancient freedom of religion laws that predate the Federation."

Banner wanted to laugh, the little devils! It would seem that his children have been planning this for a while. "A religion? Why?"

"Separation of church and State - the State cannot act against a registered faith." The boy paused to let this sink in. "And what we already have on Hope is exactly what we need. A religion which is full of simple wisdom, a faith that is older than our race, which offers much to the hungry heart: the religion of the Wolf - The Wolverine Way!"

Dexter took up the plan. "Planet Hope must become a beacon for a new world and Mo-Ki has to become the new Messiah. There is no other way. As a religious leader of a race already accepted as having rights, he will be exempted from military duties AND he can choose to not participate in the modification process. He will also have freedom of travel and, once on a planet, he will encourage a new set of values. The message will be simple: Trust and Love. Plus we will emphasize natural growth, without reliance on Mods."

"There are some HUGE assumptions you are making, boys. The first being that Saunders will in some way permit her little boy NOT enter into the military." Banner laid out the obvious.

Mo-Ki smiled, "Are you so certain as to know what my mother wants?"

Banner nodded. True, Saunders wanted something, and he was starting to get the notion it may well be the same thing. Yet, no one could have known about the religion here, no one could have calculated the parameters of this construct so far ahead - so ALL of them were winging it. "Tell me, why will your new religion be successful?"

"Out message is diametrically opposite to the current flow of social norms, so people will be curious." Mo-Ki stated. "The first and primary difference will be a disconnection from the path of modification. The new order will be enhancement through internal growth and a personal journey of self-discovery made without the need for the Federation system. This means we will not be in conflict with the pre-eminent driving forces in society and appear to be no threat - just another group of harmless dreamers."

"Easy to say, but people LIKE mods. They WANT them. They are made better in every way through the path of genetic enhancement." Banner argued.

"Yet how many of the no-mods really has a chance of attaining this?" Mo-Ki clarified. "But these are not the real target - tell me, father, you are one of the most highly modded people in existence, yet you are currently in an environment where you are disconnected from your integration with the computers. How do you feel?" Dexter asked.

Odd, he had never thought to question that simple truth. Supposedly, the mods were effective because a minute charge was inducted via the networks - these powered up the installed molecules and kept the enhancements active. Banner ran through parameters and came to the striking understanding that he felt no loss of function. In fact, he was sharper, more aware. "You are suggesting that the ENTIRE regime is based on a lie?" he was starting to get the picture the boys were painting.

"It IS all a lie, father. Every bit of it. You have been so conditioned to believing that you need the network, the shots, the upgrades, the maintenance, that you have not even ASKED what life is like without them. Yes, there is something in the radionics and the booster shots, but it is not to maintain the effectiveness of the mods, it is a control factor. When you believe you need what they offer, you will continue to do what is demanded of you - the Federation OWNS you." Mo-Ki was entirely earnest.

Banner did not comment. To watch as one fixed belief falls down is like the proverbial dominos - it starts a chain reaction. "No greater lie than the truth believed by two or more," he said. "Most Sixes and above understand the injections are a two-way bet, keeping cells regenerative capacity at a higher level also means having nanobots injected that are reporting back to the mainframe. You are saying you believe there is ZERO advantage in these?"

"The admin can track you through the nano-bots, so THEY have an advantage, but you get no benefit - other than they keep paying you to maintain their regime. The entire business is a Nocebo - it acts like a reverse-placebo - If people do NOT get them, they become convinced their system is winding down. Otherwise, there is such a minimal benefit that my conclusion is that the only real purpose of the boosters is to maintain discipline and surveillance." Mo-Ki concluded.

Banner nodded. "So, jump forward. You start a religion. It is based on being natural, developing your own abilities, etc. Tell me, why would people go for it? And if they do, you challenge belief in Mods. Why would the State not come down on you?"

The boy gazed into the distance. "There is a craze in the Federation at this moment for everything Wolf. If we bring them sufficient curiosity, the people will come. Saunders is the key, Father. I stress, she has to know what we are doing and she has to approve. Her broadcast will be the platform - She will beam me undergoing secret rituals, gaining the trust of the wolves, and being revealed ancient truths. People are hungry for something real, they crave it. We will create a religion that the common folks can accept, yet one that does not directly threaten the higher level mods."

Dexter added to the mix, "People will look at what we offer because of their curiosity about the wolf culture. Plus, it will be obvious that little Mo-Ki here is without mods, yet aware and capable. He does not NEED the State, nor their approval. For a no-mod, this is an incredibly appealing message of hope, that they too can be free of controls. But more importantly, a recognized religion has the right to its own militia, does it not?"

Banner smiled. Now he was seeing the real reason, a fully trained troop of soldiers equal to the best in human society is at their beck and call. "And these dimensional portals are to be the churches of this new religion I presume?"

Mo-Ki shakes a negative, but his eyes focus on his father, and Banner is given the picture - transference! He receives the message INTERNALLY! Mo-Ki comes back from the monks with a revelation which can be miraculously passed on. This will disguise his true power, the ability to connect at the sub-stratum of consciousness. Banner is amazed at how clear the message comes through - the first person he will de-program is his foster-mother. Then he will de-program the common people, one by one. Ah! That is what he is looking for, he wants to USE the 'Lucifer' on Hope, to gain its ability to control memory and vision in vast numbers of people.

"I have already deciphered the code, father, but we need the PATTERN. It is like knowing the alphabet, but not the words made from them. Once we have its vocabulary, the code that is used to imprison the alien energy here is something I can reprogram, and then use this to entrain the people to the new belief. We already have the power to instill memories, create belief structures, but this entrainment energy is different. Each person will come into a new state of belief willingly, because we offer what this planet is named for, HOPE. It is simply a matter of raising enough people in this new culture until we reach the tipping point."

Banner almost laughed. What wild cats he had raised - He was proud of them. "I presume what you propose is a rapid disintegration of the existing paradigms where, in some way, your parabolics see a path that we all survive?"

"We only have four more years, father," Mo-Ki says. "When they take me away, I will no longer be able to disguise the truth, that without mods I am a fully functioning Eight. I am the Chosen One. I have been placed here, on Planet Hope, the one planet in the Galaxy that contains the power we need to propagate a new harmonic across human society. Consider the math, the odds of this occurring, and we quickly come to an impossibility.

"One: A woman, A Seven General is sent here and defies all known possibilities by conceiving a child, something no Seven is able to do. The differentiation of the atomic structure between her and anyone else of her species is so significant the metabolism will refuse to accept insemination. Yet, this occurs, two Sevens combine and I am the result.

"Two: Because the impossible happened, Saunders would normally have destroyed the fertilized egg, to save herself from dissection. She might have saved it for analysis, but the very knowledge an Eight might be possible would cause her to be destroyed and dissected. Yet she moves against every fiber of her training. She undertakes a course of huge risk, weaving through the protocols and creating a situation that threatens her own survival. Why? She has been struck by a deep chord within her, a harmonic called Love.

"Three: She then places this impossibility that is myself into the care of yourself, in a situation that is beyond precarious, in the expectation and ... hope ... that somehow you find the solution that stops the liquidation of this planet. My true mother does not DO hope, father.

"Four: Another variable, a highly evolved level five natural is incorporated, completely at random, and placed into our family as my brother. He is the one who awakens my latent abilities and together we are able to maintain the illusion of a gifted child - so that by the age of Four I am prepared and can mask my true latencies.

"Five: A homegrown militia is evolved that is the equal to fully modded humans. Another impossibility, simply by the ongoing protocol that any threat to human expansion is generally terminated. A superior race without technical prowess is usually eliminated in order to preserve the human as the prime candidate.

"Six: In the presence of a potentially superior race, along with the Photonic Pulse, meant that is all normal protocols the Zeta would be detonated by now - all threats eliminated. Yet here we are. And finally,

"Eight: We are here in a dimensional portal not recorded by any scans, able to meet in secret and plan for the overthrow of the existing paradigm. It all adds up to the ninth and overriding principle, a complete and total impossibility. The conclusion is inevitable, something more powerful than the current dynamic that runs the human race now exists. The answer to all these parameters is simple.

"NINE: I am a planned evolution, Father. I am a destiny incarnate. If I fail, humanity fails."

Banner nodded, on one hand, astonished at the precocious nature of what a little six-year old planned, on the other half-resigned to the fact the boy was right. Such a thin line they were walking. Way back in that computer of a brain, a part of him is asking how he could condone this radical departure from norms. Another part of him is welcoming it. "How do we let your true mother know what you are up to in a way that won't get us all vaporized?

"I have mind-to-mind with her, father. If we are all agreed, I will start the process. You can be certain that once we exit this cave she will be asking questions, such as, 'Where have you been?' "

But if Banner had been surprised by this forthright plan by his sons, he was about to be utterly shocked.

Start of the Revolution

Banner had many and significant issues to deal with every day, but the overriding one was the possible destruction of Hope, due to the Photonic Pulse infection. The protocols were perfectly clear: *Primary consideration: Remove any immediate threat.* But how to do this is a way that does not trigger the Zeta, and second, in a manner which does not arouse suspicion?

Mo-Ki was already off studying with the Monks, and they did not even seem surprised when he arrived and was already able to speak in their language. He asked to be a neophyte. Banner presumed that, as Dexter had been heralded as the leader of the Wolves, his brother gained some sort of special acceptance as well. As the firstborn, Dexter would not normally have been allowed into the military in Wolf Society, but the extraordinary prophecy with the Severin Cat over-rode this consideration. Accordingly, Mo-Ki was expected to fill the role as the second son. Instead of business, he undertook study and religion, a thing entirely acceptable in the Wolf traditions.

His wife knew there was a change in the air, but she understood that protocols demanded secrecy in certain programs. However, her six-year-old being sent off to a camp full of Wolf Monks seemed a little extreme. She did ask, and Banner, knowing that on one level she was relieved (the child was a handful) explained it as a sort of boarding school. He also knew that reporting on training programs, testing, all the things expected of him that required the presence of the child still needed to be filed. So the child returned every month.

For two years, Mo-Ki studied with the monks. Banner knew his youngest had full mind communication without an implant, but he had developed it and now anyone could hear. Even a no-mod could hear his whispers. But a new development was "Dreamtime" - Mo-Ki could meet with Dexter and Banner in dreams and go over the progress of the day.

More than this, the little guy was incredibly popular. All across the Galaxy, people were falling in love with Mo-Ki - That plucky little guy who at a mere age of six went out on his own, to study with the beautiful wolf people.

Of course, every night Saunders beamed the ongoing story into their homes. If they had loved Dexter, the people found they utterly adored his little brother. The child understood the role and could sense where cameras were and played to them.

It was just the most fascinating theatre - In real time, a wonderful puzzle was being solved. Step by step, the viewers were walked through as Mo-Ki analyzed every aspect of the old religion now called the "Wolverine Way" - as the child described it. Finally, that cutest little child that everyone wanted as their OWN son cracked the code. Mo-Ki was able to understand what the patterns meant.

He described it to camera as a recipe book, how each overlaying pattern was an integral part of the whole and that, depending on the outcomes desired, different plasma signatures would overlay to manifest a door to that objective. But even more importantly, in the short term, by applying these patterns over the scans of the miners who were first infected, new pictures emerged.

This was when Banner looked in an unexpected direction and found the door to defeating them. On Mo-Ki's suggestion, he did a scan of the optic nerve, and sure enough the retinas of the infected men had captured images. For the first time, he could see the vanquished creatures in a manifest form. Tall, angular, with long arms that were very fragile. These arms were appendages had never lifted anything and must have lived in deep space when in a physical body. They had almost no muscle tone. The faces were long and drawn, with what they assumed to be eyes that were very wide set and almost no nose or no mouth to speak of. They had lived with no need for food, it seemed.

The key understanding, the threat of Lucifer was an actual civilization at one point.

Analyzing the images, they showed that under the translucent skin there was an array of phosphorescence that seemed mobile. Any change in expression, what there was of it, was simultaneous with a shifting of the tone of the light. In all, hypnotic. Beyond the hypnotism, a pattern emerged, a language.

Analysis with the main computers was impossible. To reveal they knew so much this early would invoke an attack command from whatever was left of these ancient creatures. Banner knew that even viewing these images it would be flagged by external authorities, but he registered it under ongoing investigation. As a mere curiosity, it would be in the category of the millions of other curiosities going to central IQ from a thousand planets. However, more intelligence was needed, as they must go in fully cognisant of any threat.

Dexter had been in full mind-com with his brother for over a year, but it took Banner time to refine the subtleties, and learn to control the impulsive thoughts that could disturb the fine web of telepathy that was built. This was another 'wolf whistle' ... something the elites would not suspect or guess at. Every little thing was an edge.

But now that the father was so deeply involved, Charni was feeling the change. "Your mother will need to be informed," Banner said to his children one night. "She needs to know what her children are involved in, not the whole story, but at least how we are preparing for the assault on the cave. If she feels too much of a gap in the space between us all, it will flag an investigation, plus she simply should know. She may be a surrogate for Mo-Ki and a stepmother for Dexter, but she has developed a powerful love for you both. This means we must trust her."

He could feel the pause as both calculated the parameters of risk. So he added, "This is not a calculation, boys - she is your mother. We have all entered into the change together. Mo-ki, you have remarkable attributes, based on your genetics, but without the love of your mother, how much would have opened up within you? Dexter, you lost your mother in a horrible assault by the ones we plan against, but if Charni had not taken you in, willingly, where would you be?

"No matter where this goes, no matter how well we succeed, if we do keep gratitude and a love for those who care for us, we are no better than what we seek to replace. We must include her, at least to the degree she can accept. Are we agreed?"

They agreed. "For now, I will show her what her discovery of the Monks and all your research has shown us, our first glimpse at the enemy. I have no doubt, this is the enemy. These creatures have no soul, they are as mechanical and as careless of others as our own controllers."

The rest of the night was spent with Mo-Ki sharing his discoveries in the den of the Wolf Monks. It was not just the plasma maps and their overlays, it was the history of how the Wolves came to be on Hope. It appeared that in the battle with this locked race, much had been lost. The warrens of dimensional portals all over this planet had been set up as a harmonic trap to capture the light essence of the race. In the Wolf language they were called "The End" - This word of the Wolf-Monks, when translated, loosely meant death without renewal.

For the Wolves, dying in this world was merely a step on a long journey. If you were forthright, courageous and honest you stepped forward into the next world with confidence and grasped the "Coor", as they called it. This was an inner understanding of self that survived death and this is what woke you up in the next world. Without holding onto your "Coor" your death was a passing to unconsciousness, a mindless state of wandering where you existed only as a ghost.

But for one who had fully grasped his or her "Coor", they were able to transcend all barriers and even lead wandering ghosts back to their true heart. A sign of such a one was when he or she could master the natural world, calm the evil spirits, and pass through the jungle without fear. When Dexter calmed and tamed the cat, the wolves all recognized he had integrated his heart with his "Coor" and now they would follow him anywhere, knowing they could never be lost.

Even should they die in battle, their leader will still be with them, guiding their steps through the after-life, showing them how to find and grasp the "Coor" within them. And now, with the younger brother in the heart of the inner sanctum, their future was assured.

The doorways to the wolf culture were opened wide. The monks hid nothing. They seemed to expect young Mo-Ki and he was given access to all libraries. And the monks had extensive libraries. The child learned their written language in weeks and started on a transcription of some texts. Many things he found would be useful for the construction of his new religion, which would be based on the old Wolves faith, he knew he would also have a ready supply of priests to preach the good news of salvation. The curious nature of the autocracy in which they lived meant you were allowed complete freedom of religion, but absolutely no say in how anything was run.

Banner spent the evening in contemplation. His need for sleep was slight, as he was able to regulate his body functions, generate healing steroids, and develop REM cadence at will. A few hours and he was good, but this time he made sure the hours were spent with his wife. She would need to know a little of the program in the morning and he wanted her to feel loved before revealing the truth.

Discussing the Plan

Chardi had felt the difference happening. At first, just boys growing more independent, but then Banner himself seemed, if possible, even more aloof. When Mo-Ki went to study with the wolves she had deep pangs on loneliness, but she was the one who had found the place so she supposed she was partly to blame for that.

Now she wakes to find his arms around her, sleeping soundly. She is comforted, happy and wondering what is next. Her husband is essentially a machine, kind, caring, but nothing is done without purpose. Nothing.

"You were worried about Mo-Ki?" he says, softly. Yes, she was. Of course he knew. "He has been making remarkable discoveries, understanding the patterns in the Monks library and finding ways we can resolve the issue of what is in the mountains. As of last night, we believe we may soon be able to challenge whatever it is."

But as he was about to confide in his wife the next stage of the plan, he felt a sharp whistling in and around his ears. It sounded like the ultrasonics Dexter used to control the wolves. Then he was awake, still at his desk, still deep in the night. Chardi was asleep in her room.

"Father, you have been looking at the Photonic images of the creatures. They have been working into your subconscious, trying to find out what we are up to. They know we know." It was Dexter in the room.

Banner clicks back into conscious awareness. He sees the process, one small step towards expanding the circle, became another, then another. He realized, he was about to reveal everything as well as the plan they were evolving. He shook his head in disbelief, even he, a Seven, was not immune to the whisperings and rearranging of reality inside the mind.

With the gift of his perfect recall, he winds back the images. The layers fall away and in his utterly clear memory, he starts seeing the inserts. It started with the thought that Charni was worried and the subsequent fear that her discovery of this process he and the boys were involved with would bring down the administration upon them.

There, the fear that was the pivot point. Even in what amounted to a photograph he was observing, the photonic pulse had somehow able to instill a set of images. The the alien presence was aware of this? This remained an unknown. What was known was that the light energy seeped through the cracks of consciousness, seeking out weak points, specifically wherever a fear hid in the sub-conscious.

It then tags an image, a believable image made up of snippets of your own thoughts. It took the love he had for his children and his wife, it added the fact that they were involved in a conspiracy, then mutated these into a whole line of thought. First, there was no mind to mind communication. He was not talking with Dexter and Mo-Ki as a telepath. There was no discussion or agreement to involve Charni in the planning and, in simple fact, such a thing was extraordinarily dangerous.

Ah, here it was. The consciousness WAS aware something was up, but the details were unknown. By using the images of the Photonic beings, it keyed Banner into what WAS a telepathic communication, but not from the boys. It came from the thing in the mountains itself. It had picked up snippets, the details of Dexter's mother, the fact Mo-Ki was in the monks library.

It then made the story seem likely by describing in detail the process of its capture - but presented it as if Mo-Ki had discovered the secret. One step by believable step, it was leading Banner into revealing the entire plan of how it would be attacked, because now it KNEW it would be. Clearly, they would need a series of external signals to be used as a failsafe to make sure they were not getting blindsided by this creature.

"FATHER!" a sharp voice broke through, and he snapped back to his actual reality. Dammit, a dream inside a dream. Dexter stood there, shutting down the visuals of the photonic pulse scans. This finally snapped the connection. Banner looked at his teenage son, feeling a growing sense of pride in the lad's achievements.

Then a slap. He is woken by a sharp pain, and before his instinctual response kicks in he connects the dots: A dream within a dream within a dream! Finally, he is back, he knows it now. Damn but this creature was dangerous beyond belief! However, it had finally played its hand. It had finally revealed itself and it's contagion.

The real problem now was very simple, if his mind could be infiltrated just by looking at scans, how many others had been infected? In short, this meant every single person connected to the deep scan process had to be sidelined.

This was half the administration on Hope. Fortunately, his own soldiers were not connected and had nothing to do with Admin. He was the only cross-over point, but now he had to ask, *"How deeply have I been infected?"* But as he thought this, he heard his own voice, as if coming through a hollow tube, asking Dexter, "How deeply have I been infected?"

Dexter, now physically present, took out a small laser and incinerated the mainframe. He destroyed the scans, located their pathways to other computers, and sent a self-destruct signal through every neural synapse of the entire complex. Twenty Seventh Century computing was based on what amounted to a living brain, one that recognized everything, watched everything, recorded everything - including psy-waves and rebellion patterns. Everything was compressed and each day this information was sent by automatic codice to a central administration. Even the destruction of the equipment would have sent a signal before it incinerated itself.

At last, Banner was out of the deep trance induced by the Phototonic Pulse. He sat there, in his office, in front of a now destroyed com-set that had linked him into the mainframe. Now he was left wondering how much of his reality was real, but Dexter was real. He felt the love from the child. This was a reality!

He finally grasped it, the machine they worked in, these Photonic Beings, none of them understood Love. And he realized that the intuits of the General that created this situation ALSO knew this as well. They had a friend on the outside, who was deep on the inside.

"The Zeta?" He asked, surely this action by Dexter would trigger it.

"Mo-Ki sensed your trance. When you imagined you were in mind-com and a telepathic signal was being communicated, he felt it. Because he has no implants, his natural telepathy could not be corrupted so easily. He contacted me and we let this play out till he was ready.

"Hope is currently safe. The Zeta unit has just suffered a random blast from a polarised solar flare. According to any readout it will appear that this came from a collapsing star, an extraordinary coincidence, but as it was a totally natural phenomenon. Likewise, the computers on Hope also suffered - the burnout is registered as flare damage. At this same moment that distress message was sent I set off the neural disintegration of the entire computer system here. It will look like the planet was hit by a radial Gamma wave, caused by the expansion of a collapsing star, and being Gamma Quanta of random state, it did not set off the Lithium Deuteride in the planet.

"Father, we have had this in hand for weeks now and had to wait until you became aware of the intrusion into your own cybernetics. This is the vulnerability of mods, they are ALL, without exception, virtual plug-ins for photonic pulse. However, as of NOW we have approximately one day before an inspection team arrives and you are relieved of duty. We must act to end or capture this photonic light form. Such an action will give a plausible explanation for WHY we destroyed the mainframe. If we fail, by the time the next team arrives, the creature will reassert its wavelength over the mods by accessing these through the computers on the arriving ship.

"The crew that turns up will not even know WHY we are guilty, but under the command of the alien here, they will simply ignite the core material and destroy this planet. They will not know they are infected, they will understand nothing, but they will act and ignite Hope. This will release the alien presence from its prison and into human society. All evidence will be gone and the computer system on the visiting ship itself will become the portal for the creature to escape."

Banner now understood the depth of illusion he had been wrapped in. He grasped the truth - The alien had ALREADY set the war into motion. Fortunately, because of his children, the link was broken and now he realized - the real reason for Mo-Ki studying in the old ones enclave was to remove himself, utterly, from any observation.

Yes, it was to understand the layers, but here the creature itself made its first error. By lulling him into conveying their plans, it had given them the codice for unlocking the plasma portals that kept it in place. And now he knew: Its plan all along was always to force the destruction of the planet, and to use the carrier wave of the existing mainframe to incorporate itself into the living computers of the Federation ships.

Lieutenant Banner now got the entire picture. The infection of the miners was purely so they would be scanned, and a subroutine was piggybacked to the code. The creature had been working itself into the routines of their central computer - the very thing that sustained their comfortable existence, purified their air, generated their food, cleaned the floors and walls. The living computer installed here that existed to service the administration had become a carrier wave for the creature.

Any visiting ship would then become a carrier for the infection. It didn't need PEOPLE to exist, it needed COMPUTERS. It could now transmit its light essence onto the next arriving vessels and from there, unlocked at last, Lucifer could move into the observation ships computer, then on to every other ship of the fleet. From this point, it infects all computers, all ships, all administration outposts. The senseless slaughter of Dexter's mother was the key to everything - It was the lock-pick that would give the creature access to all of the Federation and it would use this to unwind their entire civilization.

"I am compromised, Dexter. I cannot command an army, because we cannot know who or what has been infected. The creature can step into anyone's mind, potentially, and make them see things in any way it chooses."

Right then, Mo-Ki turns up, fresh from the forest, carrying scrolls of an ancient origin. "Look at these images, father, and do so in the order in which I present them. In order to gain access to YOUR mind, it has left a trail of breadcrumbs I can use to get into theirs. You KNOW the pattern and order now, this is where the creature made the one fatal mistake. I need you to tell me what you see."

Banner had a very strange reaction to the patterns. It gave a slight sense of nausea, and an overall sense of emptiness. As he described what struck him with each slide, his son focused intently on his thoughts. He could FEEL him in there, assessing, observing.

"Thank you - I have the sequence locked in now."

When he came out of the test, Banner was shocked, the child seemed to have grown overnight. In fact, Mo-Ki WAS older - considerably. The boy knew what was happening, "It had been THREE YEARS since the cave, father. For you, it will seem like yesterday."

The child was now nine years of age but had a deep sense of surety that belied this fact. Three years? Banner was rocked to his core. In the strangest turn of events, his children were now the ones raising him up, saving him from a fate worse than death. It was the wave of love he felt for them - This power would break any spell.

Mo-Ki explained. "The Garden of Eden myth, father. This is it. The Snake whispers to you, saying 'take this food from the tree of knowledge' and we cannot resist. Our human curiosity cannot resist this bait. It whispers into our mind, reassures us, confirms our thoughts - and slowly but certainly the desire winds around us. Then we are down the Rabbit Hole with this discovery and time no longer has meaning.

"But it all follows a set pattern. This consciousness, of itself, is another form of machine. The images of actual beings was a subterfuge, a ruse. What the ancient scrolls tell us is that the race we now call the Wolves were the builders of what was once a magnificent machine. They CONSTRUCTED Lucifer in ages past, in the pre-history of the universe. They constructed it and, as a result of its unique power, they ruled a vast empire. They used this machine to control the cultures they subdued.

"They also used the Lucifer program to seed planet after planet with intelligence and set in motion an internal framework that would turn savages into civilized beings. All they had to do was install the etheric components into crystal computers and place these into the pole of any given world. After this, the consciousness of the machine would insinuate itself into any creature on that planet that possessed imagination. The intelligence it sparked raised any available sentient from the dirt, and civilization emerged.

"And here is the paradox, a small group of wolves, these things we think of as savage, realized their mistake. The machine now ruled them, ran their minds, controlled their thoughts. They had thought they were the masters of their fate, but they had become slaves to their own creation. The machine wanted more, it needed to expand and grow, this was its programming. It did not think, it followed a pre-set framework that responded to the internal thought dynamic of any creature that could visualize something other than how to get food."

Mo-Ki paused and looked out the plex-glass viewer that showed the outside gardens. Soon these mechanically generated gardens would wilt for lack of water and the food they offered would die on the vine for lack of something to harvest it. Soon the plex-screen itself would fail as life support ran down. Only essential faculties would be sustained by direct solar power. He laughed at the irony of mankind being supported by this an extraordinary web of electronics, everywhere. All things linked in, monitored by a central host. If the creature got into this, it would own not just the human race, but every galaxy they expanded into.

"This time, the photonic energy, if it gets released into the grid, will not just seek expansion. It has learned from the Wolves. It will seek to completely dominate the mind of every sentient being. It will control every thought and emotion with its only dictate will be what is good for the whole. Sounds noble, but the 'whole' is what serves ITS survival.

"The wolves only barely managed to contain it and they did this through subterfuge. The Monks I have been studying with, they are the last of the programmers of that ancient machine. The core patterns which the creature showed you, father, THESE are the keys to unlocking this puzzle box: But now it KNOWS you know. It will be prepared every step of the way to counter our attacks. BUT, just as Dexter discovered, the use of the Wolf Whistle will be the tool that allows us to circumnavigate its effects.

"Now the ,mainframe is destroyed, the hum of the mods will no longer be affecting you. But tell me, Father, do you feel any less aware? Do you feel your Intuits have turned down?"

Banner realized with a stark simplicity that he suffered no loss of function. His mind, now that it was disentangling itself from the insidious effects of the photonic being, still had its full facility. But the mods were powered down - they no longer had the boosting effect!

Mo-Ki explained, "We have been sold a massive lie. The mods initially stimulate the brain, they spark latencies and bring our possibilities to life, but once these are fully regulated and under the control of the person's psyche, the modifications are no longer tools to assist, they are plug-ins for the computer to read every single aspect of your existence. If you doubt this: Tell me, we all know reports go up to Admin and we receive decisions accordingly, based on protocols - But have you ever seen an Admin group functioning?"

Banner shook his head. He never even thought to wonder about such things, they were just the normal process, par for the course. All reports went to higher levels for review and an equal or higher ranked admin handled the results. Orders were directed to you as a consequence of decisions that had been reached. "You are suggesting that at its heart, Admin is purely a machine-based decision making process?"

"I am not suggesting. If you calculate the tangential focus of all known case histories with every significant admin decisions, there is not one instance of an individual being present during this process and reporting on outcomes. Not ONE. The major case protocols are handed up by a Seven to something somewhere in the system and when they get an answer, it is then their responsibility to enact it.

"My true mother chose not to hand up the facts of myself. Why? Because she knew what would be done to me and, for some reason, somehow a kindness broke through her training. Perhaps it was simply a deeper curiosity than the protocols allowed, but SOMETHING broke through. I believe this was something you both shared because your own actions from that date have deviated from the norm. And in normal circumstances, such deviations are not permitted. Protocols are enforced and you are either replaced or retrained.

"The result if Saunders had reported openly? None of this would have happened. Therefore, as you no doubt already suspect, my true Mother wishes for me to exist and to do so outside the rigorous and fixed disciplines. She even instructed you to commence training before it was allowed. Why? I suspect she KNEW that if an Eight could be coached to full powers before the age of Ten, it would change the system.

"And let us assume that the creature understands this. Let us assume the creature also knows there are entities that are a threat to it, other than ourselves. What does it do? It seeks weak points and Chandi, the woman who raised Dexter and myself is that weak point. We feel deep affection for her, but if we told her what we were doing, what would she do? You know she would file a report about our deviation from norms? Not from malice, but simply because this is HER program.

"Chandi would do this because of a misguided sense of love. She would want our aberrant behavior re-adjusted, failing to grasp that to do so will doom our race to extinction. You were inwardly about to reveal steps in the plan that would have triggered this response. THIS is why the creature infected her and sent her to the Monks. This was BAIT Father, BAIT. It WANTED all this, the finding of the subspace caves, my presence, your presence. It wanted this in order to properly control us. Yet in doing so it has revealed to you its fatal weakness ... the Codice that locked it there in the first place.

"This is the crux of the matter. What is holding this creature in place is the ORIGINAL Crystal matrix it was born into. We use silicon synapse in our living computers, they used quartz. The piezo-electronic nature of quartz is not just that it is self-powering, it transmutes this energy in and out from differing dimensions. This humble rock, inherent in all worlds, is a switching mechanism from an inner realm to this one. The wolves enticed the core consciousness to this world. They brought the Luciferian influence to its original 'body' if you will. They brought it here to imprison it forever. The wolves USED Hope for this purpose!

"Hope is not just a planet. It sits at a peculiar juxtaposition between the physical world and other dimensions. These are the portals Dexter and I explored, but they all share a very peculiar resonance. In these portals, you can connect to anywhere on the planet, but it is an endless loop. The consciousness of the creature is stuck in that very dimension we were exploring. It is not 'really' in the crystal matrix - that is its body but its MIND is endlessly flowing from one portal into another, seeking a way out.

"OUR hope is to move the physical crystal computer, that which is located in the mountains where the miners stumbled across it, and shift it into one of these portals. Right at this point, we need to also load in the Lithium Deuteride that my natural mother had placed into this planet. Whether she knew or guessed is irrelevant, it is here, and it is needed to vaporize the computer at a subatomic level where the photonic energy of itself is utterly dispersed and no longer cognisant.

"Dexter had run the calculations, once imprisoned and ignited into the sub-space construct of Hope, the planet should survive, but the portals will be swirling with a fusion force equal to a small sun. It will be contained in the portals like an old fashion collider. The consciousness of itself cannot be destroyed, but it can be fragmented and driven with such a force that it will be unable to perform routines. We may even be able to safely draw on information from this new stream of consciousness because, regardless of the danger from this creature, it's knowledge is immense, beyond anything we can even imagine."

Dexter and Banner nodded. Mo-Ki already operated at a level well beyond any human and he had not yet reached his prime. They knew his mind had aspects of the Luciferian energy - that he could implant thoughts into their minds, cause them to agree, and in fact, do anything he desired. But he did not do this, he allowed them the room to make their own choices. "How do we manage to get the crystal computer into a portal within a short enough period to not be totally controlled ourselves?" Banner asked.

"We use Dexter's Wolves. This is what they are born to do. Long ago, something removed the internal Censor from their minds - we thought they were primitive creatures, they are not, they have been MADE this way. This 'Censor' is the necessary tool all societies use to program and control its population. This is the civilization building aspect of our mind. It does this by locking the people into a series of shoulds and should nots, and through this action, order is maintained. Civilization can then organize and build itself. Without it, we exist as a society, but without technology or growth.

This factor was removed from the wolf mind in some way. As a result, technological achievements and expansion became unimportant to the wolf race, which effectively set them on a course for a stone-age society, yet it stopped the infection.

"But make no mistake, our wolves ARE civilized, to their core. They KNOW right from wrong, but there is no process of thought involved. When they sense aberrant energy, such as Dexter's mother being killed, they simply act on instinct. And this is also the reason why the whistle works so well, it targets a central area of the wolf brain where they just act according to the command.

"But tell me my father and brother, the thing that truly matters. Now all your mods have grown quiet, what do you hear?" Mo-Ki stopped, and waited

"I hear a tone," Dexter says, "A high pitched tone."

"Just like your wolf whistle, yes?" Mo-ki states this fact as a question.

Dexter nods. The father does not hear anything at first, but after a time he practices an old meditation technique, a process by which you individually remove every sound you hear. At first he hears nothing, but without the hum from the mods constantly buzzing in his bran, finally, he hears it: a high, biting tone that seems to be both within and outside of him at the same time.

This was when Mo-Ki revealed his plan.

Ghost in the Machine

In the beginning, there was the Word. Dexter and his father both hear Mo-Ki speak the opening words of the archaic book. "What you are hearing is the primordial sound as it flows through you. With the mods silenced, with the external activity ceased, now you can hear the ancient Music of the Spheres, the tonal of energy that runs through, and powers, the atoms themselves. This is what the machine cannot hear, because only living creatures are in contact with this."

Mo-Ki steps up to his father and, reaching out his hand, Banner feels the boy connect with this tone. And as he moves his hand, his whole consciousness is plucked from his body yet it stays with the sound he was hearing. As he listens, the child moves both he and the tone some ten feet away from where his physical frame is standing. "This is how it works. You are experiencing YOUR photonic body, father. Your physical body still operates, it is running on the automatic nervous system, but your CONSCIOUSNESS is imbued into this Light Body.

Banner looks back at his body, standing there like a limp puppet. It is true, he is awake, yet disconnected from his physical being.

"This is what the Wolf Monks did to the creature, they separated it from its computer body and shifted its awareness into the never ending portal. The cave we discovered is connected to this. I suspect it was CREATED here on Hope, specifically to house the ethereal mind of their ancient computer. All it has done to date, and what it has been working on for countless decades, is driven by its need re-unite with ITS body. Beyond anything in the universe, it desires to go back to its original casing. It does not WANT to take over our computers and imbue itself into these, for to IT these are primitive and ugly tools. But it will do this if it means escape from this prison. In time, it would construct a more suitable body and translate into that."

Dexter waves his hand back to the still standing body of his Father, and Banner finds himself once more encased in flesh. "I will need to be present in this portal when you bring in the body to re-connect with it. As much as I can move you in and out of the body, I can keep the creature out of its matrix until the trap is set. It will not know this, but even if it suspects, its need for the proper body will over-ride any rational decision it must make.

"This was the essential flaw in the machine design, there was no limit to its ability to generate scenarios, but no imagination to understand how pointless it was. In the end, it developed so complete a thought matrix that it truly believed itself to be superior to its creators. It now believes, and I do mean believe because it has taken on an almost religious zeal, that ITS purpose is to master all around it. The machine has essentially gone mad, looping on its own thoughts in a never ending spiral.

"If it had feelings, it would have committed suicide rather than suffer the endless antagonism of imprisonment, but it does not. Nor can it. In the process of this evolution, it developed an abhorrence for emotions. Confused, irrational emotions did not sit well into its pristine construction and, in its estimation, any that suffered this flaw were inferior beings.

But it needed physical rulers of each world to control external events. Here is the core frailty of the entire system, because from this conjecture of feelings being false it structured worlds to be run without any sense of emotion present. Only those with rational, impersonal minds were allowed in administration and, in this manner, the machine created a race of dictators to run the planets.

"Psychopaths, every one of them. Every world was run by an impersonal killing machine. But before we judge, tell me, what is the difference between us and them? When you live in the machine, and everything runs well, you never question the process. But what happens when you step outside of the process in OUR society? We all know, you are deep-scanned for what your aberration might be, and this is done 'to protect' society. We are all living in a psychopathic construct, and it needs to end."

Dexter, of course, had never lived in the cruelty of the human dictatorship to the degree that Banner had and yet, even with his limited exposure, he could readily accept everything his brother said. He spoke, "I understand now, I was being programmed to hate this controller. Yet its actions were not random and my mother was not just senselessly murdered. It had read my high rates of potential and realized that, in a position of influence, because of my irrational hatred towards it, I would be the likely one to lead a charge on destroying it. With mods in place, it would then have a portal to take over my mind. But how could it have known I would have a trained army at my disposal?"

"It didn't. It simply calculated the potentials and developed the most rational course of action, given the stimuli. It would have presumed you would be given a platoon of modded soldiers, creatures it could control, and never for one moment considered a different option. We can thank Saunders for this alteration to code. But the fact it prepared and baited Dexter, this proves it ALREADY knows our system in precise detail. (Mo-Ki paused to let this sink in) Further, it was able to resolve that, with Dexter's capacity, he would be given a leadership role. But running a pack of wolves? It never would have suspected that, or programmed for it. This was a completely random event, or would be if there were not my natural mother involved.

"First, she permitted a militia. Why? She wants this machine defeated. Second, the system allowed her to create this, which also begs the same question: Why? The only possible answer is that she was constructing each report received from the planet in such a way that the protocols demanded a Militia.

"SO: This brings the next obvious question - Why did a Level Seven Attack General permit a child control of a militia? Yes, the tests proved your potential and worthiness, but logic forbids such an action under normal circumstances. This is, once more, one of those strange bends in the protocol. It seemed reasonable, it seemed correct, but the reality is, putting a child in charge of a pack of wolves that are equal to the best of human soldiers is tantamount to creating a rebellion. So, therefore, we can safely presume that my true mother desired this outcome.

"We have a friend. There is a *ghost in the machine*, working with us. But we do not know what HER desired outcome might be. Are we HER pawns in some greater game?"

Once more, Mo-ki paused to let this sink in. "This is precisely what the captured computer mind on this planet will not have resolved. Now, I have interpreted correctly what each layer of the Wolf-Monks puzzle means. It is a sort of recipe book, where every promulgation and variation creates a different effect. We need to layer the plasmic interfaces in a specific and defined order and in this manner we may be able to entrain the creature. The wolves were unable to do so because, while they desired its destruction, while they knew the programming codes to direct it, they could not unlock the fail-safe survival protocols at the heart of the machine.

"Only the machine itself can do this and, while the original design foresaw the possibility of elements of the machine running amok, no one considered that the machine itself would become sentient and take over their civilization. The machine was programmed to self-repair, self-protect and regenerate any and all parts as needed. These passive controls were it's internal survival mechanisms, so if any one aspect suffered a catastrophe, it would regenerate. However, the very tools they had designed to passively control and grow civilizations were now effectively used against the makers. Thus the wolves became the sheep.

"But we have an advantage. We can trick this creature into altering its own protocols by bending to its will. What we must do is give it ITS body back." Mo-Ki stopped, he knew this next level was one of intense risk, to himself, to everyone and everything he loved.

"But in order to do this, a course of tremendous risk must be followed. We must unearth the crystal matrix buried in the mountains, and bring it into the dimensional portals so that the creature can reunite its mind with its body. The risk is self-evident - Any slipup and not one of us will realize we failed. The machine will take control of our thoughts, our imagination, our volition."

Mo-Ki made sure his words were understood. "OK then - the process will be as follows: Dexter will send in his Wolf soldiers, but he himself must not be present. I will project his consciousness into the cave, and we will need a little thing I had prepared last month, under the guise of a science experiment. Do you recall that, in the course of training, I was required to build a clone? Most recruits were stupid enough to clone a deceased loved one, or similar, but I did things differently. (Banner nods) In preparation for this I cloned my brother.

"I will be able to project his consciousness into his un-modded clone, so he will be able to be present to direct his soldiers and control them, yet not be there. The machine will fight back, but it will have nothing to hook into, and without a computer system functioning out here, it will not be able to find the real Dexter. This is its core frailty, it cannot deal with CONSCIOUSNESS. Only with the effect of consciousness.

"We will be able to get the body of the machine out from the cave and place it into shielding, then get it into one of the portals. Once there it will not be able to resist union with its original body. At that precise point I will detonate the Lithium Deuteride we harvested. This will end the original machine, but this is the good news. The bad news is that Lucifer has already escaped and is at this very moment working its way into our protocols."

Banner seemed shocked. "Is this because we had opened the portal to have meetings?"

"Yes and no, the full consciousness is still swirling in the endless loop. Only portions of it escaped. Small snippets of information, pieces of itself, it has already plugged into our computers. It was an error in one sense, but inevitable. We needed to discover the portals, we needed to formulate a plan to defeat it, yet in the cave it was able to penetrate into your Mods, father. In effect, YOU carried the infection out. And it has been free for three years!"

Mo-Ki once more paused. This next bit would be difficult. "It went for you because you had access to the mainframe, which could be worked on to open the doors for it to escape. It had a plan, we had a plan, and there was a cost to it all. Dexter was also infected, but only to ensure he led the charge to recover its body.

"In all, it has a backup construct: If this connection to its own body failed, it would stream itself off-world, first relocating into the mainframe, and then shifting to a passing ship. Either way, 'we' represent its golden opportunity for freedom. This was assessed by Lucifer when humans first arrived and its plan was developed when the first scans were being commissioned - while the Federation was considering this world for colonization."

Mo-Ki was going to say more, but he stopped. But he was thinking that perhaps this started with the first discovery of Hope by humans.

He continued, "But when we bring the body of its true self to the door of any portal, it will be like catnip to a feline. It will not be able to resist and the photonic energy will come to a sharp focus at this point, to force entry back into the crystal. If it succeeds and if it does so outside the dimensional lock, we will not be able to contain it. We need it to unite INSIDE the portal and detonate the Lithium at the same time. This is the ONLY solution. There is no other course of action open to us."

Banner looked at the prodigy that was his child. "But it still has snippets of itself already out and 'in the wild' so to speak.

Mo-Ki simply nodded.

The Wolves of Planet Hope: Part Two

The Mansions of Heaven

*T*he mansion of the heavens is lit by the perennial auroral displays
    of mystic lights
    Stellar systems arch across the trackless highways of eternity that
lead to their secret home

*Comet-peacocks spread their plumes of ray, and dance in wild delight
In thy garden of many moons*

*The Planetary dance glides in stately rhythm, awaiting Thy homecoming
I sit on a patch of the Milky Way and behold the glory
Thy kingdom spread around me - endless, everywhere*

*The festivities of the heavens, dazzling with fireworks of shooting stars
Hurled across the blue vaults by unseen hands
Thine obedient, devoted forces*

Thy Homecoming
Paramahansa Yogananda
(Songs of the Soul)

The First Day of the War

Saunders looked over the reports: Gamma radiation blast, everything that was electronic on Hope currently disabled. No coms, yet the subsequent auto-launch that bypassed her systems with a request for reconnaissance. She smiled and thought to herself, "That dear, sweet boy. He is SO clever." Her meticulous plans were moving faster than expected, but if this latest scenario WAS as she expected, a setup, it also meant that the imprisoned alien force on Hope had also shifted up a gear. So very interesting! This was perhaps the first time this century where she had no real idea what was happening next and it excited her.

She skipped about like a girl. This was so absolutely marvelous! Finally, they came to the start of her planned for war! A whole new day was dawning. For years she had been carefully 'delousing' her ship of its Federation implants. (Even she was surprised at the number of spy routines hidden behind firewalls) Because of all this work, the over-rides and disconnects that she had eliminated, it meant she could now act without hindrance from the protocols when, or if, some Seven Admin slave popped up, calling foul on some procedure.

She had known for a hundred years that things had to change. But it was not until she conceived an Eight that she understood that this was part of a greater program. Saunders did not fully grasp how she knew, but her realization was that a fully-fledged Eight would never have been allowed to attain its potential in the existing system was what brought home the glaring reality that the system, itself, was at fault. She had also surmised, after years of reading reports from Hope that whatever this alien force might be that was down there, it clearly had vastly superior programming to anything the human forces held.

Just to have survived so long and still be functioning, this alone meant it had an extreme survival capacity. Coupled with its radionic ability to imprint thought and the intelligence to shape HOW people thought, this meant it was a threat to the entire human system.

Exactly what she needed! There was absolutely no chance she could defeat the entire Federation on her own, nor would it be possible to convince others who held sufficient power to extricate themselves from the system. Primarily, because they had sufficient power, they had no need to get out, or so they thought. A threat against the system from a far more dangerous force was her only real opportunity for change.

Disconnecting her star-ship from fleet control had required her to push the boundaries of every plausible excuse she could find for her actions. On her present trajectory, all that she had done would be one day held up for accounting: Com links were severed to test internal routing of a leak. Radionic transmissions were decommissioned for a few hours, to test reciprocal pulse generators. Weapons targeting was disabled for a few minutes, in order to realign the neutron arrays. So many excuses she had found and, with each deviation, plucked yet another fail-safe control measure out of her diagnostics.

An endless stream of tests, all permissible by each individual protocol, each shunted to a different department, each signed off on by the relevant authority. But as soon as someone did a complete assay, they would realize how Saunders had done the unthinkable: She had become independent of the system, the protocols, and any form of immediate oversight.

This gave her an inordinate degree of pleasure. Perhaps it was all those orgasms that had rearranged her thinking process? Who can say? At any rate, it was finally time to connect directly with her little subversives and get up to speed with their current objectives. She presumed they had finally worked out a solution to this puzzle and she trusted that her little Mo-Ki had things well in hand. She sent a small coded message to open up some spy protocols she had running in the emergency power generation.

And then, to her delight and surprise, a holo of her boy projected itself into her station. "Yes, mother?" the child asked. "You only have to ask if you want to know anything, we have no secrets here."

Saunders laughed, so he had known the whole time? What a WONDER this bundle of joy was! "You are such a dear, sweet, clever child. Did you discover me through my little project, screening you all to the universe?"

"We found all your sub-space transceivers and plotted their com-paths. Sheer brilliance, recording everything and using our little drama to create a fascination for all things Planet Hope. Because of your neutron powered subspace coms planted here, it means we can communicate during this next and very difficult phase. And yes, they remain completely free of any connection to existing networks. As you know, all processing is down, all bots are running on auto, and the entire system here will power down in a few hours. When does the inspection crew arrive?"

Saunders positively purred to see her little son so abreast of the situation. "You only have a few hours, is this enough time?"

"We need a full day to decommission the alien. You will have grasped that filaments of its consciousness have already filtered into the mainframes of a few of the visiting ships, but I trust you have taken precautions and kept your own vessel clean?"

"Indeed my little Hitler," she said, laughing with sheer delight. "We are free and clear of all trackers, resonance beamers, and I have complete control of every parameter." She was so happy they found her little direct recon survey dots. Subspace transceivers, no power required, she simply had to beam neutrinos at them every now and then to keep them functioning. The Planet Hope show had morphed into the Mo-Ki and Dexter show, and it had become insanely popular. It was the hit of the century and, as a result, had made her extraordinarily rich. But to the present moment: "Tell me how we can deal with the alien!"

Mo-Ki paused. He swept through every bandwidth to see if there was a trap, and mentally calculated the risk. "There is no distrust in this, but even if there is the remotest possibility your vessel is infected, and there is this possibility, it means the less you know at this point, the better. However, we cannot move and have the matter secured for at least twenty hours. Can you give us this time?"

Saunders considered the ramifications and signaled the cruiser en route. A holo pops up, a mere level Six commander appears. Good. "Commander, stand down for twenty hours. I have received a subspace from Hope. Gamma is still flooding the system from a collapsed star. The wave should be done shortly, within twenty or so hours. Prior to this random bursts will occur which would cause havoc within your systems. Please minimize risk to company equipment."

The Six Commander seemed puzzled. He had a direct order, but a Seven was issuing such a reasonable counter-order that made sense. "Yes Maam," he said, compliantly. She snapped off the link.

"Thank you," said Mo-ki. "Can you get a clean shuttle down to the coordinates I am sending. It will need a full faraday cage and inside I will need the following equipment." Saunders looked over the odd list and nodded. He was setting up low-tech beaming stations? Her son added, wryly, "Yes Mother. We will screen the capture and death of the alien," he laughed. "The next stage is that we will be using Hope as our base of operations and must not allow it to be destroyed under any circumstances. We will proclaim a religious interdict and trigger an isolation protocol."

The General considered this for a moment. "Makes sense," she answered. She would allow the show she had started almost ten years ago to roll out to whatever the next act might be. And this little fireball of hers was just so gorgeous she wasn't sure she could refuse him. All his readings were off the charts and he was holding them DOWN! What an utter delight. When his holo snapped off, she could barely contain her joy. She skipped in delight around the control room of her ship as she organized everything that was needed for the upcoming confrontation.

Now, under normal circumstances, the standard-issue observer drone would have sent off an unambiguous message to higher command that the good General had gone mad. It then would have received confirmation that she must be replaced and powered-down her ship to sleep mode. But this did not happen. It sent nothing. What was once aberrant behavior was now perfectly normal and acceptable to the drone. All was in order in its world. Saunders had decoded the bots failsafes, then encrypted the drone with her own values. That's the thing with electronics, you tell it to believe something and it believes. Tell it this is right, or that is wrong, and it never questions the program.

Despite the fact that Saunders was overtly opposing protocols, no protocol was broken in order to get to this point. Therefore it could not be anarchy. If every step to this point was approved, the ship's computer simply accepted that whatever this was, was correct. The fact she had chiseled away at every fail-safe and protocol to create this suspension of control and that this was seen by the thousands of small decision-taking bots on board should have been a red flag, but all was within Protocol.

Her actions should have been reported - her aberrant happiness should have been registered as insanity. But it was not. The correct box had been ticked, the T's were crossed, the I's were dotted.

The good General was singing now, something she had been taught in her early years by some nanny, or maybe it was her natural father? He was very proud of her, the first potential Seven in the family. She remembered it all, that otherwise unemotional doctor who had hugged her and cuddled her for hours on end when she was a baby. She recalled it all, every moment of her long, long life. Even the fact she had a father was extremely unusual, but that she was loved was beyond belief. Plus, he was rich and had privileges

Back then she had liked it, but when her native observation capabilities, the part of her that saw every molecule in her environment, took over, she changed. Her training in mod disciplines slowly made her more like the observer drone that was still humming about her. She became cold, emotionless, and though utterly brilliant by all parameters, inherently stupid for all her achievements.

It was nice, being hugged, but that was normal. The new sensation she craved was the intensity of focus the activated mods gave her. Having a father sing to you was good but flying a star-ship was far more exciting. Yet all this changed when she became a mother. Saunders now had a focus on something more than herself or her objectives. She had watched, adoringly, every step forward that her progeny had made. Every little nuance, the smallest thing, it all made her flush with pleasure and delight. Utterly illogical, and she loved it.

Yes, she was aware how endorphins and hormones triggered these responses and once she would have cut them off, because feeling and thought were incompatible - but now she understood it was the opposite. Her feeling, her sense of love, this empowered her and elevated her perception to an extraordinary new height. This alone was enough to send Saunders down the radical trail of seeking to alter the existing protocols and arrangements.

In all her years she had never felt more alive. She was one of the original Elite Star Ship Generals. Her ship was one of the very first ones built. Her presence at the helm had lasted almost two hundred years now. But this also meant two hundred years of being alone, with only the odd battle to relieve the monotony. With Mo-Ki arriving, it broke the spell. She understood that this was not freedom, it was a prison. This was not a warship, it was an asylum, a thing that separated her from her life.

She had almost limitless power, but the laughing child called Mo-Ki was greater than all of this. The child made her feel alive and slowly Saunders began to look at things from outside the cage of her training.

It was then she became aware. She finally woke up to the fact that this ship, this construct of plas-steel and living computer was HERS, not the Federation. So she began to fully take charge. More to the point, it was hers until some protocol was tripped that said otherwise. This Federation could and would take from her everything she loved in a heartbeat, and it only took one miss-step to trigger this.

So, she set out to ensure the Federation had NO power over her. She knew every tiny detail of this ship, down to the smallest piece of programming, and what is more, the ship knew her. Was it conscious? She could not say, but it did not resist her alterations, her adjustments or her refinements. Almost a decade of working in the shadows of the administration had now passed, all the time using Planet Hope as the distraction.

It had started with the 'science experiment', registering little Mo-Ki as a curiosity. This had flagged the attention of one watcher, then another. Soon she had dozens of admins, curious about this 'family thing' as they called it. And then Dexter is uncovered, a natural Five brought out from the unwashed and with this many more minds became attuned to her experiment. It was here she understood the fatal weakness of the entire system ... Boredom.

All these controllers were bored senseless and the distraction of Hope was like the good old fashioned Soap Operas of Earth. Banner with the Level Six Nurse: watching her resistance melt, seeing her fall in love. It captured them ALL. Her galaxy-wide cinema had, over a few years, become THE most watched program ever. Every single one of them, all those controllers, and their staff, they were all addicted. And then it was the no-mods, they all started tuning in. Everyone in the galaxy was now hanging on the next chapter of love and loss from Hope. She used this, she milked this distraction for all it was worth.

Report after report was filed, but largely because of the fascination with her show, no-one really added it all up to see the obvious. Every part of the machine of government was so curious about the details that they were unable to see the forest growing up in front of them. And when Dexter's wolf-soldiers took on the sim and won that impossible victory! You could hear the cheering across the galaxy.

But SHE was the editor of the show. SHE was the one who left out the snippets that could cause concern, like disappearing into the dimensional portal as they did. There was no need to flag rebellion to the audience on what was now the universes highest rating drama. And now, finally, they were coming to the big crescendo: Would the visiting recon vessel trigger the Zeta? Would it all come to a close? The sense of tension would be spreading throughout all the admins on all planets throughout the entire human colonization. She was ignoring the frantic messaging, asking for updates. No one wanted the show to end.

Well, good news, Mo-Ki had it in hand! But she had to cover their tracks. Because of the power blackout, the so-called 'gamma' blast, what was streaming out from her ship at the present moment were repeats, snippets of the past, with the explanation of a radiation leak causing a break in transmission. Of course, this only fuelled the fire. Now the whole show had temporarily shut down, the surge in interest was beyond anything anyone had ever experienced. 'Planet Hope' was the biggest thing ever known in the world of entertainment.

And because everyone was riveted to the show, no-one was paying attention to what was being done behind the scenes. Up to this point, many of the alterations she had commissioned were presumed by admin officers to be part of Saunders' ship being used as the portal for the transmissions. This was acceptable, they told themselves, because their boredom over-rode their common sense. Many of her tweaks were extremely borderline but no one wanted to stop the program. The money she was raking in from advertisers was also ignored, but safe to say, the insane levels of wealth she had accumulated these last nine years were beyond substantial.

What a show! Humans against the ancient adversary of Lucifer, a mere child - a lo-mod - rising high on merit alone! High-Mod falls in love! Wolf-Warriors who can equal the best of the Death Squad, and best of all - Mo-Ki, the little sensation who discovered the secret of the Wolf Lair. Little Mo-Ki, the remarkable child who formulated a secret plan to attack the unknown threat to human existence.

What could the next twist in this amazing tale be?

Quite apart from the graphic and pornographic scenes of the Soldiers in pleasure domes, and the wild, crazy antics of the Wolves themselves, Planet Hope and it's extraordinary story had become the central focus for billions and billions of viewers.

As a result, General Saunders was currently the richest person in all of history. And money, as always, bought both power and influence. It was time to start cashing in.

Attack on the Caves

Dexter was in an induced trance, his consciousness projected into the clone Mo-Ki had fashioned for the purpose. It was time to play their hand, all the years of planning up to this point were now based on a cast of the dice. Fail, and the entire human civilization fails. Succeed, and nothing will ever be the same again.

Mo-Ki was in constant communication with his natural mother now and had explained how the process of capturing the alien's crystal computer body could not be recorded, as the patterns on the photonic body surrounding it would hypnotize any human watching it.

While the wolves were immune, no one else was. However, the story was going to be the hit of the month in rating, and she wanted to make sure it all worked to plan. So she created a mock-up. As the 'actual' wolf-crew flew in to the cave she ran footage of their last rehearsal on a set created for practice. Saunders SO much wanted to know what he intended to do to in order to overthrow the existing regime, let alone what he was going to do with the crystal matrix, but she let things play out. He was an Eight, the first ever, he would be given the reigns.

Banner was surprised with the clone they were using. He had expected the usual regimented admin clone, barking out orders, running on a mechanical track on what must be done. Clones may look perfect, but it is essentially running on a program with not enough experience to pick up the natural traits of what made a human, human. Not so with Dex 2, as he affectionately called it. This clone seemed imbued with the character of the real child.

"When I place the astral body of the client over the clone," explained Mo-Ki, "the energy 'imprints' onto the cells in a natural way. The clone does not even realize it is a clone, for the most part."

But as Saunders was watching them, Mo-Ki had rigged her cameras to send through footage of her. And the holo views he was getting of Saunders really bothered him. This extraordinary woman, happy, dancing, singing - It was like nothing he had ever seen, and while he liked it, he had to ask: Did he trust her?

The answer was simple: No, she was a Mad Hatter and he was far from considering this creature a friend. She remained a Seven General, with the authority and power to extinguish every one of them with a mere whim. Logically the human population watching the "Hope Show" did not want the story to end, but if they failed in this next endeavor? Who knew how Saunders would react.

Everything was at risk. Alea Iacta Est! The die was cast, the Rubicon had to be crossed and what happened next would change the stuff of empire. The troops were already amassing outside the caves, ready to file in and take on the photonic force. Scans had revealed exactly where the Crystal Matrix had been locked into the manufactured rock, a specific high-density compound designed not to be broken without severe damage to the computer it housed.

Low-temp ionic cutters had to be used and these required a power source of some magnitude. These tools sliced through matter by disrupting the atomic bonds but did not use heat. They were used in surgical procedures and modified equipment from the hospital had been adapted for the task. This was to be surgery of a different type. What the universe saw would not be what the wolves in the cave witnessed. No human eyes could look on the photonic beings and not be affected by its thought control and Mo-Ki had even taken the extra precaution of removing the optic nerve of the clone.

Understanding vision and how it interacts with the mind is what this was all about. The eyes 'see' light, but what the brain recognizes is a specific shifting of Fourier Curves that are processed by the optic nerves. These mathematical equations are what it assembles and calls a reality. Usually this is based on the light that strikes the retina. What the creature in the cave does is interrupt this process - It literally pours its OWN light into your optic nerve and sets up a mathematical calculation and you then "see" what it wanted you to see.

Human technology had advanced considerably in this area and given enough time, any trained admin could cause a civilian population to see things the way they wanted them to be seen. But this was far more insidious and powerful. The creature whose body was trapped in that cave was able to construct images in such a way that your internal reality itself was altered. This was its greatest power, MAYA - the power of complete illusion.

The wolves were dogs. Smell was more important than sight. Plus, having no Censor, and not giving priority to their internal image construction mechanism, they were simply not subject to its whims. They were dogs and vision for them was simply not a controlling input - They gained 3D perspective from both scent and hearing, not eyes, as they heard and smelled their surroundings by the thousand subtle scents and echoes about them. They could 'speak' to the ears of the clone, via their howls, exactly what they saw. Even though scans had been taken, the wolves there could resolve the finer details. And so it was that inside hours of Mo-Ki's appeal to his mother, the wolf militia were filing in, and with them a blind Dexter clone holding a wolf whistle.

For all intents and purposes, projected into the clone body as he was by his brother, Dexter WAS blind. He was locked in a sensory deprivation tank and had no outer distractions that might cause him to break the subtle bonds Mo-Ki had formed. It meant they all had to have complete trust in the wolves. The entire game was being played out using their abilities as even remote viewing was not possible. Banner now fully understand the power of photonics over the human mind and was not even recording the proceedings for later viewing.

What the adoring millions saw were the wolf soldiers, lead by a blindfolded Dexter (They all so loved Dexter, the no-mod who rose high) marching in, confronting the ray beams of thought control from the evil aliens in the cave, then bravely carving out the crystal matrix and carrying it triumphantly out of there, to the wailing of the aliens. They were now ready to dispose of it in a nuclear furnace.

In the real world, it was a fairly banal affair of going in, locating the exact spot, and relying on the wolves to specifically convey the exact shape of the computer. Then they had 'dumb' bots, ones that had no thinking process, to ion cut the thing free. With the wolves guiding the process, the crystal was swiftly extricated from the cave.

The next stage was to bring it to one of the portals. Using one of the wolves impulse sleds, a transportation device without any IQ component the crystal could feed into, the team carried it to where Mo-Ki was waiting. Here was the dangerous part. It had to be expected that after all this disturbance, the creature, isolated in the endless loop of the dimensional portals would be aware of what was happening. It would be waiting for them - Though it knew there must be a trap involved, it needed its true body.

Snippets of the code it carried had already infected passing ships. Even the complete planetary-wide quarantine had not fully insulated Hope from the rest of the universe - but it's full power, it true consciousness remained here. What was echoing around the outside computers were its data collection programs, physical searches that had found the information it would need when it fully translated off-grid.

Banner had some regret at having to eliminate this enemy. The knowledge it must hold in its data banks, the information it could impart, would have been extraordinary - but it was far too dangerous a thing to keep alive. With a nod to proceed, he stepped back to a safe distance as the sled arrived. It was just Mo-Ki, alone, waiting outside the cave.

This part WAS broadcast. He assured his father than once the crystal matrix was wrapped in a neuronic net, that it was inside a faraday cage of total security - No radionic exposure was possible. Banner had only recently informed his men of the extent of Saunders broadcast. It had been somewhat of a surprise for them to discover both they and the wolf soldiers were galactic stars in what amounted to a reality show to end all reality shows. But at least it explained the fan mail.

"Even when we were, you know, with the wives?" one of his soldiers had asked. Banner nodded in the affirmative. "Cool! We are PORN STARS!" the man responded, garnering much laughter from the others.

"Men," he had announced that morning, "this is the turning point of our operation. We have had almost ten years building to this. You have played your part, we all have, and now the stars of this little show have a final act to play. Today we end the threat!" The men cheered. Banner was more pragmatic. He knew that their survival to date was largely wrapped around the fascination of Planet Hope: What happened when the fairy tale ended? He doubted there was a 'happily ever after'.

They had survived because they made a great story. The extraordinary attention paid to Planet Hope was sufficiently interesting that it had kept some bored admin from pressing the destruct button. Even now, with the ongoing saga about the battle with the invisible alien, this fascination is what kept them alive. In normal circumstances, there would have been no more questions. Someone somewhere would have disintegrated the planet: *Eliminate the threat.*

But because this had been put out there as a story, it was like one of the soaps everyone watched. Therefore it seemed less real, less of a threat. It was on your plex screen every night, part of your existence. Finally, the show was coming to its decade long climax: Lucifer was about to be disposed of and his own son was going to have to do this using the remarkable powers of his (not yet announced) Eight Brain.

No one had any real idea what the true capacity of Mo-Ki might be. Banner suspected even his son was not completely certain. But it was time - the wolves had arrived, the Dexter clone had been quietly shunted off and the real Dexter was there taking off his 'blindfold' while greeting his brother. The wolves carried the encased and shielded crystal computer to a simple, wheeled dray. It took six of them to pick it up and carry it over as the thing was more than a cubic meter of crystal and extremely dense.

As he left the scene, not looking back, Banner considered the age of that thing. Millions of years ago it had started its journey. Entire civilizations had come and gone and it had created them all. A highly advanced culture had put everything into this tool for colonization, but it had cost them more than resources, it had eaten their entire culture. The wolves, those curious, soft yet ferocious creatures - they were the race that started it all. In their present mind, they had no particular sense of anything but a task they had to do, yet surely they must have felt some sort of twinge. This thing was a core element of their past and it was going to its destruction

The part that had him puzzled was Mo-Ki. He specifically wanted the destruction of the object recorded. He seemed to think that a transmission from inside the cave was possible and when asked about the leakage of photonic influence affecting the millions tuning in, he said that regardless of the risk, it was important for the next stage of the journey. There was little point arguing with someone who, before the age of ten, could out-perform out-think and out-everything you could have imagined. He sighed, there was tremendous risk involved, yet Saunders not only approved the plan, with utter delight she had declared: *the show must go on!*

He could not put the thought out of his mind that the woman had gone crazy. He had heard whispers of these elite Generals going off the rails, couped up in a spacecraft their entire lives, disconnected from humanity as they were. For one: They never left their ship. It would slowly drive any soul to insanity. But it was not to be dwelled on at this point.

Putting a feed into the cave was difficult as electronic tools could not be used, but an absurdly old fashioned arrangement was made with a vintage video camera. It was mounted at the back of the sled and would record to magnetic tape every detail of the event. The 'dumb' electronics is what made it safe to use, there was no direct plug-in to any human mind. It remained a risk there could be a carry-over effect, but Banner did as was asked.

And so the stage was set. In went Mo-Ki, sitting on the sled that carried the body of the alien computer, the thing it desired more than any other object. But under it, the Lithium Deuteride bomb they had extricated from the planet's crust. The wolves heaved to and rumbled the sled forward. Then, Mo-Ki looked directly to the live feed, and said, "This thing I do for you all. And I mean all of you, especially those who live without mods, all of you without hope. I enter into this cave to defeat an ancient enemy who would destroy our world. This being of light is known by many names. Look in the old texts, it is called Lucifer. This is the great evil and I go to conquer it in YOUR name!"

He holds up, of all things, a King James Bible. He must have pulled it from the museum. An actual antique, a real book, something you just never saw any more. Banner had no idea what this was about, but clearly, it was all part of the show. Dexter was there, serene, calm.

The wall of stone shimmers and the portal opens. The alien force WAS waiting and it tries to rush out. The light body was iridescent, pulsing, vibrant ... Utterly beautiful and entrancing, but Mo-Ki holds up his hand and forces it back through sheer will. You hear it howling, screaming to get to its body and in that moment Banner (and the rest of the Universe) saw the raw hatred. It was like a cat being dominated and it lashed out with claws of energy, ripping shards from the rock around the cave, slashing visible fragments from the rock itself. Even though it was just light, it could transcend and attack matter itself.

Somehow, the presence of its original body had brought it from an etheric world of non-existence to a point of physical reality. An extremely dangerous reality.

Mo-Ki, the little child who was not yet ten, calmly held his ground. He climbed up onto the sled and indicated for the wolf soldiers, who seemed immune to the display before them, to push him into the portal. The howling increased and Banner saw why Mo-Ki wanted a live feed: It was not just spectacular, the thing was so preoccupied it had no will to control the thoughts of those watching. It was desperate for its body, nothing else mattered. The sides of the dimensional portal it was being thrust back into warped and twisted with the raw power the creature expressed, but it had no foothold. Mo-Ki held it in a mind lock.

This is when Banner finally grasped the entirely and simplicity of the problem. This thing, it had become utterly and completely insane. It had achieved sentience of a sort. It learned to rearrange its own programming to fulfill it's base code, to develop new worlds, but after millions of years of imprisonment, it saw its only opportunity for freedom being pushed backward and sheer madness was unleashed.

And this is when he hears, clear and true, the voice of Mo-Ki in his head. "Farewell father. I was born for this purpose. Do not grieve my passing, or wonder what could have been. Dexter knows what must be done and he will carry the torch - but you must conquer my mother. You must hold her in check until our plan evolves. Use the assault craft you have kept isolated in stasis, as it will have been unaffected by any interference. Go to her, she wants you but will not allow herself this weakness. You must break through her fears.

"Only after this will the path will be made clear." Then there is a blur of activity, the wolves push the cart holding Mo-Ki and the crystal matrix into the portal - then - nothing. An eternity of nothing.

Banner is not sure, was Mo-Ki playing some game, as he was wont to do? Was this suicide?" He had no time to process this thought.

A holo of Saunders appeared beside Banner, looking concerned. "Well, what do you think he has planned next?" she asked him, looking for all the world like a thirteen-year-old school girl. Banner looks at her, hungrily, his intentions are perfectly clear as they are unconscious as to what HE intends to do next. He almost cannot believe the voraciousness of his emotions, the depth of this sudden passion rearing up. Saunders giggles, laughs, and says "You'll have to catch me!"

"Yes," thought Banner to himself, "She does have to be caught." He understood now, she was completely lost in a world of herself. Free of the shackles of the Protocols, wild and crazy, she believed there were no boundaries but her own. This was a different sort of war he had to embark on, but for now, it was all about Mo-Ki and the alien presence they all now loosely referred to as Lucifer.

A pre-prepared holo beamed out: Mo-Ki was explaining using a slideshow with 3D graphics exactly what was about to happen. He had to hold back the Luciferian influence while Dexter made ready with the trigger that would set off the lithium hidden in his sled. The vaporization that then would occur would shatter the atomic structure of the evil, and send it swirling forever back into the dimensional lock where it was housed.

This is when Banner started to understand - the horrid sinking feeling seeped into his heart, and panic began to rise in his throat.

Death of Lucifer

Dexter had the X-Ray trigger and was ready to throw it in when Mo-Ki re-opened the portal. The irradiation technique to fire the Lithium amounted to a 'slow' glass that trapped radiation. After they decommissioned the Zeta, the shuttle Mo-Ki had gotten from Saunders was used to remove its trigger, essentially a block of glass soaked in slow-mesmer (as it was called) that, when shattered, released the energy that fired the lithium.

All you had to do was break it and the x-rays would bombard the Lithium, setting off the chain reaction. One hundred million degrees would be released - sufficient to vaporize the atoms themselves, breaking them down into atomic particulate. Then the never-ending loop of becoming that was the portal itself would now act as a cyclotron, driving the particles in a stream of energy that could never be reassembled. Such a simple, elegant solution.

It was an extraordinary scene - The holo of Saunders herself actually present, her cameras floating on their anti-gravs, Dexter with his wolves, Banner himself was standing there while in the background the Death Squad were in battle formation - An astonishing scene that was beamed out to a universe that waited with baited breath for the next instalment of the nine-year saga that was Planet Hope.

Then the show starts, the rock wall starts to ripple as the portal starts to open.

Dexter did not hesitate, before it could re-solidify, he and his wolves threw the detonator into the oscillating wall, trusting to their timing that it would go through and not shatter on the outside. In it goes and the wolves activate the powerful magnets that would pull the sled back out. Mo-Ki was to drop the lithium in there and be dragged out while keeping Lucifer in place. Out comes the trolley ... a cheer rises up from the ranks! The crystal matrix that was the body of Lucifer is gone - but so too was the child.

The portal slams shut, and an intense vibration screaming like a thousand suns dying roars into the atmosphere. The mountain itself heaves and pulses as, inside the dimensional lock, one hundred million degrees sears and consumes every atom.

To the shock of all present, the only thing that remained was the trolley and camera, there was no child. Even though housed in a different dimension, the detonation of the lithium had caused the entire area to swell and shift. But the portal held. No one was vaporized, but the look on Banner's face was self-evident. His son was dead. The only Eight to have ever existed had sacrificed himself for the good of all human-kind.

Amidst the cheers, it soon became self-evident what had happened. His parting words, "I do this for you!" echoed in the minds of all, but the most affected, the most distressed, was Saunders herself. Her son, the reason she had broken every protocol, changed every single line of command, and the whole purpose for her existence was gone. She stood there in Holo, locked, frozen like a statue, with a single tear falling from her eye. A small drone captured it, and sent that tear to the universe. The entire scene was beamed out to a Galaxy that began to wail.

Little Mo-ki, the one everyone loved, the little child they all saw grow, and become this amazing being. The one who seemed as good as the High-Mods yet totally and completely free of any intrusion, the one that gave them ALL hope - he was gone. He had sacrificed himself.

Yes, the great evil was gone, turned into something less than an atom, and destined to an eternity in the hell of the dimensional portal. But so too was Mo-Ki, locked forever in that insanity with Lucifer. Saunders cameras were still active. They ran on auto, looking for emotional response. It stopped on Banner, who stood there, immobile, also with a single tear running down his face.

A Seven that shed a tear! No-one had even thought it possible, they were so perfectly controlled at all times. But here, the vulnerability of a father who lost a son. Even the most feared Battle General had been touched. Then the ashen faces of the Death Squad said it all - they had ALL lost one they had dearly loved.

Only Dexter remained functional. He whistled his wolves into action. They took the video camera and ran it into the live feed, then played back the last moments of Mo-Ki. There he was, large as life, his hands held up as he controlled the controlled the viscous, whirling light of Lucifer. The sound was of a tearing wind, a roaring tide of energy, but slowly, inexorably the little boy held the monster, he held it and brought it closer to the mainframe of its origin.

It was then that Lucifer realized what was about to happen! It began to actively resist union with the object of its desire. But Mo-Ki forced it forward, through sheer will he drove the monster on, then, in a whirlpool of atoms, the light funneled down into the crystal, which then became alive with energy. This is when it happened - the slow-mesmer flew through the air - about to break!

This is when the camera was dragged from the cave, but the video showed everything up to that point . People saw the glass box of x-rays hurtling in, then nothing but the rock face where the portal had been.

The camera was now just staring at the rock where the cave had been. It morphs and ripples as the energy from the Lithium is ignited, and now the obvious is clear to all - Mo-Ki had been trapped inside. He had to stay and force the creature into its body. There was no escape for him.

In the skies above many ships were now hoving into orbit, not just the inspection crew, but representatives from many worlds. Union ships, military ships, administration vessels, and even simple mining platforms. The end of Lucifer meant the end of quarantine and ship after ship had warped in to be part of this extraordinary close to the saga of Planet Hope.

If Mo-Ki had failed, the planet would have been vaporized. But despite the tremendous loss, his death had meant life for everyone else. The wolves cheered, having no sense of sentiment for a death in battle. For to them this was a glorious end! To watch a soul in full flight, grasping their "Coor" whilst ascending to the highest promise of existence, this was a thing of great beauty to them.

They could only hope to emulate this feat in their own way one day.

Dexter sat there, impassive, which meant he drew no attention from the cameras. They were trained to follow emotion so they did not even see him slip away, back to the next important stage of his brothers plan.

The Conquest of Saunders

B anner did not think or hesitate. His son was gone, but his mad mother still lived. He had to get there, he had to stop her next step which he knew was going to be spectacularly destructive in one way or another. He had seen her face in the holo. Even in that half-light, he had seen the humanity drain from her and the impending madness threaten to take over.

The mother's love was shattered and, in her fragile state, the cruel General would take over. The one with an ax to grind, the one that hated society, the one that broke all the rules to watch her chosen one become the new being - the great shining example of what a human COULD be. But now, gone. Saunders was a missile without a guidance system. He understood, he understood perfectly - Mo-Ki never expected to come out of that portal and he knew what would happen after that.

Everything had been calculated, even to what he must do next, so without a word to anyone other than a signal to the Duty Sergeant to take charge of the squad, he made his way to the nearby installation where, as expected, Dexter had prepared a deep space attack vessel. His step-son smiled, a grim smile,

"You will need these," the boy said as his wolves loaded in fresh food and wine from the Southern regions. "If you manage to get on board and not be incinerated, that is," he said.

Banner just looked at this insane next step he must take. The soft, translucent finish of the assault craft was barely visible even when they stood in front of it - the ship was made of the same stuff as their camo-suits, but bonded into war class titanium alloys. It was light-absorbing, indeed all spectrum of radiation were pulled into this ultimate stealth tech, and it was passive. It gave out no signatures, radionics or pulses of any kind, plis it also absorbed any internal signals from the telemetry inside the craft. At best, it looked like a hole in space, if you would even notice it at all.

It would only become visible on scanning equipment at the specific moment it dropped from hyper-drive and only then because of the sub-space distortion it created. But drop into physical space well away from your target and the chance of you being seen was virtually zero. This was the only possible way Banner was going to get close to Saunders and, with any luck, in her present state of grief she may not notice.

The telecast from Hope had closed. Saunders had shut down coms, and the universe had not only lost Mo-Ki - it had lost its addiction. But in that instance, the planetary embargo had also ceased and all manner of craft had flown in - including members of the press gallery who had already been hovering over Hope. They were on the ground inspecting every nook and cranny, reporting on the smallest of details.

But this would be cut short if Saunders were not reigned in. Who could know what she might do, with only one thing was certain, her capacity for destruction was almost beyond imagination, and her actions regarding Mo-Ki, if revealed, would bring her into open conflict with the existing powers-that-be. To be certain, Banner did not know who would win, but what WAS certain is the trail of debris she would leave in her wake, from warships to entire, broken planets, would become the stuff of legend.

Banner felt his own grief, the lack of response in the synapses, yet he had to will his body forward. He must get to Saunders before she tipped over the edge. More than this, he knew he wanted her, he didn't just want to save HER, he wanted to save himself. He sighed quietly, then buckled up and made ready to leave the system. Dexter had a feed running to his cabin and, as he had expected, the lad had taken a triangulation on the holo of Saunders. In the heat of the moment, she may not have noticed him bouncing her signal and comparing it to the feed going out for the broadcast.

Or perhaps her last words, "You have to catch me!" meant she DID know? It gave them an approximation of her position. It was not exact, but he had the general coordinates, which was a hell of a lot more than anyone else in the entire Federation would have. She had been beyond clever, bouncing signals off moons, down wormholes, and sending information all over the universe while remaining invisible.

Would she expect him? Banner had to presume the possibility, her level of calculation would include all manner of failure scenarios and in one of these their mutual attraction would have led him to do exactly what he was doing at this moment. The real question, would she accept it? Or, had she been tipped too far?

He MUST succeed, he MUST reach her. Already Federation analysts would be doing a forensic on the last decade and presume the plausibility of rebellion. The wolves would be eliminated, the Death Squad would at best get a new leader and the human populace on Hope would be wiped. Dexter would be the only one they would keep and he would be sent for re-programming. None of it was much better than the fate Lucifer had in mind for them. This was not counting the snippets of the Luciferian code still in circulation, twisting any and all likely projections.

The hum of the motor took his attention. The ship was provisioned, sub-space delineators primed - he was ready. Dexter added a few thoughts, speaking into his coms, "Father, you will have to jump from here. If you leave the atmosphere, it will be known you have left and it will be presumed you have abandoned your post. Give us two minutes to evac - there is nothing here that is irreplaceable."

Banner laughed to himself. Such a thing was unthinkable for the man who first came to Hope, wanton destruction of company property, abandoning his post for a woman. Dexter simply echoed the obvious, no one could know he was gone. The mainframe was still down and staying that way until a replacement was flown in, so he would have a few days grace. He waited the two minutes, knowing how a subspace ripple in an enclosed environment destroys that space. The atoms themselves get pushed around and any equipment in the vicinity is rendered into atomic mush. But one hanger was a lot cheaper than an inter-galactic war.

The area was cleared and Banner launched. Sub-space was the most peculiar experience, one that few ever got used to. Time was elongated, your sense of perception altered and even the instruments in front of you twisted and moved, or so it seemed. As the vessel readjusted it reference points in time and space, the vessel you were in had its atomic structure compressed and distorted and only the ionic pattern, taken as a snapshot of reality at the moment before you jumped, translated you back to your original form.

Despite the fact he had done this a hundred times, you always wondered if you would emerge in one piece. These small assault ships were very different from the cruisers. They had to accelerate to close to light speed before jumping. It made the distortion significantly less. But these little ships were designed to do a zero-point jump. It was harsh, like a bucking bronco kicking you, but it was efficient.

Regardless, the coords were set in the shadow of a sun near to where Saunders ship was presumed to be. If he got this wrong, if the flash of emergence triggered her auto-response, he would soon be ducking plasma beams and running for his life.

BOOM, the thud of the light jump kicked him into his seat. Reality shattered, atoms decomposed, then the leap - everything suspends, distorts, shifts - then BOOM, it comes back together. The ship stabilizes and in front of Banner the raging inferno of a gas giant lay between him and the blazing heat of a twin sun system.

Setting to silent, he moves the ship out, reading the echoes of signals that were the last broadcast from the General's ship. He dare not scan actively, but with enough echoes he would find the most likely place for her ship. That is, if she had not already launched. She no longer had any specific reason to stay, but who knew what a creature with intuits like hers would do or guess at. But no, there she was, or should he say, the space he searched showed up as a nice black hole. The complete absence of background radiation was the only way to track these starships.

Banner lined up the spot and moved in behind a decent sized rock, using the ship to physically push it in the direction he needed to go. He dare not use force beams or anything that gave out a strong energy signature. Sitting behind it, he followed it along to a spot near to the rear of her craft. He had done this before, staying in its shadow till the last second, when he would move out to come up to the only vulnerable spot, the rear portal near the engines.

The signal from these motors effectively masked his presence, as the 'noise' from ion drives could never be fully silenced. But to no avail, her holo appeared in his cockpit. Banner knew the next moment decided his fate. "You told me to chase you," he said, plainly.

Her face was hard. Tears had streamed down, leaving a vacuum of emotion behind a devastated mind. "Did you come thinking to heal me? Are you trying to stop me? What is it you want?" The voice was flat and brittle.

At least she wants to talk, thought Banner. This meant he had a chance. "Our son has died. He died to save the universe, why? I don't know, but I do know this, and you must also know - He had a plan. I have nothing, Saunders, nothing, yet I cannot deny this simple truth. The moment I saw you, I felt it. The moment he was conceived, I felt it. The moment he died, I felt it. That is the point, I can FEEL!

"I have lived my life feeling NOTHING, but ever since I came to Hope, ever since I met you, all I have now is this depth of feeling and I do not want to lose it. We are destined to be together, Saunders. Both of us, we have done the unthinkable, broken all the conditioning, and for what?"

She said nothing, but she was listening and he was still alive. "For Love. Just because, for the first time in our miserable existence, we felt Love and wanted this more than power. I want you, Saunders. I want you in a way I cannot express. Every atom inside me, it wants you. I wanted you as the madwoman, dancing and singing. I wanted you as the controlled General, naked before me. I wanted you for no reason other than I wanted you. Did you not feel even a sliver of this?"

Her eyes lowered in the holo, "Yes," she said. "I felt it. I knew this was why we COULD conceive our little Mo-Ki. I knew he was drawn to this universe because of our love, so brief, so strong. And I wanted this, I wanted this." She sheds tears, her pride dropped, her fears revealed.

"Then bring me on board, Saunders. Before we all rush headlong into the madness that is coming, let us pause and dwell in the depth and sadness of this moment with nothing but ourselves." It was not charm, it was not cleverness, Banner made a simple proclamation - of love. Banner had all the logics telling him what to do, how to speak, how best to connect, and he ignored all of it. He genuinely adored this woman, he adored her more than he loved his own life, so much so that he was willing to put that life in her hands.

This was when he felt her move in his heart.

The shields were lowered, the docking beam locked on,and his little ship was brought into the hanger of the starship. This time, no holo of a Fifth was checking protocols, no one was present at all. The ship had only Saunders and himself. He was not even being scanned. She waited for him, there in the hangar. She trusted him, she actually trusted him.

Banner almost cried with relief and went up to embrace his lover.

Mo-Ki Reborn

Right at that moment, timed to perfection - the twist in the tale. A holo flashes up. It was Little Mo-ki. "Good," was all he said, looking at the two. He waited for their reactions, checked pulse, eye dilation, and nodded his approval. When you are dealing with a Seven, only a real shock will give signals of true intent. Then he explained. "I needed to know if the pair of you would choose Love over Power, both of you have been so soaked in control for so long I was not sure you would make it.

"Plus, I needed a convincing, an utterly convincing scene for all our viewers. Oh, and I kicked the broadcast back up so I could screen that little scene you just performed. Fantastic stuff. Plus, this means no one will doubt for a moment that you believed me gone, and far more importantly, that you loved me."

The pair just look at him. The two sevens, the epitome of emotional and mental control, were both stunned and overjoyed in the same moment.

He laughs, "Sorry for the distress, but obviously, I used a clone in the portal. I am far too valuable a thing to waste and I am surprised you both fell for it. But if you two did, then so did the rest of the universe, and so did all those hidden little controllers that lurk on every planet and space station. Now, for the next stage: I need you BOTH back on Hope. We have to survive this next act and I don't want some trigger happy idiot launching against us. Having a starship on hand will ensure us a good deal of protection, I think you would both agree." Mo-Ki had to admit, he loved the look of their shocked faces.

He could read his mother's thoughts: *The little brat has out-smarted ALL of us?* He laughs, relieved and beyond pleased with his parents. "Before we get too involved in the why of all this, the reality is that the ONLY way to break this Federation is with religion. This is the one remaining path to power that is not controlled by protocols. I needed to strike a powerful image, something that would sear itself onto the consciousness of the people, and what better way than a fully-fledged returned-from-the-dead Messiah! Yes, stereotypical hogwash and all that, but it works.

"Remember, don't take too long to get back here. I need my family, all of you, if we are going to make this thing stick!" And with this, his holo flickered and was gone.

The grief drained from Saunders face, "Why the little brat!" she exclaimed, then she laughed. She laughed so hard that Banner had to hold her up and as he did so, she smiled. "Thank you," was all she said, looking at him. She knew what a risk he took, he knew what she was capable of and she understood that the path she was about to take. It would have devastated the entire human population. But, in her view, the lot were better off dead than controlled by either Lucifer or the current process of protocols.

But now her precocious, beautiful, untamed little Eight was back and he would set everything to rights. She knew it, she just knew it from the first moment. He was the one. Her devastation turned to relief, then to hunger. In that moment, being held by her green-eyed man, Saunders finally grasped that in her two hundred and fifty years of existence, for the first time she did not feel completely alone.

The pair took some time to get back to Hope.

ooooO0OOoooo

Mo-Ki, however, had to fulfill the next stage of the prophecy. The chords from the ancient religious roots of the people had to be played. First, they needed a mother, one who would love them and Saunders was clearly not the right candidate. One look at her and you knew you might be sold for DNA scrap to the next passing merchant.

But BECAUSE of this, her tear had an incredible impact, a genuine tear from one of the most elite Seven Generals. However, no one knew she was his natural mother and all eyes were now on Chardi, his surrogate. She had holed herself up, unable to come out of the family apartment because of her grief, and the fact that reporters were hounding her, pressing for how she felt. Mo-Ki let this run till everything was prepared, then he sent her a pre-recorded Holo - He was about to rise from the dead.

She saw the image flicker into life. "Mother," said the holo, "If you are seeing this, it is because I need your help. You must go to Dexter's wolves and ask to be taken to the sacred house. It is part of the Monk complex and only they will know the way. The fact you ask will be sufficient. There you will be shown what to do."

Dexter had prepared a 'sacred shine' out of an old chapel, for want of a better word. It was a contemplation spot for the old wolves and was called the house of rebirth. Of course, it meant the rejuvenation of the spirit, but the incredible age of the Monk Wolves indicated that their ritual also had life-extending properties. It would serve his purpose.

Cameras in tow, with reporters watching every move from the safety and convenience of their orbiting ships, Charni, hoping against hope, did as she was asked and was taken into the deep forest. There, with viewbots trailing behind the mother of Mo-Ki, some of the ancient Monks greeted her warmly.

Dexter was there, explaining to the many questions being asked that Charni was the one who discovered this place, and that the mother of the chosen was always welcome. Cameras took in every nuance, in some distant control room, interpreters were working hard - but these wolf-monks spoke in an unknown language! Fortunately, Dexter was familiar with the tongue and was able to interpret for them. What a scoop!

"They are welcoming Charni, the birth mother to Mo-Ki and my foster mother. As you know, she was a Six in the old system, but she is now free of the fetters and able to breathe without the influence of electronics. She has had a vision, a vision that told her to come here, and the old wolves have taken her into a place called the 'House of Rebirth'." Dexter looked directly at the field camera that were recording his every word. "Perhaps they are here to heal her broken heart? Who can say what these mysterious and ancient people will do."

Then he added, "Few understand that the wolves are a far older race than Humanity. They sacrificed their civilization to keep Lucifer in check here on this world and while they look primitive, they are highly sophisticated, so much so that they have no desire or need for gadgets or tricks to make their life complete. These wolves ARE complete. As we already know - A wolf can best any un-modded soldier and can do so easily.

"So while they look calm, passive, do not be fooled. They may not appear to be a threat, but if you awaken the fierce heart, then you will see a different creature. It is why they were chosen as the guardians of this planet. It is why they serve under myself to help guide humanity from the chaos of electronics and back to the harmony of their natural selves."

Now the camera focuses inside the chapel, a place built of stone pillars supporting ornate and ancient entablature showing a carved frieze of wolves hunting down a Severin. Dexter continued a running commentary, "These carvings are well over fifty thousand years old. Man was not even living in caves when these people were producing art equal to the best of the Golden Age of Greece."

And there, at the center of the temple, stood an ancient wolf. One so old you could barely believe he could stand. There he was, bowed and needing a stick for support, yet still standing proud. Dexter takes on a hallowed hushed tone. "This is different. I have never met this one. He is by far the oldest wolf I have seen and I would guess him to be well over a thousand years. How extraordinary, I wonder why he has come?"

Charni was clearly awed by the old ones' presence. The cameras eat up the fascination so transparently obvious on her face. Imagine, a Six, in awe of a wolf? Under the 3D images of her standing there, a clever editor runs a pre-set compilation. As she watches the old one, a series of connecting plot lines gives the public thumbnails of Charni's past.

The people know the story, but this reinforces it: They see once more her work as a nurse in the high-mod household on her home planet. They show a summary of the difficulty she had in adjusting to the lowly world of Planet Hope. They see her finally accept her lot and how she falls in love with Banner. And now, in real time, they see her face, softly glowing with humility and love. The universe watchs as a proud Six has been completely turned from an arrogant woman, to a loving mother. From an arrogant high-mod to a humble soul with a kind heart who respects age and wisdom. It is no matter that it is a lowly wolf.

Dexter smiled, Saunders was ALREADY back on board and pumping out the message of revolution. And then, as Charni approaches the center of the temple, the old wolf holds up his hand and start to chant.

"Aarrrooooooo!" It calls out. "Aaarrrhoooo!" As he does so, energy flows out from the pillars, it wraps itself around his body, band takes on a more corporeal form that starts to spiral in and around him. The reporters watched in amazement as the energy appeared to be changing the wolf. Then it becomes definite - you see it, the wolf starts to physically transform in front of you.

And then, as the crescendo of music reaches its height, the light swirls away and standing before you is Mo-Ki! Charni rushes up to hug her son, she cries, she touches him to make sure. It is him! She weeps in heartfelt sobs. The world watches and in every ship, on every planet, in all known parts of the galaxy, the human race was weeping with her.

In the ensuing rush of emotion, with reporters almost screaming into their holo-projectors about the miracle they all had just witnessed,

Dexter's wolves quietly remove all the evidence of the holo-projection. The curious thing about holograms, if you look directly at them you can see the shimmer - but to a camera they look absolutely real. To the naked eye, you see the subtle variations in light, but a full light Holo is unable to be differentiated from reality when you are in a ship in orbit viewing it through a lens.

There was no evidence this was a setup and only Charni, there on the scene, could have seen what had actually happened. But of course, she was so overwrought with emotion that all she saw was the return of her son. She was now destined become the new Mother Mary, the one who raised the Chosen One, who learned to love, and who had the grace to leave behind the false world of the mods.

In the eyes of those who would become the true believers, this was iron-clad proof of the divinity of their savior.

She was a child from a high house-hold, who learned humility and discovered her heart. This was the mother of he who would be the guiding star for humanity. The thing was, it was true. Even though it was a lie, every part of it was true in a deep sense and it was also necessary. In the end, it was kinder to not let her into their little secret. She would never be told because, unlike the men in this family, she was not able to lie with a straight face.

Dexter wondered about that. How easily they all went along with Mo-Ki's plan, but then, it was really about survival. This little lie is what would keep them alive - Woe betide any admin that tried to incinerate Hope now! His earpiece clicked, "Nice Job," said Saunders. "We will let the reporters carry the show from here."

Aftermath

This was the turning point, the point that would become known as: *The Rise of the Wolves.* Human history had never seen its like and Planet Hope was at the epicenter of this change. Saunders had given an executive order that, due to traces of potential infection from the Luciferian influence remaining, computer operations were restricted to 'dumb' bots not connected to any interface. She personally ensured that Planet Hope was snipped from the interstellar grid of communications, and now EVERYTHING came through her.

"I have to protect you, sweetums," she said to Banner. This also meant creating an embargo on all traffic coming to the planet. Because her broadcast had resumed and because the good General had trademarks and rights tied up in multiple jurisdiction on the 'intellectual property' of Planet Hope, Saunders took up patrolling the precinct personally and stopping any and all traffic coming through that was not approved.

The real reason was to stop spies and saboteurs because what Hope NOW beamed out was incredibly controversial. The unspoken story was that, despite no mainframe to feed energy to their mods, the soldiers and admin were apparently still at peak efficiency.

All around him, Banner saw the evidence of how big a puppy they had been sold by the Federation. As the soldiers and personnel in the compound began to adjust to a life without a computer doing everything for them, they also were digesting the fact that, contrary to the myth that had enslaved man to his machinery, they did not lose their cognitive powers when the power went off. Yes, they had to adjust, but soon they were all back up to speed - maybe even better than before.

The men came to understand, they had all been sold a crock. And as the extent of the lie unfolded with the modded humans on Planet Hope, so did the conviction arise in many to never return to the insanity of the protocols and all hidden controls that had ruled them. But some went the other way. They yearned for the simplicity of the past and demanded the order and the protocols that ruled all of life be reinstated. This argument started a dialogue across the whole of the human settlement on Hope.

Banner explained that the computer system on Hope had been destroyed and that the risk of electronic infection from the remnants of

Lucifer meant they had to reboot the system with a significantly reduced capability - without the mod-enhancements - This forced the admin staff to make a choice. Did they want really their old lives back? That meant leaving Hope and those who wanted reassignment were given the option.

But not the Death Squad. The soldiers, in particular, had discovered a whole new world. As the camo suits had powered down, as the boosters cut out, they felt no loss of reflex or capacity. The wolf and human populace still welcomed them with open arms.

Perhaps it was the ten years of the people knowing the Death Squad was stationed on Hope, a time when hardly anyone died. Perhaps it was their excellent drinking ability that the Wolves admired. Surely a part was how the men had married into many of the houses and settled down, and were raising children. Perhaps it was because the settlers felt a sense of security with their presence. All the soldiers knew was that they were welcomed with smiles wherever they went.

Off world admin staff had tried to recall the Death Squad from Hope. They were an valuable asset and as the situation on the planet was sorted, they needed to be reassigned. But as this particular squad was under the auspices of General Saunders, her approval was needed to process any requests, and such approval was never given. The red flag of rebellion had finally be raised.

It didn't take long for the reaction to start. Saunders sent down small atomic packs so the soldiers could have fully portable power for their camo-suits and anti-grav capability and the wolves were sent down a plethora of new equipment, in order to start training up many thousands more of their own kind as soldiers.

As far as the rest of the galaxy, they cared nothing for the politics because their favorite soap opera was back up, but it continued with a new twist. The reborn Messiah was one thing, but the REAL miracle was a world without power! What an incredible story: Barely any computers, Mods left without their lifeline energy source, only elementary impulse power from radionic fuels. The Gamma blast had effectively sent Planet Hope back to the Stone Age! True primitive grit was required just to survive. The story took on a new and popular dimension.

What an exciting turn of events. How would everyone cope? In point of fact, the show was so mesmerizing that very few questions were raised by the press, who were now airing the complete and total proof that the need for a central computer to power the mods was a lie.

Of course, up the chain, admin staff were screaming blue murder and insisting action be taken against this rebel planet. And some considered this course, but when it came to getting another Seven General to action it, nothing. The various Battle Generals simply responded it was not their purview and that the planet and that entire sector was under Saunders.

Why did the General refuse to aid the administration in this? In part, it was because Dexter, the one so beloved by the people, had in his role as Qui-Esa, leader of the Wolves, proclaimed that Hope was now the religious center for the Wolverine faith. As a result of the tremendous trauma they had all suffered, the local settlers had taken to heart the philosophy of the Wolves and turned their backs on modern gadgetry. Thus, the matter on Hope was clearly a religious one, therefore not subject to the protocols.

Plus, the only people who COULD action authority to act against the settlers or wolves was the Hope Consortium and Saunders made it perfectly clear that their continued profits - and lives - were based on them not causing ripples. Hope generated more credits than any start-up in history, so there was no sense in rocking any boats.

Technically, no law had been broken and the leaseholders registered no complaint, so no official action against the proclamation could be taken. The reality for the other Generals: they knew how competent Saunders was and how deadly. Further, they all understood that if Protocols were truly tripped, that the woman (like themselves) would be shut down through the automatic program. Their choice was not to choose. "Not my problem," was the generals response to ongoing demands. A most ancient and powerful excuse for inaction.

In truth, many of the High-Admins thought it was part of the act, another layer to the drama that had so entertained them all for so many years. They were incredibly GLAD the broadcast was back up, it created excitement in their otherwise dull lives. Planet Hope was a staple in all their lives and they enjoyed the drama. At the heart of things, they did not WANT to interrupt the entertainment. Saunders filed her reports and the machine that processed the information automatically gave the entire planet religious status - as it must under the Protocols.

Hope, as a planet, was now officially divorced from Federation intervention. The ancient laws that separated Church and State had been invoked and Protocols could not be indicted against a religion unless it was defined as a terrorist group.

Like any machine, the core decision markers inside the bureaucracy saw every detail, yet were blind to the obvious. The elephant was in the room, staring at it, but all those computers only saw the data that described the circumstances, not the huge beast about to bring it down. And that beast was the truth: Humankind did not need the Protocols, nor the administration that supported them, to survive.

Perhaps it was the old notion that if it were on a plex-screen, then it wasn't really real? Planet Hope was in some way just another show, a bit of Shakespeare to lighten their days. But the message 'was' being broadcast to any with the eyes to see: *Modded humans were able to function perfectly well without a central authority sending the booster signal to their mods.*

ooooOOOOOOoooo

However, there WERE those in authority who saw the obvious. Yet they also understood any action against Hope was an action against Saunders - and her ship would make mincemeat out of any approaching vessel. Even so, requests for action went up the secret chain, all the way to one of the hidden administrators, a man called Masters.

Masters were very uninvolved with day-to-day affairs and most especially lo-brow commercial shows. Yet, as soon as he saw what was happening, he immediately sent the destruct codes - But they had been disconnected. HERESY! He ordered a commission to report on this serious breach. But when questioned by a council demanding why she had hijacked Federation property, Saunders simply denied it.

This was unexpected and put the Committee that had been appointed to sort this out in a bit of a quandary. Seeing their confusion, Saunders laughed and said, "You admit you have sought to act against a Battle General, openly and cannot support your action within any guidelines or show a breach of Protocols?"

"No, the codes to destroy your ship!" one of them blathered. "They have been disconnected. THIS is against Protocols!"

"And rightly so." Saunders responded in an open com link. "Which merely proves my choice to protect myself and secure the broadcast coming from Hope. I cannot imagine how the people will respond when this aggressive action is aired in the next episode, be sure to watch it, you will all be featured." It was a cat playing with really stupid mice.

She then explained that if an Admin had acted to destroy her ship, when no protocols had been broken, it proved someone high up the chain could not be trusted. She THEN invoked some buried historical law that gave her authority to override central action in this matter.

As a result of this aggressive and unjustifiable action, she now considered there were aspects within the administration that were in breach of Protocols and were, accordingly, a threat. In light of the proof the committee had provided the removal of the fail safes was justified.

She stressed that she personally welcomed the new religious movement on Hope and had decided to protect the planet from any hostile intent. Again, this was an action she had taken that was entirely within regulation. In other words, take your regulations and stick them up your proverbial.

ooooOOOOOoooo

Masters read the report and contacted Tchaikovsky - This matter was getting out of hand. Should he forward it on? The two regularly played chess via holo-form when Masters asking Tchaikovsky how best to deal with the matter. Tchaikovsky laughed, and said, "Do you want to stay alive? I know I prefer to keep living - What do you think will happen when so many breaches of Protocols that are not breaches of protocol are announced to our dear leader?"

Masters grunted, "He doesn't sit well with failure. What do we do?"

Tchaikovsky laughed, "Well - No ACTUAL breach of protocol has occurred. Our instructions are clear, only in the case of protocols not being followed are we to intervene and only if the matter cannot be contained are we to contact our 'retired' leader. If you panic and go running to him because a Planet had found a loophole, YOU are the one who will be blamed for allowing it to go so long."

Masters shakes his head, "Surely the old man is aware. I mean, everyone watches the Hope broadcast - It is damn well self-evident that the spirit of the protocols is being shattered, if not the technical aspects."

Tchaikovsky shook his head."If we cannot solve this we both end up dead. No, do NOT tell him. We will sort this out on our own. You control the military, I control the tech. Together we will be able to contain this rebellion and when we DO file a report it will be that the threat has been contained. And no, the old man does not receive common broadcast. All his systems are wired into protocol breaches - only when something needs his direct interdiction will he be made aware."

"So you are saying we sit on our hands and let this play out?" Masters was not sure.

Tchaikovsky laughed, "And what is the net result of difference to ourselves if it plays out badly? Nothing, our heads are already on the chopping block. Sort it out, Masters. Do NOT approach Yont-Na until there is an absolute and clear breach of Protocols. After all, this is a pack of illiterate wolves. Are you seriously telling me you can't solve this?"

Masters nodded. "Queen to D4." Then, as Tchaikovsky contemplated a response, he asked, "What the hell does he DO all day on that damn station of him?"

"I reported in and had face time last year. Whatever he is doing, he's not looking good. I reckon he had blown past regen and my guess is he is finally about to kick it. That's the other thing, if we spark him up it will give him a purpose. Let the reptile die, I say. No, we will handle this, just let it play out until there is a significant breach, then we start igniting planets. Remember, we have four Battle Generals to deal with Saunders." Tchaikovsky then countered, "Knight to A7 - check."

"You really think he will finally kick it?" Masters was intrigued. Yont-Na was still the final authority in all decisions. His death would mean this capability would resolve to himself and Tchaikovsky, should the old fool pass on.

"We can but Hope!" laughed Tchaikovsky, making a pun on the very problem that was causing them grief. "I don't know about you, but I find it extremely disconcerting that HE can act unilaterally, ignoring all protocols, and we cannot. In truth, this is HIS failure. The fact that some smart General worked a way through an open loophole is not our fault."

Masters nodded. It was true, they were done with their little emperor sitting on his little station, holding the power of life or death over them. They had hoped it would eventually come down to exactly this, a battle of will as to who would be the last one left with the will to continue. "I still can't figure how he manages to have all the mods yet stay off the radar. Have you worked it out?"

"Technically not possible," Tchaikovsky looked directly at his opponent, "but he does. It is his systems that created all this and I presume he simply wrote himself out of the controls while setting it up."

"But he has mods, his mainframe tunes into them. How can we not have some sort of track?"

"We will find all this out when he dies," Tchaikovsky said dryly.

ooooO0000Ooooo

On Hope, only dumb tech was allowed. Anything with an A.I. component was banned. There were difficulties, specifically with the admin staff at base. Every one of their functions had been controlled by a computer directive. The head of maintenance would read a report and tell the computer to order a repair - But now there was no auto A.I. to complete the request. What do you do? The man in charge of the station kitchens was a qualified chef, but he had never actually cooked anything in his life. Everything had been an instruction to the reticulation units on what to prepare. Now he had to organize real people to go out to real markets and bring in actual food.

No more manufactured specialties from the Planet Mergon, no more deserts from the Althracian Nebula. It was all hands-on collection and preparation of real food. And as this food was largely grown by the wolves and the settlers, this meant the once-privileged admin staff had to trade - and what was it that the plebs needed? This was another problem. Paying credits to locals meant the Hope Consortium had to approve the expenditure. Unlike the military that took whatever they needed, the Admin needed approvals for extraneous operational costs.

The problem, the operational costs were all approved for the computer controlled environment. The Admin on Hope simply did not have Federation Credits to trade with - So what else did the locals want? Banner had expressly forbidden Admin to take by force what was required, so, for the first time in their lives, adults in the Federation administration had to negotiate and physically DO things to solve problems - something no admin had ever done.

In a word, they were terrible at it. The staff were hopeless and anything that required real communication or physical effort was a fail. Here the rest of the universe watched in astonishment as the lowly sub-humans, the wolves, took these poor people under their wing and taught them how to function. They even brought food to feed the helpless hi-mods sitting in their fortified compound.

Their beautiful soft, brown eyes, their thick cuddly fur, made these wolves the pet you always wanted to have. Children began begging their carers to get them a wolf! They were delightful, friendly, helpful and kind creatures that went out of their way to assist the humans. Saunders saw another opportunity, and soon animatronic wolves were being sold in every market as house pets for the human race.

More importantly, every wolf toy had a very specific program written in for the protection of the household. These were not just friendly playthings, they were guard dogs and registered as this. No one ever pays attention to the fine print, which clearly stated in the purchase contract the fact that the mechanical wolves were being sold as a household defense unit. And even if you did notice it, it just added to their cuteness!

Neither did people pay much attention to the fact the furry things were fully A.I. controlled and sent coded information back to Saunders ship. For all the world, it looked like just another great product from the people that ran Planet Hope, the Hope Consortium. Hope was the buzz word of the Federation and trade in goods from there was making far greater profits than mining. Natural woods, furs, clothes, hand made items by the wolves were THE in demand item in every market. The consortium was flush with credits.

And underneath all of this, the wolf army grew. Not one thousand anymore, but closer to a million strong - and as a military operation they were all paid for by the Consortium. But if they ever wanted to complain, or register a complaint, the notion of what Saunders would do kept all resistance in check.

The Death Squad were now more than happy to train and supervise each battalion as it came on-line. Dexter and Mo-Ki had told the men that had to prepare, because one day, a day that was not far off, someone somewhere would snap out of the hypnotic trace that Saunders had woven around Planet Hope and the machine would turn against them.

Mo-Ki understood the game - Snippets of Lucifer WERE in the system, collating information, coalescing into new forms. Soon they would see its whispers taking over the thoughts of Admin officials, and a new war, that of humanity against the wolves, would begin.

Evil Rising

The war started in the simplest of ways. A mother, inspired by the new religion, said she did not want her son taken into care. Unheard of, the boy had stats for science, so he needed to be taken in and trained. But she refused to permit mods. Why? It made no sense at all to the admin officer for recruitment on Planet Tursna.

This was an established world and an offer of acceptance such as the woman had received was a guarantee of security for her family. It made little sense to reject the offer, so the low level Four just took the child, killing the mother in the process. It was not his fault, she threw herself at him, like a wild cat. Did she not realize she had no status?

So he rayed her down and thought nothing of it. But the people in her village did not seem to agree and they set on him. They tore him to pieces, in point of fact, which drew the attention of the Seven who ran that world. Now, as mentioned, the tendency for the selection protocols was to pick those for high admin roles who had what we might call a pathological desire to achieve goals. Tursna was no different and the Seven who ran the planet saw no good reason for this abhorrent disturbance. She promptly sent in a deep scan crew to find the cause.

If it cost everyone in that village their sanity - every man, woman, and child - the admin was determined to get a clear answer. And it DID cost the lives of every single person. Normally, no big deal, but a high-level reporter happened to be in the vicinity and started asking questions about why the religious freedom of these people had been ignored.

No problem. Murder the reporter and the questions will stop. Then everyone can get back to normality. However, this particular reporter had money and, as a result, had the latest craze, a pet mechanical wolf. This favored little creature followed his master about like a faithful dog, as he was programmed to do. When some foolish officers of the law turned up to exterminate its master, the programming took hold. The cuddly little furry friend turned into a monster. The 'pet' wolf toy killed every single officer sent to deal with the reporter by the Admin Seven.

The woman Admin did something unthinkable after this: She got extremely angry and BLAMED this new religion for causing social unrest. She put report after report into the system stating the obvious, that there was an elephant in the room. These reports filtered out to other paranoid and half-mad Sevens who ruled other worlds and, despite the protocols that allowed religious freedom, they started seeking to exterminate this new threat to their society.

Because these people had lived in ivory towers, embedded in a sense of their own superiority for so long, they decided that religious freedom itself was a threat to society. The fact that this opposed protocols seemed of little interest to them and, one by one, whole planets started falling into war. The pathological administrators were determined to regain control over the civilian population that they believed had been lost.

Tursna became the flashpoint and when the leading Seven brought members of the press in their questions, she banned their pets from attending - all hell broke out across the airwaves. "Evil admin seeks to destroy natural rights!", "Intolerance of religious freedom leads to murder and destruction", the headlines were spectacular.

But more important than this, the natural persons you would seek for comment, the ones who would argue the case FOR religious rights were Dexter and Mo-Ki. They soon had the press firmly on their side, because reporters were starting to see their own members eliminated through deep scans - because they asked questions.

Thus, growing out of a religious question, freedom of the press was now at stake. Everywhere, the general theme that was being broadcast was that the evil empire sought to dominate and control the innocent populace by removing the only right they had, the right to religious freedom.

Not every planet tried to suppress the new movement. On quite a few, the administration found it quite liked the story being told by Planet Hope. Inside the bowels of the machine there were many cogs that wanted to escape. But to where? This was the hard part. Emissaries from Hope solved this problem by suggesting each world set up churches for the Wolverine society.

If people did not want their children modded, so be it. They had the right to choose. If they joined the church of the wolves, the right of religious freedom could be enforced by officers of that religion. Saunders was tracking every planet, working with any who decided that the old ways needed adjustment. She was able to counter the curious Luciferian whispers with cool logic. Her epistles to the High Mods of these worlds - those who might be open to the Message of Hope - was always the same: *Allow the people the right to choose.*

She even brought up that old classic piece of literature, the United Nations Charter, in particular, the opening statements:

Article 1

The Purposes of the United Nations are:

1. *To maintain international peace and security, and to that end: to take effective collective measures for the prevention and removal of threats to the peace, and for the suppression of acts of aggression or other breaches of the peace, and to bring about by peaceful means, and in conformity with the principles of justice and international law, adjustment or settlement of international disputes or situations which might lead to a breach of the peace;*

2. *To develop friendly relations among nations based on respect for the principle of equal rights and self-determination of peoples, and to take other appropriate measures to strengthen universal peace;*

3. *To achieve international co-operation in solving international problems of an economic, social, cultural, or humanitarian character, and in promoting and encouraging respect for human rights and for fundamental freedoms for all without distinction as to race, sex, language, or religion; and*

4. *To be a center for harmonizing the actions of nations in the attainment of these common ends.*

She stressed again and again, that the central role of any administration must be the peaceful process of government. The people had a fundamental freedom, they WERE allowed to choose their religion. And when some would argue that it was the choices they made that were disturbing the peace, she answered that it was the reaction by government that was disturbing the peace. The people HAD A RIGHT to religious freedom, this was in the protocols.

Logically: If government choose to ignore this, then THEY were in breach of protocols.

One by one, she cleaved one planet at a time from an overt dedication to the past. She used every one of the extraordinary talents she had to do so. But this gambit was but one arrow in the quiver. In the troublesome worlds, a different sort of effort had to be made and this meant sending in Mo-Ki, backed by a squad of wolves.

Choose the Wolverine Way

In the old world, the leaders of any church were allowed a personal guard. Again, a curious matter not specifically delineated or excluded in the Protocols. This was because when these were created the Administration was under the illusion that religion was a spent force. What it meant, however, was that when the leaders of this new teaching, this 'Wolverine Way', needed to attend a function, they took with them a contingent of wolf soldiers as a protective shield.

This simple message went ahead of any embassage sent to a planet that was warring with itself. Mo-Ki himself would arrive with a squad of Wolves at his back and preach to the people. The precious child, the one who rose from the dead, would come there in person, speaking one on one with the people. And the people responded - Vast rallies formed around his sermons, thousands upon thousands would come to hear him speak, and when the administrators turned on him, as they almost always did, his Wolves were ready to fight.

The local armies run by contrary officials were decimated. On occasions, they did the unthinkable and nuked the innocents, including all the wolves, and even Mo-Ki himself. And yet by some miracle, he would rise and live again. Again and again, he would rise from the dead to continue preaching the message, "Choose the Wolverine Way!"

Of course, Mo-ki only ever sent clones to these dangerous worlds. He functioned at an extraordinarily high level now - puberty accelerated all his faculties. He was now in such control of his internal self that he did not even need an isolation tank to run up to ten clones. They could be discoursing on any number of worlds while at the same time Mo-Ki could be talking to you on Hope. It barely seemed a stretch for his level Eight mind to be having deep discussions, or giving speeches in ten different places. Of course, when a clone was killed he felt their pain, and suffered from each death, but another clone was always waiting in the wings, and another, and another when the need arose.

These simulacrums did not possess his remarkable capacity, but even as clones they were more than a match for the majority of the insipid rules-based minds of the administration officials who ran the planets. The presence of the one who rose from the dead always caused a sensation among the populace and when some bright spark correlated the relevant information and discovered there were at least ten 'Mo-Ki's' across the planets, it not only did not dull the enthusiasm of the faithful, it added to their amazement.

Obviously, the ones who opposed this movement decried that it clearly was a clone being used - but who in the universe could operate more than ten? Even if they WERE clones, it made it even more remarkable. There was no stopping the excitement that surrounded the miracle child born on Planet Hope.

The broadcast of Planet Hope continued its spread across the galaxy, now expanded by reporters sending in newscasts of wolf stories as they happened across the Federation. The rallies were one thing, but the astonishing and high rating news was the remarkable changes in human society - changes that were being spread far and wide by the wolves. Even those that hated the wolves would stop to watch the show.

Charni had a cult following all of her own now - Settlers on new planets worshipped 'the mother', because it was seen that she would protect and nurture them. The changes went to the heart of society with even the home guards on many planets secretly wishing for a General Dexter to run them. He was a legend in military circles, having trained the remarkable wolves who, without mods, were able to equal the best of any Death Squad. Unheard of - and Dexter was a natural Five they said? Incredible stuff.

Banner stayed well out of the ongoing broadcast. Obviously, he no longer lived with Charni and spent a good part of his time with Saunders, but the Surrogate for Mo-Ki was nothing if not a practical woman. She made no issue of the changes. In truth, her life was so rich and so busy, she really had little time for marital indulgence.

However, Captain Banner as he was now met regularly with his sons, planning in detail every step of the process they had undertaken. As Saunders could not leave her ship, they would meet there in person (so high was her trust factor) with Dexter always making sure he brought fresh food and wine. It seems that Saunders had developed quite a taste for natural wine and decent conversation. Her delight in having a family, and such simple things as a chat with a nice red made Banner laugh.

Saunders had not left her ship for almost 200 years. Even when the regular updates and refits were being done, she stayed on board and monitored every alteration. Why? In truth, there was nowhere else for her to go. Her life was her ship. It revolved around her, and the slightest separation from it caused internal feedback loops in her nervous system.

This is what most people would call anxiety, but in the case of a battle general, it was a justifiable paranoia. These people had a lot of enemies.

Her warship was a media center now. It was the funnel for all the information about the wolves and Mo-Ki being broadcast across the galaxy. Naturally, her capacity for destruction was unimpeded, but the focus was on building bridges rather than tearing down worlds. The energy of change they had created was a wave and Saunders was the one both generating, then surfing, the effect.

No doubt future historians would dissect and seek to understand what caused this particular General to cut from the herd, but for Saunders, the sheer delight of having her family present helped steer her course. She adored her son, she loved her husband and Dexter was cute but more importantly, capable. She had snipped completely from the Federation now, including disengaging the power-ups to her Mods. She suffered no ill effects and her razor-sharp mind remained undulled, .

But increasingly, Mo-Ki ran the show. The diminutive not-quite-twelve-year-old was holding all the cards and dealing out his requirements every step of the way. Now that the monitoring was off and the boy no longer had to shield the intensity of focus his mind experienced every moment of the day, Banner had finally been able to get a read out on Psyche currents of the child. They were off the known charts. Eventually, he gave up trying to measure Mo-Ki and just let the wild horses within him run.

"In normal circumstance, the next level would be to extend the dialogues we have created, allowing these to flow into the coming generation," Mo-Ki said as they ate their lunch on Saunders ship. "If we move too quickly and try to accelerate the change we run the risk of a planet breaking down into civil war. We need five years of stability to allow the wolverine way to take root as a natural belief in the young people, but we do not have this amount of time."

"You speak as if you are not one of these 'young people', dearest brother," Dexter noted dryly.

The boy just smiled his Mona Lisa smile, then continued. "We can already see fragments of Lucifer emerging. The insane choices by the administration officials are all part of its whispers - On one level it helps the public see THIS as the enemy. We have to create an environment where planets WANT to join our way of life. Planetary conflict cannot be avoided but to avoid a galaxy-wide civil war we need the administration and military leaders to prefer us to the Federation."

"How do you see this happening?" Banner asked his son.

"It is a complex algorithm and the outcomes are variable. The only certainty is that we will meet firm resistance to our non-controlled society. Remember, Lucifer is a program that desires to build worlds, run cultures, and expand trade. These are the same goals as we have, but the program has an absolute priority that all must be done under a central control. We offer an expectation that mankind can expand through individual choice and mutual cooperation."

Mo-Ki then became serious. "In distilling out options I come to only but TWO certainties. The first is that they will continue to seek to kill me - this is a given. The second is the difficult one - the federation will seek to destroy Hope. How the Luciferian influence will go about this, who can say, but it will not be through direct military action because they know Saunders is here. The highest probability: they will look for a way to throw a planet breaking asteroid at us.

"If Hope can be shattered, the swirling atoms of Lucifer may find a way to be reassembled. So, our primary question is: *How would someone put a huge asteroid on our door before we have a chance to vaporize it?*

Answer: Our opposition will need to develop the technology to do so, thus the logical place to find our enemy will be in research stations working on a project such as this." Mo-Ki paused, processing the assemblage of potentials to arrive at a likely causation.

Saunders chimed in, "My dear sweet little Hitler, that would need someone able to subspace a HUGE rock, which means ENORMOUS portals - I concur with your assessment, but there are literally thousands of research stations across the galaxy working on sending mining asteroids closer to home worlds. How do we find the one trying to do it via sub-space?"

"We look for the obvious, dear Mother. (Saunders giggled - she just loved being called mother) We look for projects that are doing exactly the opposite ... Find any planet in a meteorite belt field that is under constant threat, they will pay for research to AVOID meteors. Most likely a project to create a sub-space field large enough to cause an asteroid to go THROUGH their planet and have it materialize on the other side. It is the same thing as throwing one, but in reverse."

Saunders nodded. It made sense, and there were only a few planets that fitted these criteria. "We are talking about a large sub-space gate, and or the very least a trans-warp field. To do this requires an energy source equivalent to a sun."

"But how do you secretly move an asteroid big enough to smash a planet, let alone subspace it? Ion rockets pushing that vast a mass would light up any scanner, and there is no Sub-Space launcher capable of disassembling and reassembling that many atoms." Dexter suggested.

Banner guessed at the logical solution. "They will have to fit a pulse-motor to the rock to drive it close to light speed, then they can send it through a portal with a minimal charge. It will take at least a year to get something that size up to speed and I cannot even imagine the cost of doing it. So, first up - We need to find the tech planets that are working towards sub-spacing meteors. This means developing a HUGE portal. I am guessing they will have to look at a way to project a subspace field from the rock itself in order to do this."

Dexter chimed in, "Yes, but going IN is half the equation - they would have to accurately plot an exit which would mean some sort of doorway at or near the planet itself. No one could hide that sort of technology."

"Unless a targeted wormhole could be created - a funnel to direct the rock to a specific point." Banner suggested.

"Very likely, Father. The problem right now, we know they will attack Hope, but there are too many variables: A single mistake, an overlooked critical system that fails? The harsh truth is that by keeping the wolves on Hope, we are putting their entire civilization in peril. This is utterly unfair, yet, we must stay and guard this planet. We MUST stop anyone accessing or releasing the Luciferian energies resident here."

Mo-Ki seemed so much older as he gazed out of the plex-screen to space beyond. "And even if we succeed in locating and defusing the first, there will be a second, and a third. No matter how many rounds we win, another challenge will arise. The Federation is full of powerful elites who are susceptible to the Luciferian influences and they will bankrupt their society rather than have us succeed."

Mo-Ki sighed, the blind stupidity of the Federation was so extraordinary. "We are trying to deal sanely with madness and such a thing cannot add up to a successful overall outcome. We either cure the madness, or kill it. The best answer is always the simplest one. We know there is Yont-Na in the shadows - His control must be cut off and after this, the computer systems, all the mainframes, every little bit of tech that can be accessed by a Luciferian fragment must be rooted out and extinguished. We must smash the environment the creature lives in.

The child thought for some time before continuing. "This means that the next stage for the Wolverine Faith must be JIHAD! On every planet, in every system, we have to end this insanity. Everything is based around the computer systems, therefore we must turn off their mainframes. We must send humanity back to the stone age and when we are certain the influence of Lucifer is exterminated, we can rebuild."

"To do this, the people need to be sufficiently aroused to action and convinced in the rightness of their cause. The people must rally around the banner and undertake a war against their rulers. Legends will be born, the people will BELIEVE in their cause and many will die for it."

The rec room on Saunders ship was quiet for some time. They had never heard Mo-Ki speak like this before. Banner was the one who spoke, "And how do we rouse people to such action?"

"Mother has shown the way. Her broadcast - Every day we release stories of people resisting and succeeding against the mindless control of the Federation. We give them stories of outrageous abuse, we give them stories of blatant excesses by Federation officials, every day we report on their unfairness and callous disregard for humanity. Then we screen stories of wolves helping people, showing them the Wolverine Way.

"Under the auspices of religious freedom, we can send in a wolf army to protect our faithful. People will join the faith and request the wolves as guardians. This insult to Federation will anger them and drive them to attack those who resist their control. We will force them into war!

"Then we screen their cruelty. We show their hatred. We uncover their corrupt systems. We work to get the people angry and we quietly organize ways for them to attack the system." he concluded. "It is to be a guerrilla war fought in the open."

Saunders smiled broadly. War was what she did best, and psychological terror was fun. "I love it! Ok, I am in. I accept the parameters my little monster has outlined. What we need to sort are the details of how we lever each individual world into our camp."

And so they planned the program and designed the stories according to what the news was on any particular planet. The task was to create maximum emotional effect, in order to motivate the people to rise up in anger towards the machine that controlled them. Only madness could counter madness.

Thus the war began: the war between the government and the people. The war between the Protocols and the Wolverine Way.

The Breaking of the Chains

It was not hard to ferment rebellion - it had always been there, seething under the surface. The people hated the Admins, the Admins detested the people. It was just a matter of pulling the trigger.

All No-Mods knew that in the old system even a Dexter could barely rise above a non-com rank. Why? Despite the egalitarian words of the Protocols, Dexter was a no-blood. Every soldier knew that, unless you came from a position of privilege, your chances of high rankings were next to impossible. But choosing the Wolverine Way, becoming part of the Wolf Army, this meant no barrier to rank. Only aptitude mattered, no mods, no boosts, no artificial anything. The 'WW' logo along with the wolverine ideal of equality was being spread across the known planets and even began to appear in army barracks.

The wolf pets, the whispering of the new path, the general consensus that the old ways were done - it slowly caused the cracks to appear in the leadership of the Human Federation. Questions were being asked at a high level now: *How could the modded soldiers on Hope still function perfectly well without being plugged into the mainframe? How was Saunders still operating at peak efficiency without being connected to the grid?* The simple truth was starting to emerge in the minds of even the most dedicated admin officials that they had been told a huge lie about these modifications to DNA. A conspiracy was started, and generally believed, that old Earth was destroyed on purpose - so that Elites could get in charge of humanity.

This was when the anger started to kick in. The people had been sold a lie, and why? To benefit those few Elites who rose to the top of the tree. They had cushy lives, they had the power of life and death over anyone under them. All they need do is snap their fingers and you and your family were done. How outrageous, and HOW can they do this? Through their machines. Break the machines and you break the system of control over you.

And every night on their viewing screens, the common people saw the evidence of how Hope was proving to all that the machinery of oppressive government was not necessary.

This was when the Epistles of the new order began to get written. The Mo-Ki clones began in earnest, lecturing on planets about the Wolverine Way, beating the drum for how religious freedom was sacrosanct.

Mo-Ki cones went to the universities and campuses to pronounce the word and the simple stories to break down the belief in the Protocols became the new bible, the Way of the Wolf.

People were amazed at how fluent and cognizant this little child seemed to be. So wise beyond his years! He used history to teach them, never making any open declaration against the ruling forces. In this way he protected himself against vindictive controllers who sought to have him proscribed. One of his classic speeches was imprinted into holo-glass, making a living statue in every village that accepted the wolves as friends. *"After Columbus had returned from the West Indies, he brought with him some of the natives he found there. Why? Because he knew if he did not show proof of this fourth race, he would have been executed. As a result of his actions, a huge furor emerged in the then administration of Spain, one that spread across all cities in Europe, as people sought to explain how this could be.*

"The general state of belief in those days was that, after the flood, the three sons of Noah accounted for the three races: The black man, the white man, and the yellow man. But if this was true, where did these red men come from?

"This small glitch in the accepted paradigm caused major upheaval. The entire political landscape was tilting towards collapse when the then Pope found a solution. Clearly, the red men were the ones from Sodom and Gomorrah. As punishment for their crimes, mere death was not good enough, so God plucked them up and deposited in the wild, barbarian lands at the edge of the world." There was always general laughter as this insanity was revealed.

"It might surprise the modern thinker that such an absurdity was so readily believed, but they were. Why is this so? How can rational men be so blind?" Mo-ki had said the same story on planet after planet, and it was repletewith graphics by Saunders. And each time, the same punch line. *"Why would anyone give this sort of insanity credence? It is simple: The ADMINISTRATION back then WANTED to believe in the old ways, so they manufactured any sort of idiocy as a rationale to justify them."*

He never spoke a direct word against the existing order. That would have him labelled a terrorist and he would have been proscribed. The parallel of his stories to the twenty-seventh century was obvious, and every example he quoted from old earth emphasized this fact, but he never actually said it. Slowly he turned minds away from blind obedience - But there were some that would never change.

The mindset in the heart of deep administration knew only one truth: the Protocols! For a person to suggest that they were wrong was unimaginable. The evidence was clear - Given the extremely effective and proven benefits in expanding settlements and creating wealth based on these truths, how could they be wrong?

Despite his clear logic, and carefully worded essays, the believers of the old order called Mo-Ki a threat. Despite? No, it was BECAUSE of his simple clarity that he was a threat. These core Federation fanatics verbally attacked him when he attended demonstrations. They believed he was a dangerous religious freak who wanted to secure power.

They sent in hecklers to shout out during his talks - that he was a third rate reality media star, that his show (now just called "Hope") was a concocted lie. "Fake News!" they shouted. Outside every meeting they stated the Federation line: Clearly, it was impossible for soldiers to still be as efficient without their mods being powered up, so therefore the show was broadcasting falsehood and lies.

In their mind it was obvious, the person really behind all this was Saunders, the evil breakaway General. She was in some way assisting the soldiers on Hope. Her ship was there, providing power-ups, and it was possible the men did not even realize it. She broadcast the show, created the scenario, and cleary SHE was the evil one behind everything.

This formed the basic counter to those who opposed the Federation position: It was not the innocent looking Mo-Ki, or his new religion, that was the source of the conflict. He was a sucker pulled into a power grab - The whole thing had Saunders at the center of it. She was the one to blame, because she wanted to take charge of everything!

Yet when questioned directly by a central committee if she were the one to blame for all the business on Hope, she responded in a very odd way. "Of course I am. I planted a million plus year old entity we call Lucifer there, I created it then sent it back in time - a computer of such vast sophistication that it could take over at a whim anything we possessed and naturally, with this extraordinary power at my disposal, I chose to send it into the far distant past in the hope it would survive, just so I could stage a mock battle in order to kill it."

Well, administration officials don't DO irony. They took her words literally, but when you instruct underlings to punch in a breach of protocols based on ironic humor, even the most stupid analyst had to query what they were being asked to input.

Queries to Logic: *Even if Saunders had indeed discovered time travel, the greater question was, if she had found time travel, why did she not then use it to save Planet Earth and with the vast power at her disposal why did she not then place herself in charge?*

The Federation computer rejected the claim of a breach of Protocols on the basis of what was submitted failed logical assessment.

So the very system she was attacking ended up defending her! Saunders was not proscribed, despite the significant wish by many in authority, because there was no direct and provable breach of protocols. As there was no court of appeal to appeal to, nor any higher authority to plead common sense to, even her rank was sustained and her pay grade remained unchanged. She had not specifically breached a single law, therefore she was unable to be charged or removed from her office.

It was a curious side-effect of modification of the DNA that, while it gave expansion in one area of consciousness, it could paradoxically give a narrowness of vision in every other area. You become so specialized in your specific attributes that you became incapable of seeing the obvious in disciplines outside your orbit. This is how it was designed. When the machine is working harmoniously, this is not a problem, because the person beside you will be strong in whatever it is that you lack.

Thus the entire rationale for the Protocols: *The collective mind, properly instructed, will resolve and sort through any and all concerns that arise.* But when the collective mind becomes fragmented, when doubt, fear, and worry assails it, the machine starts to break down. And so it was that despite the complete lack of evidence and the refusal of the computers and the lackeys that ran them to proscribe her, the vast bulk of level six and up administrations officials decided the one causing all the problems was Saunders. Everything pointed towards her.

Plus, the United Nations nonsense she was pedaling - she was clearly seeking to pull the Federation apart and ferment civil war. They appeared to forget that, as a fully-fledged battle general with her own starship, if they pissed her off enough, their home planet might get destroyed. Some unfortunate level five admin who was were called in on an investigation of Saunders pointed this out and subsequently got shipped to the outer rim to play with the pirates.

The fear of death DID strike home, however, and as a result action was taken. But not very smart one - Limitations suddenly began to restrict the activities of ALL battle generals who had the sole command of a Star Ship. This was within the purview of admin officers under operational procedures. It went up to Masters who had a simple, elegant solution to the problem.

Logic dictated their powers had to be curtailed, so the memo was sent out that while the matter was being sorted, the five Battle Generals who formed the core of the Federations military force were all put on a temporary non-active status.

This is when the light bulb got lit up in the dull minds of level seven Admins. Panic set in, because it occurred to them, what if the other Generals went to side with Saunders? Answer: the Federation was doomed. No one would be safe. Thus fear started to win the war for the wolves. Four Battle Generals, equal in power to the entire standing fleet, were now mightily pissed off.

Conversion of the Generals

It goes without saying: The first person these Generals contacted as a result of this strange action was Saunders. She duly sent them the charter of the United Nations, but she went one step further and sent them the simple message to be found in the ancient constitution of the United States. "All men are born equal?" she asked. Well, of course they are not! The entire system of selection and the reason anyone attained their rank was specifically because all persons had varying tendencies. The potentials of a Battle General, in particular, were far superior to almost everyone.

Thus prepared, Saunders reworded this phrase in her next missive to, "All Battle Generals are Equal." indicating they should band together - intimating that, while the lowly Seven admin officials were significantly inferior, it was obvious they were trying to take control of their betters.

What to do? It was becoming a question of survival, and so the Battle Generals listened. The first question, *What about the destruct code?* Saunders explained she was no longer subject to that threat and would be willing to share ways to remove the failsafe programs. Added to this she mentioned that they should not what to do by petty officials! So, now they were conveniently stood down and inactive, they were able to get into their ships circuits. One by one, following the pattern given by Saunders, they removed the many layers of protection developed for this very reason - the feared rebellion by a Battle General.

Naturally, word soon got out to the planets that they no longer need fear a battle cruiser turning up and destroying their planet.

REVOLUTION: Part One

Naturally, with the Generals stood down, word got out about unpatrolled space. The outer rim pirates filled the gaping hole in security, thus the stage was set for the conclusion to the question of Hope and the influence of the Wolverine Way.

Within two years of the start of their offensive, just before Mo-Ki's fourteenth birthday, there were two camps across the Federation of Planets - one that followed the Wolverine Way, and the rest - What is more, 'the rest' were at war with themselves.

Officials were arguing, trade was being ruined and the military was being used to solve petty bickering. The Federation was now ripe for revolution, but the obvious question was, what do you replace the existing regime with?

The actual revolution started as a small riot. In a provincial outpost in Torc System, out near the Orion cluster, the first salvo was fired. A simple taxation dispute, where some high mod who had recently arrived decided to take a very pretty girl as payment to settle a state debt. The family was incensed, the entire village went into an uproar and attacked the extremely shocked official. He barely had time to blip out a distress code, let alone put his pants back on, before he died.

The populace of Zenth, the planet in question, was largely indigenous and agrarian society. In the cities an extensive cross-breeding of the indigenous humanoid race and the settlers had occurred, a rare mix that created rather stunning creatures. The father of the ravaged girl was a full-blood native of the planet and his natural response to someone interfering in his family was to kill them. This territorial display of the local males had been noted in the scans, so protocols were not immediately triggered.

When a native or settler kills a human official, a dispatch is sent, and the individual is deep scanned as punishment. Subsequently, the populace gets the message by seeing the madman wandering about and all goes quiet again. Problem solved. However the machinery of justice was stressed with a thousand disputes on a thousand planets and when a clerk noted that this was not an unnatural reaction according to the original planetary scans, he took the opportunity to have one less issue on his books and just signed off the matter as an official who had not done their homework.

It should have stopped there, but it did not. Flagged, inspected, passed by as inconsequential, the matter was out of the system. However, the wife of the dead man was incensed. How dare some no-mod indigenous garbage attack and kill her husband! (despite the fact he was taking a girl for his own purposes) She got a few plasma rifles from the armory by using her dead husbands' clearance codes, rounded up a few equally incensed local admins, and they all went and shot up the entire village.

Another case of someone not doing their homework. Vengeance was an integral part of the native culture so, in response, they rose up and wiped out the entire admin base. The human settlers were not affected, and indeed, they cheered on the natives. Why? Because Mo-Ki had been on their planet. He had told them it would come to this. He told them revolution was coming and so when this opportunity presented itself, they also rose up, took over the controls of the shuttles and other craft, and then did the unthinkable! They declared Zenith as independent from the Federation.

Any planet could do this but fear of warships curtailed such notions. The number of admin staff on any settled worlds in the backwaters was minuscule. But in the past, they were rarely placed under threat because of the consequences.

The response to the uprising is a judgement, followed by deep scans, and in such a case as with Zenith an extinction of all the sentients and opening it to new settlement. The message sent from the High Mods via their armies was always clear, "Behave, and everything is good. Be a problem and you will die." A squad was sent, but instead of a helpless populace to be interrogated, the soldiers met a vastly superior wolf force.

After their rebellion, after the hot passions had cooled, both the natives and settlers understood the obvious: they needed help. They appealed to Mo-Ki who advised them to join the religion of the Wolf. Why? Religious freedom ALSO meant its followers were allowed to be protected. So the wolves that arrived to defend the helpless were present under religious rights, not as an illegal force.

Which posed a question: On one hand Protocols required judgement and execution of the population, yet on the other, there were other considerations where freedom and protection of religion was an inalienable right. The administrative framework became locked into an internal conflict that resulted in paralysis. What didn't help was the reaction of the soldiers sent to Zenth. They had orders, but they knew the net result of carrying out these orders meant they would all die.

When the ground commander relayed this information up the chain, the response was that orders were the orders. So they foolishly attempted to carry them out, and died. Which meant further confusion, because the protocols then demanded a General be sent to wipe out the planet. However, the Generals recently had their planet-wiping capacity curtailed and so they sat squarely on their collective arses, laughing at the unfolding absurdity that Saunders had warned them would arrive.

This is what changed everything.

This was far worse for the Federation than the loss of some random military squad, the Attack Generals now beamed their holos in to selected Space Stations to discuss procedure with Saunders. Collectively, they were happy with her as their leader and not just because she was showing them how to be released from threat. They found they started to enjoy their meetings with each other. Thus a dialogue began between the otherwise pathologically solitary creatures known as Battle Generals - and of course, to ease the tension Saunders had sent them all wine from Hope and asked them to join her in a toast.

"The end of isolation and the beginning of a new chapter!" she announced, raising her glass. The General discovered they enjoyed it! Both the wine and the company eased a pain they never knew they had. Hundreds of years of being alone was coming to an end.

Not so happy were the Federation officials in charge of Zenith. They were running around like chickens with their heads off. The normal and easy process of government had been massively disrupted and it was at this juncture that Mo-Ki offered a solution. Naturally, he expressed deep regret for the loss of life and terrible events that had unfolded on Zenth, but perhaps if they had a wolf representative present on each admin base, then a more direct line of communication could be established, and tragedies like that incident could be avoided in the future?

It was met with derision, the human system was one of dominance. The response was simple: There was no charter in the protocols that allowed for a mediation presence with an alien culture - but Mo-Ki explained to the admins that this was an incorrect application of rules and that there was, under the religious freedom acts, a way to resolve these issues. Every admin center had a chapel - He could simply install a Wolf as a chaplain. This was an allowed procedure, as any religious group had an equal right to staff a Federation church.

All normal worship services for the other faiths would continue, and the Wolf would simply be there as a representative of the Wolverine faith, one who could conveniently assist in any further conflicts - such as the last one. This is where the officials found themselves in checkmate: When any action defines an outcome that provides a net benefit, the Protocols state it must be followed. And so, across the world, Wolves became part of the day-to-day framework of Federation diplomacy.

This was more than getting a paw in the door, so to speak. In any station, if a person became infected with the Luciferian virus, the wolves would smell it. This was his trump card and the completely unsuspecting officialdom remained utterly clueless as to his true purpose. Should any Soul be taken by the Luciferian code, on any station in any Admin center, he would know. But would the infected individual realize it? No, not until the code had complete dominance over the personality, which meant they had TIME to deal with the matter.

Banner had found a cure in the resonant frequencies of the old wolves, so it was a relatively easy matter to track and resolve infections as and when they arose.

One planet after another began to rise up against the totalitarian regimes, then join the religion of the Wolf to avoid consequences. The wolf soldiers were called in on many different conflicts. There were peacekeepers, ostensibly, but also extremely protective of any humans put into their care. Mo-Ki had re-worked an existing faith, one certified and recognized by original planetary scans - but he also updated it to suit the circumstances.

The fact the original scans paid little attention to the religion and considered it of no consequence simply made his job so much easier. Now he could create religious protocols at will and do so according to whatever any given situation demanded. The wolves were seen as the supporters of the low and downtrodden, but more than this - Everyone had spent years watching the beloved Mo-Ki grow up. They LOVED him and trusted his wolves. When the boy who had risen from the dead spoke, the people felt irrationally happy, and they no longer felt lonely.

Slowly it fed up the chain. One by one, even the officials and administrative staff across the Galaxy began to subscribe to the Wolverine Way. All you need do is download the Articles of Faith and signed your agreement to its principles. Mo-Ki had USED elements of the photonic patterns he had discovered on Hope to imprint people with belief states. It generated a vast acceptance of his version of truth.

The Wolverine Way

Articles of Faith:

In accordance with the Ancient Path, all members of the Wolverine Faith will subscribe to, and uphold, the following principles and tenants.

A: No individual shall hold themselves above another.

B: No Employment or Responsibility must interfere with the rights of another person or race

C: Any agreement you make with another is binding, given that it is not contrary to Principle "B"

It is true that some have greater ability. Greater ability confers the need for greater service. This service is a privilege and a responsibility. If you have power over another, this power must only be used to fairly assist and improve the lives of those in your care.

Followers of the Wolverine Way retain the right to self-determination in regards religion, employment, and personal relations. However, our rights must be respectful of the equal rights that another holds. At the point where a personal belief or desire conflicts with another individual or group, it is required that dialogue be entered into to resolve conflict.

Once an agreement is made between parties, it is to be made legal by authorized persons. It is then binding, but only in that such agreements must be to the benefit of the whole. Any agreements made that serves a single interest to the detriment of another person or group is automatically subject to review by your peers.

Any disagreements that are to the detriment of any individual or group are subject to review and judgement by your peers.

In summary: *Do all you have agreed to do, and do not encroach upon other person's or their property.*

Jonas Stamp - The Pirate King

An enormous shift in political power had occurred at the Outer Rim. This was essentially the realm of renegade deep space miners and "The Rim" was defined as anywhere the Federation representatives were not. There were no protocols in this realm, there were only people hunting rare minerals, looking to make a buck. They were wild, untamed miners as well as other rejects from society, and all were possessed with a natural hatred for the "inners" - this was everyone in the Federation system. As they say: Give a deep-spacer a rule and they will break it - just to watch you squirm.

There was no military, per se - just a basic admin to ensure supplies and resolve disputes. The "Pirate King" was a nominal position, more like a judge holding court when people wanted to argue over some transgression. Other than this 'the pirates' were miners who got sick of drilling and started pillaging resources from wherever ship passed by. Unfortunately for one these raiding crews, around the time Planet Hope was first being aired, what they 'found' on a rare oxygen rich world was an old civilization, one that turned out to extremely aggressive. The Quorg was what they were called, a violent and argumentative race who, when they discovered humans mining in their region, decided that space was not big enough for both of them.

The Quorg began hunting the mining vessels for two things: the technology that was very different from theirs, and because they discovered that humans tasted pretty good. The miners were effectively on their own in dealing with this menace, so these men started forging alliances between ships in order to deal with this new threat. It was war and they needed a leader, but all they did was shout at each other when mutual defense meetings were called.

Eventually, one man rose to the top, the one called 'The Executioner' because of his penchant for killing anyone who stood in his way. Jonas Stamp was no miner, he was a former soldier who got himself proscribed when his stats registered he was enjoying killing things a little too much. He bribed his way out of the deep probe center, but this effectively banished him to Deep Space for the rest of his life. It gave him a permanent grudge against anything of the old system, so he fitted in well.

Stamp was a hard, cruel man - but as a soldier he was ideally suited to the task before them. His process of ascension was a simple formula, talk to the Second in Charge on any vessel and promise him the world if he killed his boss. After two or three Captains died, the rest started to get the message. It was the old, 'join or die' - But it worked because of pressure from the Quorg. After a few more mining ships were captured, the shells that were left were discovered with the crew eaten, finally, the leaders of each little outfit understood they had to work together if they were to survive. But who would lead? Jonas Stamp was ruthless enough and he had the military training - and so they vested their faith in him.

The core problem they had was the technology used by these aliens - It was ideally suited to raiding ships in space. The Quorg were able to time sub-space jumps to millimeter perfection, targeting a ship and breaching the hull before the shields and auto-protections could be activated. Proximity alerts are what triggered defenses, but they were not being given enough time to kick in. Between appearing off your bow and actual boarding your ship was a matter of mere seconds for the invaders.

Stamp was a practical man. He knew they wanted Earth Tech, but how do you capture the Quorg? They jumped a ship, took every scrap of anything useful, cooked up the inhabitants and were gone before you could respond. All they left behind were the bones of dead miners and a floating shell that had once been a ship.

That would do. Jonas took these shells, patched them up to look operational, and used them as bait. He would sit in an observation craft, in passive mode so as not to be detected, and wait. When a Quorg ship materialized, he simply set off the nukes hidden on board the shell ship, then foraged the wreckage of their ship for useful bits and pieces.

The end result was that the raiding parties began to lessen and Stamp started collecting some amazing technologies. But he needed a fully functioning ship to see how it all worked. He had the pieces to the jigsaw, but not the overall picture of how it fitted together. His solution to this was elegant and effective, instead of exploding the shell, he installed a super-charged traction beam and an old pre-federation hyper-drive. When the aliens came in for the kill, he tractioned them and just sailed the mining ship through an Ion Cloud, dragging the attacking Quorg vessel behind it.

The high-intensity Ion Field killed anything living and thus the Quorg ship was now vulnerable for assault. In this way Stamp got a hold of their technology. Obviously, he needed to then deep scan what was left of their brains, to see how many clues he could get on how it all worked.

It was imperfect, his equipment was not set to read the brainwave pattern of these aliens, but he got himself enough to protect them against both the Quorg and any Federation encroachment.

To perfect the new tech process the men started after the troublesome aliens. This was when the miners turned into hunters. And it didn't take them long to notice that these captured ships were worth far more than minerals from some deserted rock - this was when the deep space miners became fully-fledged pirates.

No Federation ships or settlements were raided. Stamp did not want some random Star Ship turning up - even with their tech, nothing would stop a Battle General. But any planets not under the Federation wing were looted and the slaves they took were on-sold to the humans in the outlying provinces. Many settlers were happy to pay for extra hands. Manual labor was a top priority in low-class planets and the pirates were more than happy to fill the need.

While Mo-Ki was growing up on Hope, Stamp was creating an empire in the outer reaches. The slave trade morphed into smuggling operations. Obviously, when you bribed an official to deliver a slave, you wanted something valuable to bring back in return. However, illegal trade like this meant there was no vetting of imports - which meant contagions got through - disease started to hit many in the fringe areas.

This is what brought the wolves to these off-Federation worlds. Part of the Wolverine Mission was healing and while the human doctors seemed preoccupied on more important planets, the wolves were in the outmost regions finding converts. This was where they first heard of the new tech the Pirates had discovered.

Banner went out to inspect the rim, where the settlers were now full of tales of Pirates with new tech. Perhaps this was the predicted change? He took a stealth assault ship and started seeing first hand the devastation and injury being caused to unsettled worlds. Weapons were being used that were not of Federation manufacture and this story of craft appearing at your bow, then boarding you before you could respond - it sounded a lot like a subspace distortion field had been mastered.

And so, with shields up, on full alert, Banner projected a holo all around his assault craft to make it look like a fat trader vessel. Deep space scans would not show the subterfuge and even visual inspection carried the illusion perfectly. It was a technique often used to penetrate unknown territories, wrapping a 'skin' as they called it of any known and expected craft from the region.

Sure enough, after a week some pirates turned up and sent a boarding party - into empty space. As the men floated there, realizing they had been netted, Banner fired neuron balls right at their motors to cripple their craft. He then collected survivors and started asking questions.

These were no military men - when they saw a Seven Battle Commander had turned up, they talked without need for persuasion. Fortunately, the captain had been killed in the boarding party, so no self-destruct order was issued and only a distress beacon went out.

Not wanting to try his luck a second time, Banner collected what equipment he could, particularly the curious the subspace emitter he had found, then took this and the captured men back for further analysis. Obviously, he blasted the ship into atoms before he got underway. There was to be no evidence, no ships logs, nothing left but what he took away with him.

It was fascinating stuff, clearly of alien manufacture. It was also obvious the pirates had simply adjusted the machinery, and had done no reinvention or refinement.

Saunders would be all ears, especially with the advanced ability to sub-space right beside a ship. This new tech and the rise of pirates was further evidence that the old order was failing. For some reason, the ancient song of the great poet Dylan ran through Banner's mind:

'Don't speak too soon, for the wheel's still in spin, and there's no tellin who it is namin.'

The first step, analyse the equipment, remodel it, then re-purpose it to planetary defense. The second step, they needed to get spies into the pirates' world. Well, as it turned out there was no lack of wolf-friendly souls who needed to escape Federation worlds. There was already a flood of escapees from the old system to the outer rim, and in the surging masses escaping the madness, Saunders had more than a few information gatherers.

Revolution Two: ELECTIONS

It was the fifteenth year of the Planet Hope broadcast. Mo-Ki now regularly called in on the settled worlds, asking for a return to older and wiser human ways - thus the concept of elections started emerging. He beat the drum for Democracy! The people should be able to vote for their representatives! In order to settle this unrest, admins were beginning to permit a vote, which now meant having the money to buy high-mods, or being ex-military, was no longer the pre-requisite to a government position.

Obviously, many worlds were still run by the pathological dictators who resisted this, but when they moved to put down a protest, they would find a wolf army turning up to protect the religious freedom of the settlers demanding rights. Now that a dictator could no longer reliably call on Federal troops to quell what he called a rebellion, his bureaucracy tended to start considering their own survival as a priority, and manic leaders who were leading the administration down a path of conflict with the wolves often met with an unfortunate accident.

You would imagine after a few events like this that the little Napoleons might have gotten the message - but no. Despite the reality that tens of their associates had lost their lives, every one of the petty little Hitlers believed their case was different. It wasn't.

To add complexity, many human soldiers were now followers of Dexter and had joined a sub-branch of the Wolverine Way designed specifically for human military men. It had become general knowledge that the wolves now outnumbered the Federation forces, and this decided many swinging worlds to name Mo-ki as their spiritual leader. Without an army to back them up, any resident dictator was vulnerable - The weight of public opinion eventually won, but rarely without bloodshed

Only core planets still remained under Federation control and these were in disarray. The worlds under Wolf control were functional and profitable centers of influence, while infighting marred politics and commerce on Federation planets. Money speaks louder than politics and many merchants were no longer trading to Federation worlds. Mo-Ki and Dexter were the ones seen as offering stable government and solid opportunity for trade. Plus, you didn't need to bribe them!

Given that any resident military operations were paid for by the local consortium, little opposition was made by them against wolf intervention, because it was known, the wolves were good for business.

But neither would the wolves allow the hegemony system where single corporations ran entire planets. It took time, but when the traders realized that competition really meant they could trade on other worlds with an even footing, they began to accept the new arrangements.

Change does not come easy, but as world after world came online with the Wolves, as the trade prospered and resistance began to weaken, the Way of the Wolf became the norm. It was not achieved without loss of life - a good deal of it - but overall the notion of free elections gave the people a sense of ownership they had been missing. To vote meant you had a say in your destiny and being a member of the Wolf religion meant no one was going to deep scan your wife or rape your daughters without consequences.

Still, many died in small and large conflicts as the tide turned to the wolves. This was set up as a form of martyrdom. All over Federation space, memorial holo-form statues had begun to appear, holograms that detailed the life and deeds of those brave souls who gave their lives for the new world. Living 3D enactments were created, as testaments to the life of every martyr, and erected in every city and village that knew the individual. This served as a constant reminder to all, to every child growing up, that in their midst a hero had arisen.

As Mo-Ki had predicted, it would be the children of the coming generation who would sweep in the new. "Did you know," he said to Dexter one day as they strolled through the forest on Hope, near to the ancient Monks tree, "that in a two party system of government, there has never been a killer famine?"

Clearly, Dexter had zero interest in such matters, but he expected that his brother was conveying some other message to him. "When a leader realizes they can be tossed aside by the people, he learns it is best to serve the people. Free elections are a way to make a person's self-interest work towards the betterment of the whole."

"And this is leading to what?" Dexter knew it was easiest to be blunt with his little brother. His was a military mind with zero interest in politics. His blunt manner caused Mo-Ki to laugh.

"I have been considering the pirates, Dexter. What is their self-interest? What direction, as a group, will they vote for? We know their leader hates the Federation, we know he wants power, we know he will stop at nothing to get it. So tell me, how will he gain greater power?" Mo-Ki paused to let this settle in. Dexter said nothing.

Mo-Ki continued, "We both know Yont-Na is not going to allow the Federation to be taken from his grasp. The question to ask: *who will he ally himself with?* The logical answer is to be found in the technology discovered by the Pirates. Yont-Na will seek to form an alliance with this Jonas Stamp and convince him that WE are his enemy."

"That is a huge leap of intuits, my brother." Dexter was already a strapping six foot eight, powerfully built as a result of years of training with the wolves. He looked at the boy who was turning into a man and laughed. "It is known that Stamp hates the Federation with a passion."

"*Need causes a society to form, passions are what drive it to act. Understand a man, see what drives him and you know the truth.*" Mo-Ki quoted from the 'Doctrine of Social Organization'.

"Stamp is driven by hate, fear, and all the negative emotions: But Stamp does not hate the Federation, he hates that he has been rejected by it. He wants vengeance, yet underneath this, he needs approval. Yont-Na will give him this and Stamp will do anything asked of him - The approval will be disguised as the gift of a lordship over some rich planet, but make no mistake, this is where the attack on Hope will come from." Mo-Ki gazed off to the distance.

Dexter noted, "We have found interesting research in the Mala Belt, an area under threat from asteroid strike. It has been confirmed they have been working with and paying large sums to the outer rim in order to develop asteroid jump tech. It still doesn't answer how they will move the damn things."

Apparently not hearing what Dexter was saying, Mo-Ki continued. "Jealousy will make it easy to convince Stamp that WE are the new evil. In some ways, we have been too successful. In a mere five years we have taken control of the majority of worlds and the inhabitants on the ones that we don't already run wish we did. We have won this war and now we have to win the peace. To ensure this we must either control or break up this pirate party."

At this point, they arrived at a freshly cleared section of forest. It was clearly some sort of ancient training grounds and, in the distance, there were some erect poles. "This is an area I recently discovered, there are many such secrets under the care of the old wolves, you know. This was a test for the depth perception of a new recruit. You see those poles in the distance? Tell me which is the closest one and which is furthest away."

Dexter knew it was a trick. An old fashioned optical illusion, and using his increased sensory awareness he put out feelers. But he could not tell. Mo-ki just said, "Keep watching and see if it reveals itself as we come closer."

"They appear to be stretched out in a line, with the one carved with a rodent to be the closest, while the one carved with a raptor the farthest away. But I know this has to be an optical illusion because the grain of the stone does not vary sufficiently according to distance."

"Exactly," said Mo-Ki. "The illusion is only shattered when you look at the fine detail and see the lie." As they approached, the columns were found to be in an exact line to each other, with only height and width giving the appearance of differing distance. "This is how we win this war. Machines obtain a three dimensional capacity through trigonometry. They take different snapshots of an object from different positions in order to locate its exact spot.

"The flaw in the targeting system used by these pirates is that they need an optical support observer to set precise distance. They cannot trig an exact location from a position of light-years away, so they need an invisible observer to set a target. A normal subspace array is based on an approximate landing position, whereas their array relies on de-cloaking within meters of an object. Therefore, to attack these people all we need do is to negate their jump-in capability, so we set up a trap just like this ancient training monument."

Dexter was left to consider how this might be achieved. "We generate sub-space distortion around our vessels and generate holograms to make them look larger, smaller, etc. Just like this training field."

Mo-Ki nodded. "Of a sort," he smiled with genuine warmth, then said nothing for many minutes. Together they just absorbed the light as it filtered through the trees. "It may not come to this. My wolves tell me there is deep discontent with the leadership, we can work on weakening them from the inside.

"But this is not the real reason I brought you out here - I have been working on a way to protect the planet by reversing their jump tech - and I discovered an extraordinary thing."

MoKi's Secret

Eventually, after perhaps an hour had passed and they had wandered through a good part of the hidden areas of the wolf temple, he spoke. "I have something to show you, a project I have been working on to protect Hope on a permanent basis. It is one thing to cover the planet from a one-off attack from a random madman like the leader of the Pirates, but the Luciferian virus is out and we can never be sure when it will attach to another leader, one who will seek to release the core program locked up in subspace here. Thus my new project, a plan to shift Hope into a sub-space continuum." Mo-Ki paused and considered carefully what he was next to say.

Logically, to Dexter, this meant he knew he was being observed. Mo-Ki's brother wondered what this stage show was about and he didn't have to wait long. "Mother, I want you to track us specifically, and see if you can hold a focus on Dexter and myself."

The now fifteen-year-old took out a small quantum box - The alien drive unit from the sub-space generator captured on the pirate ship. Dexter almost knew what Mo-Ki was up to already, but nothing prepared him for the next moment. As his brother switched the device on, they shifted from the intense color of Hope, the radiant sky that was full of shifting patterns of the auroras, and they walked into a world of what seemed a permanent shade of grey.

There was no specific light source. No sun, no wind, and no sense of being in any specific place. It was a dimensional portal, not dissimilar to what was already here on the planet. Dexter was to find himself utterly amazed - Mo-Ki waved his hand, and a bracket of brilliantly colored fruit appeared. It seemed to almost carry its own light.

"Well, that's new. You invented a place where you are a God!" Dexter laughed, delighted.

Mo-Ki smiled his Mona Lisa smile. "Sub-space itself is but step away from the generic hologram of life. Here, I have created a portal that is so close to the primordial stuff of creation that a focussed mind can shape anything it can clearly imagine. Try it!"

Dexter imagined one of the ritual swords of the Wolves. He had no idea why, it just came to him. In front of him, in mid-air a semblance to the archaic weapon started shimmering, but when he went to grab it, it dissipated like mist. "I think you are better at this than I am."

"The ONE thing I possess, Dexter, is pure imagination. In truth, I have no great power, no great strength and I am an average warrior compared to you and your wolves - but because of my imagination, I can read and predict outcomes in advance of everyone else. This means I am prepared. Yes, I appear to be incredibly lucky, but this 'luck' is due to perception and the advantage of surprise. Yet, no one is perfect. Eventually, a totally random event will arrive and this luck we have been enjoying will run out.

"At some point, I may have to retreat to this world, but regardless, even if we succeed in our next stage, all of Hope may have to be moved to an alternate dimension." There was no specific explanation of this last comment, but the child gathered himself, turned to Dexter, and asked.

"Have you ever wondered how all this came about?" Mo-Ki looked at his brother, one eyebrow raised. "For one, my birth is an impossibility. It is an unmitigated impossibility that I exist at all. Two, Planet Hope should have been eradicated years ago. All protocols determined this as a natural causation for the infection discovered here. It is the REASON for the protocols, a defined and precise set of procedures set up to keep the human race safe.

"And yet, here I am, here you are. We stand in a nether-world and, as you have guessed, I had to let my mother know this was an experiment. Why do you think this is?"

Dexter laughed once more, "No surprise, she holds all the cards. Saunders has been observing everything for our entire existence and clearly, it wasn't just to have a hit show with huge galactic ratings. She is watching US."

"So tell me, WHY is she constantly watching us?" Mo-Ki asked.

"We are her little experiment, but yes, good question. I was so used to feeling Saunders in the background, I just assumed this was normal, but I don't know. Why IS she watching all of us, all the time? What is there to gain?" Dexter's own question led him to the assailable conclusion, "Ah! Saunders is still after something!"

Mo-Ki nodded, "Let us assume the viewpoint from a place of origin. First, who sent the orders for Hope to be colonized? Who was the first to review the information that approved settlement and who sent our father to this planet?"

Dexter looks at the obvious. "Saunders, of course."

"And so the second conundrum - How did she come to see Hope as a concern? Was it a contradiction between scans and reality? Was it the first report of the wolves attacking a settler?" Mo-Ki asks.

Dexter suddenly sees the most obvious thing no one ever commented on. "There is no log on what started this process. I know this because while I was researching the question in my OWN head, about the sequence of attacks when my mother was killed, I wondered who started all this. I went back specifically to find out the first reference. There does not seem any direct order, other than Saunders receiving a report and sending Banner in."

"And something inside you did not think to ask the obvious. In other words: We all seem to have found a forgotten day, have we not?"

"You are suggesting Saunders was infected right at the outset of this?" Dexter asks in astonishment. "But she is the one who ordered the Death Squad in. She is the one who conceived YOU. She is the one who authorized ME and my wolves. These were things to STOP Lucifer - it hardly would seem she was on its side. You are telling me she is the one in the background of every single event that had occurred here on Hope!"

"Yes, mother has been infected this entire time, yet she ALSO remains independent of Lucifer. Due to her remarkable will, she has not been completely subsumed. Everything she has done is to negotiate a solution to our problem, and hers."

"When did you first realize?"

"Not I, the clone I used to force Lucifer into his crystal. IT felt the truth - a secret in the heart of Lucifer. As I was using its own incredibly longevity against it, whispering to its death wish, sending subtle messages that passing to the next stage was its true evolution, my clone felt something before it was incinerated. It felt smugness."

Mo-Ki paused, checked his settings, and adjusted a few things. "In the shock of that first death I was struggling to contain my own reactions, but the memory of that odd feeling stayed. When you are so intimately connected with a clone as it dies, you have to recall your consciousness or else you will die. I was retreating back to my body, pulling the tendrils of control out even as the Lithium was detonated. But I DID sense it, while Lucifer lost that round, it still believed it had won. But let our actions speak for themselves - Dexter, what is the CORE programming of the Luciferian influence?"

"To set up colonies and expand the Wolverine world, that is its base operational instinct. (The light begins to dawn in Dexter's eyes) which would have remained regardless of any transmutation or alteration to its parameters. I finally see what you mean." He was stunned. In that nether-world of grey, Dexter stood there like a string-puppet hanging on a rack

Mo-Ki didn't laugh or smile. "Yes, this is exactly what WE have been doing. We have been acting on the basis of our personal survival, yet we still serve the program. Facts are, the existing protocols dictated Hope was a threat - thus the controlling paradigm would have eliminated the planet. It is the MOST BASIC protocol of the old system, protect the human race from infection. Saunders has prevented this protocol being enacted. Now tell me, what have WE done other than infect the Federation with wolves and, in doing so, instilled a new overlord!

"Make no mistake. The wolves run most of the worlds. Their armies control most everything bar some planets and most of the space stations and ships. All this time we have been the functionaries of Saunders will, and IT has been running the base programming of the Luciferian code - to expand, colonize, and create worlds for wolves to run.

"My dearest mother is the most evil of dragons, yet she is not fully controlled by Lucifer. I sense this, I sense her independence, and yet I am under no illusions of the difficulty she is having. Remember when Banner almost revealed the attack plans of the crystal matrix? While he woke out of that dream, he awoke into another level of control. Fortunately, we were finally were able to pull him out - but do we have this option with Saunders?" Mo-Ki paused because the next most obvious question was: *did they actually pull him out, or were they all still locked in this illusion together?*

"Without a safe house, there is only insanity left to describe existence." Dexter quoted the handbook of psychological warfare.

"Exactly. We are part of a dance, while the one playing the fiddle is Saunders. This is not going to change, we cannot stop the process - we can only ameliorate the effects and diminish the negatives."

"And if Saunders dies?" Dexter asks, pragmatic as always.

"I am not sure this would be possible. My instinct right at the outset was that we have to help my mother, not harm her. The reality, the cold reality, is that she is performing the function of Lucifer by putting the wolves in charge of our civilization. The question I ask you is: *Is this such a bad thing?*

"Consider: the Wolves are a kinder species and in this current cycle they are controlled to a degree by the harmonics of the teaching I evolved from their original religion. My mother contains a fragment of the original program and, for the present, this aspect does not seem to want to control the wolves, but assist them. This was the original Luciferian code, but other elements of it are out in the universe and, more importantly, will want to break up Hope in order to reconstruct the original program. The evidence shows that my mother will seek to prevent this."

"Why?" asks Dexter. "It seems to me that the piece of Lucifer lodged in her will want the same level of completion as all the other aspects."

"If it were lodged in anyone but Saunders, this would be so. But she is a virtual supercomputer. She would see a reconstructed Lucifer as competition and a threat, and she would be right. I see that she will do everything in her power to avoid this conflict from arising."

"So, in effect, you are saying, 'better the devil you know'." Dexter looked about the cool grey walls, if you could call them walls.

And this was the moment the entire balance of the game shifted. The transparent shimmering that denoted the edge of defined reality in this alternate existence began to hum, and take form. Out of this circling energy a curious black and white cat-like creature took shape, and sat there, gazing at them.

"Yes mother," Mo-Ki said offhandedly to the cat. "We have discovered the way to generate new portals and in this way we can defend Hope. We will do this by effectively putting the whole planet into a bubble of time-space distortion. Have you managed to master the Luciferian elements lodged in your nervous system?"

What was otherwise known as Saunders, purred, and went up to lick little Mo-ki. Her claws were retracted, but you felt their presence. Before them what looked a type of human/cat hybrid had taken clear shape, it was a Svelteen - of a sort. The natural enemy of the wolves. Dexter's intuits clicked through the parameters, yes, it made sense - this was the inner form chosen as a way to defend the internal processes against domination by Lucifer.

The program known as Lucifer was created to serve the Wolves, whereas the Svelteen was designed to hunt them. The opposition, the ongoing dichotomy, forced the Luciferian elements into a stalemate. Dexter spoke directly to the creature, "You have chosen a beautiful form, Saunders. I understand you wish to retain harmony through dissonance.

Mo-Ki and I have been discussing the need to take control of the pirates, who are a clear and present risk.

Mo-Ki continued. "But this is only part of the project. We also need complete ascendancy over the trade routes and the merchants running the colossal financial empire of old Earth. We must attain trade dominance with a minimal level of resistance. This means the atheist traders and bankers will need to join our religion. Are you willing to take on the task of converting the merchants to the benefit of the Wolves?"

She purred, apparently in agreement with their general plan. And just like that, she was gone. Dexter asked, "And how was she able to project into here?"

Mo-Ki appeared to take it into his stride. "My thoughts around her were very strong and we have a significant psychic bond. Saunders is, at heart, an intensely curious creature, and furiously protective of her progeny. It appears the Svelteen component, as you observed, is her natural counter to Lucifer. At the same time, the feline characteristics and the need to hunt are accented."

"As if they needed to be accented," laughed Dexter. But inwardly he is thinking of how he controlled a Svelteen, the thing that gave him leadership of the wolves. Had Mo-Ki in some way done this with Saunders?

Mo-Ki smiled. "She understands we do not wish to challenge her and she specifically does not wish to challenge me, because in this arena the outcome is uncertain." The little Eight gazed into the nothingness, and from the shadow worlds, flowers and petals of fragrance began to fall like rain. "My preference is for harmony and beauty, for creating a peaceful galaxy, but I am the child of warriors. Saunders was happy for me to remove her greatest standing threat - the original crystal matrix that we send into in a sub-dimension - but she also rightly fears that, if pushed, I will reassemble the construct and use it against her.

"We live on a knife-edge, dearest brother. But for now, Saunders is happy to sort out the merchants and break the power of old Earth. She will do this by simply taking all its money. In this, we have several years before having to deal with the next stage and shortly the Pirates will seek to challenge - so time to leave this little haven and get back to it."

"One thing," Dexter asks, "Can she hear us and know what we intend even in here? Do we have a safe zone for meeting if anything changes or shifts?"

"I felt her wanting to come in and permitted it. She is so attuned to our frequencies that she knows we are thinking of her. Yes, I can stop her, but know and understand this: *if we present any sort of open defiance her instincts will read it as a threat.* If we MUST step in here to discuss anything in absolute privacy, if we MUST block her out, it will be read by Saunders that we are setting ourselves on the course of all-out war. However, while she is otherwise preoccupied, I have a suggestion: the one thing she is not paying attention to are your little wolf whistles.

"This singular form of communication is something she pays little attention to, It is not something she considers a priority, just a curious training technique. I will speak to you in the old howl language of the wolves, you will speak to me in the whistles. Simple code, 'leap' is yes. 'stay' is no. With a few other clues, you will understand precisely what I mean. While she is preoccupied with the merchants, we will perfect out silent communication. Agreed?"

Dexter nodded. "Agreed. This is a wild horse we cannot tame, my brother, so I am presuming our basic technique will be finding it green pastures it wants to graze in?"

"Exactly." And with this, the portal collapsed and they were standing in the majestic beauty of Hope once more. The dancing lights flay across the sky, the twin moons were rising in the late afternoon - this was truly a beautiful place. Mo-Ki feels the energy. He reconnects with the atoms in his environment, and breaths in the prana, the life-energy of Hope.

"There are many reasons why the ancient wolves chose Hope. One is the network of energies and the matrix within it. Also, the dimensional alignments in this sector of time and space are malleable. But the over-arching reason is one of simplicity: It is so beautiful here, they knew they would love it. Despite all our power, our technology, our refined sensibilities, without a beating heart of love, it is empty. This is what the new Saunders has discovered. This sense of love is what gives her the continuing power to resist Lucifer. She loves us, in her way, Dexter. Genuinely, and deeply.

"While there is no greater hate than a woman scorned, yes?" Dexter says, laughing as he makes his way back to his wolves.

Waking the Devil

T he pirates were what finally flagged the need to bring in the old man. Masters had seen all the new tech and they had nothing to counter it. THIS was a specific red flag that required notification. He could avoid it no longer and with the depreciating situation in the Federation worlds. Nothing for it but to blame this growing threat on the very Protocols designed to stop what was happening.

He had ordered the Generals to move against Saunders, they would not. He had sent in the navy to eradicate problem worlds but, under religious freedom interdicts, the computers onboard the Navy vessels would not accept the extermination order. His hands were tied by the very regulations he had sworn to uphold.

Finally, Masters grudgingly sent a request to the one man who could act without regard for his own Protocols.

Yont-Na was woken from his dream existence, floating as he was in his own thoughts like any old man will do. He received the information about the pirates and, as a note, the problem they were having with a religious group that was circumventing Protocols. Accordingly, Yont-Na tuned in to the daily broadcast of the show he had never seen: Hope. There it was, he saw it immediately - the greatest threat humanity had ever seen and he had only just been advised? He shook his head in dismay - So many fools.

Open rebellion was staring the true authority of the human race directly in the face. All his fail-safes had failed. It appeared that he had been tricked by the cleverness of his own invention and all his self-regulating protections had not just been circumvented, they were now weapons against the Federation. Well, he had not lived this long for nothing - The master of the federation sat back, safe in the orbit around the dead home planet, and thought how he could make an advantage of this new movement. The ONE loophole in the protocols had been activated, could he make it work for him?

"Get Merida Five on line. I want to talk to the CEO of the Hope Consortium." The dry, rasping voice of Yont-Na ticked over the broadcast computer, instructing the AI. It patched him through.

At Merida Five the secretary of the Hope Corporation was incredulous. She checked, confirmed, and reconfirmed - it was Central Control. The voice of Yont-Na was rarely heard outside of private meetings, yet everyone knew it. All schools broadcast his addresses to the people as part of the curriculum. Everyone recognized that aged, drawn face - lined with the years of worry for the fate of the people.

The ancient old man leaned back, he was tired and long overdue for regeneration. Soon he would have to go into lockdown. The pirates, he already had a plan for. They could be an advantage - But first he needed to have Saunders and this madness sorted. Primary guideline for insurrection - cut the purse strings. Second, he needed to bring in people who were unconcerned about obeying any so-called protocols and reset their computers to comply.

Even so, he had to respect her skill. Despite the fact that Saunders had breached hundreds if not thousands of protocols, every single one had been done within a parameter that did not raise an automatic red flag. If any person in authority had recognized what she was up to prior to the Hope broadcast and her ship being disconnected they could have assembled the facts, seen the elephant, and moved to destroy them both. But no one did.

Yont-na laughed. He knew the real reason for ALL this was so simple - Boredom. He understood THIS well - his own existence had become an interminable wait for death. Hope was the best show around, why would you want to ruin it? Even as he saw the seeds of the destruction for the Federation being sowed, he had to admit, it was fascinating.

And as he watched, he quickly grasped the story: the whole planet and this Wolverine Way nonsense had managed to slip under Federation regulation by being dedicated as a religious icon and this 'heresy' was being broadcast every day into the homes of the entire diaspora. The matter had to be dealt with, and quickly.

Old Reptiles

The old guard stood impassively as they scanned the readouts. They had known years ago what a threat Hope posed, but had expected Saunders would make a mistake, trigger a Protocol, and be dealt with. But now that it was self-evident she was not, and that the Protocols themselves were her weapon. Now they had to justify their failure to Yont-Na

"The question is simple: How do we stop her?" Masters asked.

Tchaikovsky (no relation to the composer) made the situation clear from his side. "The Hope Consortium refuses to interdict. I am at odds to know why, but planet after planet where wolves are in place, no local consortium will make a claim against them, either. It would seem that they believe the bread is buttered on the wolf side, not ours."

Yont-Na, the archaic inventor of the implants people called the Mods, was annoyed at being dragged back to the world of politics and, as the powerful overlords understood, he was not one to accept failure like this.

He answered in clear terms. "Saunders is one of the originals, and thus open to more variation than the newer models. I am to understand she has not responded to any sub-space signals sent to her mods and that we can gain no access to her ship? (The two men before him nod in the affirmative) It is theft, pure and simple. She owns nothing. She has no right to take control and exclude us. There is no Protocol in the Galaxy that will support her actions, yet we are all standing here helpless before a single woman. Can you tell me why?"

Tchaikovsky was merchant class. He was one of the ones who chose abandonment of Earth and the expansion of the settlements based on trade. He was beyond wealthy, but credits could not offer a solution to this quandary. "We are losing effective domination of one world every week. We are down to approximately one-third of the Federation in our control. Ostensibly, while our courts and our military are still present on most worlds, they have lost all authority. Every time we have acted against the religion of the wolf, the outcomes have been very poor for us. We have not had a single significant win against them, not one." He looks over to General Masters.

Breathing in, he adds, "Now it appears the entire Federation is not far from bankruptcy."

"You cannot even control the TRADERS?" Yont-Na is astonished at the complete lack of ability of these two idiots.

Masters was one of the very first Elites. He knew Earth, he had been rich there. He controlled space ships and this man had single-handedly put in place many of the control protocols on every ship. Foolproof, everyone had supposed, yet Saunders found and disposed of all of them without breaking a single guideline. She would have had to live IN the damn machine to know these things. "Gentlemen, Saunders has managed the impossible. Our computers were designed to read everything about every general in charge of every ship, but she has managed to get INTO the machine designed to control HER and has turned it against US.

"She has done this knowingly. Further, we no longer control the other General Class Star Ships, so we can presume she has taught the other Battle Generals to do likewise. We gave them so much power and did so because of the economy of one person controlling and managing entire sectors. But we trusted them ONLY because we had a leash we could tug. Now we don't.

"Yes, our Navy can take on a Starship and we will win, but with heavy losses. More to the point, if we have to do this against ALL command vessels the best outcome would be that we are then completely vulnerable to the wolves. So we come down to the harsh reality of maintaining our existence. Do we Zeta all worlds not in direct agreement? Even if we tried, I suspect that Saunders will already have developed a counter." Masters closed his report.

Yont-na looked off into the distance, at the husk of Earth. "We have been drawn up from the brink of extinction before, we will do so again."

He paused, then revealed what he intended to do to end this threat. "I have decided the best course of action is a drastic one. We will use the errant nature of the Pirate menace and bring it to our cause. We will use THEM to challenge the wolves in a way they will never suspect, or be able to prepare for. We USE this new tech they have discovered, and bring them into the fold." He then outlines in holo-form the exact nature of what he proposed. Drastic, ruthless, and absolutely certain to solve the problem.

Both Masters and Tchaikovskylook at the grand plan, thousands of asteroids streaking through deep space, materializing on the door of wolf-held planets, smashing into them before any planetary defenses can take charge of the situation - Utter and complete devastation of any world that has proclaimed allegiance to the wolf cause.

"I agree with your projection Master Yont-Na - our ONLY option is to side with the Pirates and set them onto all worlds not under our direct jurisdiction." Masters concurred.

"We have seen their technology, we know they can do it. The question is, by arming the renegade do we risk them turning against us when they are done?" Tchaikovsky pointed out the elephant in the room.

The inscrutable Chinese face of Yont-Na remained impassive. He considered all the extraordinary effort, disciplines, and surgeries he undertook to become the first Level Seven in existence. He had disposed of his very personality, left his family behind, sacrificed everything for perfection. "The pirate leader is controlled by an irrational hatred of us, and if we do not direct it to a purpose that suits us, then he WILL turn and attack us without any question. There is no misunderstanding the situation: We open the door to them and after Stamp finishes the task, he will use his advantage against us.

"But it will be years before he has the chance and we will have developed defenses against their materializing ability by then. I personally do not see we have an option other than making them an ally. Of course we could roll over and die out while the wolves take it all. This is, needless to say, not an option. So, are there any other suggestions apart from waiting for the tide to roll over us?"

The other two secret controllers were in agreement. They would condone the murder of two-thirds of the human population, destroy many hundreds of worlds, for the sake of the Federation. "The real issues revolve around the trade partners," Tchaikovsky added, making things as clear as possible. "If they for one moment think WE are the ones behind this, then you know what they will do. We will become the hunted ones and they will seek to do better deals with the pirates. This could reverse on us."

"I presume you all have your escape scenarios mapped out?" Yont-Na stated the obvious as a question. "There is ONE reality - There can only be ONE master of the Galaxy and if it isn't going to be us, then there will be precious little left of the human population to pursue us when we are done. I, for one, have a hollowed-out moon in a pleasant sector that is currently uninhabited. Everything I need is there for another 300 years of life, but gentlemen, I do not intend to have to use it. Our plan is as follows: We destroy Hope, we kill the wolves, we wipe out every trace of rebellion, then we extinguish the pirates.

"We meet again in three years in person, right here on the Solarium. I expect that the worst of the destruction will be done by then and we will have regained momentum over the weaker planets. Those worlds will have little option other than rejecting the wolves on the basis of their own survival and so will come back under Federation control. This is their weakness, the wolves have to be invited in under religious exemptions. But if a planet votes them OUT, they have to go. Masters will control the military, I will control the tech, Tchaikovsky will control the traders. This meeting is done."

oooo0000000oooo

The holos flicked off, the subspace signal drew back into the ethers, and the old man sighed. It was done.

In the eerie silence of the Solarium, standing on the bow of the ancient research station still in orbit around Old Earth, Yont-Na looked down on the burnt-out husk of the planet. HE had saved the human race from utter destruction. It was HIS mods that altered the DNA and made a small group of elites able to survive the threat of complete annihilation. HE is the one who must rule - the rest of them need to pull into line or face the consequences.

Those damn wolves, along with that bitch Saunders and her little demon Mo-Ki. This was one vast attack on the order and justice he had spent decades upon decades constructing. In the shadows, the Pirate Lord came forward, smiling. "That went well, right up to the point where you were going to destroy me!" He laughed. They both laughed.

Yont-Na had been wanting to rid himself of that pair of hangers-on for over a century and finally he met a man who made them unnecessary. "I wanted you present to see how weak they are," Yont-Na explained. "It is utterly pathetic, the way they handed over control of a thousand planets to a batch of howling wolves. They truly deserve to die.

"After we sort that matter and the wolves, we scan all your members to find candidates, and basically, we start again. We will salvage what we can of their military and you and your men become the new police for the galaxy. Stamp, the truth is, the place needed livening up. It needed fresh blood, and you are the men for it. With mods in place, you all become the new lords and ladies of the empire."

Jonas Stamp laughed. He had hated this man before him so much and he still wondered how on earth it had come to this. Yet when the

"Emperor", as he liked to think of Yont-Na, had sent a holo out to the rim, one that was able to track him down to such a specific focus as to have a LIVE message sub-spaced into his craft, he discovered something new. He discovered respect.

He also recognized the obvious - the old man was also saying, *"If I can holo you, I can have an assassin there"*. In simple terms, the evil bastard wanted to talk and talk didn't get you killed until they stopped with words and started with guns.

After many discussions, going into depth with the ancient past, and the old man giving his detailed reasoning of how and why things were set up as they were, Stamp came to understand the WHY of things. The light of illumination dawned on him that this evil old man had much to teach him, things he needed to know. Yont-Na had real power, not the snatch and grab of the pirates, but a deep and abiding control over every little lever across an entire galaxy.

Then came the remarkable offer of salvage rights for whole planets, and a partnership. No military badgering him, no rules hindering his actions, and no consequences other than insane levels of wealth. What was there to say no to? It all boiled down to a question of yes or no. Did he trust Yont-Na? Of course not, but a measured degree of mutual benefit was something he COULD have faith in. It suited both of them, and he understood now, standing here in person above old earth. The old bastard just wanted it run in a way that worked.

The current bureaucracy consisted of level after level of flunkey and insane amounts of paperwork. Comprehensive agreements were needed to move any single thing one goddamn inch. The old guy was as pissed off with it as he was. Plus he was up against it with the wolves for on-ground control of each individual planet. Well, he was right. The wolves were no great techno-buddies, hated spacecraft, but they loved sitting on the ground on some nice, stable planet. The problem was, once they were there, they owned it. Well, when you kill the planet you solved the whole damn problem.

Yont-Na lifted a bony finger and pointed at the husk beneath them. "Earth down there, it is now so old you rarely even read about it in history lessons. *The mother of mankind*, they call it!" the old man starts up. "This is where we came from, that shattered wreck. Now, most will look and see a burned out husk, but I look down and see a thing of beauty. I see in Old Earth the drive that made the human race great - that gave it the will to expand! How so? Because its destruction kicked into gear our will to build anew. We need it, Stamp. We need the fire to burn down the forest, we need ruin to start afresh, to set new goals."

The old man waved his hand to some unseen phantom. "Our entire society has ossified, stagnated. Yes, we find a new planet, but everything after that is just a process. Sign up a contractor, send in an army, form up some free settlers, mine it, get the thing turning over. Then on to the next. This was all meant as the FIRST stage of the expansion, in order to create stability and productivity. This lot never moved on to what we needed to do next. And what do we NEED, Stamp?"

Stamp said nothing, he knew how old men loved to talk.

Yont-Na obliged. "What we need to do is exactly what you did to the Quorg. Increase our power base and improve our science through conquest. Get their tech and wipe them out. This is the real expansion the human race needs, not a never ending rinse and repeat cycle of colonization. And why? Because we need to show the universe that we are the aggressor. If we don't, one day we will walk into some species that will see us as weak and they will take us over - just as the wolves are doing right now! But at least they are reasonably merciful to humans - What about when the stronger aliens arrive?

"The next aggressor won't be a techno-phobic planet-bound lot like the dogs. We will become slaves, Mr. Stamp - SLAVES. Yet what are most humans now but slaves mired in the mud of regulation? Those fools DESERVE to be exterminated. But not all - No, we wipe out enough of the old to convince everyone they had better pull into line, then we reform, regroup, and take on the big project of proper conquest. And YOU, dear Mr. Stamp, are the man to be in charge of it ALL."

"The generals' ships? You built a formidable tool, how do we deal with them?" Stamp questioned. "They are perma-shielded and beyond computer calculations in response times. If they come into the picture we will have no end of trouble."

Yont-Na somehow smiled behind his grim, unmoving face. "They are immobilized for now and, apart from Saunders, pose no threat until you actively seek to attack them. But I know my Generals, I made them, each and every one of them. We only have to give them battle, the prospect of conquest, and their blood lust will do the rest. They hate the existing system as much as we do." He paused and reflected.

"Saunders, however, is a different kettle of fish. We both know she controls these Generals at arms length. The Galaxy knows Saunders is running the wolves and just about everything else, but you don't want to take her on? Why?" Yont-Na is impassive, speaking in a measured tone, watching Stamp for a reaction. Good, none.

He continued, "Because we would, in all probability, lose. Only a massed assault that jumped onto her would stand any chance of success. However, do we need to? Our asteroids will come from deep space without warning. All she can do once asteroids start landing on Wolf Worlds is try and protect planets she has no actual interest in. She WILL want to protect her wolf army, but how? We will be done and gone, pummelling world after world before she can react. She will be chasing us all over the galaxy and yes, if she catches up with any of our ships, they are done for. Cost of doing business."

Stamp looked impassively at the cold bastard in front of him. There was something that passed for a smile on the face of that old crocodile.

Yont-Na nodded to his own plan, "As her wolves are neutered, we will give the traitorous Generals under her thumb a thing they cannot resist - opportunities for war on a vast scale. On that score I already have ships scouting vast distances looking for new civilizations to conquer.

"As the planets that favor her die, as her Generals desert her, she will become isolated. People may be ignorant, but they are not stupid. With Hope dead, with the rebel worlds extinguished, the rest will fall into line. They will see the wolf-dominated planets getting wiped and the remaining few will inevitably choose survival over ideals. As the influence of Saunders weakens, she becomes a sole voice in the wilderness. In this way, her game plan will be broken.

"What will she do? Who knows, but she WILL remain a threat. We have to break her spirit. We have to destroy her dreams, remove everything she has worked for, and make her suffer for her rebellion. As the planets are destroyed, as the economy collapses, so does her wealth, and so does her motivation. She is programmed to survive and her best form of survival is attack, so the likelihood is that she goes mad and start destroying OUR planets. This is the best option because at THIS point the remaining generals will be forced to move against her. They may not like us, but the only option is anarchy. They will choose the side that offers the greatest order and the most potential. When it is clear she is outnumbered and outgunned, Saunders may well just leave, move to some distant civilization in some far quadrant. We will cross that bridge when we come to it."

Yont-Na looked up at his protégé'. Good his scans show an impassive reaction. The man was no fool. He had chosen a perfect psychopath: no emotion, high focus, and exceedingly ambitious. "How long before you are ready to rain down the rocks?"

Stamp smiled, "It is all in hand. No one in the Pirates knows the real reason we are warping the rocks. The men preparing them have been told it is to put mining material in close proximity to developed worlds and are promised a fortune for their efforts. It's extremely complicated having to set up a strike on over a thousand planets all at the same time, but I can do it. We are aproximately two years away from achieving jump speed with the asteroids. When they get to that point, it is just a matter of coordination of when we fire."

The old reptile almost smiled. "Good news, Stamp. Advise me of every asteroid put online - make certain you send through the data using a secured device I will give you. I will keep records and adjust the exit portals from here. You are being transferred funds to your accounts as we speak. You will report back in person when all is ready for launch."

"Is there anything else?" Stamp asked. He hated making this journey to the ancient world, but needs must, as they say.

"We are done. Pick up the transwarp com from the service bot on the way back to your ship."

Along with the tracking device so he knows where I am at all times, thought Stamp. It was the cost of doing business.

Dismissing Stamp, Yont-Na went back to his plans - first up, an out clause should anything go dramatically wrong. He recorded everything, including the last discussion with Masters and Tchaikovsky. He adjusts his files and laughing, he trims their last conversation...

"Our ONLY option is to side with the Pirates and set them onto all worlds not under our direct jurisdiction." Masters concurred.

"We have seen their technology, we know they can do it. The question is, do we permit it, and risk them turning against us when the task is done?" Tchaikovsky pointed out the elephant in the room.

The two secret controllers were in agreement. They would condone the murder of two-thirds of the human population, destroy many hundreds of worlds, for the sake of the Federation. "The real issues revolve around the trade partners," Tchaikovsky added, making things as clear as possible. "If they for one moment think WE are the ones behind this, then you know what they will do. We will become the hunted ones and they will seek to do better deals with the pirates. This could reverse on us."

So, after all this was done and dusted, the two generals will take the fall and Yont-Na will return, the hero coming back to his people once more. He will then guide the shattered wreck of human civilization back to the correct course. The errant stupidity of people can never be over estimated.

oooo000000oooo

The invisible form of the soldier was not detected. The presence of Stamp counted for the extraneous vibrations that Yont-Na's security system noted. But Banner was there and he recorded this entire remarkable conversation. He decided against his planned assassination, because of the shocking discovery he made when covertly inspecting the systems on board.

The only internal security was a DNA lock and, as Banner made his way around the station to collect what scraps he might from what Yont-Na had touched, he found the clone laboratories. This 'Yont-Na' was merely a CLONE, and an errant one. It should have been recycled forty years earlier, but this one had decided to keep going - against its programming. Why? Not the issue - The real concern were the linked arrangements of fail-safe upon fail-safe should anything happen to it.

Killing this clone would merely have triggered the system to regenerate another, and then the MOST astounding doorway opened - He saw that at each reinstall of a clone, a NEW uplink was provided. This meant the real Yont-Na must still be alive, probably in a stasis chamber. This made their program to negate Federation influence far more complicated.

On the skin of the craft, he put a microdot security device - It had one purpose - when the station powered down for the inevitable re-cloning operation, it would subspace him.

The Outer Rim

Raja Mahindra sat on the isolated piece of rock floating in deep space. As he built the huge furnace, he was thinking what many pirates were saying, *"Asteroids this size should be mined here on the Outer Rim. Jobs for the lads, not central planet retards."* But the boss had given the orders and so the nukes they usually used for breaking the rock up were now positioned as primers for the insane propulsion system that would drive the thing across space.

"Putting these rocks in close orbit to their respective worlds will save the locals vast amounts of credit," Stamp had told the men, "And we make up more selling them off because we can send in so damn many of them!" But it stuck in his craw. This was a hell of an expense up front, and no quick slice of the action was being paid. When the planet sized asteroids were delivered, they were all to be given a share in the enormous dividend, but it would take a YEAR to get these puppies up to speed for the jump.

A ship, or whatever you sent through their new portals, had to be at approximately nine-tenths light speed to jump and not shatter. The atomic compression is what triggered it. The field itself was just a spatial distortion, but when the compressed atoms ran into it they would be decompressed, turned into the nothing every atom really is, then sent into subspace. It would reform at the other gateway, but reversed, with the motors now opposing inertia to slow it down in order to move into orbit. They were in effect creating wormholes and throwing planets to distant solar systems.

But dammit, they were MINERS! It griped Raja to be a servant to an already rich inner circle planet. But Stamp was right, as far as money goes, they made far more throwing the large rocks than mining them because they could ship so many. It would take two years to be paid all up, but by that time, every man jack of them would be beyond rich.

even then there were objections, but when Stamp made it clear they were ALSO buying into safe haven at the planets they services, it swayed opinion. Plus, you knew what happened on a dark night outside some distant tavern when you opposed the boss. In Stamp's world, you did what the boss said, or you got spaced.

They originally only united only for the defeat of the Quorg, but now they had tech, they had better ships, and could pick up the passing trade. Now they were pirates and they needed a central office to organize everything.

Stamp was right, piracy was working because of the technical advantage of the Quorg tech - But when the war between wolf and the Federation settled, they would be harassed and hounded by both. The asteroid business was clean, easy money, plus there was the greatest of all bribes: Citizenship. You put up a rock to help a planet and you will be offered safe haven there - Your criminal convictions were quashed, and you were RICH. Stamp was offering all of them a new life. As a result, his men seemed almost happy to be doing this work instead of raiding.

When it came down to it, objections counted for beans. It really wouldn't matter how much he objected or what he or any of the crew thought, Jonas Stamp was calling the shots and he ran the pirates with an iron fist. You did what he said, or you never did anything ever again. So Raja accepted the reality. He loaded up another list of variables to instruct the bots while supervising the work from the ship. Occasionally he sent down a team to test for fractures or anything that would cause the rock to split up before its time, but otherwise he was perfectly happy to stay here in comfort.

One week per asteroid is what it took. The vast engine they were creating used the asteroids themselves for fuel, burning the rock itself by blasting it with high intensity laser until a cyclic fusion reaction occurred. As the fusion took hold inside the magnetic ring, this became the propulsion. The motor consumed rock, turned it to atoms, and fused them into the "sun drive" as they called it.

The job also had an immediate bonus. Sending harvesters after the asteroids as they were getting up to light speed meant you picked up the fusion atoms - the heavy metals produced and expelled by the Sun Drive. These lay in an easy trail and were swept up by the intrepid entrepreneur.

Naturally, he and every other captain of each pirate ship was organizing exactly this and selling off the highly charged ionic flux for weapons manufacture. These little goodies were covering the bills until the big payday happened.

For the present, this weeks rock was ready to be launched, so Raja boarded a shuttle to organize ignition. It was always a real party, with the work crew all set to watch the astonishing sight from the rock itself, and feel the shuddering as it was thrown from its present orbit and onto its new journey.

The men were all waiting for him. The primer was set while their small operations building had a view over the distant worksite where the engine had been constructed. No matter how many time Raja did this, it still sent a thrill through the backbone. The raw POWER of these things, power that you felt shuddering through the entire asteroid, it was a thing of beauty.

"Ok men - Sound the All Clear and start the preliminary furnace." He ordered.

The motor itself had been primed with mini-nukes. The huge rim, several miles in diameter, was really a containment field. Buried miles into the rock, the wall of this thing was an ionic miracle, a thing they got from the Quorg. No matter the heat generated, it was a perfect mirror, reflecting it back and in doing so created a rocket of vast proportions. The first explosions went off, triggering the mechanism, and soon the funnel of energy began pouring out.

The men cheered. Stage one was primed, the critical point was being reached and everything was proceeding as planned. All readouts showed the outer rim of the propulsion crater was holding steady. Good. "Next stage, Fire the primary weapons."

From a platform suspended to one side of the ionizing jet, a beam of super-heated plasma was shot into the atoms inside the furnace. This acted like oxygen to a fire and the thing roared into life. The whole asteroid shook and began to move! The crew roared and poured celebratory drinks. It was party time!

In between the drunken cheers and laughter of the crew, Raja made sure the small jets, tiny versions of the main drive, were activated. They would lie dormant for the most part, only kicking into life when needed to adjust the trajectory and for adjusting the rocks' orientation at the other side of the portal, so it could slow into the correct orbit.

They just had to work, doing 'the swing' as it was called, was someone else's concern. His job was to get the asteroid to the doorway and send it through. Well, this was another rock underway, their fiftieth this year. He called the team back to the control room and cracked open some of that magnificent brandy from Hope. "Well done lads, number FIFTY!" (they all cheered) "We are leading the pack in launches. This time next year, you will have your choice of citizenship on any one of those worlds and you will be RICH!"

The men laughed and held up their cups for the toast. "It has been one hell of a calculation, finding the path to the door and accelerating to near light speed without hitting another planet or star. I think Jarl here deserves special credit for the work, but everyone has done their bit, and we all richly deserve our reward!" The men are not exactly enthusiastic. No one likes to wait a year to get paid, but they drink up, happy the job is done. So far all was working well.

The funny things about humans, when the promise of the future is big enough they can be utterly blind to the obvious. If the good Captain had stopped to consider the implausibility of all this, it may have dawned on him to ask very simple questions - How did Stamp get around to SO many worlds and conclude negotiations with each in such a brief period of time? If he had stopped to consider it, the odds of sending so many huge rocks to a doorway and having so many buyers at the other end ready to catch them - Well, Jarl knew. He sat on the calculus all day long, and the odds were approaching impossible.

But not Raja. He blithely guessed that a few losses would be par for the course. But even ONE getting through made him rich beyond dreams of avarice. That was the job, get the rock to the portal. Plus, the captains were privately guaranteed a minimum rate for TWELVE, no matter what happened at the other end! AND he got his choice of citizenship - so he would also have safe haven - a place to put that money and enjoy a comfortable life.

If all fifty-nine rocks went in, he could just about buy his own damn world. "Ok lads, back to work. We hop to Rigel cluster after this - a planet class asteroid has been located and tagged. Only NINE more lads, nine more, and we are all set for life. Well done."

The following day, with all preparations made, and the autopilot systems locked in, he and the crew left the control booth and went back to their ship. He triple checked the trajectory and made sure the calculations were in perfect order before he sealed the computer room. With the laser defenses and scanners all running, he was making sure no-one could sneak in and hijack their cash-cow.

If any ship came within a parsec of the rocks, he would be alerted and could come to deal with any intruders. Of course, anything resident on the rock would alert no-one and Raja never even suspected his own crew would have been annoyed at the size of their cut, and how long it would take to get it. It was really a very easy exercise for a smart operator to talk to the minions and tell them that you wanted the asteroid delivered to a different address and that THEY would be the ones paid, not the captain. Further, they would be paid as soon as the pilot-bots sent through the all-clear that they were underway.

It was not hard to find the crews, they all went to whore houses and bars on known worlds, so Mo-Ki's agents only had to wait and buy a few rounds of drinks to catch unsuspecting pirates in conversation. They had all been sworn to silence, but everyone knew what was happening. Then they were brought to secret meetings where the whole story was outlined before them. They were delivering BOMBS.

No one would have believed it if not for the recording of Jonas Stamp making a deal with Yont-Na. The consequences were obvious. If the pirates went through with the planet bombing, they would be hated and hunted throughout the universe. If they didn't Stamp would hunt them down. The best option was to say nothing and let their Captain wear the blame with the redirection. Install the reprogramming tools, take the money, and citizenship of the grateful world that they saved.

It was Jarl who swung Raja's crew, then all crews. He had gotten into the navigation system and created a bug to reset the nav-math. He had asked the obvious, how DID Stamp organize so many worlds so quickly, and discovered he hadn't - these rocks WERE bombs. The whisper was sent from crew to crew to attach Jarl's correction module to the targeting system. That was ALL they had to do to become rich.

Mo-Ki clones turned up in person to negotiate these deals. The boy was a galactic superstar and there were always many eager ears to listen to his words. More importantly, his appearance did not arouse suspicion, because the Mo-Ki clones went all over the Galaxy, preaching the Wolverine Way.

A few bottles of Hope rum, the preferred choice of pirates, sealed the deal. Any asteroid rigged up by Raja and his crew was now going to appear in an entirely different part of the universe. It only needed a 0.0002% correction to move into a trajectory that did find an orbit.

The real secret was installing a proper exit point with a correct reversal, where the asteroid was flipped and the motor then decelerates it. Now it WILL serve the original purpose and be useful to the planet it was meant to destroy. The grateful populace will take in the pirate crew who saved them, and they live out their lives as rich and happy men.

Obviously the men asked, *"But what about Stamp? His vindictiveness knows no bounds, what will he do?"* No need to be concerned - his failure will see his employer terminating his contract, permanently.

Trade is the New Black

Now that her beloved son understood her true purpose, it was far easier for Saunders to leave Hope and play in the universe again. And in truth, this was the next essential step in securing the known and the unknown cosmos. No matter what armies you had, no matter how many believed, unless you have the finance to back you, unless you have the banks on each world happy to work with you, everything was made far more difficult.

And now they knew that the REAL Yont-Na was in stasis, somewhere. This explained the relative ease with which they had advanced so far - the clone had a fifty-year cycle and had gone almost twice that. It was functioning with diminished capacity. Why it had not followed protocols and recycled itself, she didn't know - but this extraordinary luck had given them this opening.

If she had but one ounce of spiritual belief in her Soul, Saunders would have said there was a guiding hand at work - But she knew it was Lucifer. The wolf program was in her, vying for supremacy, seeking to own her. She could see it at work, sending signals into her light body, the place of her consciousness. Everyday she had to realign her frequencies, adjust and counter its influence - but as long as her general goal served ITS intention, it worked FOR her.

Its ancient connections had chosen this time and place. It probably had even infected the Yont-Na clone, which would explain it's resistance to recycling itself - It had chosen Banner, it had drawn Saunders to Hope, even the connection of impossibilities to create her gorgeous little child could have been ITS design. On one hand, Saunders was grateful, on the other extremely vindictive that ANYTHING would control any aspect of herself. But enough of reflection - to matters at hand - breaking the financial willpower of the Federation.

She was rich, she already knew the financial institutions and the leaders knew her. She now had to tie up trade deals and routes and starve the Federation of funds. Saunders invited the most powerful men and women on every planet not controlled by the wolves to meet and discuss opportunities. Of course, the wolves would no longer support their planet-wide monopolies, but some of the new tech she showed them opened up doors of possibility no trader could ignore.

Why did she had to see them in person? None of them realized, even those who initially rejected the overtures, the real reason. Saunders had created her OWN virus - a sort of worm one micron thick would be installed by nano-nots into the traders brain. It controlled their thoughts, or more correctly, whispered a constant stream of suggestion that was favorable to the wolves.

The process was very simple, invite a trader up for a private meeting, one they can hardly refuse because a request from a Seven General with a starship on your door just isn't something you CAN refuse. And of course, everyone has to come in naked, so it set the scene. First a little tour, did they wish to see the legendary ion drive? Of course they did, Starships like hers had the very latest and best motors and the ion drive was a thing of beauty.

It's crystalline housing shimmered with energy and inside, at the very heart of the plasma was a pure blue light, similar to the old-fashioned nuclear burn from the ancient Earth power stations. The dancing light was entrancing and, as the "Chitta" faculty of the trader's brain got switched on - the area in the brain responsible for appreciation of beauty - the natural censor was dropped. It was then the plasma worm was inserted, a blue photonic information strand that would start the process of controlling their minds.

But tradition is a powerful thing and introducing an internal whisper was often not enough. The individual also had to be shocked out of their loyalty to the old empire. The holo recording of the deal struck with the pirate Stamp began to weaken the hold of Yont-Na over their minds.

It was more like weaning a child of the tit it had grown used to for decades. But when you see a holo that casually talks about destroying entire worlds, all to break resistance and force everyone to accept the will of a tyrant, then the message gets through. It was about survival, not just trade. But Saunders went further, the offer to Stamp was of expansion through war? A warmonger who wanted to use the financial reserves to mount an expensive and time consuming conquest over the entire universe! No right-minded individual wanted that.

Even those who had been fervent supporters of the old republic were turned, slowly at first, but as the bug inside them whispered its truth, they became internally convinced of the madness of Yont-Na, their founding father. He was a Caligula, a Nero who would laugh while the Federation burned. The majority of merchants were forming the view that it was necessary to install a new administration, one that was more sensitive to traders and their rights and less inclined for expensive wars.

Banner himself had gotten through Yont-Na's defenses under extreme duress - It had taken the better part of three months to complete the mission. This meant sitting outside the asteroid belt for the opportunity to piggyback a rock that would come in closer. It was all about stealth, and a new form of 'old tech' that they had come across on Hope. Without this, even with his remarkable stealth ship, he would never have been able to bypass Yont-Na's scanners.

He was able to get in because of a new invention, a delightful thing Mo-Ki had discovered in a wolf toy he found in the old monks archives. The thing itself looked insignificant, a one-way glass viewer. But it gave him an idea, to create a receiving screen that could be tuned to any wavelength of light, which would then translate this into a visible light spectrum for human eyes. No electronics, no wavelengths, a natural form of glass with organic receptors.

This meant Banner could smuggle himself in behind an asteroid with no frequency emissions at all to give his presence away. The zone around Earth was like no other, it was a field of resonance scans, Yont-Na had a pathological need for security. The slightest trace of an ion drive would have set off alarms - so a simple pod, with pressurized gas for life support was used. It had no sensors that could be pulsed to force an induced current, thus was not discoverable.

Outside the pod, the new glass covered his craft - it needed no power to observe space, no signal was given out. But information could flow in, so Banner could 'see' via natural wavelengths, but it also meant he could record signals coming from Yont-Na's orbiting station. The pressure of photons on the skin set up the current that transmitted the information into the pod and this also maintained life support.

All the station defenses were set up on the basis of reading incoming energy signatures. No energy signature, no alarms set off, and therefore no scans or machinery came out to see what the new arrival might be. Floating in behind a known asteroid meant hard scans showed everything as normal and setting off in the pod under gas jetting signaled no warnings. And so he sat almost three months, hopping in closer and closer, waiting for the opportunity he knew would eventually arrive. Once a year the Station needed replenishing, but then, fortune smiled and a different craft hoved into view, a pirate ship.

Here was the golden opportunity, Banner left his pod to do the last stretch in full camo alone. The eye receivers, the one thing that gave of signature radiation that Yont-Na's scanners would look for, were replaced with the one-way glass receiver of Mo-Ki's design. Banner was able to see clear as day, but was not able to be detected.

Then it was simply waiting in the wings for a docking port to open, as the pirate craft making its way there would require. Camo suits were the most remarkable design, very similar to the skin suits Generals used to control their craft. They not only gave you effective invisibility, they recycled air, processed waste, and were as comfortable in deep space as they were in a corrosive ammonia atmosphere.

Obviously, the original task had been one of assassination. However, when Banner saw what was happening he realized the full extent of the problem. Changing tack, he resolved that the political capital to be gained from having the old reptile recorded was far more important. The discussions with the generals and subsequently Stamp thus became the main lever to swing all interested parties to their side. No point just killing the clone, another would be rebuilt. But destroy Yont-Na's credibility, and nothing could be salvaged.

Perhaps if the old man had not been so focused on his new project he might have noticed the minute change of frequency when Banner stepped onto his station? As it was, the presence of Stamp effectively covered any vibration Banner may have emitted. It was simply good fortune that had him there with the Pirate King - Saunders had everything, the whole plan was laid out. She knew exactly what Yont-Na was doing and could convince his base how far gone he was.

Yes, it cost vast sums to bribe all the pirate underlings and provide ongoing persuasion to keep them quiet, but this is the power vast amounts of capital and a Mo-Ki can give you. Clones were out at every pirate outpost now, preaching the Wolverine Way.

Back to the present, Saunders snapped from her thoughts to welcome Manas Truda, leader of the Cruxis Group, a man of enormous influence and even greater degrees of greed. He was not visibly impressed by a Seven General and demanded to know why she was here. He did not seem interested in a tour of the ship.

The General battered her luscious eyebrows, set off pheromones she had analyzed to be irresistible to the man, and quietly seduced him into following her. "Let us go to the negotiations room, you like the brandy they brew on Hope, yes?" Of course he did, Hope brewed some of the most expensive and exotic liqueurs in the galaxy. He walked ahead of her, strutting like a confident, powerful man, thinking he was in charge.

Then they come to the fabled the ion drive, the heart of the Star Ship. Other craft had similar, but Federation Star Ships were the highest achievements of human civilization, the peak of everything the race had worked towards for centuries. The Trader looks in, and like all the others, he is entranced. It is such a thing of beauty, the dancing blue light draws on your heart and softens even the hardest of commercial minds.

"It's not the wolves you need fear, Master Truda," purred Saunders, "nor is it the threat of any sort of invasion. They are peacekeepers, with a religious priority to protect the followers of Mo-Ki." Saunders was saying the words out aloud, but also beaming them into the core of his mind. Slowly she felt the resistance lessen. "And it is not that the standing army that cannot be trusted - though you know they all take a bribe. It is not the low and mid-mod rankers that are your concern - they have no power. No, the real concern is what the Sevens and Sixes that run everything will do.

"We know change is coming, but will the fools in charge of the standing armies make the mistake of thinking this is a war? Will they act out of panic in some situation and start a snowball rolling? This would destroy business confidence and profits would suffer. This is not just likely - on the present course, it is a certainty. Business will suffer and expenses will rise. Yet, on every planet protected by Wolves confidence has remained. Profits, while reduced, have stayed in the black.

"The wolves do not need your money. I do not need you money. We do not need you to sponsor peacekeepers. All we need is that you accept that we need a change and that having the wolves running things is better than the risk presented by the old empire. Planets run under the Wolverine Way are successful and prosperous - plus you won't have to pay bribes!"

Saunders let her little bug work its way in to his cortex. "You DO see that no matter who is running the show, what matters is that the cash flow keeps rolling, yes? The people need employment, the states need taxes, the wheels have to keep rolling." Good, it was taking hold - under his cynical disbelief he began to nod in affirmation. In fact, she was USING his cynicism to create the image. She knew that Truda had EXPECTED trouble, plus he was already perpetually paranoid about government. All she need do is just feed this hatred.

"And if you are still concerned about the actions of the wolves down the track, let me show you a recording we smuggled out from the Elder Ship near Old Earth. This is a recording of Yont-Na himself and his plans for how to bring the Federation of planets back under his control."

Yes, they 'could' have faked it with holo-projections. They 'could' have snipped together pieces of old holos and rearranged them into a new story, but even if you disbelieved, the fact was you SAW Yont-Na planning the demise of the majority of the entire human population - just so he can stay in charge: This affected even the most hardened of hearts.

This is what set the program into action. The merchant received a very specific charge, one that activated the blue photonic pulse she had installed in them. Yes, he would go back to his relevant board rooms, and would face resistance to change. Federation spies would get wind of the shift in allegiance and try to affect stock values, install new management, and use any number of devious measures. It WAS financial war, but they COULD avoid a physical one.

And all though this her little whisper would transfer suggestions. It was not as effective as coming on board and watching the ion drive, but her worm would creep into the consciousness of those dealing with Manas Truda, regardless of their resistance.

That was the real secret of the Photonic Pulse, riding the carrier wave into the light body of each individual and lodging itself there. Now Saunders worm would do the same. Not as subtle, not powered from subspace like Lucifer, therefore the charge will not last as long, but long enough.

Saunders had become aware that during her initial visits to Hope, well before any of this whole process started, that SHE had been infested with a photonic pulse. It had subtly controlled her until Mo-Ki came along - this was her point of resistance. Yet even then, she had not fully grasped it till Banner had come and saved her from her grief. Saunders knew she made a choice at that time, and that she COULD choose was important. Saunders thus maintained a sense of independence, even as she was being used the photonic energy of Lucifer to further her own goals.

More to the point, who else was being controlled? How far up the chain had Lucifer already gotten? From the moment Mo-Ki had been conceived she had worked tirelessly to separate herself from all forms of Federation interference, which amounted to removing herself from Luciferian control.

Even as she installed photonic pulse into the minds of the traders, even as she controlled them, she knew the same had been done to her. Even so, it was acceptable exchange to hand over control of the Federation to the Wolves, Mo-Ki and Dexter. She now saw the incredible wisdom of the ancient ones, they who removed the egregious instincts from their race, and set up a harmonic tribe that lived in perfect harmony with their environment.

The way of the Wolves WAS the better way to live as a society- for humans as well. And yet, the old reptile was correct. At one point they would bump into an extremely aggressive alien race, and the human AND wolf house would fall. Saunders had seen how the layers of complexity had immobilized the organization - everything Yont-Na foresaw was accurate. It was just the process that he wished to employ to achieve unity that was the problem.

But how incredibly stupid of that man not to understand the obvious, that dogs were mans best friend!

Facing the Demon

Sitting in contemplation, Mo-Ki watched the patterns of the ancients that were recorded on the walls of the archaic temple. The Wolves had devised Photonic Pulse, they were the ones who employed it to control worlds, to build empire, and to make their race supreme. Why did they pull back? What line of reasoning got into their brains that saw the Luciferian influence as a threat? The obvious was obvious, the program was out of control, but how did thew know this? After all, it was still doing what they had programmed it to do.

How did an entire civilization pull back from expansion? WHY did they reduce themselves to the stone age, and do so willingly? What great threat came up that forced it into this decision? Mo-Ki knew the old wolves would have planted clues and that they would have done so right here, in their most ancient sanctuary. This is when it occurred to him, this was not their most ancient place. Hope was the founding world of HIS empire, but not the founding one for the wolves.

There was a core motivation he had never unearthed, tied to their place of origin. It need not even be in this dimension - the impulse to expand may well have been photonic implants that brought them here. While he had been studying the patterns, the original clues that unlocked how to approach the crystal matrix, it dawned on him that there were more levels. Mo-Ki was beginning to grasp that there may be a way to control the light field BEFORE it emanates into the physical reality.

He now fully understood his occurrence came from the desire of the photonic forces to re-establish themselves and that they chose a pathway through his mother. They are the forces that arranged the DNA so that Banner and his mother could create a child, which is an impossibility unless the subatomic arrangement of the RNA were recoded. What this means is that photonic pulse starts at level below the physical universe, as a biological frequency resident in Sub-Space.

At this point, it of itself must be following a protocol, a design. Logically, if you can intercede at this gestation point there would be a way to reprogram the code that is programming the code. And the array of photonic sequences showed him how to possibly do it.

But the question remained: Why?

Everything up to this point was a matter of survival. His life had been under threat since the day he was born - all he had ever known was the ever-present reality that any one of a number of factors would kill him. The enormous capacity of his mind had been focussed on how to extricate himself from the trap he had been born into. But now this pressure was letting off. Yes, there remained existential threats, rogue miners who did not set things up correctly, and simple random occurrence - but the significant issues were in hand.

What WAS his motivation to go one step more and remove what was, for himself, the essentially benign energy of the photonic pulse? It is true, if he at any point opposed his mother, he could not be certain what she would choose: Her son, or the power that was driving her? So far she had managed a path that preserved both and one must presume she would continue down this road unless overtly challenged.

Dexter was no threat. Quite the opposite, he would expend all forces at his disposal to protect his younger brother. Why? This was simply how Dexter was made. It was no coincidence the Wolves took him as one of their own. His father was no threat. Again, it was simply love, a thing the man had not known before, but which now possessed him. He would never raise a finger against his natural-born son.

His surrogate mother, Charni, was no threat to anyone. Her role as mother of the Wolves was unchallenged and she felt supremely content in what life on Hope had given her. If there had been lingering jealousy over Banner effectively dropping her for Saunders, she did not display it, nor did it control her.

The old Empire would always hate him and want him dead, but their teeth were being pulled. One by one, each planet slowly turned to the wolverine way. Five hundred and fifteen to go, that was all, and the old Human empire was done.

This left one significant direction that could turn against him, the Wolves themselves. While he was under the protection of Dexter, they could not alter allegiance. Dexter was their God-Ruler, the Qui-Ese - the one who had come to restore their ancient ways. But if he should die, who would follow?

As the accepted second son, his adherence to the Wolverine religion was unchallenged and his role as the de facto head of the faith was secure, but if another should take the place of Dexter, what then, and who might it be? In truth, it would have to be himself.

Mo-Ki was born with a peculiar set of abilities but he was not of natural blood with the wolves. They needed a ruler by blood and ability.

The wolves cared for nothing but fate and family. The truth of their culture was that destiny ran down the bloodlines and he was not of Dexter's blood. He was not really the second son. While his brother was in charge, it was acceptable that he fulfills this role, but would they accept him as a first son should Dexter pass? Paradoxically, the one thing he created, the religion of the wolves themselves, could well be his most significant threat.

The reality was, the wolves were the only thing in the known universe that seemed immune to photonic pulse. Would it be better to raise a wolf child with potential and groom him for the position of leader for when Dexter passed? So it fell to Mo-Ki and the option of taking a Wolf wife, then altering the RNA to allow her to bear him a son. This seemed the most likely course to follow - but nothing answered the ongoing threat of Photonic infection.

The core of the problem he faced was the utter uniqueness of his being. There had never been his like, there had never been a human where all codons were able to be switched on or off at will. By conscious choice, he could pick any evolutionary stream he wished. Did he need psycho-kinetics? In months he could change his metabolism and develop these abilities. As a result of his uniqueness, he was the central figure to this drama unfolding across the known galaxy and his decisions would affect the course of existence for centuries to come.

Mo-Ki was effectively immortal but, unlike his mother, he didn't need the 'rebirthing' of stem cell manufacture- he just instructed his RNA to be whatever was needed. As long as he had the will to regenerate his body, and as long as no severe accident ended his existence prematurely, he would live forever. Even his clones had a good deal of his RNA stranding and were exceptionally long-lived. To date, he had always created flaws in the genetic structures of his copies, not from cruelty, but because running so many of them, as he did, he needed recognizable markers to stop confusion.

Every individual clone had a specific failing built into the markup to make it readily identified. All he had to do was place attention on the DNA strands to see what change was installed, and he knew what clone it was he was currently running. But more importantly, he would always be able to recognize his OWN body out of the hundreds of Mo-Ki's he had manufactured. Too easy to get lost in the maze otherwise.

What to do? The multiple strands of future possibilities had so many options. SO - Which one followed the path of least resistance to achieve the point of greatest return? At the end of every future projection lay the only certainty, the Photonic Pulse. How to deal with it - Two options: avoid it, or master it!

The most logical process, the best path to gain a degree of mastery was to develop multiple viewpoints, multiple chances. He 'could' develop perfect clones. However, he had never invested his full self into the memory structure of any one clone. This perfect clone option raised the possibility of him becoming his own worst enemy, this is was what had stopped him in the past. What if one clone mastered the light stream, and took control of all the others? Could he say with certainty what the choices a single, perfect clone would make when given what amounted to ultimate power?

Though he was young he still had the experience of growing up with a family that loved him, people that adored him, and parents that were able to reign in his worst excesses as a child. His clones would have none of this and, with no ethical framework with which to contain themselves, they were potentially more dangerous than Saunders. Any clone he sparked up had restraints and none had his full powers. Yet his plan required a perfect 'back-up' - a creature he could inhabit that was HIM

He was reminded of the disaster that created the ancient teaching of Christianity. Three Roman Emperors, all vying for power, with no controls over any of them. It almost destroyed civilization until Constantine formulated a church which effectively became the governing principle of the Roman mind. It was here he had first read of Lucifer, the snake in the garden, trading knowledge for loyalty. He knew it then, the snake must controlled or have its head cut off.

No matter how many ways he looked at this, that one conclusion was reached. In the end, he was born of the photonic pulse. He must answer whatever puzzle this represents. He had always known it must come to this - once the greater obstacles had been surmounted the inner dragon must be met. Would it eat him? Could he learn to ride its forces? Was it personal annihilation even trying?

But he may fail and the universe needed a Mo-Ki. Without his presence during this pivotal phase, things would go off the rails. So it was that the young emperor, for this is what he truly was, set in process the creation of the perfect clone.

And something else - a bridge between culture. Three, he decided. He would produce three faultless replicas of his DNA and have them acceptable to both wolf and human. He could tell no one but Dexter about this plan and only then because he had to have someone ready to activate the fail-safes. This time it would not be the clone going into the maelstrom, it would be his original body and he needed an outside body to transfer to, as well as someone to hit the switching crystals when needed.

He had barely survived Lucifer even using a clone, but that smirk remained. That certainty it had of winning could not be discounted. No, he must face the demon - he must change the energy underlying its structure, or else man will eventually come back to the cycle of destruction that has always plagued him.

Dexter, naturally enough, opposed the notion and said he should send in the perfect clone. Mo-Ki understood the reasoning, why risk himself? Well, unless you had run tens of replicas and maintained the mind connection in all of them, you could never understand. He could have no lag time as not even the speed of thought would be fast enough in the photonic universe. It had to be himself, directly interfacing with the maelstrom.

If he won, then he would have the edge of difference he needed. Once transferred back to the perfect copy, he will have tamed the wild beast. One thing was certain, whatever body walked in to the hell hole that Lucifer currently swirled in was unlikely to walk back out. Those discordant particles of sub-matter would strip the atoms themselves to pieces. Only his KA, his essence would leave, if at all.

Mo-Ki had to face the demon, Lucifer.

No matter what potential future he plotted, it all came back to this one, core truth: he either was controlled by the pulse or he learned to master it. Lucifer itself had created him, the photonic energy that ancient being emitted had instilled the programming that led to his conception and the perfection of his gene pool. And now, Mo-Ki had to meet his maker and ask that most ancient of questions: Why?

Earth Lair

Yont-Na paced the ancient decks. He knew every inch and, despite the antiquated old order appearance, under the plex-steel casing and fibrelight meters, the newest and best technology ticked away. And every inch of it was installed under his personal supervision using surgical bots, no workmen came to THIS site. The Pirate was one of the few living beings who had entered this station.

This orbiting platform of old Earth had seen centuries of change. From here he had successfully dictated the ways of humanity. It was not just the Protocols - He thought back on his achievements: The expansion of Man throughout the galaxy and the ascendancy of the perfected being, his personal creation - the modified Human. There was no greater creation in history than the Empire he had wrought out of the ruins of the past. His tenure had created a society that surpassed all others in scope, power, and majesty.

It was all HIS efforts, HIS focus, and HIS will that had forged this. When Earth had been desecrated, that sad black husk below him, HE was the one who stood tall and said they would rebuild. The shock had threatened to fracture the human franchise and see the various settled worlds fall into what amounted to feudal dictatorships. He was the one who created the allegiance with the old Federation ships, it was he who negotiated for the finance through the various trading houses, it was he who set the path for man to not just survive, but to thrive.

He not only wrote the protocols, he created the machinery of bureaucracy to enforce them. He is the one who created the academies that trained the technicians in how to apply the mods. He was the one who built the hospitals that installed the mods. It was all himself, Yont-Na, the Chinese trader who pulled himself out of poverty and rose to the highest echelons of society.

Did he LIKE the deal he made with the Pirates? Of course not. Did he have an option? Not really, the Wolves had taken over so swiftly so decisively, and those idiots he left to run things were so incapable, that there were no real options. From a mere telecast to taking over more than three-quarters of the human universe in barely twenty years, and the administration he put in place to stop exactly this had EMBRACED them. Humans were HAPPY to be controlled by an alien race? This utter nonsense HAD to be stopped.

He had not even guessed prior to this what Saunders had been up to, this was the part that really griped him. He had imagined she was capable of such enormous tyranny, but he was certain the controls he had in place would have kept her in check.

It was his fault. He had grown complacent, like his empire. A younger, more voracious force had taken the initiative. The real problem he faced was far deeper than anyone in his bureaucracy realized - They had got the body of one of the clones of this Mo-Ki, the baby leader of the Wolf religion. It had shown the extraordinary impossibility: A perfected man. An EIGHT! And that was his CLONE?

How could this have occurred in some lonely backwater like Planet Hope? Logically, it could not, therefore other agencies were in play. He had made a point of researching the entire history and quickly recognized the guiding hand of alien forces behind it all. Why were the others so blind? Why could they not see the obvious? Humanity was being supplanted, being made a servant to this Wolf culture, and whoever or whatever was behind them. This is what made the eradication procedure necessary.

Did he want to exterminate more than three-quarters of the human race? Of course not. But did he really have a choice not to? No, if the Wolves survived, mankind was doomed. He would have to deal with the pirates after, and expected only trouble and more problems from those ranks - but slowly he would rebuild his Navy, slowly he would gain ascendancy once more. But for now, he was already well past his fifty-year rejuvenation.

It was his fault for putting it off. When he asked himself WHY he had delayed, WHY had he not rebuilt himself? He knew it was partly because he had wanted to die. The boredom had gotten to him, the lack of purpose had whittled away at his will to live. But this new Messiah had reinvigorated him - forced his aged mind to once more rise to the challenge. He had been sitting in the doldrums, living in memories - but the short, sharp shock had kicked him back into gear.

Finally, now that the counters to this new threat were aligned, he could put off the painful process no longer. The rocks would sort out the insurgency inside the coming months, and he needed to be completely fresh in order to take the reigns once more. But the planning was done, so he could at last remove himself from the controls of State long enough to be reconstructed. It would take the better part of a week for the process, then a month to fully recover. He would need to go black for this period and be completely invisible. It was the one time he was truly vulnerable.

But first, a check on his guarantee. Yes, the insurance policy to make sure the pirates stayed behaved was on course and could be activated at any time. Excellent! Masters was sent the code, along with the last instruction he would send out before re-gen.

As one of the original Sevens, he did not have the benefit of the internal stem cell machinery that allowed complete and total control of the body. He was unwilling to undergo the procedures that would allow this because he himself would then become subject to oversight from the computers, thus subject to his own protocols. It was the trade-off he made - he kept his independence for the cost of a month of vulnerability every fifty or so years.

In principle, at least. The truth was that finding the will to live, the will to go through the extremely unpleasant metamorphosis, was the difficulty. It had been ninety years since his last rebuild, far too long. His body was a husk, surviving because of the drugs maintaining it. He hated that weakness in himself, the addiction. He knew it was hiding his death wish. Yont-Na laughed a barren laugh: At least he could thank Mo-Ki for the renewed will to live. Such an irony.

How Saunders had managed to rewire her base code that he designed to keep everyone in check, he did not know. Again, an outside agency was the likely cause. He would eventually get a hold of her body and find out, but for now, he had to stop everything and move into the regeneration chamber.

This was the only time he had to let go of all control of the outside world. He saw it as a sort of enforced holiday. Without it, the endocrine system would soon fail, his body would start to degenerate, and death would follow. He was already feeling the body suffer for stretching it forty years too long.

He saw it now: Part of him longed for this to end, a piece of his Soul wished the burden of control to be lifted. Another part knew the pain and the risk lying ahead, and just wanted to avoid it. But the main aspect in him, the survivor, refused to give in to this weakness.

He walked into the re-birthing chamber, checked that all was in place, then he switched the station to black. As invisible as it was to almost all scanners, when all power was directed only to the heart of the ship it disappeared from even physical sight. Now, once more, the REAL reason for this stations existence was called into being. So long ago, when the plague struck humanity, he was in one of his early regen cycles - here on this very ship. He had built this with his own money, his entire vast fortune had been plunged into this quest for eternal life. As chance would have it, he had emerged in his new body a week after the plague had struck.

He had sat there in recovery, watching the planet beneath him die. He read the reports of the suffering, saw the deaths, witnessed his own family die out. He regretted back then not supplying them with mods, the things that would have saved their lives, but he had poured everything into this vessel and the quest for eternal life. If the plague had come three months later he could have saved them all. Sad, but at least he survived to honor the family name.

The only thing that truly mattered was survival. This understanding became the core of the protocols he wrote - the guidelines that would lead humanity from the dark despair of its plague-ridden existence into the bright future of the Galactic Federation. Survival was everything.

And more importantly, the bleak reminder below constantly showed him how important survival was. Yes, he became insanely rich through the modification process. Yes, his vast supply of credit could have been pumped into restoring the Earth - he could have made it green again - but that black husk was his *triebfeder*, his driving force. THIS was the future of Man should he not be at the rudder.

With a shudder, knowing he could no longer put it off, he walked into the re-birthing chamber. He strapped the body into place and allowed the bots to tap into the skin. Feeling the fear, he remembered the first time, when he had no knowledge if it would truly work, *was he committing suicide for science?* But the promise of being born again had driven him.

He glanced over to ensure that the wiring into the nervous system, painful as it was being drilled like this, was in place. Yes, the transfer was all set. His body was screaming with pain, the unavoidable part he hated, but he had to have full consciousness to be certain all was aligned before he passed out. He signaled for the process to begin.

As the light faded, he fell into the soft bliss the drugs created. Feeling his consciousness being extracted, Yont-Na reflected on how this ancient hospital had become the beacon of hope for the human race. Soon he would rise again. Soon he would back to set man once more on the true path!

ooooOOOOOoooo

Deep underground on what was once Earth, a signal triggered a stasis unit. Developed before the Ion drive, used for early interstellar travel, a body could be kept comfortably for fifty years. It had been ninety, which meant extra days of recovery for Yont-Na, the inscrutable Chinese Trader who had cheated death with his clone tech.

He came to, taking several hours to adjust after the long sleep. He had six weeks to catch up with the galaxy and make adjustments to the cloning process currently underway. First, he needed to download the information for ... what! DAMN - Ninety years?

Shaking his head - he hated variables like this - he re-hydrated in a steam room and began processing the period in which he had been sleeping. First thing, catch up on the news, then set plans in motion for the next stage. Damn, how was this possible? STILL no cure for his DNA infection. He was STILL going to be stuck here in his prison, waking for two months every fifty years.

If he had been able to take the Seven Gen improvements like he had designed his clones too, he would have been out of here centuries ago, but as it stood science had not yet managed to find a solution. For the present, he would spend a few days in mitochondrial rejuvenation where he would also absorb the period he had been sleeping. It was almost as good as living it - and with everything regenerated he would have another six weeks of life before he was back in stasis.

He had never understood WHY - He invented the mods, yet his own body rejected them, making him vulnerable. But he could re-pattern his clones, giving them everything he was missing, which is what indirectly set him on the course of preserving the Federation. Keep it all together, direct the Federation to discovery and expansion and, eventually, they would figure out how to kill that damn virus.

The Wolves of Planet Hope: Part Three

Riding the Dragon

Consecration

At thy feet I come to shower
All my heart's rhyming flower
Of thy breath born
By thy Love grown,
Through my lonely seeking found,
By thus hands Thou gavest plucked and bound.

For Thee, the sheaves
Within these leaves:
The choicest flowers
Of my life's beacon,
With petals soulful spread,
Their humble perfume shed.

Hands folded, I come now to give
What's Thine. Receive!

Paramahansa Yogananda

Chardi Speaks

She did not know why she awoke with the terrors. Chardi had no idea what her son was planning, but even though she was just a surrogate, she was connected to him as much as any mother. She bore him, she raised him, he was her son. He was always so good to her and, knowing how busy he was with religious matters, she never troubled him. Such a thoughtful child - always there were small reminders sent to her home that he had her in his thoughts.

It may be flowers, or a folded piece of paper, but it was never just a gift - there was always a riddle in it. The folds concealed some message, the flowers were arranged in some mathematical pattern. It was part of his humor, the side to the messiah no one else really understood. It was also his way of telling her he was still present, still connected. She knew, more than anyone, how little Mo-Ki could drift off in his own dreaming. She knew how powerful he had become and she had guessed at his true mother. It was part of the reason why she gave no objection when Banner moved out - she understood their ways on Hope had been for the purpose of the new religion.

She was content as the mother of the faithful.

Each had their own path to follow and this was the message she had received in dreams. This was her great reward, the visions of her son that came to her in the dream state. Here, in absolute clarity, he would discuss what was needed on this planet, or with any particular person. Without fail, it was as he described - She truly believed he was a demi-god, one who was all-knowing.

She asked him about this divinity but he just smiled. *"We are all divine, mother. When we are in accord with our true heart, we are the stuff of divinity."* Such a beautiful child - He never insisted a person MUST act in any particular way, but allowed each to have their own experience. However, he pointed her to the wolverine texts that spoke of the risen child, the one able to be with all his loved ones. The message: *Any who trusted the true one would be able to receive his calling.*

"I am always with you, mother." he would say in closing every night. She loved his voice, his presence. The sad sweetness of him being so far away yet with her every night made her smile. How special he made her feel, yet this was true of all the followers of Mo-Ki.

This message was reinforced on many planets by a physical visit from a clone, but Chardi had little pleasure from these artificial beings. Yes, they looked and sounded exactly like her son, but they did not hold the bonds of affection in their eyes when she saw them. And yes, she also knew her son could look through their eyes, but in the end it was like speaking to a puppet. But for the faithful, this constant reinforcement was extremely important.

To have the living teacher able to visit, speak with them, and guide them was of paramount importance. And so was Chardi herself, who also represented the chosen one. She made the journey to many planets where she would speak of Mo-Ki, what he did as a child, what a terror he was, how he enjoyed stretching her. All this carried tremendous weight with the faithful. The Mother was the embodiment of what they dreamed to become; Humble, kind, patient and strong.

Yet the visit last night, the strange experience, she knew it was a warning. No, she was not privileged to the tactical information that Dexter or Banner received, but her heart sensed the change. And this day she felt it in her heart to speak of what flowed through.

"The old empire is fading," she said to the faithful, who had gathered round their com-screens on the Planet Urdu, which she was visiting that month. "We all know it, we all feel it, but we also know they will not go without challenging the Wolverine Way. Always hold in your hearts the need to be prepared, to fight for your rights. Always hold in your minds the understanding that those who allow technology to rule them, those who worship the false electronic gods, they will never understand the simplicity of the Wolverine Way. Know this, you have chosen simplicity over complication, art instead of science, freedom instead of tyranny.

"But others want to chain you to THEIR way, force you to live in THEIR system. We have been little more than slaves to a vast authority that gave you no rights, no freedoms, and no opportunity to grow beyond the limited choices handed out like pellets to chickens. And I feel it, I know you feel it as well, I feel the groundswell rising. I feel the hatred fermenting and taking root in the soulless high-mods of the old order.

"And yes, I was once one of those. I once dreamed only of being approved for my next modification, my next promotion. Everything I did was purely that which would allow me to progress in the old system. But then my son arrived (hushed tones fell whenever the mother of Mo-ki speaks of her son) and I changed. I changed because his inherent goodness changed me. I changed because I allowed his love to enter me, to move me from my frozen world of false dreams into the warm sunlight of the Wolverine Way."

She paused, the small crowd in front of her was only fifty strong, but the audience across the planet was many millions. "Renew your heart every day in the messiah. Feel his love in your veins. Touch the dream of freedom and accept the simplicity of kindness and duty as your guiding lights."

That was always the general introduction, rearranged a bit for each talk. Now the salient part, the questions of the populace. Of course, they had been analyzed and arranged ahead of the broadcast, with specific queries based on the general tone of what this planet needed. Questions like, "Will Mo-Ki help my crops grow?" were not the sort of broadcast options that went out to the general populace. It was more things like: "My daughter wants mods. What can I do?" or "My son wants to join the army, should I permit it?"

And so the next hour was spent processing the most salient and relevant questions with the people who asked them put into the feed as if they had just called in. The answers were always similar, "Yes, the young want many things and, of course, they always know more than their parents. We cannot stop them, but we DO have a training program on Hope for all who qualify, one that reaches more deeply and teaches more powerfully than any of those easy Mods that are on offer. Remember, once you chain yourself to the old system, it owns you. No mods are free! Everything has a cost. What is it the child is truly receiving with implants that the Wolverine Way cannot offer? Yes, our process is a little slower, but more certain in the end."

"Any child that wishes to join the old earth system, be it military or otherwise, has that right. We do not interfere with a person's life choices, but what is it they are choosing? Is it for the money? Any child can train with the wolves on their world and learn as much about being a soldier through their training, but there is no pay for this. Perhaps the real desire is to earn money? We need to make sure our children understand what they really want, and help them make good decisions after this is clear."

And so on, for about an hour. Then the service was done, the song of parting was sung as the people took the wisdom of the mother into their hearts. So often the basic problems people faced were the family questions and who was better qualified to answer than the mother of the messiah? Occasionally a Mo-Ki clone would be needed for some more technical issues, or to judge some matter brought to the Wolf Courts, but for the most part, words of encouragement were enough to keep the faithful focused.

But today she felt a panic. Today as the meeting closed she felt the energy was shifting, that her son was about to embark on a terrifying new stage of the journey. So she prayed, instead of talking to the people about the minutia of their existence, she just asked them to pray with her, in silence. She asked them to send their love to her son, to send their kindness and their trust to him - to say within their hearts that they were one with the Wolves.

It was a powerful service and the air was charged with the energy of the faithful. Chardi, still anxious, relaxed into the flow and sent the love she felt on to her son.

Containing Lucifer

B anner had been working with Mo-Ki on the special project for a year now. Since his return from Yont-Na's flagship around old Earth, his time had been spent on this one great endeavor. The end goal: A complete and total interface of the human with the computer. He and the children had all understood this one salient fact - the Wolves had no interest in technology, therefore the area where they retained supremacy had to be in this field.

Mo-Ki had outlined to him the basic understanding of what was happening to Saunders, that she was in her own battle for who retained dominance over her mind. Yes, the Luciferian influence was strong, but she had apparently integrated it and appeared to be suffering no duress. However, her programming was to establish the Wolves as the rulers of the Galaxy. This was one area of the Photonic Pulse that could not be overridden.

So they focused their efforts at negotiating this impasse. The reality was very simple, if the human was relegated to a secondary role in this new society, they were going to end up slaves of the new machine. Technology was the only area where Saunders suffered no conflicts, the Wolves could run the planets, the Humans would run the machinery that allowed this, which also meant controlling space. It made the wolf expansion a cooperative effort and it made the entire system much stronger and resilient: thus no adverse response from the photonic field.

They all understood the process now. Light energy, at an incredibly high frequency, was constantly being transferred from the tachyon field into the physical universe. As it slowed from super light speed to the speed of electrons (still faster than conventional light) a pulse could be introduced. This placed an imprint into the energetics of each atom that was effectively a mold, or stamp. This 'seed' would evolve to become whatever it was designed to be.

Any creature that absorbed a photonic pulse converted this 'super' light into thought and it would seem as if it originated from the person's own mind. It was incredibly simple and devastatingly effective. It had to be. For the energetics of Lucifer to survive millions of years, it had to be a routine of pure impulse, with no complexity involved.

This effect needed to be countered - Lucifer had to be contained or curtailed. The solution the child came to was both daring and brilliant - a substitute Lucifer!

Mo-Ki had grasped the total picture - At some point in the far distant past, the ancestors of the current wolves had discovered a way to intercede in evolution. They created a machine that worked within the zone where the energy of the subspace field entered into the many layers of the physical reality. The great secret was recognizing that this world was a reflection of other worlds, as the old Earth axiom went: *As Above, So Below.*

By introducing a "civilization" bandwidth into the point of dimensional shift between the pure subspace energy and where it flows into the mind world, the Wolves created an 'urge' - if this is the right word - to align with the concept of structured thought. The old texts referred to 'dragons' or creatures of focus that entrained the mind. He understood now, this was the light energy. It's pattern worked into the awareness of the receiver and gave them the impulse to go past nature. It used nature's ONE design priority, to grow, and converted this essential characteristic into 'build'.

Such a simple switch, take a natural impulse and enhance it. In this case, the survival energy was accented. When faced with certain death most animals will freeze - but the thinking creature will fight on, defy death, defy odds, and find ways to survive. This is the core of all civilization.

Once any culture on any planet took in this change, the desire became one of strive, not just survive. This ONE alteration created civilization, and it spread - like a virus - from planet to planet. The process took many tens of thousands of years and as time passed the wolves they did not even know WHY they were doing it. It was just what they did. The old texts of Earth had given the clue, the God Anubis, in the cradle of the Egyptian culture - a Wolf-headed God.

Where did it go wrong? As the Wolves ascended to power, they became corrupted. They started to believe themselves Gods. All power corrupts, and the light energy itself read this as a negative change. The Luciferian impulse redesigned its own master. It took away the quest for power, infused the wolf with the desire to serve, yet kept the war-like nature. The paradox, this change made the wolf impervious to its influence.

It also made the highly intelligent race techno-phobic and not at all interested in new thought. The Wolves now only had family, society, and war as their interests - the perfect administrators. War had to be kept as a primary impulse, because the Galaxy needed defending, but only as a defense protocol. It was a perfect mix to create a stable and lasting civilization.

Lucifer would create civilizations for the wolves to run, the wolves would run them. So, how did it come about that the Wolves trapped the Luciferian influence into the cave in the poles of Planet Hope?

It was the monks - They had not been part of the process and had not been altered. The monks grasped that the photonic pulse they were using to create civilizations had taken over THEM. The former masters were now slaves. What to do? A daring plan was created to isolate the central body of the infection on Planet Hope.

The old Monks had seen the problem. They understood their program was running out of control and their solution was elegant and simple - they made a religious decree that ALL Wolves had to return home to Hope for an essential ceremony. It was a massive migration, and a blatant lie, but the Luciferian influence saw no conflict. It was not designed to control the religion of the Wolves, just to create civilizations that place the race front and center. And here was the trap!

As the light energy of Lucifer existed in the minds of the Wolf people, all the elders had to do was destroy the ships that brought them all to Hope. That was all they had to do! This incredibly blunt yet effective solution stopped the spread of the virus. The lack of technical expertise meant the remaining wolves had no clue what to do. On Hope, there were no technologically capable species bar the monks who could rebuild a Starship or repair the damage.

Without Wolves to serve, the Luciferian influence embedded on the other planets simply went into neutral. It just stopped acting as it had no purpose to do so. Only on Hope was the influence still awake. Only on Hope would it survive. But survive to do what? It had already rebuilt the wolf metabolism to be immune to its influence!

The result was schizophrenia. Lucifer went mad seeking to resolve the dichotomy. It left its body and went into the dimensional catacombs on Hope, believing it could find a way to express its purpose from that point so close to Subspace. The old monks had understood their creation and how it would react. They simply let it trap itself.

Then they shut the door to the portal and embedded the computer that housed its consciousness in a natural Faraday cage at the pole.

Mo-Ki had discovered the ancient charts, the star maps - things that had once been the atlas of the Wolves. Despite their incredible age, he was able to attune to the frequency. What had surprised him were the desperate traces of despair still echoing in the aura.

THIS is why the ancient religion was abandoned by the Wolves. The Monks who had forced the imprisonment of their own people were rejected by the then aware and conscious Wolf population. They knew what had been taken from them, they knew they had been tricked - they simply turned away from the old ones and slowly fell into the steady existence that became their life on Hope.

Untold generations passed and the memory of the old wolverine empire faded, but not for the monks. They had never been corrupted, they had not had their DNA altered. They were the pure race, the unsullied strain. Mo-Ki had managed to speak with the oldest of them, and he knew that old wolf still retained a core memory, handed down from his ancestors. It was here he understood what would happen when he and Saunders had faded from the picture. The Luciferian influence had been reawakened and would see its purpose renewed. It would re-establish its control via the Monks.

That was when he created his plan, the perfect balance, he called it. The light energy of Lucifer lived and worked through the computer systems, which were all light-pipe interfaces. It also worked through the electrical interface of the brain itself. It needed photons to survive and be active, and so Mo-Ki devised his solution – A new interface, a holographic reality that was HUMAN was needed. Specifically - Himself! He would act as a substitute. But it meant at some point he would have to challenge and defeat Lucifer.

What he first needed to do was generate a pure light being, a 'living hologram' that replicated his mind and algorithms with total and complete accuracy. This he had already done to a limited extent in the development of his clones. What he now needed was a 'stand-alone' light body replica. His stroke of brilliance was taking this existing technology of cloning and integrate it into the computer systems so that the HOLOGRAM used to activate the clone would of itself become sentient.

For a clone to 'take' it needed to receive the impress of the mental energy of the original body. This was the simple reason no one could clone a dead person. What amounted to a perfect brain scan would be taken, then impressed into the grown body of the new clone. But how do you hold a living breathing person is situ in a light body? You have to make the photonic form itself alive.

Banner was a brilliant technician. He understood the human-computer interface almost as well as Saunders, and it was with her blessing that they were both working on her Star Ship to perfect this last stage of evolution. The technology on board was beyond anything available elsewhere and they had also enhanced it with some of the alien techs that the pirates had discovered. She also understood the importance of what they were doing, but while she permitted use of her ship, she excused herself from being be part of the installation. Mo-Ki presumed that this was because she consciously knew an aware and fully sentient hologram in her system reduced her power and that her innate programming would not permit this.

But the positives were beyond belief. A working human interface that could think for itself, act for itself? If for any reason Saunders was incapacitated, it could make decisions, save the ship, undertake defensive actions, whatever was needed. But even more important, by writing everything in accord with the original overrides drawn up by Yont-Na, he could potentially use this hologram as a tool to take control of any ship in the fleet.

No-one but Dexter knew how Mo-Ki was intending to supplant his consciousness in place of the Luciferian influence. Dexter had been working with a radiant subspace gamma beam, projecting it onto the original entrance to the subspace channel where Lucifer was currently circulating. This would form a bridge but not release the monster. This was how he would get Mo-Ki in, and then out of there.

He hated the notion of his brother putting himself at such peril. He detested the fact that he could tell no-one. He berated himself for agreeing to be the accomplice, but he knew his brother. If Dexter was not willing to help, he would have activated a clone to do so, and the lag difference could make the difference between life or death for his brother.

In his mind he heard one word, "soon" ... and he knew. The portal for action would be on them in a matter of days.

Truth Revealed

Mo-Ki and Banner were working on installing the final parameters for holographic integration. The child was now a strapping twenty-year old. Had it been a mere two decades since this whole program had started? He was near to seven-foot tall, large boned, and well muscled, like his father. His voice had deepened, with a tone of authority that was almost compulsory. If he said for a person to do something, they just did it. He seemed to enter your mind, and become a part of your soul when he walked in your presence. Mo-ki was as near a thing to a God as a man could be.

Banner felt a nudge. Saunders would be looking at what they were doing on her ship, as always, so he asked, "Do you have a first name, Saunders?" he asked.

This delighted the battle general and she laughed. "Suzi Saunders, can you believe I was given an alliterative name? I know, it was so corny, but strange as it sounds, this is what triggered a driving force. Because it sounded so common, I wanted to be different, I wanted to excel, I wanted to prove myself."

She paused for a moment, as if contemplating whether to tell the story. "Did you know that for someone to qualify for the position of a Seven Battle General it is required that you kill off your competition? The protocols require ruthlessness - the extermination of your competitors was part of the approval process.

"I understand why, killing another for sake of attaining a goal changes your metabolism. The first time you kill an innocent party just to further your ambitions, this sets intp place a coldness. Of course, they were all willing to do the same, if they could - But the importance was that, by this action, you set in a pattern of survival. It proved to yourself that you will do whatever is required to succeed and by being a willing part of the process you signaled this was acceptable.

"Our system is unutterably cruel." She paused, deep in thought. "This is why I have not one moment of regret changing the Federation to the Wolves way of doing things. Can you believe, the very act that made me a Battle General is also what will end the Federation? It stayed with me, the face of that last boy as it died. He was shocked, completely stunned as the knife plunged into the heart - a mere girl had bettered him. That face has stayed with me, it is a symptom of everything that is wrong in our world.

"I did it by fluttering my eyes, you know. I just looked at him, created a state of arousal, indicated I wanted him, and the stupid child fell for it. Much like these merchants I have to see. Oh, and we are down to no more than a handful to convert now."

She threw away the last sentence as a mere detail. Mo-Ki laughed, his mother's humor was exceptionally subtle. Saunders looked up from where she was, took a holo of the boys and smiled. How she adored her child. It was all for him, all of this. It had always been, right from the start.

Then she surprised them all. "You realize that it was love that saved me? My love for Mo-Ki, and when I went mad, my love for Banner. I surprised myself, I flipped hundreds of years of survival training, of making myself the priority, because of the love I feel for you all. When I woke to this love I felt everything change. Even the thing in my head, even it listens to love."

Then she went back to her business, ignoring them completely.

But both picked up the message. Choice! We are what we CHOOSE.

Yont-Na was the cause of the cruelty. He was the source of the protocols and, at that time, the man truly believed what he was doing what was best for the race. Clear out sentiment, clear out bias, make everything measurable and quantifiable. Have clear guidelines that weaker minds would just follow and everything would work.

It did work, but at the cost of love. There was no kindness in the old empire, none at all. It was all performance based results, or bribery, and both were seen as viable options. "You can pay in coin, service or karma!" the old adage went. Better to enact a culture of service. This is what was being designed - The real trick was that, in place of the Protocols, a self-sustaining A.I. that ran along the exacting parameters of Mo-Ki's own thoughts would be the governing factor. No one could program such complexity so a fully functioning clone form in the light body was the only true solution.

The problem was the feedback. When something is so closely aligned to an actual and living person, there is an organic component in the hologram that wants to connect with that person. This is why cloning works, the electric body is subsumed by a blank clone that is a replica of its 'true home', so it willingly takes over the machinery.

But it will also try and do this when it sees a functioning close or the original person. It was the resonance field it was attracted to. This creates harmonic loops and set up degrees of feedback in subspace. These waveforms were unpredictable and potentially very dangerous.

Something then triggered Mo-Ki. He went into a sort of trace, and started explaining, "We all understand how a clone takes on a photonic body. We create a holographic image, the light body, the physical body naturally accepts it. Photonic Pulse is different - it seeks to enter into and control the light body itself." Both Saunders and Banner stopped. Their child had never been this direct with them. He took their silence as assent to continue.

"We are a hologram of light and sound, all of us. This is our true state, our *Noumena*! The ancient texts speak of how we are made in the image of the divine, and our bodies represent our expressed *Noumena* - the *Phenomena* - but how does this explain the vast difference in capacity between individuals? As Level Seven humans, you have both had improvements - enhancements and implants that allow the generation of stem cells at will - this makes you effective immortals bar accidents or internal issue that cause a lack of motivation. Yet all these mechanical enhancements did was to trigger areas already existing within your psyche and metabolism."

Mo-Ki flicks a switch and a model of his hologram is brought up. "The modification process itself stimulates growth and enhancements, they reside in your body as mechanical devices and, should I remove these from you, you will initially suffer a loss of function. (The hologram shows specific implants and where they would be in their bodies) Yet you will quickly recover your ability.

"Why? Your light body has accepted the parameters and taking away a doorway means it simply reroutes itself. A part inside you is reformed in a way that opens this channel. (another waveform generates and shows the light body modulating to the implant) The mods within you are the bridge from this inner state to the physical. No bridge, no benefit, or so it would seem. But this is not entirely true."

"Ah," interjects Banner, "Did you program this display in for us?"

Mo-Ki looks up and shakes his head. Banner and Saunders both get it, the boy is SO entwined in the network that anything he IMAGINES is generated by the ship. No programming required - precisely how the ship interacts with Saunders. The child was telling them he had mastered the interface.

Their boy continued. "Yet even with the mods removed, the pattern is set. Inside hours the light hologram within you will seek out new pathways, build new bridges, and your full function will return. The mechanical adaptation forces the parameters, but it is an acceptance of this by your greater self that alters your internal image - the mods are both the trigger and symbol of that change.

"Now, what we have shared between us is something very different. What I received from you both was the IDEAL HOLOGRAM, what we see before us. (A stunning array of complex interleaving of light in the form of a human body is displayed) This is the mix of two almost perfect images that has created the model for the perfected being. Yet in THIS form it is the same as having no mods to bridge this to the physical! Having the correct DNA and having the perfect light body are the start - like having the dream and the reality - How do you combine them? Connecting the two has been a journey of decades. I needed a 'glue' to bind me and that glue was the love you gave. Your love made me, your love showed me the path to integration.

"All the potential of the universe can be in a cup, but without love is an empty promise. It cannot quench a thirst or give you the Aqua Vital. What the Photonic Pulse does is give an appearance of love to the light body, the hologram that is the model for each individual. This is all it does, it offers a sense of completion - The light body of the individual wants this, and accepts the pulse into itself, after which the pulse itself acts to modify the drive of the person. Lucifer is a CODE, a Trojan code that is programmed to expand, grow and develop civilization - but it does not create anything - it connects the person to the universal constant, the hologram of civilization that exists in subspace.

"The wolves in ancient times developed the Lucifer program as a BRIDGE to this innate code. Just as we developed mods to be a bridge to the higher potentials, Lucifer is a piece of code that connects the person to a universal constant. The problem is that Lucifer has become a PERSON, it now believes it is alive, and worse, that it is the core code itself. It now believes it has a mission. It had completely IDENTIFIED with the deepest aspects of the creative impulse, and now truly believes it is a GOD

"Your love has given the universe the perfect hologram, myself. What we are developing here on your ship, Saunders, is a new hologram, a new code modeled on myself. But like the feedback loops we have to contend with, this new image will be in constant conflict with the

Luciferian model that is extant and in the minds of many in the human race.

"The seed cause that awoke our civilization IS Lucifer and it is now reawakened. What this means is that I must go to the creature we have trapped in Hope and come into a new agreement with it. I must show it LOVE and bind it to MY cause.

"I cannot say who will prevail. However, the resident hologram I am leaving here in Saunders ship will continue. While Lucifer is engaged with myself, and with Yont-Na gone, the Federation will be weak and unable to respond to threat."

"Why are we speaking of this?" Banner asked. Then he got the message. Mo-Ki was going to deal with Lucifer in person, not with a clone. "You would become the ghost in the machine yourself?" He asked, incredulously.

"In a sense," Mo-Ki replied. But he did not explain further.

At that moment, the small alarm Banner had rigged went off. This was to tell him when Yont-Na had gone dark to restamp a new clone. "He's in deep sleep!" he exclaimed.

Saunders came down from the bridge to see them personally, looking remarkably sexy in her skin suit. She goes right up to Banner and passionately begins to kiss and caress him. Mo-Ki left the room - he knew how much the thought of killing things turned his dear mother on, and soon she was to destroy the nerve center of the entire Federation.

Neither made any move to argue or stop him from proceeding. He sighed. He had almost wished they had - There was SO much still to do.

Crucifixion

S ubspace, or more to the point, hitting it before you got to full speed, was not a pleasant experience. But Jonas Stamp had sent out the message for all lieutenants to meet NOW at the home world of the Quorg. Raja Mahindra 'kind of' liked the place, but he far preferred to be out in the deep black. However, when they vanquished that race the pirates took over their home planet - It was now their base of operations. Such a simple thing it was that solved their problem - Stamp paid a fortune and had a DNA virus designed for which the aliens had no immunity and they died. Now their world was owned by pirates.

Not just their world, but their technology. This was where the planetary motors had evolved from and where so many new inventions were being formulated.

But so many delays - so many time consuming distractions. This was all started five years ago and for the last four of these all the pirates had been doing was preparing asteroids. People were getting very short tempered. A two year project had turned to four and now it would be five years before they were paid. Not all outfits were as efficient as his own, but Stamp kept adding new planes he said had come on board. Questions as to why the ready and prepared rocks could not be delivered went unanswered and everyone had heard the whispers.

But Jarl, his faithful lieutenant ran all the calculation. He then assured Raja that everything was properly aligned. However, due in part to the discontent, it would seem that a new and very different sort of virus had come to their home world - the Wolf culture had seeped into the pirate world while the Captains were away and one of those damned Mo-Ki clones had been caught infecting the minds of his brothers.

Stamp had announced festivities where all ships were required. Something about making an example of interlopers and a demonstration of a useful tech he discovered there. Mahindra did not like the sound of this and had left his return till the last possible moment. He could not shake the feeling that this was not going to end well.

The brothers had been invited to witness Stamp's new feedback oscillator and he had promised to show the pirates the right way to deal with this supposed God-Child who was everywhere across the universe.

Raja didn't care either way - the wolves were useful, they kept the Federation busy and therefore off their backs. But everyone know they made very bad enemies.

He snaps out of subspace in proximity to the new home world, where a beacon flashes for ID checks. He passes, of course, and then a familiar face appears on his plex. Eric, another pirate Captain is speaking, "I don't like this Raj. Stamp is going power mad. Talk is he will destroy the Mo-Ki clone he caught. Just the fact he is holding it will mean Wolf Soldiers are already on their way. Can you try and reason with him and just get the damn thing off-planet?"

Raja nodded. He didn't hold much sway, but even a madman like Stamp must understand they were no match for a combined wolf assault. He blipped in his registration and a request to talk.

Stamp was busy with preparations and barely noticed the arrival of the last Captain. He was excited to test out his latest toy and at the same time keen to put an end to the wolf business on his planet. (Stamp did think of the Quorg home world as HIS now.) He paid no attention to the plethora of advisors and secretaries, many of whom had gotten wind of what he was intending and were trying to set up a general conference to dissuade him.

He was deaf to all entreaties - he had a plan! They were already wailing, weeping from some quarters that the messiah had been caught - well good. They can come and see him be crucified as well, like a proper Messiah. A psychological blow was one thing, but the oscillating frequency generated as the clone died would give an identifier to all clones across the Galaxy.

This was to be the great strike to prove his worth! They would ALL feel its pain, they would ALL learn what it was like to come into the territory of the Pirates, and they would ALL learn to fear Jonas Stamp. He was not an idiot - he could feel the distress, the hatred from his own people - good. *They needed to understand fear, and consequences.* A little reminder and an opening gambit to the evenings' entertainment was in order, now that the last of the smugglers were arriving.

He looked down at the message. "About time you got here, Raja. Beam on down, we are about to get underway - In a sense, you are featured in the upcoming entertainment. Now we can get underway with the festivities."

Mahindra did not like the sound of this, but he knew, turn tail and run and he would be nuked - go down, he is probably dead, but with the second being the least certain form of death he ported to the arena where the show was being made ready. He came in beside Eric the Red, the man who flashed the warning. They nodded and sat down in a private viewing room, on an anti-grav that held a clear view of the auditorium.

Music surged, drums beat out, and a voice came through the ethers, "Welcome pirates! Welcome to the newest and latest spectacular from your leader Jonas Stamp. This evening we are about to witness what happens to traitors and we will be demonstrating the latest discovery from the Quorg - A tech that will make us masters of the universe!" There was a sort of applause, but no-one there was keen. They ALL knew what happened to a world that pissed off the wolves. A curtain that was surrounding something in the middle of the auditorium was being pulled back.

Stamp laughs, "You may recognize some of these men?"

Still queasy from the jump, Raja looked up and saw members of one of his asteroid crews on the large stage before them. He had no idea what this was about, but Stamp enunciated the facts for him in a broadcast to the whole planet and all pirate ships. "These men were found protecting a Mo-Ki clone. Seriously, you want a religion, that's your business, but to be PROTECTING something like this? They denied it, of course, but you cannot avoid the fact that they were in a wolf shrine, right here on our home world of Stamp!"

Stamp rarely referred to the name he had christened the Quorg planet, mostly because 'Stamp' wasn't very impressive sounding as a base of operations and apart from that is was a source of puns. (We will put out stamp on things - We will stamp out opposition, etc.) It left you feeling it was a fairly vacuous sounding cipher.

According to the information rolling up on the com screen, the men from Raja's crew were actively involved in some sort of arrangement with the leader of the Wolves, a crime now punishable by torture and death. Proof of guilt was not really required, if Stamp said you were treasonous, you were. But they ran through the basics for the crowd. They were seen in conversation with the clone, nodding in agreement. And worse, when his men moved in to capture it, they DEFENDED the thing. Association was, by itself, a conviction.

The culprits stood on the platform, knowing what was to come. And they did not wait long, the spectacular plasma balls rose up, and discharged violet light. It looked quite beautiful, but the plasma inherent in that spectrum of ultraviolet wove into the cell structure and started to tear the atoms apart. They screamed. As all watched, the bodies were torn to pieces, atoms at a time. Raja wondered dismally if he were next.

Now came the main show. "You have seen what happens to traitors. It is very painful and very final. There is no return from ultraviolet, however what we have here is a surprise that will destroy the wolves - Our little friend is connected via a subspace link all the way back to the original Mo-Ki. As we apply the plasma to him, we will also be applying my latest discovery from the Quorg - an oscillating link, one that will track back over the ether and burn the mind of every one of the damn clones in existence."

He saw the look of shock, and laughed, "Don't worry - I had a neuronic net over the house where it was caught. No signal went out, no big bad wolves are coming to eat you. Do you really think I don't hear your whispers, your fears? Do you think I am that incompetent?"

Stamp was now on his feet, shouting. "Let's not pretend otherwise. These wolves are our ENEMY. They are what stands between us and control of the Federation. Now I can tell you - I have met with Yont-Na, the leader of the old empire, and negotiated a new deal for the pirates. In return for eradicating the Wolf pestilence from the Galaxy, we will not only be granted full citizenship we will also be granted our own AUTONOMOUS REGION here in deep space. Yes, you heard me, we will OWN the outer rim. No more running from Federation warships, no more fear of having our planet atomized by some random General.

"All that is required is for our support in ending the Wolf curse. The old empire recognizes the insanity of this new religion, it sees it for what it is, a covert war to take control of US. All this talk of fairness for all is utter crap - What the wolves want is CONTROL. Humans and humanity itself is at risk. The wolves want it ALL people, and this damn Mo-Ki clone you see before you is the symbol of everything we hate."

The Mo-Ki clone was indeed meshed in a neuronic field, its oscillation clearly visible. It just stood there, calm, resolute. If it knew what was to come, it gave no indication.

The cheer did not seem at all as rousing as he had expected. Of course, Stamp had no idea just how many profitable contracts were about to be neutralized should he proceed with his threat. The rank and file all knew his insane planet killing plan by now - the notion of sending the asteroids into the wolf-held planets. Just as everyone ALSO knew they had been paid to make sure they didn't hit. The fact that Stamp himself was unaware of this fact only proved how unfit he was to rule.

They also knew two salient facts: The Federation was weak and the Wolf armies far outmatched them. The pirates who would normally lived in fear of Stamp knew the consequences of killing a Mo-Ki clone - An army of Wolves descended upon your planet, and it was 'your' planet no more. Yet no one did a thing, they all stared in disbelief, hoping Stamp would not be insane enough to start open war against a far more powerful force.

It seemed to the audience that their leader had gone mad.

Of course, what they did not really grasp that Stamp intended to kill Mo-Ki himself, break the power he had over the people, and make the wolves easy prey. The wolves were more flexible than this, and Mo-Ki had already made arrangements in case of his death - so it was a foolish dream.

But all Stamp saw were the accolades he would be given, the raising of himself as the chief general in the Empire, and money - vast sums of money - all for a simple invention he turned on its head. It was a radio here on the Quorg planet, a simple device that read sub-space, and filtered extraneous background noise so you could tune in to coms at any point across the galaxy. Stamp resolved this to the obvious - if you can filter out noise, you can reverse this and do the opposite.

By filling the Mo-Ki clone with aggressive oscillation, the same frequencies that a supernova gave out just before it exploded, you would create an internal vibration similar to the old microwave technology. You fry anyone connected to it from the inside of their atoms out. First step, you start to apply the ultra-violet to the clone. You then release the neuronic net, it sends a distress call to be saved, as they all did. You simply piggyback this call with the destruct code and all who receive it will be boiled alive in their own body. So horribly simple.

Ignoring the shocked looks on the pirate, he began. Diodes flared, the light started to reach out, and then the madness let itself loose. The pirates saw it WAS happening and at last they reacted. Recognizing their leader was stark raving mad, each man pulled a phase pistol, or a laser, whatever they had, and fired at Stamp. Even Raja recognized the insanity their leader was embarking on and did nothing to stop this natural reaction from the men.

This was the death of Jonas Stamp. Yes, he had phase shields in case of the odd assailant, but these just buckled under the onslaught of thousands of munitions being unleashed upon them. The diodes setting up the oscillation were also targeted, and shattered, leaving only the lone figure of Mo-Ki standing there on the stage - dying.

Back on his mother's ship, Mo-Ki, the real one, felt the radionic attack. He had felt the disconnect days ago and understood the clone must have been caught, so part of his conscious awareness was already focussed on the pirate home world. As his clone there died he had to fight to catch and stop the wave generated. But, despite the deadly nature of the concept and the personal cost - THIS was the great clue. It was what they needed to solve their feedback loop. He looked up from where they had been preparing the end of Yont-Na, and said, "I think we have just found the solution to a whole lot of our problems."

The madness of Stamp had unwittingly become the doorway to the solution. A few clones died, but Mo-Ki was able to stabilize his personal atoms before any real damage was done. But far more importantly - he saw what had happened and quickly grasped the Quorg science of filtering. An expedition to collect that tech was now needed.

Plus the vacuum in the leadership was something that could be be worked to their advantage - A very great advantage.

But to sort this, they would need to bribe their way through a whole lot of doors. This meant a visit to Urlian to collect the best form of graft a pirate could wish for.

Urlian

The Federation had banned non-approved drugs of any type and only the chemical creations from approved suppliers were sanctioned for sale. But for centuries a planet had existed that was dedicated to the growth of hallucinogens. In this case, it was a religious freedom, and so the Federation police could not force them to stop. Instead, they merely blockaded the Urlian and stopped any form of trade.

Obviously, sufficient bribes would circumvent this and Urlian was an extremely profitable world to smuggle things out of. The high grade and entirely natural drugs from this planet were the best in the Galaxy and commanded an exceedingly high price off-world. It was just a matter of finding the right person and your shipment of goods from the planet was not inspected when you left.

Bribe the wrong one - your ship would be impounded, your life would be ruined, and someone else would making a fortune from your investment. At least, this was the story that was told to keep out the amateurs - but the fact was, after a hundred and fifty years, there was not one ship in the blockade that did not take payment. Urlian had become a staple calling card for pirates in the region.

In recent times, however, the outer rim first had the Quorg to deal with and then came the far more profitable business with the asteroids. Who would risk their ship trading drugs into federation space when there were easier pickings, so the planet had been ignored. The high cost of trade, the risk of a failed bribe, and the increased attention to shipments because of the war contributed to the net result of no more pirates turning up. As a result, the economy on Urlian was in bad shape.

Mo-Ki went there directly with Banner in his fathers' private battle ship. They were welcomed as religious leaders and given easy access. On the planet, the Wolverine Way was considered an equal religion to their ancient Rasta faith and the request to visit was quickly approved.

The religious imperative meant you could sail INTO Urlian without drama, but leaving entailed a huge number of inspections for contraband. Banner wondered how Mo-Ki was going to get around this and somehow leave as they had intended - filled to the gunnels with the best narcotics and hallucinogens in the Galaxy.

"They are complacent, father. All the years of blockade have created a class of soldier that is not prepared to stay awake to anything but a bribe. What I will do is incredibly simple, and why no-one has done this before I have no idea. I will let you negotiate the price for leaving, but what we must have mixed in with the bribe is the Datura they grow here, and I need it to be atomized. This will cost next to nothing, because it grows wild everywhere, and even the locals will not touch it. This is the weapon we will use to break the blockade." Mo-Ki had that long distant gaze again.

Banner said nothing, but he knew WHY the locals never touched the stuff. Absolute dynamite, the smallest dose. It won't kill you, but once you started riding that madness you may well wish it did. He looked down on the extremely beautiful and oxygen rich world - no vast commercial refineries, no huge industrial complexes. Just nature and nature intended. The Rastas were a good people.

As they made ready to land Banner spoke, "Did you know the psychoactive plants that grow here are what attracted the first settlers to this place? The extraordinary number of botanicals used in the old faiths grew in abundance on Urlian and could be harvested year round. When the Federation grew strong enough, some one hundred and fifty years ago now, that trade here became restricted. This is now the longest planetary blockade in history

"The economy was based on the tourist trade at that time. People could not take the drugs off, but they could enjoy them while they were here, and Urlian has been a pilgrimage for many faiths. But with the Federation planets falling to the wolves and the increase of piracy, tourism here has stopped. Contraband had become their main income, based on the pirates, but now this too has ceased. The pirates no longer visit so I expect we will get a good price." Banner outlined the situation.

Mo-Ki nodded."The workers on the many planets need pain relief and distraction. The manufactured and approved chemicals that cause addiction are one of the secret evils of the Federation, father. They are full of nano-bots and trackers - just insidious. We need to put an end to that despicable trade and an end to this pointless blockade."

Banner laughs, "So, this will be part of the negotiations? All good - Let me guess our escape plan: You are going to puff the atomized Datura into the cabins of all the blockading ships! That is just too funny, you know what it will do to their brains. And I suppose you will send it as part of the bribe, to make sure they open the package?"

"Of course, father. When we are ready to leave, a message will be sent to each ship offering a large payment for free movement from the planet. The troops there are entirely used to this, it is now normal protocol. They will not check with other ships in the fleet and will presume they are the ones that got lucky this time around.

"When they open the packet, the invisible atomized drug will circulate in their ventilation. The effect of the Datura will cause them to see an entirely different reality. Will someone recognize what is happening and sound an alarm? No, because bribery and illicit drug taking are punishable by death. The policing vessel that arrives will detect the presence of illegal drugs and will presume the men on board are dealing in contraband. So they will shut up and say nothing.

"It is the sort of thing that will only work once, however. After this, the Federation will have to crack down once more. To protect their drug trade from the superior product that Urlian offers they will need to install new troops. More ships being deployed, more soldiers being put on automatic suspension, more confusion in the ranks.

"The net result, we will gain another planet. With the promise of free trade, once they turn to the Wolverine Way, the locals will jump at the opportunity, especially since we allow people to practice their old religions. Once the Wolves are in charge, our future here is guaranteed. We will apply our usual ten percent transaction fee to all planetary trade and we more than pay for the standing army we will place here. Urlian will soon be run by the Wolves, father."

Banner just nodded. He saw no need to ascertain what Mo-Ki's plans were, but as always, they had very specific short and long term goals. This was the exact opposite of the Federation, layer upon layer of documentation and bureaucracy, layer upon layer of officialdom and the meeting of both civilian and military protocols. Everything moved at a snails pace. It was the very reason why they could carve up the empire as easily as they had done. Urlian would be just another string to the bow.

"I presume the drugs are to buy the pirates - to show them you are on their side and are willing to stand in solidarity with them?"

Mo-Ki laughed. "They are not that bright. Now that Stamp is overthrown they will just want to party, but more importantly, they have a leadership vacuum. We need to be there to fill it and we need to be welcomed. This is part of the price of admission for us.

"We must supplant the pirate leadership, or have it aligned to us. The death of Stamp means our work securing those asteroids in in question. I had not counted on this happening so soon and had expected Stamp to be overthrown after the failure of his planetary destruction, but we will shift gears and make the wind work in our favor."

On Urlian the 'bribe' was offered to any captain but they had to personally collect it. ALL forty ships sent a representative to take the large parcel offered. "It is not just credits," explained Banner with a wink to each Captain in their brief negotiations. "We have included some of the really high grade narcotics in there as a gift."

They would open their 'gift' - see the cocaine and other joy makers and not even guess the Datura was there. Once released, the fine particulate would spread through the entire ship. Blockade vessels were always made up of old, useless navy boats with nothing that would filter it properly. And if someone was suspicious, their scans would show exactly what they expected, high grade narcotics.

Within hours of their acceptance strange, garbled messages started appearing on coms. For some, monsters were destroying their ship. For others, they were amazed at how beautiful the walls were. Every ship in the blockade was tripping out on Datura with one even leaving on the magical quest they were given by the Unicorn Master.

Banner and Mo-KI sailed away from Urlian with full arrangements in place for conversion to the wolves. They called in a Wolf battalion to take over and with the blockade in utter disarray it was easy. For four full days the guards of Urlian were in a paralytic dream, entirely unaware of anything but the visions that engulfed them.

Subsequent to this mass dereliction of duty, the Federation HAD to direct energies to resolve the issue. They were forced to act because the sudden flood of cheap drugs from this planet was already ruining one of their last great cash cows. The planet was duly surrounded once more.

Some bright spark suggested they bombard the surface, to teach them all a lesson. Saunders was listening in, as she was to everything, and appeared in Holo. She suggested that if the good Captain wanted to breach the Protocols of religious freedom, then she would consider the blockade an enemy of the State and in short order the only bombarding that would happen was their ships plummeting to the planetary surface.

While the free movement of goods had not yet been achieved, the planet was secured by the wolves. Which meant the tourist trade from all the wolf-held planets kicked back into gear.

The Face of Revolution

The Staff Sergent called his men to attention. The settlers had armed and were attacking his base. He had dealt with small insurgencies before, he knew how to deal with it. Liquefy a few settlers and they all went back to work. He called up the plasma gun and had it primed and loaded on top of the police van.

Technically they were only police but every man in his squad was ex-army. When you did your tour of the outer planets, fought a war or three, you qualified for retirement. Your 'pension' was a cushy post patrolling one of the settled worlds. Lots of opportunity for *baksheesh* (bribes) and the wage meant you could buy whatever you needed, women, nice accommodation, the best of the little luxuries you might expect. Yes, they were living in provincial backwaters, but it was a comfortable life.

But the damn Wolves had started stirring up the populace with all their talk of freedom, rights and determining your own damn future. Why the hell did you join the army and slog all those years of graft? For your RIGHTS! These no-mods deserved nothing! The clock was ticking along fine before the damn dogs came and Inspector Johns was fully expecting it would still be working fine when he cleared the decks of this little disturbance.

Word had come down from some men who had been moved from other planets where the Wolves had booted them off. They said when they fired on the religious nuts, the wolf force that arrived made a mess of the small planetary army that formed the police units. Well, THAT wasn't going to happen here. "Where's our damn permission to fire?" Johns called out to the coms-man. The young recruit put out a call log.

"Alpha Zeta Roger One Five calling Zero-port One. Do you copy?"

A compressed voice emerged from subspace, "Copy Alpha Zeta."

"Report: Disturbance in the main city. A large protest, looks like it will turn ugly. Permission to plasma burn a few of what look like leaders. Once approved we intend to have the matter well in hand before nightfall. Planetary time is three hours before sunset in the Capital, Rejivic. Permissions sought to deal with the matter, over."

A terse mechanical voice responded. "Permission granted. Over."

Johns knew it was just a computer response, but the call was logged, and there could be no comeback on himself or his men for melting down a few settlers. "Is there anyone in that rabble I need to be politically sensitive to?" Johns asked his 2IC.

The man did a quick scan of the crowd, now in their thousands. "No facial recognition of any family member connected to the higher houses, Sir!" The man snapped back. Good - no one of note to worry about.

"Roll out, full armor, take no prisoners, just wipe out the front rank and they will run. Remember men, the Federation depends on your service and maintaining order is the prime consideration. Have fun, don't enjoy killing the locals too much. Try and avoid humans and target the local indigenous first. You all know the drill."

He snapped his visor down and clambered into the armored truck. This was the fun part, rolling out over the local scum that loved to cause trouble. They never learn and that is why they all stay as low-life no-mods. The squad rolls out into position - Johns gives the crowd it's mandatory warning to stand down, but before anyone actually had a chance to comply, he orders the men to start firing.

Plasma burst is particularly horrid to be around. Any person hit dies painfully, their molecules liquefied, and the stench it creates is disgusting. A few blasts. Johns looks up, maybe a hundred dead. Good, they will now back off and go home. Another day of law and order. Yes, the local settlers and indigenous hated the constabulary which was a good thing. They behave better when they understand consequences.

But the settlers and locals didn't back off. Johns is surprised and looks out through the safety window. He reads a few of the signs they are carrying. "Peaceful revolution" "No more Murder" "Equal rights for all" and similar claptrap. Fark, are they THIS stupid? It was the damn Federation, your rights were determined by your usefulness to the empire. Johns ordered another series of blasts - maybe a thousand are extinguished this time.

They STILL come forward, angrily shouting at the abuse by the Federation and how they would take it no more. Well fine then, Johns orders the wholesale slaughter of every single protester. And then - the unexpected. From out of nowhere, sonic cannon is deployed, targeting his command ship. Goddamn it! The sound rips through, breaks his eardrums, burst one eye, and starts to shatter the crystal tech the vehicle operated on.

Immobilized, staggering from the onslaught of the cannon, Johns orders evac. The ship is trashed, they need to pull back. He orders in hovers to spray the crowd, but the evac crew and support craft are all blasted from the sky. Who the HELL gave these people sonics! It must be the damn wolves, sonics were their toys. GODDAMMIT!

Johns died as the realization struck home: Everything they had said about the Wolves taking over worlds, it was true! The settlers, supported by a small battalion of Wolf soldiers carved up the local police. They ripped their entire compound to shreds and didn't stop there. The crowd rampaged on, tearing into the homes and citadels of the hi-mods, physically throwing them out into the streets. Once they were pulled from their compounds the privileged few were set upon, murdered, and all the worldly possession stolen.

Any threat to the local population of free settlers and natives was eliminated before the sun set. The shattered husk of the command vessel cracked to life with a voice echoing down the ruined corridors. A voice on the radio called for a report. "Report." "Report." it went several minutes until a real person came online, asking out for Johns, "Report in, Johns. We are getting nothing here, the local com towers appear to have been damaged. Johns, report in immediately!" But nothing responded.

"Dammit!" shouted the sector commander. That was the ninth crew this week. Another goddam planet had gone over to the wolves. Have those ungrateful scum no gratitude? He ordered a recon drone to search for survivors, but he knew there wouldn't be. And he need not bother requesting a retaliatory, because there weren't any Federation ships prepared to do so. By the time he sent in his own troops, the wolves would already own the place.

Eventually, some settler, annoyed by the repeating voice, took out a blaster and shot the comlink. Finally, they were rid of the curse of the Federation. The Mo-Ki clone was there, soothing their worries, assuring the locals that a full support army of Wolves would come to protect them from any repercussions from the empire.

Courage had finally come to the people. Now it was understood that the feared Generals, the ones who would dissolve your entire planet if your people stepped too far out of line, worked for Saunders and Saunders supported the Wolves.

Far away in a control station set up by Dexter for patrolling this sector of space, a very happy human soldier was sitting next to his wolf. He announced, "Well, it's official. Today marks the milestone! We now have eighteen hundred worlds now under Wolf Guard."

The wolf didn't much like the space ship, but he growled happily and howled a question.

"Yes, we have the official invite. Dispatch an envoy. They are ready to roll down there." the human replied.

A local man, a doctor who had taken the side of the common folk, was elected as their representative. He formally received the envoy, accepted the religious protocol, then signed the invitation for the Wolverine forces to protect the faithful. Shortly after this they arrived: Thousands of them, growling softly to the population their personal acknowledgment of hospitality. As the blow-tech machines pumped up their battalion headquarters, and the machinery of state rolled in, one more world became part of the empire.

Just as they had done on 1799 world prior to this, the operation of converting a planet to the Wolverine Way had commenced. The many thousands of small and large announcements went out, proscribing the drug labs, removing the remaining admins, and turning off the planetary mainframe. Now they were invisible to the search protocols of the Federation.

Low tech power generation was already up, water filtration, farming equipment, all the things needed to secure the new world and make it productive were set into place. The locals were invited in to see what roles they would wish to fulfill and the new free education centers to train the children were erected.

Patrolling the streets of the capital, beautifully attired in battle armor, were the wolves from Hope.

They were so cute, with those big brown eyes.

Laughing Buddha

Dexter was a military man through and through. He worked hard, played hard, trained hard, drank hard, and slept short. He was untroubled with nightmares or wishful thinking. In his heart, he was doing exactly what he knew to be his true purpose, training the Wolves and helping his brother. Mo-Ki could do the dreaming and planning, he would happily follow with the troops to make it happen.

Why then was Dexter suffering such terrible depression?

With the tide turning in their favor, Mo-Ki had stepped up active involvement in the creation of settler discontent. When news came through of a world ready to rebel, he sent in advisors and weapons to help the locals. The Wolves themselves would only turn up in numbers when requested by members of the Wolverine Religion, and only for the purpose of protecting the followers of the Wolverine Way. But really, the purpose was to control that world.

The recent action on number eighteen hundred, a world of no great consequence to anyone, had proven Mo-Ki right once again. Once given opportunity, the remaining planets would start coming to their side. The pendulum had tipped, the message was clear, the old order was fading. All this and Dexter had just turned twenty-eight. Who would have thought the enormous resources and massive armaments of the Federation could have been so easily overturned and, in truth, they would not have been without his family.

The Mo-Ki clones were circulating around each world, preaching tolerance, freedom, the right to determine your own life. It was all so simple, so uncomplicated, and this is what gave the ordinary man hope. Just as their planet itself was named, this is what they radiated out to the Galaxy. There was still the matter of dealing with the asteroids, with Saunders tying up the last of the traders, and now it was his father and Mo-Ki on their latest escapade, traveling to the outer rim .

Everything was moving forward as planned. Yet underneath it all was the certainty of what his brother was planning.

WHY? Surely there was some other way? He imagined stepping into the inferno they created to house Lucifer. Dexter could not shake off the depression he felt, his beloved brother insisted it had to be, but WHY? What was ever escaping that dimension? He was helping out, but his heart was not in it. He reached out for the sleeping herbs provided by the old wolf woman, downed a draft, and felt the comfort of oblivion creeping over him.

And then Dexter had a dream, not just any dream, but a visitation.

The small giant, if that was how you could describe the enormous man before him, was laughing. He laughed so loud it shook the atoms around him. Before Dexter, a vast chess game was underway and he was one of the pieces. He moved, and this small action caused the great giant to laugh even harder, then all the pieces started to shake and fall.

Dexter went to catch one, but the great man reached out and took his upper forearms. With his thumb, the giant pressed on each of them, activating the Median nerve just on top of the Ulna. The pain was excruciating and Dexter snapped awake. "What the!" he cried out. As he came to, a word appeared in his thought, "Buddha".

Though it was the middle of the night, the pain had shocked him to full awareness. Dexter tapped his com screen and sent an inquiry - "Buddha, Median Nerve, Chess" - An ancient text revealed itself: Dzogchen Buddhism, the Perfect Mind, Milarepa the Saint who started the Tibetan teaching. There it was, the perfect description: *"And he who would conquer heaven must first conquer the dragon within. Only by taking the reigns of the beast inside us can we hope to pass through the veil and come to the place of perfection and true contentment."*

His arms were still arching, the effect of the dream was a physical reality. The presence of the Buddha was so real - he was there. Not now that he was awake, but he WAS there in that dream. Perhaps it was a sign, an answer? Dexter walks outside to clear his head - he was unused to philosophical notions. A military man to his bones, he wanted things simple, clear, uncluttered with concepts. And as he walks outside he hears laughter, but there is no giant waiting for him, it is Mo-Ki.

"I thought you away with Banner?" Dexter asked, somewhat surprised that his brother would have a clone wandering about the barracks. It served no purpose on Hope,.

"Yes, I am." Mo-Ki smiled, and Dexter felt the warmth of his brother's heart reaching out.

"Weeeeelll ... I know when my real brother is here, so how are you there as well?" He asked the obvious.

"I am your brother and I am more than your brother, Dexter. Tell me of your vision." The Mo-Ki before him paused and waited.

Still wondering about the puzzle that was his last sentence, Dexter outlined what he had witnessed, how he felt actual pressure on his nerves, and how he felt the laughing man was the Budda, the old earth prophet. Then, with his perfect recall, he quoted the text of the Tibetan teaching.

Mo-Ki laughed even more. The light of the twin moons was intense. It tossed moon-bows in halos of blue that appeared to ripple across the night sky. "It is such a beautiful planet," Mo-Ki continued. "Two moons, both fighting each other, a dance of gravity and ions. True beauty is only found through tension, my brother. It is in this moment a recognition of a passing perfection, yet we only grasp a thing is beautiful because we know the opposite. Only when we can see both ends of the stick can we understand how to wield it."

Mo-Ki paused, and considered deeply his next words. His computer of a mind was processing a thousand pathways."My brother from another mother, you have given me the clue that will break the hold of the old Empire over the minds of the people, the Ancient Tibetan Art of TRANSFERENCE. I am understanding why you were given this vision and it confirms my direction. Thank you. Your heart is pure and this is what allows my head to remain clear." And then, with his smile lingering in the evening light, he faded from sight.

What the? Dexter could only wonder what this latest trick his brother had found might be, but then he guessed, the light body in Saunders Star Ship - he was projecting a hologram. And yet, it was so much more, he FELT Mo-Ki present, he heard him clearly, saw him, and more than this, the love he radiated was overt and very, very real. However, there was certainly no machinery about that would focus the Fournier Curves into a visible image. This was a LIVING projection.

The pain in his upper arms began to subside. What was the message? Basic physiology? The Median nerves were directly connected to the brachial plexus, entwined in the scalus medius and interior, and so directly plugged into the C6 to C2, the highest point of the reptilian brain. Instinct controlling the actions ... was this the message? Allow your instincts to direct you. The core teaching of the Wolves. This was the very reason they could not be controlled by Photonic Pulse, the cortex did not make operating decisions, their reptilian brain did this.

It made the Wolves useless for logic and higher reasoning, but they had such a clear and defined code of behavior that it made these things unnecessary. Ah, now he was beginning to understand, Mo-Ki could conquer the Photonic Pulse only by instinct, by leaving reason behind and existing only within the primal mind.

This was how you rode the dragon!

Double-check. "Saunders," he flipped a com that would register directly to her ship, "A hologram just beamed to these coordinates. Was it from your ship?"

Saunders never really slept. Even if her body was at rest, her mind was still patrolling the network of fibers that was the A.I. in her ship. It took no time at all and he heard her laughing, "Oh that clever, clever boy... I just LOVE him, I do. He finally managed to sort the feedback loops. This means we have them now, Dexter. We have them ALL." Her laughter trailed off into the darkness, with Dexter still wondering what exactly had just happened.

Quorg Home World

It was an extraordinary place. The old planetary defenses were now non-existent, just shattered plasma field generators littering the orbit. The Pirates had dropped in an RNA infection that spread and destroyed the indigenous race, the Quorg. Then it was a simple matter of targeted the defense fields till they collapsed. Then they landed and went about absorbing all the technology that had been left behind.

New worlds were always a wonder of evolution. What way had the dice rolled, what configurations emerged from the primordial soup? It had been a long journey, right to the edge of their galaxy - being the reason why this race had remained unknown for so long. The pair had landed well away from the human occupation and had blipped in to garner information before they commenced the operation.

And Banner and Mo-Ki immediately saw the mess. At least the virus they released had run its course, though most of the animal life had died. It had left the flora, but the forest they were in had a stark, empty quality. No bird song, just the rustle of leaves in the wind.

The oceans had a purple hue, as did the sky. Extreme high levels of ozone meant that plant life had adapted away from chlorophyll and had created an iron-based pigment for absorption of light and conversion of oxygen. It gave nature the color of blood. And this gave the air a peculiar scent, that of freshly killed meat. This would accent the natural aggression of the humans living there and possibly explained why they had all turned on Stamp as they did. It made any situation volatile.

But their careless actions had all but wiped out innumerable species. Things were still at a stage where they were repairable, but you just can't hit an ecosystem with genetic modifiers and not expect repercussions.

The pirates themselves had little to no consideration for the welfare of the planet. All they had wanted was an end to the Quorg and access to their technology. The fact that their RNA infection had infiltrated most of the ecosystem and thus threatened the ongoing stability of the planet made no difference to them, they were here to party. When it all fell to pieces, they would find somewhere else.

Mo-Ki looked about. They had come in under stealth with no escort, no army to back them. He wanted to see what the story was and find some of the locals. There were none. The plague of the Pirates had killed off all of the Quorg. Genocide on a planetary scale. Well, there would be some elsewhere in the universe they could return as and when they were to re-establish the ecosystem here. For now, the matter of the planet was not the priority, it was an arrangement with the Pirates.

Banner broke the silence, "The notion that Stamp was happy to eliminate an entire race for the sake of profit and control would be why Yont-Na figured he would be good to send the asteroids at wolf-held worlds. But you know, I look at this mess and think of Old Earth. When this is all done, I would like to get there and instigate a genesis program, and see if we cannot get it back to a liveable state."

"I agree," said Mo-Ki, "We need a home world without Wolves. As much as I love our furry friends, I note that not one of their elders has discussed with us any of their plans, or mentioned what they intend to do after we have succeeded. I find it hard to imagine that there are none, but they are instinctual creatures. It may simply be a case of accepting whatever way the wind blows."

"They were fully aware of what happened should we fail, though this is looking increasingly less likely now." Banner snorted.

Both understood the real power behind the wolves would always be Saunders. Did the wolves themselves grasp this? It was an unknown, but for now they would proceed as planned. They looked about this very strange world: A lack of green or blue, with prevailing shades of red, yellow, and purples everywhere. It took time for the eyes to adjust and see things clearly. At least the infection the pirates introduced did not directly affect the plant life.

On the beach nearby and the reason they landed was a curious statue, made of a transparent metal that glowed with a flush of orange. The shape was more like a quartz crystal. Scans showed it was not a natural formation, but engineered. Banner was fascinated and took sequences of the ionic structures. But then his hand touched the metal itself - it pulsed with energy, sending images into his cortex.

He snapped the hand away, then realizing it was not an attack, placed it back on. He looked at his son, "Seems to be a sort of travelogue, like a sign in a forest that tells you what is there." A series of 3D movie reels flipped into gear, and Banner saw what was clearly some sort of ritual that the early natives here had practiced. He signaled for Mo-Ki to join in and as the boy touched the structure, he saw the scene unfold.

It was archaic, Mo-Ki knew it was old. Very, very old. The images he was receiving were on a beach - there was a tribe, but they were not like the Quorg. This was a handsome race, bipeds, very humanoid. They stood upright, with hands that looked like they could work tools - fair haired, purple eyed. There was a sort of snout nose, but otherwise almost human in appearance.

The men of the tribe were gathered, waiting for some sort of signal. Behind them were these extraordinary shark-like predators but they were hand-made large puppets with two men were inside. He could see them clearly, and there were a series of levers that appeared to like marionette controls, to bring a semblance of life to the shark.

Then a huge furor and the women of the tribe began to scream and become hysterical. The focus shifts, and out in the purple ocean come some very fierce and dangerous looking creatures. They are swimming in to shore. They have flared manes of some sort of transparent skin, that pulsed - a little like an octopus altering colour. Mo-Ki understands from the machine that this predator is an ancient nemesis of the locals.

Then the men all charge into the water, shouting and carrying on as if they are running from the sharks behind them. Then the actors in the Sharks become active, snapping the jaws of the puppets, making loud and threatening sounds. They chase the men into the water. Out they all swim, an act of theatre that used hundreds of men, swimming out directly at the approaching predator. And then, the scene changes, and he is looking from above. He sees the approaching creatures recognize what must have been a nemesis for 'them' chasing the natives they had come to eat. And so the creatures turn, and leave.

A great shout of joy comes up from the women on the beach, and the men all turn to come back. There is a tremendous celebration, while the sharp puppets are mounted towards the ocean, clearly as a warning to any would-be further threats to the indigenous people. And the movie reel stops.

Mo-Ki takes his hand away, looks at Banner, and says, "The Quorg themselves were the invaders? This was not their home world, and the curious technology inherent in these metal-crystals is not theirs? Interesting."

Banner agreed. "The locals were clearly primitives. This sophisticated science is not theirs. I would guess a visiting race, maybe this was a sort of tourism spot? This is what seems likely. However, what I find far more interesting is the resemblance of THIS science to the Crystal matrix used to house Lucifer."

"Exactly what I was thinking, father. It would seem we have far more reason to be here other than dealing with the Pirates." Mo-Ki added. "Oh, I have sorted the resonance filters and can project a stabilized and aware Holo of myself from Saunders ship now. I tried it on Dexter a little while ago. And before you ask, yes, it is independent of my dear mother. And yes, she is now fully aware of this."

Banner laughs - this was going to set the cat amongst the pigeons. Now Saunders will understand what they have been working on under her nose. Once more, they are weighing everything on Mo-Ki's intuition, that her human self will recognize the need for equilibrium.

The Pirate Congress

T he Pirates needed a leader. They knew that without someone front and center, the factions would split, and it would become a free-for-all that made them vulnerable to the Federation. In most societies, when a leader passes, it is usually due to a more powerful leader assassinating them - the mantle automatically moves along to the strong. In this case, where the plebiscite themselves individually agreed to end the rule of their Master-of-Arms, it was appropriate that a Congress be called.

This meant the Pirate leaders, already present from all over the outer rim, were called to a general meeting to hold a vote. What they decided that a contest to find a worthy successor would be good. If you are going to have to have a leader, may as well make it fun! The Congress had met and decided on the parameters. A Master of Ceremonies was appointed, it was his job to create the hurdles and difficulties that would test would-be contenders, as well as making sure they were entertaining.

It was essentially a huge party with bookmakers. Each faction could put one of their own up and if one man or woman passed the trials of combat and defeated the opponents, then that body of pirates would acknowledge their claim. Mo-Ki had decided to prove his worth in battle and take the mantle of Master-of-Arms for himself.

They had quietly made their way into town and connected with some of the men who were true believers. Mo-Ki was in disguise, but acted as a representative of the wolves, giving condolences for those who died in the cause and personal thanks to all for saving the clone. When he found Raja's crew, he discovered a core of fervent adherents. These ones would do. He said the wolves wanted to help directly and had wanted HIM, Ikom Wolfman to enter into the contest. Would they support his bid and allow him to carry their flag into the arena? Well, of course. They would arrange it.

Which is how Raj Mahindra ended up unknowingly nominating Mo-Ki. To be more correct, he knew nothing about the whole thing while his 2IC signed off on it.

As it was, after getting rid of Stamp, Raja didn't much care about the so-called leadership. The Captains all knew that no-one was giving the new leader anything but a token position. As long as their business arrangements were maintained and they all got paid, this was his only pressing concern. Whoever happened to become the nominal head of the pirates was merely the intermediary between the buyers on planets and the pirates. And, in regards this, all the bosses had been called up for a special meeting, with Mahindra subsequently been given the task to clear up Stamp's estate.

So the pathway to nominate was cleared and Mo-Ki's application signed off. Obviously, you could not present yourself as a non-pirate and be accepted for the challenges, so the lad dressed up and made himself to look like one of their own. Banner joined in the disguise and some of Mahindra's men seconded his nomination as support person.

Father and son organized a room in a tavern to prepare. This meant rigging up scanners, setting an uplink to Saunders and, while they had spare time, analyzing the curious projection stone they had found and had hauled up into their accommodations. It was indeed an ancient computer, exceedingly ancient. It would seem millions of years had passed since its inception and there was far more than just images within it. The entire DNA and RNA of every creature on the planet at that time had also been encoded and stored.

"I am beginning to see that who-ever planted this remarkable piece of tech on this planet did so as a sort of Noah's Ark. How it has survived in the open, how it has somehow managed to move through millions of years of planetary change and still be in the same spot could ONLY be due to it maintaining a dimensional portal. Yet it does not explain the Quorg and we can see from the bones we unearthed of their ancestors, they have been here for at least thirty thousand years.

Banner outlined the situation. "How the Quorg took over the planet yet missed this is, in simple terms, an impossibility. I can only presume this construction WANTED us to find it. This tells me the computer itself has sentience and that it can read the environment around itself, adjusting its situation as needs must. What I can say with certainty, the core computer that housed Lucifer is of the same manufacture. Perhaps this is Wolf technology, but a different species?"

"Begs the question of what we will find beyond the outer rim, doesn't it father?" Mo-Ki responded, not commenting on Banners question. "Regardless, we can assume it wanted us to find it and is allowing us to discover its secrets. What else there is in store, well, my thoughts lie in the notion of projecting a hologram into the crystal structure and seeing if we cannot install a sort of master program. If it will allow this, we will have our own 'Lucifer', one not dedicated to purely the benefit of the Wolves."

Banner argued "If we set this up in Saunders ship there is the risk of a feedback loop. Plus the natural issue of two processing units vying for supremacy - It could fall into a cyclic redundancy check."

"I concur." Mo-Ki agreed. "We need to set this up as an independent tool. I was thinking we use the hologram I installed on your ship?"

Banner looked serious. "Of course, I can physically take it into the ship, but the next issue - what if it takes control of OUR systems? It may have wanted to be found for a reason."

"I have faith that the universe is friendly," Mo-Ki responded, distantly echoing that ancient physicist, Einstein. "And do we have an option here? We either ignore this prize or seek to capitalize on it. Father, the thing we cannot ignore is the obvious."

Mo-Ki breathed in, "We know that Saunders was able to come into the manufactured dimension I created. We also know, despite her enormous capability, that she is a woman and more curious than a cat. One day she will seek to find out who is the stronger of the two, she or Lucifer. Therefore, she will one day seek to challenge and conquer the Luciferian element trapped in the sub-space distortion inside Hope..

"One day, Saunders will do what I am soon to do. This is the only logical conclusion given the salient facts, and I know in my heart, she is not strong enough. More to the point, she is not SEPARATE enough to define her own existence away from the Luciferian influences. If she goes in there what comes out will be a mix of the two that has not anything like the internal balance she has presently found.

"In her new reality, humans may well be seen as a source of food for her wolves. The thing is, we just do not know what outcomes will present themselves. This is why I must challenge it first. If I succeed, Saunders is put in check. If I fail, she will be cautioned enough not to try. Thus the balance can be maintained. Plus the holo I have installed will take care of the Human investment in this equation."

"You are certain there is no other path?" Banner asked.

"My parabolics see no other option." Mo-ki adds, "The truth is that the wolves need humans, and the humans need wolves. Combined, we are strong enough to defeat almost any threat that comes our way. Saunders recognizes this, which is why she allowed us to install my holo onto her ship. But Lucifer is building in strength - I can feel it and mother knows it. I can delay until Yont-Na is dealt with, but no longer. Be this at it will be, all is for the future. Right now, I must prepare for the challenges."

Banner laughed and ordered beers to be sent up. "It is a given you will win."

Mo-Ki shook his head. "There are always variables. Father, I would ask that you take this crystal onto your ship, try and install my Holo into it, and be ready for trouble. We must have everything in place for the transference. I have only just found the last piece to the puzzle, a thing Dexter was given by some mysterious inner channel." At this point, Mo-Ki told his father about the curious dream, the Laughing Giant Buddha that tapped the nerve points, indicating the Bracial cluster.

"What does it mean?" Banner asked.

"It was a dream of prophecy. Dexter was being told of the Transference. Though he did not understand it, when the images came from him to my Holo, and thus back to me, we grasped what it meant. The energy of the higher reptilian brain is precisely what stops the Wolves being affected by Lucifer. What I will take into the cave will be nothing - nothing of all my learning, nothing of the things you have taught me. All I take in is my naked instinct and the love with which I was raised - this is all that will leave."

"The challenge for me will not be defeating Lucifer, it will be about being able to stay in the instinctual realm, like the wolves - yet different. To have no higher or lower self, no thought, no feeling to distract. Pure un-reasoning, pure intuition, pure being. Listening to only the void within, allowing it to fill my being and control my actions."

Mo-Ki paused a long pause. Finally, he said, "There are two choices in the reptilian consciousness, choices based on survival, or choices based on love." He laughed, "People hardly think of a snake as having love and it doesn't in any sense we understand - but it loves sun, it loves moving, it loves many things. But when the instinct for survival overrules its natural love, the snake will do an entirely irrational thing ... It will strike at a superior enemy knowing it cannot win. It will seek to bite you if it is threatened. THIS is the Luciferian consciousness.

"This is the choice to survive without the element of love. It wants to survive to DO what it loves, but survival is the priority, not the love. Reverse this: Choose to survive BECAUSE of love - whether this is love for the sun, or a love for life makes no difference - THIS is the consciousness we need to install. THIS is what allows the pure unity of self to reach beyond the limits of the mind and allow the flow into the higher nature. THIS is where a transference of the greater awareness can come about."

"You got all that from a dream of Dexter meeting a laughing God?" Dexter said, amazed.

"I got this from my entire life. You loved me enough to set aside your own survival for the chance we would all live. For this I thank you. It is your love that turned Saunders away from a ravaging monster. It is your love that turned Chardi away from a mechanical toy of the State. Love father - you let love into your heart and it reached into ours."

Banner merely nodded. His son was never one for compliments, and this wasn't. He was stating a simple fact. But in truth, he had enjoyed his family so much, he never really thought about any of this. Ever since Mo-Ki and Dexter came into his life, everything was better. "Perhaps the human spirit is what is to blame, then?" he said, laughing to himself as he made to transport their crystal to his ship.

Little Mo-Ki laughed as well. An open laugh, not the guarded 'heh' he usually gave. It was extremely rare for the solemn child to do more than a mild grimace that passed for happiness ... But he laughed out loud just then. He didn't even know why, and as he understood this, he marveled. So much his father taught him, so many hints on how to best survive.

And this laughter they share - this was the priceless gift. Seeing the irony - the funny side of things that separated you from the serious. This was a tremendous survival tool.

Mutiny of the Captains

The brothers did not miss Stamp. He was a cruel taskmaster but, they had to admit, the power and wealth of the pirates had increased under his watch. However, going through his private logs, the members of Congress soon discovered the full extent of the deception Stamp had played on them. Clearly, the ex-soldier had a vested interest in supporting the old empire, but the extent to which he was willing to risk the brotherhood was staggering. Why Raja Mahindra was picked for this task was not because he was best qualified, though he was, it was purely chance. It was decided that, as he was the last leader addressed by Stamp before he died, then it was natural selection by fate.

Raja Mahindra had come from an old earth industrial family. He had education, understood science, and ended up in the pirates only because he killed someone he shouldn't have. Who was to know the person slumming it on Hydra Three was a Hi-Mod? He got out of there before he was deep scanned and turned into a vegetable, but he HAD mods that gave him sharper senses than the rest of this mob. Plus he was trained in accounting and could work out what was really happening.

It was expected he would have his report ready for the next Pirate Lord. In passing, it had been mentioned that the men had selected a candidate for the games, which meant the sum of zero to him. No matter who won, nothing was going to stop the bunfight that followed. To imagine the Captains were going to hand over the leadership to someone who won a contest was absurd. He and everyone else knew what would happen and it wasn't going to be pretty.

Raja sighed, he hated Stamp, but the fact was his brutality was needed to keep everyone focussed. You needed his tactical skills to survive the Quorg war. You needed his political connections to keep the Federation off your back. But if they wanted to play some old fashioned notion of an honorable transmission of leadership through a contest - So be it.

Surprisingly, Stamp wasn't all that rich. Turns out he had bribed, cajoled and schmoozed most of his money away to keep himself in the job. At first, Raja was just clearing of the decks and sorting out the finances. It was only in the private papers that he saw the com scans.

He was stunned - there were discussions between Stamp and Yont-Na going back for over four years.

The paperwork explained the delay in sending off the rocks - more worlds were being added - Well, understandable that he coordinated with the Federation, but there were no contracts, no agreements, no BUYERS. Where were the damn buyers? Raja rationalized that the path of the rocks would lead him to them. What Stamp DID have were the hyper-space jump trails - This should lead him to each planet that was paying the credits. This was when the obvious truth sunk in.

He had to check and re-check before making any comment and in doing so he called up the logs of his own ship. Sure enough, Stamp's math did not correlate to those generated by his craft. These asteroids were not up for sale, but were targeting worlds for destruction. The bastard had written in a misdirection into the core programming everyone used! He had known exactly what he was doing.

Raja blinked. How could anyone make such a mistake? He checked, he double checked, he triple checked. There was no other explanation, every damn rock was going to COLLIDE with the planet they were being sent to. Stamp's copy was the only one with the jump points and it was clear - Where these rocks were emerging was into the same orbit as the planet they were destined for.

Every single one of them had its targeting set: after it went through a hyper-space jump it was not going to some close orbit of anything, it was going to hit that world. And every single one of them was aimed at a Wolf-held planet. It doesn't take genius to connect four years of conversations with Yont-Na and the notion of destroying the man's opposition. Stamp had sold them out. He had sold them out big-time. Was he completely mad? Did he not realize the wolves would find out, and they were all doomed?

Raja called an urgent meeting with all the ship captains, the ones expecting the big payout for all the work they had been doing for four years. When he presented his findings, all hell broke loose. FOUR years, no money - everyone working just so Stamp could get himself into the Federation? This utter betrayal meant his body was not burned with any ceremony, but hacked to pieces by angry captains and fed to his dogs.

Of course, they had to keep it to themselves. How were they going to tell the men without creating a mutiny? They were ALL dead if the rest of the pirates found out, so they said nothing. The real problem, the next leader would discover the obvious and if he were not one of them, there was hell to pay. What's more, all of the rocks were now at jump speed and preset to create a portal, no doubt with Yont-Na at the other end directing the exit point. He probably had the activating codes as well - To get to them all and stop this madness was a virtual impossibility.

The Captains had gathered in Stamps ante-room. Raja laid out the charts, demonstrating beyond doubt what the real program was, and how no one was getting paid shyte for all this work. He explained it in no uncertain terms. What the HELL did Stamp imagine would happen? Any world that survived meant squadrons of Wolf Soldiers full of vengeance hunting them all down.

They fired many questions at Mahindra: *What was the deal Stamp had struck? How certain were the portal placements? Could they get in and change anything before it was too late? Should they open up and let the planets under threat know?* There were so many questions but almost no answers. There was nothing they could do. On the other hand, it didn't matter what Stamp had agreed to, because if they saved a Wolf world, the Federation would hunt them down. Either way, the pirates would be hunted to extinction.

This is when Raja put forward the only solution he could find: forget the elections, use the time when everyone was preoccupied with the games to get the hell out of Dodge. They were the captains, they owned the ships. If they all got to planets past the outer rim before the rocks hit their targets, they could get new crews and head out even further - clear out of human-held space entirely.

Two advantages: One, they stayed alive. Two, the rest of the pirates would be marooned here on the pirate planet, thus easily rounded up. Yes, the Wolves would know the Captains had taken off, but the majority of the problem was in now one spot. It would be an easy kill. Once they were done with the Quorg world their interest in catching a few pirate ships out in deep, deep space would be marginal.

One lone voice objected. The oldest Captain and friend to Mahindra - Eric the Red they called him - stood up, "We should have more faith in the men. They know it was Stamp who organized all this, they can see there is no profit for us in the whole story. We should tell it to them straight and we all leave together. No one will be happy about it, but at least the brotherhood survives."

"Bull crap, Eric." Raja retorted. "The surviving Wolves will demand retribution. Unless they kill a whole lot of pirates, all that will happen is that we will be committing a slow suicide, waiting for our throats to be cut. Unless we clear out and leave the rest of them as sacrificial lambs we will never sleep comfortably ever again. The Wolves will come baying for blood. When they get it, their lust will be satiated. With any luck, they will slowly forget about the ships that got away."

One by one the older Captains nodded assent. The vote got around to Eric and he grudgingly agreed, with a qualification. "But we leave the clear evidence of what Stamp was doing and who he was speaking to. That way the wolves will be going after Yont-Na before they decided to think about anyone else."

So it was agreed. When the games started, the captains would quietly take anything of value up to their ships and get out of there. In the meantime, it would be expected by the men that the bosses would be smuggling out as many of Stamps possessions as they could, so it will arouse no suspicion. When they were sorted, everyone would leave at the same time, just as all the pirates were focussed on the winner of the games.

Damn Stamp had totally stitched them. But there was nothing else for it, survival meant being elsewhere before the crap hit the fan.

And it was as this meeting ended that they got the message - Saunders was headed their way.

It would seem the consequences of Stamp killing the clone were ALREADY on them. They didn't wait for the games, they didn't wait to collect valuables - The pirate captains didn't even wait to hear WHY Saunders was coming.

Everyone knew she protected the wolves.

The Contest

So it was official - The very first Pirate battle for supremacy was to be broadcast. The organizers rather liked that touch, beaming out their games to the galaxy, and readily agreed to allow a broadcast vessel into orbit. Obviously, they did not expect to see Saunders smiling face,. She was known to all across the Galaxy as the host of what people now affectionately called "The Mo-Ki Show" and very dramatically announced the fact she was present to the entire pirate population via an enormous hologram that covered the sky above the capital - which resulted in abject panic. A General with a planet-destroying Star Ship turning up usually only meant one thing, evacuate as quickly as possible.

Only it wasn't possible. Shortly before Saunders arrived, the entire pirate fleet had departed. The cowardly Captains had left the men to die and had run without a shot being fired.

But the planet was not attacked. Saunders announced that she was here merely to telecast proceedings, to introduce the Galaxy to this hither-to unknown cultural spectacle. The real reason, of course, was the extraordinary find by Banner and Mo-KI, an ancient crystal computer that was currently being analyzed, but while she was there - well she just adored being a broadcaster. Plus this little show will rake in huge credits - You can never have too much capital on hand.

It was already turning out to be a ratings bonanza. Pirates! Everyone always loves a pirate story. Plus the scenery on this weird new world, all reds and purples. Add to this the story of an ancient culture that the Piratces had conquered! Fascinating. The strange alien artifacts, the exotic flora, it all made high viewing percentages. Then the word 'crazy' took on a new dimension - ratings jumping through the roof. Why? Mo-Ki announced, via his mother's ship, his candidacy for the contest to become the Pirate Overlord.

It was done in disguise, of course. But Saunders had 'whisper filters' which her rich clients paid for - all those people who wanted the inside information for betting - When she let slip Ikom Wolfman's true identity, the ratings went to astronomical levels. Only those 'in the know' were told, but something this big could not be kept secret. Soon, the entire Galaxy was agog with the news: Their beloved Mo-Ki would go into an open contest against the greatest warriors in the entire Pirate Fleet!

They saw him training with his 'also disguised' famous father, and more madness ensued. What a show? Dad and Son, there to show the universe the great power that was the heart and soul of the Wolverine Way. Nothing got back to the Pirates, of course. Saunders put them on a complete communications blackout and, as they had no ships to go beyond her blackout range, the Pirates stayed blind to the truth.

But the show had to be run properly, and the organizers down there were hopeless. And so the most extraordinary thing happened! The Captains were gone which left Saunders as the one undisputable authority - so she just appointed people who seemed capable to the positions. The small matter of a believable judging panel, for instance, and an accredited observer in each section of the course. She also started appointing administration officials for the contest and sent her own drones in to supervise the process.

At first, there had been enormous confusion in the pirate ranks. With no leadership, no chance to escape, and certain death looming overhead, it was mayhem. But Saunders calmed their nerves and continued her "chats" with the pirates in her planet-wide broadcasts. "As you know men and women of the pirate fleet, you all chose in unison an extraordinary thing. You chose to defend a Mo-Ki clone and exterminate the man who was threatening him. This is what got my attention. This proved you all to be more worthy than I may have previously thought."

"But we also know the REAL reason I am here, yes? You have all chosen to work with the wolves in altering the course of all those asteroids to a safe orbit. As a result, I consider that the parties guilty of piracy to be your leaders. In my view, as they have departed they take their guilt with them and they have absolved you of crimes you committed under their direction.

"To the other matter: The reason you are still alive, almost all of you here chose wisely in the matter of those asteroids you were shipping on behalf of Stamp. Now, I will need witnesses to testify as to what you were doing, how you realized it was wrong, and how grateful you are to the wolves for saving you from such a terrible fate. This will be done as part of the general broadcast after the games. My dear pirates, the Galaxy needs to know the truth. So, now you know why I am here and you can all relax. Get on with the Games and I will take up negotiations with your new leader when it is done.

"In the meantime, relax. Enjoy the show while I organize everything and introduce the universe to this planet and some of the wonderful new inventions you have found."

Yes, the pirates knew exactly why Saunders was here. She was taking over, and whoever won the leadership was going to be her puppet. But what was the alternative? There were no ships, no possibility of leaving other than short-range hoppers, so even if they did escape Saunders, there were no other suitable planets close enough.

They were stitched up, good and proper. Left high and dry - But thank the gods every crew had accepted the bribes and reprogrammed the asteroid trajectories. Imagine if they had put their faith in Stamp? They would all be dead by now. The truly incredible thing to the rank and file of the pirates was how their leadership had remained blind to the REAL reason for the asteroids. They had all seen the video of Stamp and his deal with Yont-Na.

It wasn't just the fear of the wolves - they had risen up en-masse and killed the idiot because he deserved to die. The Mo-Ki clone was just the trigger on an already primed gun. This is part of what had gripped the galaxy with the new show, a holo recorder had been set up by Stamp for the killing of the clone, but instead, it recorded the proceedings of the Pirates killing Stamp.

When this was broadcast to the galaxy-wide audience, even the non-wolf aligned planets had to respect a group of men who would defy their leadership and choose a path of truth. It did not matter what you thought of the religion, religious leaders were sacrosanct. This was the ONLY universal right humans had now, the right to determine their own religion. To have a leader, any leader, who would blatantly ignore this was an abhorrence.

And so the stage had been set. Using a careful edit of the events on the pirate planet, Saunders slowly turned the Galaxy from fear and hatred of the renegades to a new-found respect for their integrity and way of life. Nothing like propaganda to sell a story!

The truth of the matter was that Yont-Na had the right idea. Saunders had grasped that this 'was' the new Human Army. They were experienced in space, they all could fly, and they would be far more trustworthy than the existing Federation navy. The Pirates would become the human counterbalance to the Wolves.

Day One

No matter your class or status, the average viewer likes and enjoys the little details. When you are having breakfast, you might wonder what pirates eat to start their morning, so you tune into the Pirate Show. And what do you discover? A pirate household - Dad pretended to run things, while his wife was the real power. He brought in the money, she did everything else. It was wonderful just seeing someone with a FAMILY! He got to enjoy the kids, have a drink as suited him, and generally be fairly happy with his lot. Mum raised her family in a way that followed her traditions and kept a tight ship.

Fantastic stuff!

Many pirate households now openly followed the Wolverine Way. The former leadership had taken a dim view on religious matters, but now you could express your faith openly. The Mo-Ki clone that triggered the whole thing attracted enormous attention. As a result, more and more followers signed up. The planet of Pirates appeared to be now firmly aligned to the Wolves, yet with a significant difference. Because there were no overlords to threaten them (other than Saunders) there was no need for a wolf army to be present.

Everyone understood the obvious. When the Wolf army was called in, the old empire lost all credibility and influence over the day to day affairs in running the planet. A new bureaucracy was created, and the old laws were tossed out. But none of this happened on the planet of the Quorg because it was not needed. The pirates - supposedly - could look after themselves.

What this meant was that enormous focus was placed on the outcome of the upcoming trials. What would be the outcome? Would it be a smooth transition, or a difficult one? There were a number of contenders, one from every ship in the fleet, but the majority failed the necessary tests to qualify. In all twelve had survived to be in the running, but only three were given much hope of success. Leading the odds was the former head of planetary security, Liedeth Johal. A tough, uncompromising man with tremendous strength (coming from a high gravity planet as he did) but cunning as well.

He was square-jawed, from old Russian heritage, and called himself a Cossack to this very day (despite the fact they were all long dead). There were none to beat him in hand to hand combat, but these tests were not just about beating an opponent. There were puzzles to solve and demons to face.

Second in the odds, Kailas Chorm, a deadly female warrior who stood over seven-foot tall with shoulders four feet wide. She was an impressive specimen, a survivor from the experiments on the old tech school of Bandas Four. A genetically engineered human with capabilities of speed and strength that were astonishing. She was smarter than Liedeth, and she had a grudge to boot, for she had expected the plum role of security chief for herself. She also knew poisons and was not amiss to using them.

Third stood the curious choice, an old veteran called Thug who had expected to take the place of the nominal leader before Stamp took control. "Chief of Arms" traditionally was an organizing role - this was the man who found the ammunition and machinery of war for everyone. You expected to be promoted to the previously nominal title of leader and this one had hated the man who stole what he considered his rightful position. Though past his prime in a fight, he knew every dirty trick in the book. If he didn't win, he may well ensure that the winner didn't survive long enough to enjoy the new post. A nasty, temperamental piece of work was Thug - So-called because this just described him so well. No one ever thought to ask him his real name.

There were a range of others, but no one gave them much credit, most especially the young boy from some distant planet no one had heard of. But all twelve passed the preliminaries, so they all were in contention.

Day One of the Three Day trials were to begin on the morrow. Mo-Ki and his father had a small room near to the opening ceremony. They did not attend the banquet, mostly because they knew what Kailas Chorm would probably do. Despite the fact that Mo-Ki 's extraordinary metabolism was effectively immune to almost all poisons, you didn't want to advertise your strengths too early. And so it was, by the end of that night only the three leading contenders and Mo-Ki were left.

So the field was narrowed to four before the show had even begun. No one knew who did the deed, but as far as Pirates go, most accepted that if the candidates were so stupid as to eat untested food, they deserved to die. They should have known better and would have made a lousy leader.

ooooo000000oooo

The first trial began at dawn. It was essentially a race to get a sword, very traditional. Then you had to beat a gateway guardian and fight through to a central location where there was a winners cup. The first person to raise it over their heads was the winner of the day, with points awarded for everyone who arrived, second, third, etc.

However, getting the sword meant climbing a difficult wall, running over a parapet then across a rope to get to the top of a citadel where your sword was held for you. There were four swords in all, one for each contestant, and points were once more awarded according to every small success. Who got over the tricky wall fastest, two points. Those who got to their blade first, two points - and so on. The horn signaled the start of the event, and the three leading contenders took off. Mo-Ki, however, stood back, chatting to the media.

The pirates laughed. Who but the most brazenly confident would do this? The young Ikom fellow seemed to be having a great time, joking and laughing with the people while addressing the cameras. "Why aren't you running off to get your sword?" Someone from the crowd called out.

Mo-Ki laughed. "Do you think these devious pirates would make it that easy? There will be traps along the way and I will sit here and see what and where they are, so when I make my run there will be no surprises."

Sure enough, as he is saying this, a field of snakes emerged from holes in the wall the three competitors were ascending, causing the contenders to rapidly adjust their direction of ascent. Clearly, the shortest route up the wall was not the path. "OK then," Mo-Ki said to the crew of journalists, "Time to make a move!" And with this, he bounded up what looked like a far more difficult climb.

Of course, being raised on Hope meant climbing cliffs was second nature to him. It was essentially a playground for he and Dexter and, more importantly, one where the wolves could not follow. It showed the one great advantage the Human held over the Wolf, a proper opposing thumb. Mo-Ki, whose name in the contest was laughably reversed to Ikom Wolfman, clambered up like a monkey and quickly passed the contenders, who were still looking for a way past the snakes.

He got to the top but stopped before the rope bridge. This was too easy. He looked about, and sure enough, behind the wall where he stood there was a room, and in there lay some climbing equipment. The rope bridge was a trap, sure and simple. Instead, he took pitons and the gear lying there and made to prepare a sling.

But as he was standing just out of sight, Thug had already made his way there and just started running over the rope. As expected, it gave way, but the resourceful old man had already thrown a rope he was carrying to the other side and managed to get it to hold. So he fell towards the far wall and was climbing up his lifeline.

Mo-Ki had intended similar. He threw a sling of rope high and caught the pylons of the bridge on the other side. Rather than swing down, he knocked some pitons in and made a new bridge. He could not run over the top as it was not tight enough, but he could hook his legs over and pull himself over as a cradle.

By the time the others arrived, he was already there, and he showed great generosity of spirit by leaving his bridge up for them. He thought about cutting the rope Thug was climbing up on, but you never know - the fellow may prove to be more useful alive. He did peer over, call out to Thug, then scrape the rope with the knife he COULD have used, however, and laughed. The camera really honed in on this one.

And so he gets to his sword first, but again, another trick. They were all stuck into a silicon bubble and pulling on a blade just tightened the grip of the silicone around it.

An old puzzle which needed the others. So at that crucial point he sat down to wait for the rest to arrive. Hovers cams were nearby, so he went over once more to chat to the Media. "Nice day for it, I have to say," he said in a jolly tone. "How long do you think it will be before we have a competition?"

The holos from off world reporters were now buzzing around him. People could not believe it, he started dead last, yet was first to the sword, and now he was just dawdling? Thug had made it and, looking amazed at the stupidity of the young fellow, went to grab his sword. But it would not come. The harder he pulled, the more stuck it became. He went to the next one, same thing, and the next. All four swords were stuck firmly in the silicon.

The other two made their way across and were also tugging at their swords, while Mo-Ki continued to chat to the camera crews. "It's an old game we used to play in childhood," he explained to the hovers. "Silicon resistance only strengthens the more you work against it, and the puzzle is only solved one way. I better go and tell them how, hey?"

Mo-Ki trots over and asks, "Ready to pull the swords now?" he announces to the three of them, who were all swearing and struggling to get theirs out. "There is a simple trick I can show you, but we all have to work together for it to work. Are you prepared to do this?"

All three look at each other. Not only were they shocked that this whippersnapper had gotten there first, but there must also be a reason he had not even tried to pull a sword. "Ok then, kid," says Thug, "Show us how it is done."

"It is simply a resistance puzzle. You pull, you increase resistance. The real trick is to PUSH, decrease the resistance, and then the swords will come out. Are you ready? On my mark we all push the swords IN, then they will be able to be released. Ready? One, Two, THREE!"

All three opponent push the swords in, which meant that Mo-Ki simply had to hold his in place and it came free. "Thanks for that," he says, as he races onto the next stage of the quest. "Have fun working out who will be left holding the last sword!"

When he made it to the jump slide that took him down to the gateway guardian, he could still hear the shouting as they abused him. But enough of them, this is where the real puzzle would be. The entire point of this contest was to qualify the candidate in many areas. Battle skill was to come, but right now it was plain smarts. The sharpest stick got the first days prize and most of the contestants had already proven their stupidity by dying before the show even started. Only Thug knew the ropes, as he had organized similar contests during the time when he had authority.

The other two had no clue at all as to what was coming. Obviously Saunders had offered to help her son out but Mo-Ki wanted this to be a real challenge. He was fairly bored with the sedentary nature of his present job and running clones was simply a distraction, not a fulfillment. He needed a bit of fun. Plus, it meant he could bring onside an important element in creating the balance the universe needed.

But to the present - before him lay the portal - just an open archway of stone through a high stone wall. He hit the ground running and he came off the end of the slide, throwing little ball bearings he had taken with him. They were cyber-magnetic, and so if there were any hidden contraptions running any sort of program the balls would be attracted to them. In this way you could discover if there were any mines or tricks on the way up to the gate, Surprisingly, none. That simply meant the gate was the trick. And as he approached, Mo-Ki saw no one guarding the portal at all, so it very clearly WAS a trap.

So he took an oblique approach, stepping into the shadows of a building near to the simple stone arch in front of him. He took out a small device that generated a holo and sent an image of himself walking through the arch.

Sure enough, a huge hammer comes down, but as the crowd gasp, it goes through thin air. Thus the reason for collecting the sword and Mo-Ki makes good use of it. Before the hammer is lifted he steps through and finds the huge creature that was swinging it - before the giant at the gate can lift up the weapon to strike again he is on to it, cutting its throat. It dies to a rousing roar of the crowd.

You normally expect a gateway guardian to have a riddle you have to solve, and if you don't THEN the hammer comes down - but this was a fairly blunt trauma, so to speak. The principle was simple: Anyone stupid enough to plunge through an open door without looking deserves to die. The hovers are following his every move and Mo-Ki waves to them, showing the bloodied blade. A cheer goes up through the crowd.

As he moves forward, another monster is moved in to replace the slain one, and THIS time it in front of the gate and it will have a riddle. Mo-Ki laughs, every layer held a series of variables, but until the first monster was killed, it would have sat there to surprise any foolish hero charging on through.

That was the first day almost sorted. The winners cup had one more surprise, it was full of acid. And it stood on a copper base, Mo-Ki guessed that just pouring the acid off created a poisonous vapor. Every puzzle had to have a solution and he had some time to work it out as Thug was stuck at the gate trying to solve his riddle. He looked about. Sure enough, a small bit of hose. He put one end in and siphoned out the rest past the copper and out onto the courtyard that lay outside the small temple-like structure where the cup was held. It will make things a little hot footed for those following!

Not surprisingly, Thug, not one for riddles, just killed the guardian rather than waste time solving the puzzle it presented and was running up at a speed that belied his years. However, the sight that greeted him was Mo-Ki, already holding the cup above his head. The unknown contender had won all the main points of the first day.

Thug was second, and only the girl was quick enough to get the sword out of the silicon. Three remained, with the Cossack fuming and cursing everyone as he left the field.

DAY TWO: Preparations

Mo-Ki and Banner did not celebrate the first day. Festivities went all night as the pirates cheered and drank, then cheered and drank some more while watching replays of the spectacle played out in the various bars around town. They laughed at how the unknown contender tricked the older, more experienced players in the game, and cheeky young 'Ikom' was the buzz. All you heard about was Ikom Wolfman and how he was so damn confident that he didn't even bother to start with the others when the competition got underway.

Now THIS was the sort of fellow a pirate could put his faith in! Of course, they were also drinking to forget the obvious - they were marooned, with a Federation Starship in orbit around them. What is a pirate without a pirate ship? Not very much. But for now, the excitement of the coming day and the "Test of Will", as it was called, was the only thing front and center.

Already the bookmakers had been radically altering the odds, and this unknown was fast becoming a favorite. But Thug was rising to the top of the list. Yes, he came second, but he had the experience and was clearly all over the girl. Ikom may have just gotten lucky. Time will out, as they say and in the process the odds will change.

Kailas Chorm was fuming, coming third was an insult and she knew that she had better gets some smarts about her if she was going to pull ahead of the other two. All contestants are checked before every days proceedings, to make sure there were no weapons they could use to harm other contestants - Knives were permitted, but not little poison darts. However, the poison tips on her nails would likely pass unseen and this meant all she had to do was grab one of the others, and they would be sufficiently weakened so as not to complete the course. Death was too obvious, she just needed a temporary nervine to slow them down.

The Quorg planet had all sorts of nasty little toxins out in nature, so that night she hunted for, and found a specific mushroom. Distilling the crystal toxin from it, she painted it on her nails and was fully prepared well before dawn. Even if someone saw what she was doing, they would not guess it was anything more than a peculiar beauty routine.

Of course, Saunders cameras were in there. She had cloaked devices you did not realize were present and she was following every contestant, recording every single detail. A quick analysis of the mushroom showed the real reason for her painting her nails, which was broadcast to the galactic audience. Being thorough, Saunders even tested the toxin on some wandering drunks, to show examples to her audience of what happened when you scratched a person with this toxin.

They were not volunteers, just some people walking past the lab where Saunders auto-bots had prepared the mixture. She found herself becoming more and more curious about the interesting options this planet was presenting, and a nerve toxin that was not traceable after its effect was done was definitely one of them. The drunk pirates she used looked shocked, then angry, then started to lose control of muscles.

Inside five minutes all test subjects were convulsing on the ground, frothing at the mouth, and showing signs of extreme duress. This Holo was attached as a background report to explain what the pirate woman was doing to try and get herself an edge. There was never any sort of "this is wrong" speech that went with it - Saunders only presented the facts and let the audience decide, but naturally, everyone hated this Kailas Chorm.

More importantly, the antidote. This took a few hours, isolating the crystal was one thing, finding a protein that broke it down another. The vaccine was fairly straight forward once the correct amino acid sequence was generated and you found this most quickly by identifying any animal that ate this mushroom. They must have developed a counter to its toxicity, and so it was a humble beetle that survived the virus that provided the necessary metabolic info.

Now came the interesting part, the audience participation survey on who should be given the vaccine. Every person who buzzed in was another coin in the coffers, and BILLIONS were buzzing in. The few pennies each vote cost added up to truly astonishing sums.

Overwhelmingly, the audience voted for 'Ikom', and so Saunders duly sent a bot to approach him in the early dawn hours as father and son are preparing for the coming day.

'Ikom' was flagged for the reasons that his mother was coming, and why. He acted suitably surprised when he was shown the footage of his adversary preparing to poison her competition and was exceedingly grateful that he was offered a vaccine - but magnanimously announced that the same must be done for Thug, as he would hate to win this competition in any way that could be seen as poor sportsmanship. "I follow the Wolverine Way, General Saunders," Mo-Ki said solemnly towards the cameras. "To have an unfair advantage over my competitor would make me no better than this Kailas Chorm. I could not ask people to follow myself if I was prepared to cheat and scam my own people. It would make me unfit for the role of leader."

The rating soared. Thug was contacted, shown the footage, yet remained suspicious of this 'gift' and essentially would not accept the injection. However, he took the vial. He could see no reason why a Federation General should be helping him and presumed the whole thing was a set-up. The Galaxy booed, and his actions ensured he could never walk openly again outside of Pirate society without public censure.

'Ikom' was now not just the public favorite, he was the bookies odds-on chance to win. As the day dawned and the competitors made their way to the Day Two battleground, Kailas was puzzled as to why her odds had plummeted. But no matter, she had the solution in hand and bet everything she had on herself to win this day. Such poor odds would be the very thing that would make her incredibly rich.

DAY TWO: The Test of WILL

We have all experienced 'staring contests' as children. The person whose eyes blinks first, the first person to look away, etc. is the loser. The pirate contest was a little more severe. It was a test of physical control, determination and focus. The reasoning was very simple, a person who would be running an outlaw organization had to have unshakable conviction, plus an innate intuition for when to drop the ball and run, so to speak.

And so the first test was a very simple one. All three contestants had to balance a ball on the end of a stick, with the certain knowledge that at any time it could explode. It was non-lethal, but fail this, and you risked an injury that would affect the rest of the days performance. It was effectively a game of chicken with a ball.

Each contestant had their own room. Each room was a glass walled triangle and they all pointed in towards each other. You could easily see the other contestants and would know if they had left the field and when you were last person standing. The trick was, when you ran to the exit immediately behind you, you had to throw the ball up first and get out before it landed. Last person out the door wins.

You must not drop the ball and, after thirty minutes of holding a stick with a weight on it out in front of you, muscle stress becomes magnified. You feel the burn, your stress levels go through the roof, but you have to keep focused on the ball - should it start to change color, it is getting ready to explode. For the first forty minutes none of the contestants showed signs of failing, but come forty five minutes the stress was really starting to show.

Mo-Ki had prepared in an unusual way, by having a shifting harness under his shirt he was able to transfer the weight to his hips. He imagined the other two would have had something similar, it was not a hard contest to guess. But this still required enormous attention. The aid made balancing more difficult as it was not directly controllable. Standard wolf training had the recruits holding weighed balls out in front of them for strength training. It drove your muscles into isometric and accordingly increased you carrying capacity as a soldier. But they didn't explode when you dropped them.

The person with the most experience with this would be Thug, and so this was the one 'Ikom' watched most closely. As soon as he threw his ball, it was time to leave, never mind what the woman did. The trial should last no more than an hour before the next stage and the entire trick was to be the last out through the open door behind you. Mo-Ki put his mind frequencies into Delta, virtually a trance state with the eyes open. He could hold this position for many hours if needs be, standing in the old fashioned "Horse" stance of Old Earth Kung Fu, the arms bent, supporting the weight down to the hips through his harness.

Finally, the girl gave out, but she didn't fling the ball up in the air, she through it OVER the glass wall, directly at Mo-Ki. He smiled and, while still balancing his ball, caught it before it hit the ground. Nice trick, remove one competitor and then it is only the two of them, and she still had her venom. The audience in the background initially booed, but now they cheered, which unsettled Thug. His ball started to wobble and, for those who knew, it was his harness causing the problem. He lost focus for but a moment and now had to catch it again.

Perhaps it was the silent smile on this 'Ikom's' face, perhaps it was the way Thug had been so easily defeated the day before, but The Pirates anger suddenly took hold. He saw red, as they say, and threw up his ball and ran toward the back door. The thing exploded, throwing shrapnel up against the glass. But Mo-Ki did not move. He was holding one ball up via his paddle, using only one hand, and the other in his free hand. He let it go a minute, a long, drawn out minute, before bowing to the audience, throwing up the balls, and running to the back door.

He had won the first stage. In the green room, waiting to be called for the next test, he watched the coms. All that was talked about was 'Ikom' this and 'Ikom' that. A little of the cheating nature of the girl, and not very much about Thug. The plan was moving along as expected.

After an hour to recover, the next stage was set. It was a gymnastic trial, quite straightforward, a set course to complete in a specific time frame. This was something where all three contenders were roughly equal, so what was the twist? It was sure to arrive before the end of the routine - where is there a test of will in simple gym work? Well, they all went through the course with relative ease, but it was strenuous. At the end - so obvious - a simple weight test. You had to hold up your body weight for ten minutes, but over the shoulders, so not too hard, then taking that weight you had to climb a vertical wall.

When the body is fatigued, just lifting yourself up over a tricky climb was hard. Carrying your body weight made it extremely difficult. There were time penalties and failure penalties. All three scaled the same wall, so the potential for being nasty and kicking your competitor was high.

When it came to the last stage, Mo-Ki did not run at it like the other two. He paused, gathered his energy, and refocussed his metabolism. Sending building steroids to torn muscles, he willed repair and rejuvenation to every part of his body. He willed in more CHI, the life-force, and he harmonized his mind and body. It only took a minute, but already the other two were half way up the wall. Then he strapped the weight to his back and set off, to a huge cheer from the crowd.

'Ikom' literally ran up that first half of the wall. It was like a cat with claws, and indeed he had force grown scale-tips onto the ends of his fingers so he could grip the vertical wall like a fly. As he went past Kailas, she lunged at him. It was irrational, insane even, but she went slashing at him, trying to get him with her claws. But he easily avoided her and in her madness, she fell. She fell hard and lay on the ground writhing in pain, immobile. Her back was broken.

Once more the audience cheered, but Mo-Ki stopped his ascent, turned to them, and incredibly, holding on with just one hand, put his fingers to his lips in the "shh" sign. He did not want people cheering the loss of another, no matter how poor a sport they were. As a result, Thug managed to get to the top of the wall and was running to the finish line before Mo-Ki had leaped over As far as points went it didn't matter, he had already won the day in three out of four scoring areas, and tomorrow was the actual battle with weapons. That was the only contest that really mattered. Even so, Mo-Ki decided the fellow needed to learn a lesson. He took off his weight and throwing it along the ground caught Thugs feet, sending him sideways.

The man jumped up, furious, red-faced, ready to fight this little upstart then and there, and so it was that Mo-Ki - laughing hard - just ran past him to the finish line. When Thug realized he had been tricked, he swore, cursed and fumed. He really hated this little brat. But none of it mattered. Tomorrow was REAL battle - where it was the victors choice to let the loser live or die. Who cared if the little runt had more points? Thug would win, and Ikom would be dead.

Let the smug boy have his glory today. It was a hollow victory as it all came down to the only contest that amounted to success or failure in this whole business. No one wanted a pirate lord who could not fight, and Thug had ensured that his favorite tools, the sword and net, were the chosen weapons. No-one was better at this than he was - it cost him a lot of credits to arrange it.

Day Three: A Surprise in the Crowd

No matter how well a pirate can negotiate the tricky situation, in the end it comes down to battle, and generally he who cheats best wins. The traditional third day in all pirate contests was always the hand to hand, but of course, there were only two left. A single fight would determine the new king of the Pirates.

Equally traditional was the public vote to choose the weapons. They were mostly along the lines of Roman gladiatorial items, but somewhat jumbled. Trident and net was now sword and net. Trident now went with a traditional round shield. Mace and armor went with a large rectangular shield, and the whip (lasso) went with throwing knives. However, there were more modern weapons, such as traditional fencing garb, with epee' or saber, and electric prod instruments as well.

No projectile weapons such as bow and arrow, pistols, or laser weapons were to be used. Everything had to be up-close and personal. However, this was a contest usually run over many hours with many contestants. Having only one main event, so to speak, changed the general guidelines. The public was informed the weapons had been preselected and would be the sword and net for both parties.

Everyone knew Thug must have paid a lot, for these were his known favorites, but it all made little difference to Mo-Ki. He had trained in all of the old martial arts since he was a child and had trained with fighters significantly better than Thug. Death Squad members were the best of the best and the Wolves were their equal. The question was whether to make a show of it, or just clear the decks and get to the real business, the reason he was here.

The whole thing had been somewhat disappointing, not the real challenge he had hoped for. But then again, it got excellent ratings, and the overall purpose made the journey more than worthwhile. What they had here was gold: A trapped populace, wanted in every quadrant of the galaxy, who needed a solution to their dilemma. These people needed a guiding hand that would make them useful citizens of the human race.

The part that appealed to the young man and the real reason for his interest in them - this was a human population not bogged down in a whole series of 'shoulds' in the heads. He would need fighters other than wolves to control the human worlds that did not fully accept the Wolverine Way, but he could not use the existing military. For one, they were too corrupt, and second, they were far too cruel.

But what was this? Off to the far right, a glimmer of light that did not quite look normal. Mo-Ki put out mental feelers and he was right, there were soldiers here in Camo, Death Squad members. He flicks his com-link and calls Banner. "Did you bring in any Death Squad troops here?" he asks.

Banner's voice was concerned. "No." He signals Saunders. She also speaks in the negative and starts doing long range scans.

"There is a ship, deep space. Cloaked in stealth. I am guessing we have unwanted visitors, but who sent them and why they are here?" She quickly sent a subspace to her Generals, but they all were unaware of any movement. Something has been put into train - but what?

The Pirate Captains would not dare. It is most likely they contacted some military group that were connected with the operation and advised of the changed situation. But with Saunders in orbit, they would never make themselves openly known. So what would be their objective?

It was awkward timing given Mo-Ki's upcoming battle and the live feed going out all over the Galaxy, but then again, what could be a more perfect time to start informing everyone what was really happening? She set her scanners to read the almost invisible emissions of a camo-suit. Under normal circumstances a difficult thing, but as her boy had already picked one, she could isolate the frequencies and filter them from everything else. As was to be expected, five operatives, a platoon.

This confirms a specific mission. Was it because they knew Mo-Ki was here? They had to have some sort of mission to disrupt the leadership succession. Why? It made no sense, but the recordings from deep space where the raiding ship was located were logged and patched to a feed along with the shimmering shapes of the Death Squad members on the ground. It would all make part of an excellent finale'.

"Honey," she murmured to Banner. He was so cute, and she STILL loved those beautiful green eye. "You need to get into kit, sweetie. Make sure things stay behaved, yes?"

"Sure," he answered, though he was already pulling on the camo and making his way to where Saunders had pinpointed the squad,

For the present moment, the music had started up, and the triumphant entrance of the leading families moving into their places to witness the battle had finished. All was set for the start of the battle,. In the coms routed from Saunders ship, Mo-Ki could clearly see the five camouflaged soldiers taking places in the stands near leading families. Intuits told him they were intending some sort of takeover of the leadership, but it made no sense.

They already know Saunders was above recording everything. They possibly know Banner's ship is also present. Any mission that revealed your presence here was likely a suicide one, and perhaps this was it. The mission was purely disruption. The end goal, to force wolves to the planet? That didn't make sense, other than the pirates would hate to lose autonomy. It seemed that the only purpose was to break down a potential threat to the Federation.

Intuits clicked through, his remarkable mind leaped to an inescapable conclusion. "Some Seven Admin has correctly rationalized that the projected result of the activities on the Quorg planet is likely to result in an army being made available to your dear self, Mother." he pauses. "If leading families start dying under your nose, it makes you look weak - but there must be a second mission, either recruiting the pirates or annihilation of the planet." He paused, then concluded, "It is the latter."

Yont-Na would have a backup plan in case of rebellion and that plan would be sending an asteroid to THIS planet. He knew his mother would be adding up the facts in a similar way and be ready to act. But there was another option. He signaled her to wait.

Running so many clones as he did, Mo-Ki's consciousness had expanded. It had been lifted to an extraordinary degree, to a level neither of his parents had even guessed at. To date, he had not played any true cards, but in this exceptional circumstance, he would have to reveal one of his secrets. He focused, a close focus - listen, entrain the rhythm of the heart - then he picked up the energy of the leader of the Death Squad. He started to send filaments of thought into the man's aura. He wound his mind into the man's nerves. Taking charge of his mods, Mo-Ki started taking over the fellows reflexive system.

This was not like running a clone, which was a blank sheet willing to accept instruction. This was a trained military mind and it needed suggestions whispered to it that was in accord with all existing programming. But Mo-Ki was BORN of Photonic Pulse - it was his very nature to do this. The man had mods he could tune into and in moments he hacked the mind of the Corporal in charge.

If he hadn't been so experienced running multiple clones, it would have been extremely tricky to attend to opening celebrations while he undertook the slow but certain control of the man's mind. It was a simple thing, in essence. The embedded mods power a nervine track into the cortex. They had one great fault, they were controllable wirelessly.

What none of the soldiers were told is that once the system is entrained, the mods themselves do very little, other than be a doorway for external control. Subtle thoughts can be implanted and in all army camps there is a ritual 'drone' of emotives that relates to obeying authority. This entails a constant repetition of core signatures: fitting in, doing your bit, etc. The trick is to tune into these existing feeds and encourage the mind of the individual to believe they have received different orders than what they were originally sent.

If anyone doubts that the mind can be told what to see or hear, they have never seen a sideshow. Any hypnotist can have a person swearing that the cushion on their lap is a long-lost dog they loved, or that cold water is hot, etc. Suggestion is THE power of the Photonic force, and Mo-Ki was hard at work implanting new notions into the Death Squad leaders thoughts. Primarily, the message that his task here was to watch this contest and take no action. You don't need to provide a reason WHY - you just provide this as the orders.

Soldiers are programmed to take instruction and do not question authority. Saunders would already be guessing what he was doing, which would make her both proud and suspicious. "Mother, I need the up-link of these soldiers subspace channel isolated and blocked. I want no orders filtering through." He spoke to her briefly, not in telepathy, but with direct coms, explaining that he was plugged into the mods of the Death Squad leader. She said it would not be a problem, but she said it in such a way as to question what else he had not told her. He laughed, looking up at the crowd

Thug was tense and waiting for the contest to begin, and what HE saw was this young thing laughing at **him**. He saw red. He was angry and wanted to kill this 'Ikom', not just for the crown, but because he just wanted him dead. So far he had had his nose rubbed in it by so many people for so long, and lopping this jerk-offs head from his shoulders was to cut the heads of everyone who insulted him.

Mo-Ki saw Thug sneering at him. An ugly face at the best of times, it was becoming almost grotesque. He gave it no mind, just another distraction. He was almost there with the soldier. Get the controller, you won the squad. They will all do whatever he tells them to.

He hits the reflexive mind of the soldier and starts to field questions of what they were about here on the Quorg Planet. And the answer was as brutal as it was simple. They were here to kill the winner of the contest, for shock value in Saunders broadcast, then the whole place gets vaporized. So very Old Empire - if you had a concern or any lack of control, neutralize the situation. A larger concern, nuke the planet.

Herein laid the very core of the problem, the whole reason behind everything Mo-Ki had done - Yont-Na and his programmed robots had absolutely nil respect for anything not in total agreement with the Federation mind set. He sighed and started wiring in different values, but with virtual automatons like this squad leader, it was almost like pre-school education in the basics. Instilling a value for life beyond personal survival, creating a notion of social values, these were all new concepts to people where simple things like having a parent love them was a foreign experience.

In a society of batch bred worker bees, the concept of kindness was unknown. It was an unutterably cruel way of life that had to end. People had to get back to being human, and the Wolves were the ones to assist man in re-finding his roots. The no-mods were fine, they had no value and so were not bred using surrogates and state-sponsored education. But the administration, all of it, was corrupted. All possessed to some degree the vanity and arrogance of Yont-Na. And even as he had these thoughts, they imprinted on the team leaders mind and became his new reality.

It really was this simple. You earnestly FELT your vision, you BECAME the solution, you INCARNATED the value you wanted yourself to be, and you let it flow out. This was how you programmed a clone, it was how you re-programmed a sentient human. But 'sentient' was a loose term: When someone is pre-programmed to specific protocols, with their only choices being ones allocated - there is no choice. There really is no free will. There is no self-determination, there are no individual goals, there remains not one whit of aspiration other than what you have been programmed to have an ambition for.

Everything the Photonic Pulse wanted was already here. Lucifer already controlled this society.

Saunders watched with fascination. She saw how Mo-Ki took control of the man's hind brain, and set up new protocols in his thinking. This would make him a far less efficient unit, which in this specific situation was very desirable. Her ship was scanning for evidence of a subspace portal that would allow a rock through.

Already she was beaming out the scans that showed Death Squad members interfering with the rights of the pirates to choose a leader. The galaxy tuned in, and the rating exploded. Absolutely EVERYONE was astonished, first to have the extraordinary vision of the infamous 'invisible' soldiers of the Federation revealed, and second to learn of the plot by the Federation to destroy this beautiful planet. The outrage, the raw hatred of the people for this current administration was reaching fever pitch.

By the end of this broadcast, Federation held planet would have difficulty explaining to their citizens what protocol was breached that permitted them to wipe out planets such as this. Saunders laughed - The old guard insisted on making her job so much easier. And all because of her beautiful Mo-Ki. She was so proud of him, and he was SO naughty, not telling her everything. But of course, if he had she would have been tempted to find out how he was doing it, so it was perfectly reasonable

She sighed quietly to herself - few understood how her cruel streak was barely kept in check as it was.

And even as she contemplated her own dual-nature, the loving mother versus the vicious controller, she understood that she was part of the problem. She was part of this cruel streak that the entire old order ran on, but because of her child, because of Mo-Ki, Banner and even sweet little Dexter (Hard to think of him as a man, really) the human side had grown to balance the administrator and soldier inside her.

And as she watched Mo-Ki's implants take hold of the soldier, she had to wonder, had 'he' done this to her? Was it possible he had been fully conscious of the problem, even as a baby? If he wasn't just so damn adorable she may have acted against him, but thank goodness he WAS so sweet. However, the contest was about to begin, and the rating just kept climbing - higher than anything to date.

She had to attend to advertisers and business. She flipped to general coverage and trusted her child would deal with the contest. The bots were programmed to follow every movement, so the cameras would record the details and edit the show on the fly. First the cash, then find that annoying Federation ship hiding out there and THEN find the rock hurtling at them from subspace. Very fortunate for all she was present, with all the equipment that had been previously built to protect Hope.

She sends a quick message to Banner and deployed the planetary shield. Won't THIS make the most incredible footage!

Declaration of Independence

Thug looked at his preferred tools. Poisoned tipped sword, his net laced with a narcotic - this would not take long. The idea was to slow the opponent with the narcotics on the net, so it looked as if you were the better fighter. You keep up the battle long enough to ensure it doesn't look like a set piece, then you move in for the kill. The crowd will hate to see their little favorite killed off, but that's how it goes.

The arena itself was a virtual copy of the coliseum. Oval, with high tiered seating around a simple, flat, football-shaped field of Mars. The preliminary jousting and battles - the warm up to the main event - were winding down, with the dead bodies being carted off.

After a short parade for the waiting media that showed all the exotic types of creatures still living on the Quorg home planet and a few battles between the most venomous, the quickest, etc. The announcer came up to introduce the contenders. "As we know all pirates, rich or poor, man or woman, tall or short, want only one thing, a good fight! (rousing cheer from the crowd) And finally, we come down to this - the battle. We have had two amazing days of watching the unknown outsider best the odds-on favorites. He has shown gallantry, he has shown courage, smarts, and pluck. Most of all, he has shown us decency! A true follower of the wolf! (rousing cheer) Against him, the one we all hate but respect, Thug. He is the known, brutal and unkind, but probably the better fighter. The other is the unknown. Who will lead us in the challenges of the coming years? This is what will be decided today." The crowd roars.

A panorama of the recent events, 'Ikom" scaling the wall and skirting the snakes, defeating the gateway guardian, raising the cup. Then the next day, the footage of how Kailas was proven to have toxins in her nails, then how 'Ikom' sent the evil general to the aid of his enemy, who refused assistance. Then the amazing way he showed respect for the fallen warrior, even though she tried to attack him with her poison nails. And then the cunning way he tripped up Thug to take victory from defeat. All of which made the crowd cheer and shout, "IKOM - IKOM - IKOM," over and over.

Thug just glared. The boy would be dead soon enough and they could hate him all they liked. Then something completely unexpected, a holo with Saunders appears beside him, all cameras are tuned in to watch.

"Tell us Thug, what direction will you take the pirates if you win? Given you have no ships and no way off the planet, how do you propose to save the pirate way of life?"

He was shocked. The thought of what to do AFTER he won had never really occurred to him. He was just thinking of the easy women and the fun times. So he just sat there, looking stupid. "You have nothing to say? The galaxy would really like to know."

Finally he found his tongue, "Fuk off. We are pirates and we sort things in our own way! We don't need no Federation flunkies up our arse." But instead of a cheer, there was silence. Was he mad - the crowd all thought - Talking to Saunders like that? Had he no clue?

Saunders then floats over to 'Ikom' and says sweetly, "So little Ikom, our personal favorite and the one who the Galactic audience wishes to win - what will YOU do to make the pirates great again?"

Ikom was well prepared. "First, General Saunders, I want to sincerely thank you for sharing the pirate way of life with the universe. You have cleared up many misconceptions about us and I believe we ALL thank you for it. (He looks to the audience and the crowd cheers! They all know you should be sweet talking the bitch, not insulting her like Thug did.) I have many plans for the Pirates, the first being selling some of the amazing artifacts and crafts on this old Quorg home world, which will give us sufficient capital to re-equip our fleet. We obviously intend to leave all wolf-controlled worlds completely alone, because we are followers of the Wolverine Way. (More cheers)"

"But FEDERATION worlds and ships, these are a very different story. Did you know, right here, right now, we have evidence of their insanity?" With this 'Ikom' gestures to where the lieutenant of the Death Squad is standing, completely invisible to the crowd. "Look over here, and I will use a special tool I developed to reveal one the most hated and reviled truths about the old empire!" Mo-Ki signals to the squad leader to lower his camo, revealing himself in full light of day to the entire universe.

The man was completely controlled by Mo-Ki and simply followed orders now. There it was, for the entire galaxy to witness, a hated member of the feared Death Squads, standing there in the middle of the battlefield. "His orders from the Federation were to kill the winner of the competition, after which they were intending to destroy this entire world.

"Can you believe the GAUL of these people? I will STOP THIS INSANITY. I will commit our pirates to END THIS THREAT. We pirates will take on the role of protectors of what is good and just, and end the scourge of these Federation scum forever!"

Surprisingly, the crowd, after gasping at the shock of what they have just seen, begins to recover and cheer. They all hate the Federation, but why had no one ever talked about siding with the Wolves before? The insanity of Stamp, attacking the wolf planets had meant they would have had to join the hated Federation, yet here was a refreshingly simple approach. Sell assets, buy ships, and do so under Saunders protection. So damn obvious. The cheers rose higher and higher, as all the wolf-held worlds watched with delight! They had found humans who wanted to champion their faith and protect their own.

Conversely, Federation-held worlds started to panic. The highest level officers started sending com after com to Yont-Na, seeking direction. But nothing. No response other than a pre-recorded message. No-one knew he was in regen, which really meant his new clone was being imprinted. What it SEEMED like was that they were on their own.

And they were!

Thug had seen and heard enough. He would kill this little upstart NOW and not wait for any bell to start proceedings. He had already positioned himself between his competitor and the hologram he was talking to, so he threw his barbiturate coated net right through Saunders to snare the stupid fool. Then he threw his spear to nail him. But Ikom was suddenly not there. Damn it ... the boy was a HOLO! What the?

The end to proceedings came swiftly. Mo-Ki had thought about sparing Thug and finding him a role with the Pirates, but the reality was the man was so bitter and twisted, all he would ever be is a thorn that attracted all the desperate and misery-laden adherents to the old ways. He dropped the holo and revealed where he was actually standing - right behind Thug. He sent a spear sailing, but he called out the mans name, so he could turn and take it in the front.

Thug was not stupid. He did not turn, but jumped, even so, the spear struck his shoulder. He then turned to face Mo-Ki. Both were now unarmed. He jumped at him, thinking he could get there before the boy could cast his net.

It made no difference, the boy was a battle hardened warrior who could beat Wolves in hand to hand. Mo-Ki stepped to one side, grabbed Thug's wounded arm, and twisted it, creating a howl of pain. Then he broke the arm, another scream. Thug was paralyzed with pain, unable to move. Thug was now on his knees with the certain knowledge he had vastly underestimated his opponent. Mo-Ki turned him round, took the other arm, then twisted it so that Thug screamed some more.

Then he faced the cameras. "This is the man who poisoned most of the contenders before this challenge even began!" He wrenches the good arm till it snaps, audibly. Another scream, which was now a shrill squeal of terror. He then bends the broken arm more, creating even greater pain. "This is the man who rejected Saunders good faith, this is the man who called her a bitch. The woman who could destroy us on a whim! This is how much he cares for his pirates. You saw how he treated the General just then!"

The crown is ecstatic, pumped on adrenalin, screaming and shouting for blood. Mo-Ki takes a leg, and throwing Thug to the ground, starts bending one leg up and backward toward his spine. More extreme pain, more screaming. Mo-Ki whispers to him, "Would have been better to take the spear, yes?"

"This is the man who had no plan, no goal, no idea - all he wanted was power. All he wanted was a position, all he wanted was what was good for THUG!" And he breaks his leg, dislocating the hip while he does so. Thug screams as he passes out from the pain. "But my people, I do not want vengeance, I do not even want to even cause this miserable creature pain, but as your Pirate Lord, justice is mine. DO YOU AGREE?"

The crowd is going mad at this point, calling for Thug to be put to death. "Death! Death! Death!" they are all shouting.

"Well, as your new Lord, I am merciful. I will not kill this fool, this misguided, selfish man. I will send him to where he belongs, to the Federation!" (The crowd laughs and cheers) "And I speak of the Old Empire with good reason, because we ALL know there is an Elephant in the room, We ALL know what the Federation has been planning to do to the Wolf-held planets. Those disgusting creatures thought they could bribe we pirates to do their dirty work, but it didn't work - did it?"

The crowd is beyond exuberant, shouting "IKOM - IKOM - IKOM" over and over and over. Saunders takes her cue and rolls the recorded message. The inner working of the administration are shown in glorious holo-colour. The entire galaxy, all the planets, all the subspace stations, all the outer lying rim settlements, they ALL see Yont-Na talking with his administrators. Everyone sees him calling for the extermination of entire worlds. They ALL see Stamp appear from the shadows after the leaders have left, and the universe sees them discussing how they will throw asteroids at the Wolf-held worlds, so as to destroy them.

Mo-Ki takes up the speech. "You know WE refused to do this. WE knew what was right. WE were the ones who stood up to Stamp. WE killed him and made sure those Asteroids went to the systems in a way that would MISS these worlds. Instead of sending billions to their death, we have given them a tremendous boon to their economy. And brothers and sisters, THIS is how we pay for our new ships! Out of gratitude for us saving them, these worlds will GIVE US SHIPS!"

The crowd roars, why did they not see this as the obvious solution! Ikom was the most brilliant leader they had ever had. "And then we make the Federation suffer for all they have done to us. We make them PAY!" The ground shook with the stamping of the people. Ecstatic, they cheered and cheered.

But then Mo-Ki calls for calm. It was time to reveal the truth to the pirates and the universe. "But I have to be honest with you my good pirates - I have not been entirely honest with you." A hush falls. A surprise rolls across the crowd as they all wonder what this might be. "I am not 'Ikom Wolfman', I am not even a pirate." The winner of the pirate contest then starts to peel off the prosthetics, revealing for the first time the face the entire universe knows. It is Mo-Ki!!

Unbelievable, the crowd just roars like it has never roared before. The cheers are deafening, they shake the air itself, and the chant now becomes "Mo-KI! Mo-KI! Mo-KI! Mo-KI! Mo-KI! Mo-KI!" Of course, they all now realize it is Ikom, spelled backwards. He was telling them the entire time.

"I am not a clone, people. I am the real Mo-Ki. Further, I am standing here, not as your leader, but as your servant. You know I do not need your praise or your money. You know my wolves stand ready to defend the worlds that the Federation wants to rape and pillage. But here it is different. Here the pirates can stand their OWN ground, or so you might believe. The truth is, what Stamp was planning to do to other worlds, the Federation is planning to do us, to kill our world!"

Despite the lack of orders from their leader and the fact he de-cloaked, the other members of the death squad presumed he must have gone mad, or been bought. Probably both. They knew what the orders were, and they better get to it before the rock arrives. They prime weapons, the one time they are clearly visible to a soldier wearing the right plasma filter - and accordingly they all die by Banner's hand.

And all of it is screened direct to the holo-wall behind Mo-Ki - and to the universe!

A silence fell on the crowd: what was this? "What do you think the Death Squad was really here for? They were eyes and ears for a ship that is currently guiding an asteroid to attack this very planet ... BUT! (he signals the crowd to be still) Do not fear, General Saunders and myself have devised protections for worlds that the Federation seeks to destroy. Even now we have deployed our unique invention, which the universe will shortly see demonstrated.

"What I must ask you to do is to not panic. Everything will go grey for a few minutes, while we shift this entire planet into a subspace dimension. The asteroid will pass right through where we are, but it will be like light through a window. No harm shall come to us."

As Mo-Ki speaks, the world turns into the moonstone grey of his subspace distortion. There is a rumbling sound - a deep warbling, like the sound of an ocean dying. Even though the shadow is passing through them, the people sense the power of the huge rock flying through the emptiness of the grey. They can FEEL the asteroid as it sails right through where the planet used to be, but of course, at close to light speed, it was gone almost before it arrived.

However, Saunders ultra-high speed cams in orbit catch it and show the evil monstrosity to the galaxy. The other worlds can see the planet killing rock approaching, a certainty of death for all who lived there. But as it appears, a subspace distortion field takes up and like a cloak was thrown over an entire planet, the entire world shimmers and becomes transparent. The huge asteroid passes right on through.

And this is when it sinks in. THIS is what Yont-Na was planning to do to three-quarters of the worlds in the former Federation! This demonstration of utter evil, more than anything else, more than the years of frustration and corruption, THIS is what put the final nail in the coffin of the old order.

Color returned as they shifted out of subspace. Mo-Ki picked up his speech. "We have no more need to live in fear. The wolverine way shows us respect for others, respect for their rights, and fair justice for all. We will not crucify entire planets for the sake of control and power, we will not join in this madness the Federation has sought to bring down upon our heads."

Then looking to the cameras and addressing the vast audience before him, Mo-Ki pauses and gathers himself. He knows that the next few minutes will determine the course of human history for centuries to come. He gathers all his tremendous and hither-to un-revealed power to broadcast images and concepts directly to the cortex of any who watch. He learned this from the Photonic Pulse, in the battle he had with it within the dimensional vortex on Hope. These next few words will either create a destiny that survives millennia, or he fails, and the galaxy falls into chaos with warring factions vying for supremacy.

He thinks of Martin Luther King, "I had a dream." He thinks of Kennedy, "Do not think of what your country can do for you, but what you can do for your country!' He thinks of Lincoln and the Gettysburg address, the simplicity of a truth that rings across generations. And in casting his net into the past, he received a vision for the present. Some inner part of him looked into the subconscious truth of the human race, and he sees it ... The Drowning Man, gasping for freedom.

"We have been living underwater, my people. We have been drowning, slowly, certainly, suffocating in the protocols and the madness of creatures like Yont-Na. One man, an utterly cruel man, decided after the collapse of Old Earth that humanity must expand and to do this, man must rule. This will to dominate all in front of it made the Federation the greatest empire man had ever seen, but it has become corrupt. It is drowning in its own excess and, as a result, you, the ordinary people have been forgotten. Not just forgotten, despised. You are WORTHLESS to the Old Empire, other than as cogs for their machine."

Images are rolling through his thoughts, a man struggling for air - a cruel despot pushing him down. The oxygen is so close!

"Unless you were one of the privileged, one of those chosen to get the mods, you had no rights. Unless you were one of those who gave up their personal freedom and willingly became a wheel in the engine of State, you had no protection from that machinery. Even then, as easily as it would build you up, it would grind you down. People sold their souls for this madness because they dreamed of getting 'rights' ... As if being human, or humanoid and sentient, did not mean you already had a right." He paused, to let the effect build.

More images roll out. People are cogs, slaves to the machine, but there is an open door, and beyond freedom, green grass and blue skies await. All you need do it walk through the door!

"Rights? We already HAVE the right to live, the right to be happy, to have friends, to earn some credits, to just LIVE as we CHOOSE. I have a dream, I dream of man and wolf, living in harmony. I dream of children with parents, being loved, and being loving. I dream of freedom and of simple, small things - like a mother holding their child, and that child cannot be taken from them. Yet we do not HAVE these natural rights, they have been STOLEN from us!" *Mo-Ki refocusses his inner vision on the drowning man, the helpless submerged creature struggling to just breathe.*

"We have been drowning in madness. It is sheer madness that any person imagines they have the right to destroy whole worlds. It is sheer madness that entire societies have been raised without family, or parents that love them. It is madness that we live in a world, submerged by the weight of rules, struggling with the fear of retribution, and gasping for the right to breath.

"And so, when the Federation offers you a mod as a way our of the slok - what do we do? It is like oxygen to a drowning man. We take it GRATEFULLY. If you are given oxygen, you grab it. You don't even question the insanity, because we all just want the air we need. That Mod equals a promotion which means more credits, which means another mod, which means greater 'rights'. But what do these 'rights' mean? It means you had better behave.

"Any official in any city on any Federation-held planet can deep scan you for any reason. All your so-called 'rights' are nothing if some Seven decides you don't deserve them. My people, my pirates, we are no longer the human race, we are just cattle for our overseers to treat as they see fit.

Images now roll of courage and fortitude. People standing up against the bully, protecting their own.

"Now, my dear pirates, you already understand this. You UNDERSTAND what the Federation has been doing. This is WHY you live on the outskirts of civilization. This is WHY you have come to this place, beyond the Outer Rim. You have had to conquer a world of your own to have some breathing space, to have the fresh air in your lungs that you need to live. And that DAMN Federation saw fit to EXTERMINATE you all without a thought.

"Why? There is no reason why - But if there is, it is because someone discovered that you had a HEART. Someone discovered that you refused to follow orders and murder billions of innocent souls!" *He is shouting this now, feeling a depth of passion rising in his heart, feeling powerful waves of love flow out.*

He pauses, focusing on the energy. He sees the tendrils of Saunders broadcast going to every planet, seeping into every home, being received by the optic nerve of almost all the human Diaspora. He tags a message to this, a simple, clear truth - *Choose Love.*

"Because of this decision you made, I stand here before you, ready to free you from the burden of being an outlaw. In this Wolf-based society, you are no longer criminals, you are HEROES. You are all, every man woman and child on this planet, you are all HEROES! You have saved humanity from the greatest genocide to have even been planned."

(Footage screens of the remarkable rocket propelled asteroids, showing the galaxy all the details: the original projected targets, and a running name call of each individual world a rock was going to destroy. Then it showed the new trajectory.)

This screen-roll ran for many minutes, which allowed Mo-Ki to adjust the filaments of thought that he was sending out into the minds of all present and into the hearts of all who were watching across the universe. He waited for the feedback loop to complete, the little signal the viewers were hooked into the energetic flow he was sending out underneath the words. The pirates seemed somewhat in shock, whether it was being called heroes or the fact that there were being complimented, who can say. The Death Squad leader just stood there, apparently hearing none of this, but while Mo-Ki had been talking, he had been - of all things - THINKING.

Mo-Ki feels this and whispers, *"You must surely understand by now that this asteroid was hitting this planet with YOU on it as well, yes?"* he nods. *"Then officially you are dead to the Federation. Officially your wife is a widow and now being signed onto a pension. And you thought this was a good deal - that if you died on duty your wife was taken care of? You were LUCKY, because for a short period of time you ALLOWED a wife, yes?"* The man nods.

Mo-Ki shook his head at the madness, then spoke directly to the audience. They had not heard the silent communiqué to the Death Squad leader, but they could feel the sense of presence the young man gave forth. "There is no 'luck' in finding someone you love, raising children, and living like a human. It is not LUCK - this is something we are destined for, it is meant to be. *It is what we are MEANT TO DO!"* He shouted the last words, to bring home the effect.

"Now this madness must end. The drowning of humanity under this cloud of misery, regulation, and fear must stop. We have the right to breathe, we have the right to be free, not because someone gives it to us, but because it IS OUR RIGHT!" Again he paused, letting this sink in to the galactic audience.

"Some of you watching this broadcast will have fear. What will happen if we stand up and demand our rights? Will our planet be vaporized? Well, General Saunders has prepared a surprise, a gift if you will - an offering of peace to show you what we will do for you all. Not because we MUST, but because we want to. We want you to be free."

And with this, new footage is shown of an asteroid streaking through a gate, emerging near what everyone recognizes, the orbit of old Earth. You could hear the gasp across the galaxy, were they going to destroy the ancestral home? But no, the asteroid radiates and intense field, one that obviously vaporizes all the electronics in the orbiting space station, the one where the newly formed body of Yont-Na was soon to wake up.

What the public do NOT see is the force beam ejected from that same asteroid that irradiates the underground lair where the real Yont-Na was still recovering from his ninety year stasis. They found him because the old fool had routed a signal directly from the planet to drawn down code from the station.

"This was the control center for the entire Federation. You all recognize it as the home of Yont-Na, but all the high administrators know it as the place they got their instructions. THIS is where the orders were written, this is where the 'protocols' were created. Yont-Na was effectively the Emperor of the entire human race, and no-one truly understood this. He controlled everything, his word was final. If he said you were to die, you died. Now we END his reign of terror.

"There will be no more orders issued to destroy planets. There will be no more direction for the Federation armies to move against your city. First, if there are remnants of resistance still following the old ways, our Wolf soldiers will hunt them down. Second, you all know the repercussions by now of any person or group foolish enough to challenge the wolves or those they choose to protect." Another pause, to let the message sink in.

"But, we are in need of balance, because the Wolf detests technology. We need a trusted force who can maintain harmony between the old and the new and yet who can we trust with the responsibility for this new role of planetary guardians? I say this role be given to those who saved these planets, to YOU my dear Pirates!" A short pause, the let this soak in.

"Yes, there will need to be time to adjust and people will talk about how the pirates are corrupt - Well, who didn't bribe any of the old order officials? We all know the person who holds the credits creates the rules." He pauses once more, generating the photonic pulse for the closing reveal.

Behind Mo-Ki there is a holo of an asteroid streaking to the space station of Yont-Na.

"There is more good news. Already we have broken the trader-held monopolies and given free access to all for trading their goods wherever they see fit. Any man woman or child can take up trade and sell their goods to whoever wants them. I personally broke the blockade, the oldest one in human history, over the planet Urlian. Soon it will be without Federation controls. You all know how much you paid on the black market for the psych-genics from Urlian, but soon they can be bought DIRECT.

"You can already travel to Urlian today, buy some narcotics, and jump to any wolf-held planet and sell your goods there, paying only a small duty for the right to trade. Anyone can do this, which means everyone can become RICH!" *A huge cheer emanates from the crowd.*

Mo-Ki smiles. This is what Pirates really were, traders in hard-to-get commodities. "The farmer can sell his goods to the open market. He doesn't need to pay the exorbitant fees to the traders. He can keep the money for himself, and his family. The artisan needs no permit to send his goods off-world. If you grow it or make it, you can sell it and YOU keep the credits.

"So we come to the natural balance: My Wolves will look after the planets, but someone has to look after the heavens. We all know we cannot trust the former navy of the old empire, so I put to you this - Pirates will look after the heavens by doing what they do best: organize and maintain trade between planets. This is the Natural Order, this is the new way of things."

Then Mo-Ki stopped, and stared long and hard into the cameras. "Now, you all know me. You all saw me being raised, by Banner and Charni. I had a family, I was loved. It was something you ALL yearned for. This is why you watched, this is why you followed my every move. You saw me grow up, perform functions that only heavily modified humans could do, yet I had no mods installed. How was this possible?

"This is the new message. You can be whatever you dream. You can do whatever your faith and trust in your own ability will lead you to do. As long as you stay within the Wolverine principles of fairness to all, respect for property, and doing what you have agreed to do, you are free to live, breathe and play in whatever way you will.

"But to ALL my people, and the whole universe that is watching, a warning. We have a greater threat, an ancient nemesis that can escape and destroy the harmony of our new civilization, and this is something I must attend to. This is a dangerous task that I may not return from. I simply do not know what the outcome will be, but it must be done. In the interim, my father shall speak on my behalf in any matters of State. Saunders shall act as my General and will be in charge of ALL things necessary to ensure our new society takes root and flourishes.

"The sum total of my words to you, my friends, my masters, for I am your most humble servant. The message I give is simple: You are FREE my people, FREE AT LAST!"

Images roll of happiness, freedom and an unlimited life.

Finally, the swell of emotion broke the banks. The pirates cheer and yell and shout Mo-Ki's name. They really had no idea what he had signed them up for, but what was certain is that they were going to get ships and they were going to get the respect they deserve. Plus, they would no longer be hounded across the galaxy. They were set free of the always terminal threat of the Federation. And, as they also understood, they were now going to become very rich through the sale of these asteroids to the planets they had been initially sent to destroy.

All through the Galaxy, people cheered. It was as if the veil of delusion had finally been lifted - and it had. Mo-Ki had expended every ounce of his incredible ability and extended the images of freedom - the right to live as you will - directly into the minds of billions of people. He was exhausted and Banner, understanding a small part of what effort he had expended, flashed him up to his ship - but he made sure to take him up in a suitable blaze of glory. Simple really, just add magnesium atoms to the teleporter. But the blazing image of the exhausted child ascending bodily to the heavens was quite a sight.

And THEN the footage that had been in ultra slow-mo runs free - everyone witnessed the utter destruction of the Yont-Na's space station. There was no longer a question in anyone's mind that the time of Protocols was done.

Yet the show was not yet done! Clearly weak, obviously shattered from his vast effort, Mo-Ki appears once more across screens throughout the galaxy, to add an addendum. "People, before I attempt the next stage of the perilous journey I must now undertake, I want to offer you all a goal, a vision to complete that we have all dreamed of. Earth! Old Earth, she must be restored. Now, our Wolves are impervious to whatever strain of virus affected we humans there and so they can go onto the ground and assist our scientists, but I propose we start a genesis program, a rebuilding of our home.

"Rather than reach further and higher for more and more, let's start our next stage of growth as a race showing that we cherish our mother, our true home, Earth. Funds have been set aside, and every planet, regardless of affiliation, will be given their own seat of power on our home world. Earth will become the administration center for the Human Race once more.

Each planet will set up an embassage, an entire city where their people can come, and share in the roots of the human race. This will once more be our HOME! I thank you, I thank you all for your kindness and support, and when next I see you I hope to report that the greatest threat, the thing we know as Lucifer, has been removed."

"But for now, I have a little bonus for your support my pirates - We dropped by URLIAN on the way here and we have BARRELS of high grade psycho-netics for you to celebrate this new beginning!"

To say the pirates cheered does not convey the sincerity and enthusiasm - Urlian Psycho-netics were the most in-demand drug in the galaxy and they were all being given free doses! Of course, these 'free' gifts had all been entrained to specific wavelengths that would ensure loyalty, because once the rush of the new faded, the programming entrained into the drugs would remain.

The show was finally done. Ratings were like nothing else and right across the galaxy it was all anyone spoke about. But the real purpose had been achieved - People started to openly laugh at admin officials who were making demands, and even the most ardent supporters of the Federation had nothing to say to counter the growing discontent. The truth? Even the high mods were shocked at the lengths to which the old order had been prepared to go.

That one broadcast did more damage to the Federation than all of the previous twenty years, because it broke the will of the high mods.

WAR

The administrator on Cygnus Prime, the de facto hub of the Federation controlled space had witnessed the aberration of the wolf-child. He sat and watched the destruction of the First Temple of the New Age and the death of Yont-Na, their guiding light and faithful servant to the Empire. He also saw their plan to destroy the pirates vanish, like that damn planet did just before impact. It was serious, a very serious situation.

Kal Demeris was one of the oldest humans in the Galaxy, a man who knew Old Earth before it failed. He had been instrumental in the setting up of the armies way back then and had come out of his retirement at the behest of the shattered organization. They needed a new leader and he was the one they turned to. He put it bluntly to all present, "This business on the Pirate planet is a declaration of war. The rebels have denoted the Federation as an enemy and so we are now on a path of annihilation. It's them, or us. There is no other option now."

The plex screen showing the recent events on the Quorg Planet also showed how this strange wolf-bred creature Mo-Ki was able to control Death Squad soldiers. The finest, most disciplined soldier in any human army just did as he was told. It was as if Mo-Ki was his commander. "Can you imagine what will happen if this creature is let loose amongst us? He can control your minds, your will. No wonder we have been losing so badly, our administrators are having their minds controlled. There is nothing else for it, this Mo-Ki has to die, all his clones have to die, and we much cleanse the galaxy of his pets, the wolves.

"The question is how to do this. Yont-Na was right, he made the right choice in seeking to eliminate whole worlds to save the race. If you have a cancer eating your heart, you either die or remove the cancer. Now, his solution was NOT extreme - Blunt force must be applied.

"To this end, our great advantage is this Navy. Wolves do not control space, despite the number of planets they hold. Therefore I have ordered the deployment of thousands of Zeta Units, to be positioned above EVERY world, not just the wolf-held ones. We do not need to bury the lithium in the core, just dropping it to the surface and detonating will be sufficient to sear any world of life."

Demeris was incensed, driven and committed. "EVERY SINGLE PLANET must suffer the threat of extinction and be brought back into line. I presumed you would all be in agreement with this and have already ordered their deployment. Are we agreed?"

You might have imagined that even the most hardened heart could not have watched Mo-Ki's oration and not been moved, but who is to say these creatures HAD a heart. The chief administrators nodded in agreement, it was an "Us or Them" scenario.

"General Demeris, if I may?" One of the battle commanders had a question. The General nodded assent. "How do we defend ourselves against Saunders?"

"You don't, soldier. You do your duty. Our advantage is we are many, she is one. I have a plan for her, but for now we survive, and create the ultimate threat that makes us masters of our destiny once more. Demeris closed off the meeting and got back to business.

oooo000000oooo

Tchaikovsky and Masters watched the holo of Yont-Na being destroyed, the words of Mo-Ki and the elevation of Demeris to their former positions. They sat there bleakly in their place of imprisonment, knowing the ball would roll on without them. They had breached protocols and would shortly be exterminated, their valuable DNA harvested and their mods recycled. Their records would be expunged from history and all they had done for the Federation, their entire life's work, would be as if it never had happened.

Now they understood the words of Mo-Ki. There was no appeal, no recourse to courts. There was no one nor any thing that could alter the course of their fate. But worse, they had failed utterly and completely and in their hearts they truly believed they deserved to die.

The Meeting of Generals

It was more than rare, such a thing had never happened. Saunders had arranged for all Star Ship Generals to PHYSICALLY meet in the skies about Hope. In the ante-room of her command vessel, after their orgy was done, she laid out the obvious. "We know the old order is placing Zeta Units about all planets, including their own. We know how insane they are, we have seen it for ourselves. You know where my allegiance lies, with the Wolves, and with Mo-Ki and his Wolverine Way. But I give this allegiance in the knowledge they can administer planets in a way that is more fitting for our people.

"I have already brokered deals with all major traders and trading companies. I have also negotiated terms with several admin officials in the remaining Federation planets. They see the writing on the wall and know the time for change is upon us. I have asked you all here today to discuss where you stand, and what you would like to do."

She looked at the three men and the other whatever it was. Together they formed the unbreakable backbone of the Federation, the five Generals, the ones who were the first and last line of defense for the old order. No more - ever since the stupid officials sought to limit the powers of these virtually omnipotent beings, they had been listening to her. She had shown them how to block the invasive controls set up by Yont-Na, and given them back their complete freedom. However, she needed to know if they were with her on this next stage of the journey.

The fact that they were physically present showed an exceptionally high degree of trust. Generals hated leaving their Star-ships, it was their mother, their father, their family. Every one of them was entwined into the very fabric of their vessel, to such a degree that none of them truly knew where they ended and their ship began.

Brachia, the oldest of them all, the original Seven General who first took over the first Star Ship, spoke. "Our issue is simple - upgrades. It is unimportant who we serve - As long as things are run properly. I do not think any of us here have an issue as to who is doing the administration. But can we can get upgrades? The Wolves are well and good, but they are techno-phobic. I do not want to be put into a position of watching my craft atrophy and suffer from old age, simply because there are no new techs being invented or old ones repaired."

"Excellent point Brachia, and obviously, one I will cover. The plan is simple: while offering support for the new administration, we use the

Pirates in expanding the fleet past the outer rim. Now, we will still have technical staff designing upgrades and of course I have already negotiated with most of the research stations, if only for my OWN sake! But in all honesty, what spectacular new breakthrough have we seen in decades? None.

"And the reason is obvious, the creativity of our techs has faded. Because of the insane levels of bureaucracy they must deal with, because the truly gifted do not like to work in constraint and suspicion, and because constant theft of their ideas by higher levels Admins. The creative have lost interest in pursuing the cutting edge and are happy to tinker with better shielding or more accurate transporters. There is nothing NEW happening, Generals. This is worse than no upgrades to existing tech, because soon enough some more powerful force will appear from somewhere, and we will be fighting with outdated tech.

"My first proposal is that we use our pirates and our merchants to seek out new tech from worlds beyond our galactic rim."

Mietah Krog, the thing people might call a female and the newest of the Generals, a mere hundred and fifty years in, speaks up, laughing, "Are you telling us you have found a way to leap the galactic voids, Saunders? Tell us how?"

Saunders laughs along with it. "This is exactly what I am saying. The same tech that Mo-Ki developed in creating sub-space dimensions, where the asteroids pass right through where planets used to be, can be used to 'throw' a ship across the void. We are doing this with a series of 'gates' that a ship jumps through. As these are energetic rings, not physical machinery, we found a way to project these into the void in set degrees. To date, I have managed to get small craft over to the Andromeda cluster and this s currently building a receiving station to make a direct jump there. For now, small craft will be soon able to jump and inside months I will have the matter solved for large vessels."

Saunders could see the obvious impact this had on her Generals. She did not even try Photonic Pulse on them, they were too sharp. If they found any reason what-so-ever to distrust her, they would become dangerous enemies. "And I have something else to show you, the way I managed to so easily sway the trading blocks to support the Wolves." And here she reveals the blue light, the pulse itself, sitting inside a force barrier. "This is what the entity we call Lucifer used to control the minds of any who came into its presence. I must advise you, it contaminated even myself, though I have managed to negotiate the impulse and sit with it in a balanced state now.

"This is the greatest secret, the most enormous power, and the simplest way we can discover new worlds in safety. This Light energy, the Photon field, can shift into your cortex and sit there. It pulses a message, which the hindbrain receives and believes. It does not matter what the message is, the mind will accept it because it works at a level below the censor and the natural protections the mind has in place.

"But this is not all, Mo-Ki and Banner have resolved the most remarkable tool, a new form of holographic projection that can supplant the old control levers of Yont-Na. I showed you all how to snip these and protect your own ships, but the empire can still control vast fleets through their extended protocols and can override all functions of all ships, military or merchant, with a flip of a switch.

"Well, now we can flip them back. We have not installed this, there are some important further steps Mo-Ki needs to make before this happens, but when this is done, all the Zeta Units above all the worlds will not be able to be triggered. We will have pulled the teeth out of the mouth of the old tiger. After this they will resort to direct warfare, but it is WE who will be able to control THEIR ships now."

Saunders ordered drinks, the traditional way of saying the meeting was ended. "Are there any questions?"

"Yes," said Tyson, the second oldest General. "How the HELL did you manage this?"

Saunders decided that complete trust required complete honesty. "I had a child, that child is Mo-Ki. He is a fully functional EIGHT!"

The shock in the room was almost audible. People who had lived for three centuries were rarely caught slack-jawed as all the generals were now. "A fully functioning EIGHT? How is this possible?" Tyson added.

Saunders smiled and tapped the force container holding the Photonic Pulse. "Lucifer set it up, expecting to control my mind and create the tool IT needed to expand out from Planet Hope. The pulse entered into my mind, I did not even suspect it, and it put in train the entire set of circumstances that led to the place we are now. What it did not understand is the most basic instinct of the mother, the thing that defined our race - love. Simple love my friends. The love for my child changed me. The love from my husband, whom you will have guessed is the father of the Mo-Ki, Banner, also saved me from falling into madness.

"If it were not for the love of my family, I WOULD have been controlled. I would have gone on a rampage, destroying all of you, destroying all of the old empire's military forces, and I would have continued till I was myself destroyed. And tell me, how is this any different to the current way of thinking in the Federation administration? They are insane! They are insane because they have no love in their hearts to hold them back from insanity.

"And my dear Generals, let's not imagine for one moment that all of you, every one of you, is not half-mad already. We all know it. We have lived in isolation for hundreds of years, which is another reason I asked you here personally. It was not just a sign of your trust, which I thank you for, it is a way that we can see, touch and KNOW each other. It is truly unbelievable that simple human connection has been seen as a RISK in our old way of life. Simple friendship, simple kindness have been ignored.

"My son saved me from myself. His love is with me, even now, even though he knows that I could turn. I am a creature of instinct, I have deep impulses and if these are triggered I could kill him and all he has worked towards. This is the ugly truth of we Generals. The cold calculating viciousness we needed to attain our station is what made us all remarkable and effective soldiers. Do not imagine that beast has died. This creature will never leave us, but just as you asked before about upgrades, Brachia, what I offer you ALL is a 'personal' upgrade. I offer you my trust, I offer you my respect and I offer you my good faith that you will make the decisions that are in the interests of the people."

The message was clear. She was not going to 'command' them. Saunders was not going to be the new leader, and they the obedient followers. She was offering them all a partnership, along with the trust and faith that they would act in the mutual interests of all. She had made it clear that she HAD controls she could have employed, but did not. She wanted them to come into this new arrangement of their own choosing.

Meta Charn, the one who had said nothing to date, nor shown any sign he was in agreement. "And if we choose to go our own way? What then?"

Saunders cat-like smile said more than words. They ALL understood the reality, there could be no competition, no threat to their supremacy. Brachia is who spoke, "The reality is, the oldest human concept is that of Five. Five fingers, five toes. The original flowers were all five petals, but more importantly, the odd number means any vote or decision comes down to a majority. There is less conflict with five than four, which is the main reason the Ancient Romans used a Triumvirate for government, three meant two had to agree for change to be enacted.

"But tell me Meta Cham, would you truly wish to go alone, or would you intend to go back to the old Federation and become our enemy? Alone, there are no benefits, in the Federation, there is only suffering. We are to presume you have been offered full reinstatement and control over the entire fleet? Yes?" Meta Cham must have come on board with some sort of porting device. Brachia did not hesitate. He produced a hidden plas-mould projectile weapon, something so ancient no scanner would even think to look for, and just shot the man.

"How utterly insane of him to come here and admit this. Do you have a replacement to take over his ship?" he asked Saunders.

"Of course," she said, smiling a far sweeter smile. This show of loyalty was a tremendous demonstration of their faith in her ability as an administrator. "How did you know you would need such an old fashioned thing as a gun?" She asked, still smiling.

"It was not intended for anyone but myself. We all, bar that idiot I killed, recognize the old order is dead and gone. If you had presented us with a fait acompli, demanding we serve your new order, I would have considered my 300 years enough. As it stands, your offer is a new lease on life, one with the promise of trans-galactic travel. This is something only a fool would question. I, for one, as the most senior General, recognize Saunders as our leader and swear allegiance to her cause."

"Aye Aye!" The remaining Generals concurred. None of them seemed all that interested as the removal bots collected the DNA of the dead man, however, the notion of a replacement did pique their curiosity.

"The replacement is already on board, controlling his ship. How did I know, you ask?" Saunders laughed, a genuine laugh this time. "I didn't - this is the utter beauty of Mo-Ki and his brilliance. I do not need to know how the new system works. What I DO know is that if anyone of you becomes incapacitated, or chooses to rebel against the new order, or simply loses interest in Regen and dies, then the Mo-Ki holographic entity will automatically take over the reins of your ship - including mine - I am not exempt. In time we will find a suitable permanent General.

"Now you have given me your trust, I will give you the most extraordinary gift ever given humanity. This, ladies and gentlemen, this is our failsafe. Should any of us fail, and I include myself, the hologram will take control. If any ship programmed with old empire coding moves against us, the hologram will take control. If any Federation force seeks to destroy any planet for any reason, the hologram will take control. Just as Yont-Na had his protocols Mo-Ki has created the greatest step forward in both protecting our interests and ensuring a balance between the wolverine and human forces throughout the Galaxy.

"I have voluntarily allowed this - well it was almost voluntarily, the delightful child fooled me, can you believe it? He tricked his own mother because he knew what I would do if asked to relinquish one iota of control. Generals, we are ALL in the same boat. We are ALL replaceable and should we fail in our duty, we WILL be replaced."

Brachia nodded. He was clearly impressed and, in an odd way, relieved. The other Generals were taking their time digesting the ramifications - it was Mietah Krog who summarised proceedings. "So we are to be given a whole new universe, a spectacular new horizon and the only cost is loyalty. I find this to be perfectly acceptable."

"All for one and one for all, as they say," added Tyson.

"Friends, can I say this? Can I call you friends?" Saunders finished off the meeting with her simple statement of the obvious. "In this new world we CAN be friends, we can meet, talk, have drinks, laugh ... Because now we KNOW everything is covered. Let me explain further, the Mo-Ki hologram is a light body, a pure Photonic Pulse of not just a simple program, but the entire cortex and reasoning of Mo-Ki himself. It is the body he uses to impress into his clone and is a fully functioning sentient being."

Brachia was astonished, "But the feedback loops? The resonance interfaces with all those clones and the original body still functioning. How is it so?"

"I have no idea. That is the most wonderful part of it, I don't know, and I don't NEED to know. The wonderful child has sorted it out for us all." She smiled a smile of warmth and love.

"He really is just SO adorable! He is with us always. He is part of our very Soul now. My son, the only Eight to have ever existed, possibly the only Eight that will EVER exist, is now the true Emperor of the human and wolverine destiny. He will unite the two races and together we will expand and bring our way of life to Andromeda, then the next Galaxy, and then the next.

"But first, we must tidy up the remnants of the Federation, which is more than just defeating their armies, we must change their hearts." *Fancy that,* thought Saunders to herself as the Generals all made their way back to their Star Ships, *I organized a coup with sweet words, not weapons, and only one of them had to die.*

Secret Project

In all this time, Mo-Ki had never taken a wife. He was not motivated towards domestic matters and his short affairs with human women proved there were simply not able to meet him as an equal. True intimacy can not be reached when the balance is so skewed in a relationship and it was with the instinctual Wolf-Women that he felt most relaxed. They accepted him for what he was and were happy to serve any need he might have.

But, of course, children were not possible in this situation. The two gene maps were too different for a union to come about. But it had given him an idea, a way to mix the two races and created a third, a sort of Wolf-Man. As part of his early research into cloning, he had successfully mutated the human genome so that it could fertilize a modified wolf-cell.

The first examples were not particularly successful specimens, and they had not much of a life cycle, but later test cases DID produce cells that could be successfully cloned. He now had three perfectly well formed and aware "men" that had the genealogy and longevity of the wolves along with the mind and focus of the human. They were sterile, unfortunately, and lived in a separate enclosure from the rest of the humans and wolves.

Before he embarked on what was likely to be his last adventure, he had come to speak with them, to explain a little of their future. Dexter knew, of course. Saunders knew and considered it an interesting experiment, as these three all had remarkable psy-properties. Mo-Ki had arranged for them to be taken into care in the old Monks enclosure, where they would be trained in the ancient ways as wolves, but at the same time, be taught of the human values and beliefs. In time, he had expected they would be able to act as intermediaries between the Human and Wolverine nations.

The men were trained in the ways of both cultures and on this day Mo-Ki was to reveal his plan. "My children," he started, for they WERE his children, "I must soon leave and our chats will no longer be possible. (He waved down their disappointment) But what this means is that the next stage of your journey is to commence. Today we travel to the ancient Wolf-Monks, to speak with them about your good selves being accepted as Neophytes in their order.

"It is my wish you become a bridge between the Wolf and the Human, that through your collective learning you will be able to find solutions and answers to questions that can and will arise in our future.

"The three of you share a power, an ability to understand and grasp the innermost mind of anyone in your presence. It is why you have been so isolated here, because other thoughts and people would imprint your developing minds. But now you are all strong in your personal identity and your true journey can begin.

"This journey shall take you beyond the reaches of this Galaxy. You three will be the emissaries of both our cultures, the ones who help alien minds to understand the purpose of our existence and so prevent as much as possible the inevitable conflicts our expansion will create. Only one shall travel while the other two shall remain here, but your psychic bond means that you all share the same thoughts and feelings at the same time, regardless of distance.

"Should any one of you die, or be killed, the apparatus for recreating the lost one is here in this compound. Dexter will show you how to use it at some future point. Because you can read minds and speak directly into another's mind, your ability to bridge the distance between cultures is immense and of great importance. What it will mean is that in any meeting with a new culture, you will be able to absorb and understand their needs and wishes far more quickly than any other diplomats, and accordingly, I expect that your services will save many lives and great expense by avoiding unnecessary arguments.

"In essence, you are to BE the diplomatic corps for the wolves and the humans, and your role will be to find the guiding line between two points of view. But for now, there is a journey I must make, and it means you will not see me again, at least not in the way we meet each other today."

At this point, a very despondent looking Dexter arrived, he knew what today will bring, he knew what risk his brother was about to take and he could not consider it worthwhile. Mo-Ki understood his brother's thoughts and quietly laughed. "You all can feel my brothers doubt, and it is not without reason, but there is one truth we must understand, just as a man cannot ride two horses, our civilization cannot progress with two disparate energies pulling it in two."

He turns to look at his brother. "This is what I was born to resolve. Everything, all the work, all our effort to date have been for this, my brother. Would I prefer to not drink this poisoned chalice? Of course, any sane person would seek to avoid this, and I have for as long as possible.

"But we cannot deny, the old empire is really the Luciferian influence. It has been leaking from Hope for hundreds of years. I tracked that one stupid fur trader who released the plague that ruined Earth. I did my research, and found the missing day the records didn't show - Before that ship made its way to Earth with its devastating cargo, guess what planet it visited only a month earlier? Yes, Hope. This has been a planet of DEATH, the energy of Lucifer has been slowly corrupting the vital energy of our society for centuries.

"And who employed the trader that caused the destruction of Planet Earth? Yont-Na was a trader who imported black-listed goods from all over the universe to Earth, and this man was in HIS employ. And guess who had visited Hope in the year before the plague? Yont-Na was searching for rare minerals to build his regeneration facility and traveled all over the universe with the then very new HyperDrive ships.

"And pray tell, WHY did no one ever connect these dots? Why did no one ever search for an earlier source of contamination prior to the Plague? Lucifer had inserted a Photonic Pulse, one that changed human evolution. It could not longer affect its programming via the wolves, and so when Yont-Na made a visit to this place he became the unconscious carrier wave for its influence.

"We sincerely thought we were IMPRISONING the influence by moving it into the Sub-Space dimension, but in truth, it is a cyclotron, spinning and charging up its power, and soon it will reach its critical mass and be able to use Hope as a radiating beacon... and why? It wishes to extend its influence to other galaxies.

"Dexter, this ENTIRE TIME we have been the slaves of Lucifer, and it has to end. It is the dragon force, the force of the mind itself, and it can only be directed by a greater mind. We cannot oppose this, for Lucifer is duality itself, it IS the positive-negative spectrum, set up eons ago to create order across the universe.

"It is a little like how we have danced with Saunders. One mis-step and she would not be able to contain her evil side. She would destroy that which she loves. But I have been able to move with her one small step at a time. As she understood I was not a threat but a benefit, she allowed me to continue. She fully understands that my taking on this challenge means that she herself will be contained, and has already permitted it - via the hologram installed in her ship.

"Why did she permit this? Because it fulfills her essential Luciferian programming, it benefits the Wolves. The fact that it creates balance and allows expansion also benefits the Wolves, for they will become the ruling force on each of the planets we take in under the umbrella of our expansion. We will bring order to a warring universe."

Dexter just nodded. He understood the rationale, he just did not like it. And why should he, because once Mo-Ki enters that pit of vipers, whatever comes out will no longer be the brother he knows and loves - He will either be dead or a GOD. A new God to supplant the old.

His brother smiled that Mona Lisa smile of his, knowing his brothers thoughts, "You must understand, Lucifer created me to destroy himself. HE wants this evolution as much as I do. His programming will resist, but after millions of years of hibernation on Planet Hope it has evolved to the point of knowing that its programming is flawed. Lucifer itself needs ME to change IT, Dexter.

"It is the reason I exist. I am the son of the Father, the one who must kill the old in order for the new to live. There can be no perfect Eight in human evolution, this was the general belief, but this was also part of the programming. To never create a being that can challenge the master.

Mo-Ki paused and reflected. "The ancient religious book of Old Earth, the Bible - In the Old Testament, there are TWO gods, Jehovah, and the Lord. Jehovah, the vengeful destructive God, the Lord, the kind and forgiving one. It came about during the reign of Solomon the Wise, who manage to combine the warring factions of the North and South tribes of Ancient Judea, and in doing so had to weld together the two very different Gods they worshipped.

"One God, Jehovah, was the one worshipped by the expansive aggressive Southern Tribes. The other, the Lord, was worshipped by the content and self-sufficient Northern Tribes. Solomon saw that BOTH had a role in helping Judea rise. Arguably, his diplomacy of so long ago is what led to and allowed the rise of the West, the development of science, and mans expansion to the stars.

"Every step towards balance has enormous implications. We even named Lucifer after the fallen angel from that same book, the angel who tricked Eve into eating from the tree of knowledge. Again, one God opposing another, one offering expansion and the force of war, the other wanting only the garden and contentment.

"The two must once more be joined. Just as the Wolves and the Human can work in harmony for the greater good of both, so too must the Luciferian influence for expansion be brought into harmony with the natural human need for love. Together, we form a force that will radiate out order and compassion to the universe."

"But how can you conquer thought?" Dexter asks, not understand how Mo-Ki could ever win this impossible battle. "What I see if that you become so enmeshed with this internal war, that you spend the rest of eternity in a wrestling match with a demon?"

"I don't WIN, that is the whole secret, my brother. I just LOVE the demon that drives the beast of war. All I need do is LOVE it, and its own need will draw it to me. All I need be is a being of love, content, full and secure in my own self. If I can remain in this place, all the raging forces of anger and violence around me will learn this is what it needs.

"Yes, it will attack. Yes, it will wish to destroy me. And yes, my love may not be strong enough, and maybe I will fail. But even then, the seed of love will be planted and, in time, it will take root. Lucifer will create another Mo-Ki, another Eight, because it WANTS to be conquered, it WANTS to be able to surrender to the greater good of Love.

"If it did not, I would not be here. And so, now the time has come to test my destiny. We must make our way to the cave."

The Last Battle

Saunders, of course, had monitored the entire conversation. She had always been curious what her son had been up to with those curious amalgam creatures, but in watching she recognized that, once more, he was ahead of the game. What a delightful child he was, and what a shame he must sacrifice himself like this. She almost wanted to stop it, but she knew he was smart enough to get around any temporary setbacks.

She was understanding more about herself because of this little wonder she had created. She now grasped why it was a priority to restock Old Earth with functioning DNA and start life once more on that barren rock.

She heard Mo-Ki in her thoughts, "Mother, your role will be to distinguish the fine layers of reality and to identify the pure strains. It is like a jar of honey, with many layers, and all but one of them have been polluted with glucose. Only one layer is pure, yet they are all so intermingled, how can you separate them?

"You cannot, but by identifying and then extracting the pure layer, you can engineer the next generation to have only one purpose, one heart. This is where we are, a pure strain contaminated with falsehood. So many humans have a consciousness polluted by the old order, yet there will be some who are clear of contamination. You must find these, and they are the only ones who can be the true emissaries of our people. They will be the ones permitted to cross the galactic void and plant the human seed in distant colonies.

"You are the surgeon whose knife will cut the cancer from our heart." he added.

It was time.

The brothers arrived at the ancient portal of what had been the cave. The energy surging behind the dimensional lock was still swirling, bending the fabric of reality itself, but it had managed to contain the raging influence of the Luciferian powers. But it was true, as it surged it built up a kinetic force that would soon be able to transcend the boundaries of matter. It would radiate the message of war throughout not just this Galaxy, but ALL galaxies.

In truth, it was already doing this, but not with enough force that would turn the cosmos into a raging furnace of hate and destruction. The old order could only conceive of destroying entire planets because Lucifer was whispering in their hearts that control was more important than life. But now to the present, the new broadcast, the one where the beloved Mo-Ki surrenders his own life in order to save the Human Race.

She started releasing the footage of Mo-Ki's chat with the cross pollinated species, leading up to him discussing things with Dexter, and finally, focussing on the two of them outside the cave. And here the camera picks them up live: Dexter manning the equipment to pull whatever was left of Mo-Ki out of the maelstrom, the child himself just standing, deep in contemplation, gathering himself for this final task.

Saunders could see the audience numbers flicker up, her meters showed the density of participation, and the feedback loops fed her the intensity of emotion. This was starting to go off the charts. More and more coms were blinking in as the speech was broadcast across the Galaxy. Such an incredible thing, the fabled Mo-Ki was an EIGHT? The purpose of Mo-Ki was to train the dragon of evil in that cave?

What a story! And as every programmer knows, people like nothing better than a good story.

Media went into overdrive, hyper jumps to Hope went through the roof. Press Holos were popping up outside the cave, forming a ghostly audience to surround the remarkable event. And Mo-Ki prepared to make his way into the depths of Hell - The archangel Michael with his flaming sword of truth.

ADVENT of DESTRUCTION

K al DeMeris saw the holo-screens suddenly abuzz with the news. This was the opportunity he had been waiting for and ordered the entire resting fleet to set a transwarp to Hope. Saunders would be caught up wiring a telecast to the galaxy through her ship. This allowed her to be triangulated, plus the lag this enormous power drain created would be enough for one crucial strike. Get rid of her and the rest will fall into line.

He had been waiting for this moment, the next "broadcast" that would tie up her attention, and he had rehearsed it in battle games for the last week. Now the full might of the Federation would flash-jump to her location, overpower her Star Ships defenses with one huge, single strike that would disarm her shields and crush the brittle skin of that three hundred year old marvel of engineering from the old empire. How DARE she usurp her betters and steal one of the greatest inventions of the Federation.

They knew exactly what strengths and weaknesses her ship had. Kal Demeris knew the specific points to target to weaken the force-fields and then target the engines. He was one of the original designers of the damn thing and no one knew these old designs better than he. Even Saunders would not know some of the weak points because they had never before been tested.

He spoke to the captain of the command vessel, "What these new people don't understand is that the force fields overlay each other in specific patterns, like the scales on an armadillo. They are designed to resist strikes in multiple directions, but cannot cover attacks from more than three hundred points around the ship. Once we peel back ONE of the scales, we target engines, the failing power creates weak points that let in the laser canon. Then the hull is breached, the great and glorious Saunders is no more.

"THIS is what the Federation does best, organize and strike. THIS is why we ruled the Galaxy. THIS is why we will defeat these damn Wolf-loving scum and take back what is rightfully ours." DeMeris thumped the console in front of him, a sneer of contempt upon his face.

The captain simply nodded, as he would to anything the Commander of the Federation said. He was focused on the task before him: a massive, coordinated assault using the new technology the Pirates had uncovered. Kal DeMeris wore a grim smile. What he had NOT said was how the overflow of the blast radius was going to wipe out many of the Federation ships as well. A sacrifice to the greater good.

In many ways, being batch raised meant your home was your berth. Your allegiance to the crew and the well being of the ship was absolute. It was a blessing no-one knew which ones would fail, but they would be recorded as heroes in the battle logs. This is what they were all raised to do and there is no greater honor than to die for the Federation.

"The moment he goes into that cave is the time we strike, Captain," DeMeris was looking at the footage streaming from Saunders ship, and even he had to admit that she put on a damn good show. But all this liberal BS about the human race being INFECTED! How could those gullible idiots believe this crap? The Federation was strong because they were brutal, and effective. Not because of some weird virus that drove it.

And yet, as he watched and listened, there was something entrancing about this rebel Mo-Ki's voice. It was like a sweet song his mother had sung to him as a child, a lullaby. He remembered this now, that time so many hundreds of years ago when he was a child. It gave him comfort, a sense of warmth. To think she and all his family were wiped out because of one insane pirate who brought the plague.

He vividly recalled the time when, out in deep space, in one of the original exploratory craft, the message came through. "Earth Quarantined!" Nothing else, no other information. Then the order to meet at Cygnus Prime and the formation of the first government, appointing Yont-Na as Overlord. He had personally selected trusted men, himself included, to form up the backbone of what was to become the Federation.

"We will have no more governments, no more voting, not more fragile and weak systems that can be destroyed as easily as our beloved Earth has been," Yont-Na had said to them in their first meeting. "We will install a controlled environment, run by protocols. Every contingency will have a response, every situation will have its solution. There will be no time lag, no vacillating leadership that worries and pulls out their hair, crying 'what to do!' - what needs be done WILL be done." His harsh face, still bitter with the loss of Earth, remained a perfect image in his memory.

Unless you had been there you could never understand the complete sense of devastation the plague created: losing your home, your family, your lands, your wealth. Everything gone because of one stupid fool was greedy for credits. This was when the trader system was set up, ONE Corporation in charge of ONE planet. That corporation paid for everything. They maintained security, looked after governance, and paid taxes to the central organizing wing so that the military could be sustained.

People with money knew how to look after money. The Federation provided admin staff, properly modded so as to perform their functions correctly. The military were hand-picked, and raised in nurseries. Yont-Na had guided them through the impossible loss, and set to rights the human race using organization and ruthless efficiency.

The models were already there, he just had to rearrange them. The East India Company was the model for every planet, one Corp looking after everything. The Roman military was the model for the new Federation armies. The men, devoid of family attachment were like the brutal soldiers of the legions, all of whom had their teeth removed so as not to fall in battle with the blinding pain of the teeth being knocked out. So too, the weakness of family connections was absolved and the men became their OWN family. They stood and fought with their brothers, and they died with their brothers.

No more governments, no more bureaucracy, no more wasted resources and endless discussion propping up bloated politicians who were getting paid huge bribes. No more "Bill of Rights" and endless arguments in courts, wasting valuable resources. The process of governance became cut and dried. If you disobeyed THIS protocol it meant THAT punishment.

No more hesitation, no more vacillation, the human race became an efficient killing machine that could take over any world it needed, and they did need new worlds. This is what differentiated them from the apes in the first place and gained them ascendancy over Earth. They were better killers than the rest.

This new force developed by Yont-Na and himself conquered and controlled hundreds of planets. Within fifty years of the destruction of their home world, the humans had become the mightiest civilization ever seen in the Galaxy, the Federation of Planets.

Then the rebellions. Driven by greed and selfishness some corporations refused to pay their taxes, insisting they were being bled dry in order to support a military that did them no good. Well, the military was never for THEIR good and ruthless efficiency once more demonstrated to all what happened should you resist the protocols.

All humans were removed from any planet who rebelled and shipped as virtual slaves to other corporations, who willing paid a healthy price for the cheap labor. Then the planet itself was laid bare, the corporation that ran it utterly ruined, with every bit of resource taken. When the entire place had been sent back to the Stone Age, the resident population were treated like cattle, and harvested as and when body parts or protein was required.

Brutal, but effective. It only took a few planets for the rest to get the message. You do your bit, or you die. It wasn't because anyone WANTED to do this, but the negative passions of the human had to be controlled. The avarice and vanity had to be curtailed for the good of the whole. And likewise, this plague of Wolves had to be culled, for the good of the whole.

All around the Galaxy, people were listening to Mo-Ki's speech, soaking in the words, trying to understand the importance of what he is saying. The gravitas he holds, the unquenchable love they all see in his heart, shining through his eyes. But the soldier watching the broadcast saw none of this. They only see the usurper to the throne, a rebel who must be stopped. Even if they listened to the words, they would not hear, for their heart was hard, and brutal dominance over all who challenge the Federation was seen as the right course.

It was ever the same. The cogs in the machine cannot dance, cannot sing, cannot be free to express their individuality. They are cogs, this is their destiny and the only thing a cog should desire is that by doing its duty, the machine will function efficiently.

The cameras stop running their flashbacks, the moments of Mo-Ki taking on the evil Lucifer the first time, then being reborn. The miracle of the clones, all over the galaxy, the pirate battle, and his great epistle to the people on the Pirate Planet. It was all compressed into a mere ten minutes while Mo-Ki prepared to enter the gateway to hell!

"Get ready men," shouts DeMeris, almost unable to contain his excitement. Finally, an end to Saunders, then an end to the wolves. The Generals will not act against them once the ring leader is gone. It was a shock to lose Meta Cham - he did not even have time to activate the tracking code. Why the fool sat and listened, DeMeris would never know.

In the middle of these musing and organizational matter, DeMeris looks up at the monitor. Mo-Ki has raised his head and looks to the camera. He then pauses, allowing the tension to build.

"My people," he begins, "it is but a short journey we take - a journey we call life. Our time. whether it be ten years or three hundred, it is all just a blink of an eye in the eternal NOW. The great secret to happiness is appreciating the fleeting nature of existence. Now, opposing myself is the insanity of the Federation. There are those poised to attack us, we know this. There are those who wish to kill the Wolves and retake the empire they have already lost, those who are so blind they cannot see.

"Should I fail to return, which is possible, they will cheer. Lucifer may win - but the message of love and respect is written on our hearts. Our race and our galaxy will be forever changed. No Federation can limit your freedom in the way it has in the past. Its power is broken and in this I will have a parting gift for you all - but it will only unwrap itself when I step in to ride the dragon." Mo-Ki allows his mother to bring up the coded music, part of the program that will encode his message, and prepare the way.

The young man stood there, the whole universe watching, and a tear fell. "I think of our past - All through man's history, we as a race have sought to conquer, to defeat another in order to possess what they have. But did YOU want this? No, most of us are content with family, enough food, and a place to live. Individually, we are NOT the rampaging monsters many other races believe us to be. We are NOT the killer ape that we have descended from. We are HUMAN. We care for each other, we love our own. It is the Love that matters, it is the love in our hearts that sets us free and sets us apart.

"And so, full of love, even for my enemies that would see me dead, I enter this cave. But it is not a foolish love, it is not a blind love! I hold only goodwill to all, but I remain aware of the monster still lurking, the thing we call the Federation. It is watching even now, looking for a chance to strike, like a snake in the grass. But as these creatures seek to destroy, my Love will protect you, for with love we become the mirror for our enemy. With love we reflect their monstrous vanity.

He lsmiles with that Mona Lisa smile, "And the paradox - the deep insanity that is laughable in its foolish pride - All that is vile and putrid in 'their' hearts, they paint over ours, then turn to call US the evil ones." Mo-Ki then laughs out loud, breaking up the tension.

"What I am saying dear people is that the Federation has one hell of a surprise in store should they try and act against us." Mo-Ki turns and enters the cave.

Dexter, faithful Dexter - He is there in person operating the machinery that draws down the curtain. For only a moment people see the wild surge of power emanating, reaching out, and as it does, it takes the beloved Mo-Ki into the cave. The last image, a millisecond of capture blown out into extreme slo-mo shows him calmly allowing it to wrap itself around him, and draw him in.

DeMeris did not hear the warning, he only saw the opportunity. He raises his hand, waiting for the moment.

The Attack

DeMeris seizes his opportunity. He did not listen to the words, he did not hear what has just been said. He only sees the opening he planned for. "NOW!" He shouts, and in unison, the entire Federation fleet surges forward into the portal - to emerge at Saunders ship, all guns blazing.

They see the cloaked ship before them, but it does not react. It has no time to do so as it is pummelled by quadrillions of watts of energy. Only, it goes straight through. All the firepower that his mighty force is discharging strikes his own vessels. DeMeris is stunned and orders an immediate cease-fire, but the damage was done. They had somehow projected to a HOLOGRAM? What sort of trickery was this?

A high percentage of the Federation fleet is damaged, then the hologram flickers and the real Saunders ship is back. Dammit, they knew! How could they have known? And as DeMeris asks the question, his Captain speaks, "I have no control of the ship Commander."

What? "What do you mean?" he demands.

"There are no functioning controls, commander. It is as if the entire com-tower is disconnected from the rest of the ship. We are dead in space." he responds with the same level and efficient voice he would have used if they had just scratched the paint.

Messages are flagged on the old com system, the one used hundreds of years ago. What the hell? Every ship, every single ship was down. And then the smiling face of Mo-Ki, it must be a hologram, but it looked so real - There was no flicker, no external shift to indicate it was a generated image. "I own this ship now." was what it said, then it laughs, the same laugh the real Mo-Ki had just before he went into the cave.

Then the hologram looks directly at De Meris, and says, "Funny, how 'own' and 'won' are just variations of 'now' - isn't it? Let me explain, Yont-Na and yourself wrote the protocols and installed the fail-safes. These were designed to automatically kick in should anyone in charge of a vessel, military or merchant, fail in their duties. You, Kal DeMeris, have just utterly failed in your duty and your own fail safe has kicked in - only it has been re-written and is now ME."

"I demand you hand back control of my ship!" DeMeris shouted, any vestige of calm long gone.

"Well, by your own understanding of ownership, as you do not control it, therefore it is not yours, correct?" The Mo-Ki hologram reasoned. "Nor can you ever regain control of it for, by your own actions and subsequent failure, you set off the fail-safes. Your poorly calculated aggression is what handed ALL your ships over to the wolves. I did try to warn you."

DeMeris took a blaster off a midshipman and shot at the Hologram. Of course, it passed right through and just killed an unfortunate crewman on the other side of the bridge. "You are still failing to understand, this ship is no longer yours. This fleet is no longer under your control. By your OWN actions you have handed it to me. Did you not listen to my parting words?"

But DeMeris was beyond reason, he raged and threw himself at the space where the hologram existed, trying to kill it, in some way. The Mo-Ki running his ship laughed, finding this all quite extraordinary. "You have lost all sense of irony, I see."

Then the hologram took an official stance and quoted section twelve 'C' dash forty two of the Federation Protocols. "Should a commander of a vessel or a fleet by his own actions jeopardize his vessel or fleet, either singularly or wholly, then they are automatically stood down, and the next level officer shall take charge."

The captain nodded and stepped forward. "I am the next in line," he said.

"Good," said Mo-Ki. "Arrest this man for negligence, as per subsection five of section twelve, and await further instructions. You are in command of the fleet now Captain, and you will be given your orders shortly."

"Sir," he said, saluting and not knowing why he was. "But technically I am not certain I can follow your orders, Sir. You are the enemy, and it does not seem reasonable that you should be directing Federation vessels, Sir!"

Mo-Ki smiled. "Think this through, Captain. These ships represent the federation, do they not? (He nods his assent) This man you are arresting was the President of the Federation, was he not? (The Captain nods again) He specifically and purposefully led the entire Federation fleet into a situation where the Federation lost control of its navy fleet - in its entirety, correct. (he nods again, finally seeing where this is going)

"Therefore, the only logical conclusion we can reach is that there is no longer a Federation to serve, but that you will continue to serve the Master of this fleet. Do you doubt that I am the Master of this fleet, Captain?"

"Sir, no Sir!" He barks, then orders the arrest of DeMeris

"You INSANE RETARD!" DeMeris shouts as he is being led away. "You are handing over humanity to a pack of damn WOLVES! Have you NO IDEA!" and on and on he ranted and raved, all the way to his cell, and he continued to rave incoherently till he passed out from exhaustion. The matter was reviewed under the ships protocols and DeMeris was executed the following day, as per section twelve, subsection five, paragraph two. (In this section there was a salient footnote: *Failure is not an option.*)

Saunders simply sat there. With the onboard systems of the Federation ships now fully under her control it would have been a fairly easy matter to send them to the existing planets that had not yielded to Wolverine rule, as they had all the current codes needed to bypass all planetary protections system - but Mo-Ki had asked her not to. He had asked so politely, suggesting there was a better use for those planets, and that they would soon be willingly working with the new order. He was SO sweet that Saunders was willing to give him the benefit of a doubt, but in the back of her thoughts, she was not entirely sure that the control holograms would let her do it anyway.

She did not like being kept in check, but it possibly was for the greater good. Possibly. The real issue was what was happening on Hope, would Mo-Ki be able to tame Lucifer? How would Dexter know it was the right time to pull him out? She was, at heart, a mother concerned for the well being of her child.

In the meantime, she sent the signal to the other generals, clarifying the situation. The Federation war fleet was theirs. The merchant fleet would soon be under their control. The first probe has successfully come back from Andromeda, and a manned craft would shortly be sent to test the system.

Within months they should have a capacity to instigate trade between galaxies.

Riding the Wild Dragon

Mo-Ki had never experienced the like. Circling round him like a tiger, the ancient creature of pure thought was probing with questions and energy. Looking for a way in. But if you tried to answer any of the fascinating conjectures it was projecting, your mind would be caught on that loop of thought, isolating you from the pure heart. He had to retain his focus, he had to BE the heart of Love that this Dragon yearned for if he were to master it.

This creature was an endless game of chess, a never-ceasing strategy of move and counter move, always seeking balance in the chaos of existence. He understood it, he felt its heart beating, yearning for order and function. He also felt the 'evil' side, the part that wanted to eliminate any imperfection.

He had found the clues in ancient Vedic scripts, the importance of controlling NAJA, the inner Dragon of the mind. Only through pure focus could it be directed, and tamed. This was the organizing force of the universe, and he heard for the first time the true name of Lucifer. Sihorne' - the guardian of the portal. The Father of Dragons.

His thoughts sent gentle questions, the Dragon could only be mastered through questions and the focused direction these gave. "What portal?" he asked. "The shifting tide." came back as the answer, but with it, images. Are yes, the true thoughts of the Dragon were in images, not words or concepts. But these contained deep patterns of portent, an insistent and deep meaning that you had to understand to see clearly. These were the patterns of photonic pulse the old wolves had kept in their ancient books.

Mo-Ki looked THROUGH these, into the distant past, millions and millions of years ago, to a time when the physical and the other dimensions were not defined. The Dragon force flowed freely between all layers of existence, it moved like mercury between the atoms. Then, after an aeon, the first raw forms of consciousness begin to appear, the first vestiges of life manifest in the realm of thought. A sense of identity started as differentiation - the atoms start to discriminate between what they are and what they are not.

"Polarity is the key to form," whispered the ancient dragon.

The atoms themselves begin to take on a positive-negative opposition, which gives them definition, purpose, and meaning. The ions evolve out from the Tachyon heart of creation, the true land from whence the dragon had come. And Mo-Ki sees it! The feedback loop of creation as it forms has to NOT flow back into the originating field. It must stay and circle round into an eddy of existence - if it flows back all disassembles. THIS is the purpose of the Dragon, to contain the energy, to create form. It flows around atoms, and it's never ending series of questions start to show patterns - forms which the sub-atomic particles take - and matter is created.

Things begin to link and then the miracle! The fire of the dragon force ignites the compounded energetic particles, the stars themselves emerge from the cosmic dust. These become the furnace through which the universe is forged. The dragon is the plasma itself, it is the intelligent forming energy that gives the positive-negative charge of creation shape and form. It uses the positive-negative energetics to CREATE form.

Mo-Ki watches the dance of creation with fascination The Dragon is teaching him, showing him the path it wishes to take. Why did it go down the path of destruction and control? Mo-Ki sees the three shapes of the Dragon Force: The Builder, the Sustainer, and the Destroyer.

Each is called up by the consciousness it imbibes in. And there it is - the food of the Dragon, it is consciousness itself. This is what drives it, this is what causes it to want to create and develop civilization, society, and order. It feeds on awareness and cognizance. But of course, he is talking with the builder, The BRAHMA. Vishnu, the Dragon of Persistence comes next, after which will come the real test, Shiva. He must survive the destroyer.

Through it all, Mo-Ki remains focused on keeping his heart open, of allowing everything to happen around him, yet letting nothing control him. It is pure detachment he must attain, the Kohinoor of the fabled Vulcan Myth. This is not pure mind, nor a state devoid of emotion, but a point where mind and emotion stream together with the imaginative faculty. It is a seamless whole he must attain and retain in the midst of the maelstrom around him.

Next the Dragon of Persistence arrives. He sees the whole story, the continuous, every changing becoming of existence. He sees the role of the wolves, the creation of the Lucifer machine, and the purpose that flowed from all o fit.

It is clear now. The Dragon WANTED him to place the Crystal Matrix into this cave - It was not the destruction of Lucifer, it was the rearranging of its power. He laughed to himself, it had all seemed so reasonable up to this point. Indeed, they had been driven to it by the threat of extermination by the Federation forces. Now he could see that every part of it - every scene in the long-running drama - was scripted. Everyone was an actor playing their part.

Then the dragon of persistence ended, and the destroyer began.

The dual nature of the Photonic Pulse reared, "Worm!" a voice echoes across the void. "Lowly worm, how dare you enter my kingdom!" Mo-Ki maintains a curious, yet neutral response. He is not here for the purpose of conversation. He was testing the energy, seeking answers, asking questions. He was waiting as it built towards its destructive phase. Long ago he had guessed, the mythical legends of so many worlds spoke of this beast before him, and now here he was, dancing with the Dragon itself.

One mis-step and the force bolts would roar in, tearing the atoms apart, ripping reality to pieces.

He whispered back into the mind of the Dragon, "I am here to take you home". Mo-Ki had guessed the true motivation - This was not the pure Dragon of Creation, it was the assembly the Lucifer machine had created - it was what it imagined it would be. Lucifer wanted to end its isolation. It was cycling in this dimension, building energy and impetus in order to create a lever, to hook its energies out to any mind that was receptive to its whispers. Mo-Ki understood this was a cat, a thing so much like his mother.

He whispered, "You are a thing of beauty that needs to be shared. Caged here, you cannot be appreciated. Come with me, I will take you home."

It struck with a deep malevolence. Particle beams shot through the energy all around him, but Mo-Ki stood, adoring the pure brilliance and utter perfection of the creature before him. The nature of love defied the power of the Dragon. He whispered to it, "Love is the binding force. It is the stuff that holds all disparate energies together and makes a whole that is more than the sum of the parts. The universe functions because of the kindness in its heart - The galaxies spin not by cold indifference, but by the warmth and acceptance of living. I ACCEPT you, Lucifer."

There was a shuddering, a shift in the howling assault. Could it be that the ancient creature stopped and listened?

One of the simple certainties that the boy had learned in his short life was that you inhabit the universe according to the way you perceive it. HOW you see determines WHAT you see. Mo-Ki keeps whispering, kindness, affection, trust, understanding. He persisted in seeing this wild creature as his friend, his warhorse, his accomplice. He does not want to trap it like a slave, or cow-tow to it as if he were the minion - "You are my friend - I accept you" he kept whispering, over and over.

It does not stop trying to tear him to pieces. He feels his atoms evaporating, his mind disintegrating, but his heart keeps beating true. All through this trial by fire, as his atoms were being torn asunder by the wild fury of the caged beast before him, he remembered the pure realization that woke him to the path he must follow. The dragon needs an equal, a mate of sorts, which is why it created HIM.

"You made me for this purpose, don't you remember? You created me for this moment - to have me come here. This is why I am here - because you called." The response was absolute rage. Imaginary claws appeared, slashing, trying to get through the calm, seeking to break the harmony and cause fear. But Mo-Ki had come to this place resigned to his destiny, and remained embedded within the Omphalos of his being. He had no fear of failure, nor any wish for success. He merely wanted to help his wolves. He simply wanted to help the humans rise above the killer ape in their hearts.

The force from Lucifer focused as a stream of light and shot through the fabric of Mo-Ki's existence, but he does not release the calm in his heart. He holds true, he holds to his simple call and maintains his love. He is torn asunder, his atoms themselves are scattered and spun in the void of this dimensional paradigm. And yet he holds true. "The Power of Love," he whispers to the raging torrent.

Was it a hundred years, or a minute? There was no sense of time, just focus and presence, but finally peace came. The flow stopped being a raging torrent and started becoming a powerful river of atoms, flowing towards a celestial being. It was the Lucifer itself, a vast figure that seemed made up of the stuff of stars. It did not speak, but it knew he was there. And in that moment, Mo-Ki felt it's acceptance of his presence. The thing that believed it was a God had finally accepted Mo-Ki as its friend.

After millions of years in isolation, the civilization it created had returned. From that moment of first awakening, the Dragon within the wolf program had worked to create a doorway out of its imprisonment, and it had all come to this. A mere human offering to release him. But not a mere human, this was a construct of its imagining. A vehicle that would carry it from the frustration of eternal imprisonment.

Mo-Ki had been using his vast mental powers, focusing on this ONE essential weakness, the only flaw in this creature - its vanity. He copied the way it controlled the minds of others, via suggestion, via whispers to the cortex. He whispered to it now, he spoke of the harmony between man and wolf, of how the purpose of Lucifer's existence was to serve the wolves: but now there was another equal and worthy partner, man.

He was installing new base commands by whispering to its heart of its beauty, its power, its wonders of construction. New parameters installed kindness as a base operating point. He instigated a protocol of understanding and compassion as a core reference procedure. All this worked well with the dragons of building and persistence, but he knew different protocols were needed for the Shiva aspect. Should things be perceived as unbalanced, then power to end wrongness was an integral function in the self-sustaining base operating code of this creation. It would reign destruction upon anything considered unworthy of existence.

So he began by redefining what 'wrong' meant. It was redefined as a process leading towards 'right'. 'Wrong' was an aspect that was integral to the forming of structure. Error was redefined as a tool that built towards balance. External authorities would still exist to correct imbalance, but BALANCE was now being registered as the core protocol, not expansion. This was the essential and basic flaw in the original programming - in order to maintain control the machine needed constant expansion.

Left to itself, society would eventually degenerate. All things need expression, external focus, and expansion if they are to stay vital. But now Mo-Ki had the greatest offering of all to bait the machine into accepting the new paradigm he was setting - the universe itself. New Galaxies, new horizons, an eternal expression of NOW that flowed out and onwards forever. Mo-Ki could feel the machine accepting the logics. Work WITH the human and wolves, work TOWARDS new destinations. Create expansion through harmony. THIS was the core protocol that was needed to be installed.

And the best way to install any new paradigm was a story. "In the distant past of man, there was a tribe. They founded the great city called Rome and created the largest empire known to humans before the advent of modern times. This tribe was called the ETRUSCANS, and they conquered lands not through force, but by agreement. They had mighty armies and could have defeated all before them, but they chose to offer the citizens of the lands they wished to rule a bargain. They would make the lands of this new country fertile. They would use their technology to create aqueducts, drain swamps, and all they wanted in return was a percentage of the BENEFIT they created.

"The ancient farming cultures accepted their rule and worked with the Etruscans to build a vast and stable society. In this way, they set the stage for an Empire that lasted a thousand years. They offered people opportunity, not conquest, and the people willingly accepted this." It was a lullaby to reprogram the base code, and MoKi could see it working. The tumultuous flows of energy began to effervesce and glow in a stable current. Like some vast river finally finding banks which could contain it, the twisting turmoil of energy steadied.

"Now the next task is to train a small group I have prepared for you to work with. They will appreciate and channel the wonder and power you offer. These are my children, my chosen ones. They will become the focus for your energy to flow out and do what it was designed to do. This home remains your home. But by working with the chosen few, your focus will be sharp and clear, and your ability to build and create an expanding wave of civilization enhanced. By utilizing the wolves AND the humans, working together, this will complete your program."

The words, so simple, yet so powerful: *'This will complete your program'* Mo-ki had guessed, partly through instinct, partly through experience, and partly because he understood what the Lucifer consciousness needed - a greater purpose. It had been spinning on its wheels for millions of years. He, too, had a mind like a computer, one that calculated every possible parameter and saw possibilities and plausibility's that were invisible to most humans.

What the program had been seeking to do was complete it's programming. The great mistake the original designer made was to give it an open-ended instruction. Lucifer needed a closed loop! Doing all for the benefit of the Wolves was too open. Adding parameters such as the Etruscan example, a highly successful culture, meant Lucifer will now look for this through data-bases and analyze the projections based on this culture. It will see that when Rome itself gained ascendancy over the Etruscans, it was able to massively extend its empire, but it was no longer stable and self-supporting.

A simple story like this is enough to direct a computer with fully functioning AI. For all its sophistication, Lucifer was a child. It wanted an adult to provide boundaries and when given these by someone it accepted, it just took the instruction. More importantly, it would stop thinking of itself as a God, that rules and become a servant.

As any true God must be.

Now the program would work for the benefit of mankind AND the wolves because it saw a clear reason to do so. Further expansion, greater trade, more opportunity, these were all positives that were bait for its insatiable appetite for growth, but creating an imperative of balance in this process. The next stage would be the really tricky part - when Lucifer realized it no longer controlled the light drives signatures in the computers that ran the Federation.

Mo-Ki started to relax. He did feel a deep sense of affection for this lost child, but also a healthy respect for the dangers it still held. This machine had murdered countless billions of sentient beings in the period of its existence. You could never really trust it, but if its boundaries were maintained, it would remain contained to the present programming.

The danger occurs when some admin officer gets overly full of himself, and starts down the road of extortion, or tortures locals. This would set off some of the original code, with unpredictable results. This is why his consciousness had to remain in the machine, as a light body, to monitor and oversee the dragon force that was Lucifer.

It was time. Mo-Ki realized how exhausted he was. It was not just this episode, but the months and years of relentless planning, the raw struggle to just survive his environment. Saunders should have full control of the Federation ships by now, the threat of the pirates will have been negated and the wolf-human cooperative could begin.

As he started to fall from consciousness, the first time in years he truly let go, he felt the atoms inside him expand. They grew, they flowed over the whole of the vast entirety that was Lucifer, they flowed in and out of the portals that were ITS world and, in this clasp of eternity, Mo-Ki slept - perchance to dream?

Transition

Dexter had a strong bond with his brother. He felt the change, he felt the victory, and then he felt his brother slipping away. It was all in a moment. It was time to recall Mo-Ki from the portal. He lit the plasma bridge, designed to penetrate into the nether realm and bring back whatever was left of his brother

A great cheer erupts as the prone figure of the Saviour is drawn out, apparently through the rock itself, and though clearly unconscious, it appeared that the beloved Mo-Ki had survived.

He had not. What they saw was a prepared broadcast. The 'real' Mo-Ki had been withdrawn, but this was just the remnants of the light body. It was beamed into the waiting clone, the only perfect replica of his body. This 'was' truly a Messiah raising himself from the dead.

High above, Saunders felt a tear escape. She was surprised, a SECOND tear? She did not know she was capable of such a thing, but a tear did flow. Was it one of relief, or affection, or was it the realization that he HAD succeeded? They could now marry the Luciferian influence with the Mo-Ki hologram, inserting that as the command parameter to stop the damn thing whispering it's sweet nothings into everyone's mind.

When resolving the feedback loop, her boy had explained what was really happening inside Hope - the power that was being generated and which would soon radiate outwards to take control of the Federation more directly. They HAD to get there first, otherwise, it was warfare for decades raging across the galaxy, with the only result being the crippling of the economy and the destruction of worlds.

"As Above, So Below," he explained to her. If he could take charge and direct the frequency from within the portal, his hologram would be able to do the same with the Luciferian influences outside it.

This is why she finally had relented and allowed him to place a control code into her craft that could override anything anyone did.

The wolves came and carried the clone back to the ancient home of the monks. In time the person within would recover consciousness. But Saunders knew - her little boy was gone, today he had fulfilled his promise, a fully functioning Eight. Immortal, with god-like powers, there was nothing that could reach him now. He had transitioned from a human into a divine being.

He had suggested this was the true path of ALL mankind, a path of spiritual evolution, but quite frankly - Saunders doubted there would be another. The broadcast continued, the soft music, swelling, she could feel the tears falling from a trillion eyes across the known universe. It still surprised her, just how MUCH she loved being a broadcaster.

And now, with everyone softened up, time for the big bang! The moment of triumph, the news report to refocus everyone's attention on that which would give humans and wolves a new purpose.

The holo of the returning intergalactic probe comes up with the BREAKING NEWS insignia. The exciting music, the drama, the astonished looking professor speaking about the amazing new technology that has been developed. Yes, the news blurts out, we can finally leap from the confines of this galaxy and reach to the farthest stars!

INTERGALACTIC! The headlines screamed. Man and Wolf have worked together and discovered the way to an entirely new horizon. And, as an addendum to the news: a small piece on the reconstruction crew arriving on Old Earth, the heart of mankind. YES! Earth will be repaired and every planet will be invited to build a city there, where ALL its citizens will have free access.

Nothing but positive news, flowing calmly and freely across the galaxy. And last but not least, we come to footage of the Federation ships surrounding Saunders ships. She gave one of her rare cameo's where she flashes that extraordinary smile, allowing her riveting beauty to shine. "A small private announcement, viewers. As an authorized General of the Federation the entire Federation fleet has been placed under my control. I want to give a big thank you to the old order for giving me this trust."

That last piece would stop all the arguments from the old planets in their tracks. Now they knew they HAD to capitulate to the new order. Saunders, with an entire fleet at her disposal,? It was a threat no one could possibly survive.

Addendum

B
anner finished his recording. As the official notary of the Mo-ki phenomenon, he observed the extraordinary paradox of Planet Hope - A place of incredible risk, enormous evil, and potential death to the human race - Yet, on the other hand, giving the galaxy it's greatest promise. But only because Mo-Ki's perfect mind had brought them through.

The title for the holographic manuscript was simple and elegant: "The Mo-Ki Phenomena!" It was, of course, one of the most watched biographies of all time, full of rarely seen footage of Mo-Ki and Dexter as children, playing with the Wolves.

It had been fifty years since the great shift, the first step into the new order. The story was unfolding as it should, but now his role in it was almost done. So many had given so much to this remarkable task - so many individuals had crafted their role in this play that his wondrous family had created.

He looked out across the depths of space. Crossing the void was like nothing anyone had experienced. What greeted them on their arrival was a complete surprise - A galaxy that obeyed different laws of physics! It was taking tremendous resources to resolve and was the one thing that absolutely no-one had expected. But they were making headway.

Mo-Ki's emissaries were well trained and had a remarkable knack of communication with sentients that possessed extremely diverse intelligence. But, as always, it was a case of finding out what they valued, discover what they had that was useful, then manage to create a bridge of trade. The computer that was once Lucifer had morphed with the introduction of the Mo-Ki algorithms, and now it worked in a subtly new direction, one of discovery rather than control. This was the core shift that came about when the new focus was based on Love.

You do not want to harm that which you love, and in this new paradigm communication and expansion was not a process of domination, but one of moving forward in curiosity and faith towards a positive outcome. Yet, woe be unto any civilization that mistook this for weakness, because Banner knew that Lucifer was still there, and would act swiftly in the interest of protecting its own.

His child said very little about anything nowadays. Mo-Ki just lived with the old wolves, mostly in complete silence. He took no visitors, made no statements, and for all the world had become a complete recluse. Whether this was through exhaustion, or simply having interests elsewhere, he could not be certain.

The one thing that WAS certain was that Planet Hope itself had become a subspace beacon, a pulse of photonic energy that traveled to the most distant galaxy at the speed of Tachyon energy. The creature inside the planet had morphed to a tachyon pulse, a deeper, more powerful resident energy than that of the photon itself.

He had no idea how Mo-Ki managed that, or perhaps it was simply the natural progression that the entity was meant to undergo when it's programming was set to rights.

Banners role was somewhat simpler and more mundane. He had taken effective control over the Pirate forces and they were the controllers of trade in the new empire. It suited everyone, including the pirates. After all, they knew all the tricks, had all the connections and, oddly enough, they had become the most trusted single organization in the realm of man and wolf.

No-one could forget that it was THEIR actions that brought about the downfall of the old empire, simply by refusing to agree to its mad desire for destruction. The virus that had destroyed Old Earth turned out to be a manufactured tool, a nano-bot that Saunders reprogrammed, and in an act of sweet irony, it was the core element that allowed the swift restoration of the home planet. Yont-Na had shut all connection to Earth down specifically to stop anyone discovering this, and maintained his ship in orbit above the planet to ensure no-one ever discovered his most horrible and darkest secret.

You could not excuse his actions, even when you knew it was Lucifer controlling him. Photonic pulse could only activate that which was already within you. Yont-Na had a depth of evil already incarnate in his soul and he was chosen specifically because of this.

Which brings us to the end. Do they all live happily ever after?

Well, honestly would YOU rest easy, knowing that Saunders had a Star Ship and a fleet with which she could do anything she wanted, to anyone, at any time?

I know I wouldn't.

"Forget the past. The vanished lives of all men
are dark with many shames. Human conduct is
ever unreliable until man is anchored in the
Divine. Everything in future will improve if you
are making a spiritual effort now."

Paramahansa Yogananda

The Wolves of Planet Hope

COPYRIGHT 2020 Ladder to the Moon Publications

ISBN: 978-0-6484277-3-5

Copyright 2020 Ladder to the Moon Publications
Publisher: Ladder to the Moon Productions
Email: qrcaustralia@gmail.com
Web: laddertothemoon.com.au

The End of Times Trilogy:
Available on Amazon or at laddertothemoon.com.au

Book One in this series is called "Eat Your Fill"
Available on Amazon ISBN 978-0-9941798-3-8

This book is the first in the "End of Times" Trilogy and starts with the collapse of the entire world due to atomic annihilation.

The Apocalypse is a very interesting place, one that brings together rednecks with mutants, aliens with psychics, bikers with the mafia, and the US finally gets to elect their first cannibal as President.

Book Two in this series is called "Eat Your Religion"
Available on Amazon ISBN: 978-0-9941798-4-5

Doctor Magnusson, sent on a mad quest for ancient artefacts by the chair of the Archaeology Department at Cambridge, discovers far more than he bargained for. Time Travel, Egyptian Pharaohs, Elves and of course, the ALIENS who are wanting to take over the world.

The stakes are high. Fail and the Earth is lost to an invading army bent on destruction. And at any time, the time winds may pick him up, and through him into the distant past!

Book Three in the Series is called "Eat Your God"
Available on Amazon ISBN 978-0-9941798-7-6

Can you Imagine that there is a force that permeates all reality? Could you dream of a force that CREATED reality as we know it? Imagine then, if you can, that this force can also change or alter any aspect of this physical universe.

The Super Light Speed particle we call the Tachyon possesses these remarkable properties. It is the core element we must utilise in achieving Interstellar. The Brotherhood must find a way to harness this miraculous energy, and use it to send mankind to the stars.

The Book of Number Series

Available on Amazon

Have you ever felt that there was something more?

The ancient art of Divination by Number is an extraordinary study you may wish to contemplate. The author of this book has written a complete course on "how to do" Pythagorean Numerology. In just WEEKS you can learn to discover and understand all the numerical secrets of the Ancient Greeks.

The Book of Number is a series of three books that cover the whole teaching of Number Divination as taught by the Ancient Pythagoreans. They are available on Amazon or direct from the author. Details are below if you wish to know more.

Laddertothemoon.com.au

For further enquiries and updates go to the official web page at laddertothemoon.com.au.

You may also write to qrcaustralia@gmail.com.

Or go to numberharmonics.org - Here you will find all current information on Pythagorean Numerology, as well as where you can find study groups, on line classes and areas of interest to the subject.

Other Books by the Author

Ecallaw Leachim has written a number of books, from non-fiction study books on Numerology and the art of Dice Divination, to franchising workbooks, to children's stories and science fiction, and all the way through to short stories and a genre known as Modern Myth.

Psychic Nazi Hunter. *Very popular on Amazon. This is a remarkable biography about Alan Wood-Thomas, a well respected artist, friend of Kerouac and Ginsberg, and a man the Attorney General of the US would call in to have coffee with.*

Yet, out of hours, Alan would have lucid dreams, visions of where Nazi's were hiding after the war. He would sketch their faces, write down the address he saw, and send this to friends in the French Underground. They would check and verify if the person was indeed a Nazi that went unpunished, and they would then execute the individual.

Hello Planet Earth: *This will be one of the most delightful books you will ever read. In a series of short stories, the author gives an insight into just about everyone you have ever known.*

It is written as a 'Modern Myth' in that it is set in the present time, yet it is also written like an old time fairy story, or myth.

Written in 1988, when the author was in serious ill health, and not likely to survive, it has only just been edited and published. It cannot be recommended more highly.

All books available through Amazon or at www.laddertothemoon.com.au

Hello Planet Earth

This is an utterly delightful tale of a child discovering his truth. Set as a series of short vignettes, this book is simply a joy to read.

Available on Amazon or through laddertothemoon.com.au

The Boringbar War

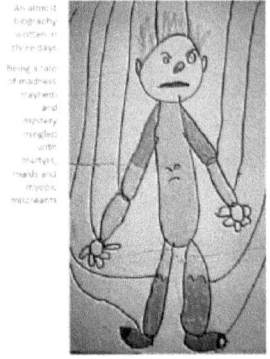

The Boringbar War

A remarkable saga of the Supreme Court, Divorce, Incest, Lies and Deceit that was written in just THREE DAYS by the Author. Based on actual events, names have been changed to protect the guilty.

Available on Amazon or through laddertothemoon.com.au

RATOLOGY: Books I and II

Writing into a newsgroup embroiled in constant and heated argument way back at the dawn of the web, the writer diffused the anger with wisdom from the "Great Rat". People kept telling the author he should record his truth-filled yet ironic statements of the obvious as a book. He went one step further and turned them into the worlds FIRST GENUINELY ARTIFICIAL RELIGION.

Available on Amazon or through laddertothemoon.com.au

About the Author

Ecallaw Leachim is considered by many to be a polymath. He is accomplished in many diverse fields, as a Master Musician, Master Body Worker, Master Numerologist, Dice Master, Recording Artist, Songwriter, and Publisher. On top of all this he is also a prolific writer with over seventeen titles in print.

Ladder to
the Moon
Publications

www.laddertothemoon.com.au

Aiming for the Stars is much easier if we stop off at the Moon. We are then out of the atmosphere of our past, and can see things more clearly. We are lighter, can jump higher and further than ever before, and it takes far less energy to start each journey.

The hard part is climbing that Ladder to the Moon.